THE
ANNOTATED

THE ANNOTATED

CLASSIC

FAIRY TALES

EDITED WITH AN INTRODUCTION AND NOTES BY

MARIA TATAR

TRANSLATIONS BY MARIA TATAR

W. W. NORTON & COMPANY

New York / London

Illustrations by Arthur Rackham, Edmund Dulac, Gustave Doré, George Cruikshank, Kay Nielson,
and Walter Crane courtesy of Department of Printing and Graphic Art, Houghton Library,
Harvard College Library, and the Department of Rare Books, Houghton Library, Harvard College Library.
Illustrations by Maxfield Parrish reproduced by permission of © Maxfield Parrish Family Trust,
licensed by ASAP and VAGA, NYC, courtesy of American Illustrated Gallery, NYC. Illustrations by
Arthur Rackham reprinted with permission of the Arthur Rackham Estate/Bridgeman Archive.
Illustrations by Wanda Gág reprinted with permission of the artist's estate.

For information about permission to reproduce selections from this book, write to
Permissions, W. W. Norton & Company, Inc., 500 Fifth Avenue, New York, NY 10110

The text of this book is composed in Goudy Old Style
with the display set in Delphian and Edwardian Script
Composition by Sue Carlson
Manufacturing by The Courier Companies, Inc.
Book design by JAM Design
Production manager: Andrew Marasia

Library of Congress Cataloging-in-Publication Data

The annotated classic fairy tales / edited with an introduction and notes
by Maria Tatar ; translations by Maria Tatar.
p. cm.
Includes bibliographical references.
ISBN 0-393-05163-3
1. Fairy tales. I. Tatar, Maria, 1945–

PN6071.F15 A66 2002

398.2-dc21   2002070131

W. W. Norton & Company, Inc., 500 Fifth Avenue, New York, N.Y. 10110
www.wwnorton.com

W. W. Norton & Company Ltd., Castle House, 75/76 Wells Street, London W1T 3QT

1 2 3 4 5 6 7 8 9 0

For Lauren and Daniel

CONTENTS

Biographies of Authors and Collectors

Biographies of Illustrators

Appendix 1

Appendix 2

Appendix 3

INTRODUCTION

For many of us childhood books are sacred objects. Often read to pieces, those books took us on voyages of discovery, leading us into secret new worlds that magnify childhood desires and anxieties and address the great existential mysteries. Like David Copperfield, who comforted himself by reading fairy tales, some of us once read "as if for life," using books not merely as consolation but as a way of navigating reality, of figuring out how to survive in a world ruled by adults. In a profound meditation on childhood reading, Arthur Schlesinger, Jr., writes about how the classical tales "tell children what they unconsciously know—that human nature is not innately good, that conflict is real, that life is harsh before it is happy—and thereby reassure them about their own fears and their own sense of self."

"What do we ever get nowadays from reading to equal the excitement and the revelation in those first fourteen years?" Graham Greene once asked. Many of us can recall moments of breathless excitement as we settled into our favorite chairs, our secret corners, or our cozy beds, eager to find out how Dorothy would escape the witch, whether the little mermaid would win an immortal soul, or what would become of Mary and Colin in the secret garden. "I hungered for the sharp, frightening, breath-taking, almost painful excitement that the story had given me," Richard Wright observes in recollecting his childhood encounter with the story "Bluebeard and His Seven Wives." In that world of imagination, we not only escape the drab realities of everyday life but also indulge in the cathartic pleasures of defeating those giants, stepmothers, ogres, monsters, and trolls known as the grown-ups.

Yet much as we treasure the stories of childhood, we also outgrow them, cast them off, and dismiss them as childish things, forgetting their power not only to build the childhood world of imagination but also to construct the adult world of reality. Fairy tales, according to the British illustrator Arthur Rackham, have become "part of our everyday thought and expression, and help to shape our lives." There is no doubt, he adds, "that we should be behaving ourselves very differently if Beauty had never been united to her Beast . . . or if Sister Anne hadn't seen anybody coming; or if 'Open Sesame!' hadn't cleared the way, or Sindbad sailed." Whether we are aware of it or not, fairy tales have modeled behavioral codes and developmental paths, even as they provide us with terms for thinking about what happens in our world.

Part of the power of these stories derives not just from the words but also from the images that accompany them. In my own childhood copy of the Grimms' fairy tales, held together by rubber bands and tape, there is one picture worth many thousands of words. Each time I open the book to that page, I feel a rush of childhood memories and experience, for a few moments, what it was like to be a child. The images that accompanied "Cinderella," "Little Red Riding Hood," or "Jack and the Beanstalk" in volumes of classic fairy tales from an earlier era have an aesthetic power that produces an emotional hold rarely encountered in the work of contemporary illustrators, and for this reason I have returned to earlier times and places for the images accompanying the stories in this volume.

Fairy tales are up close and personal, telling us about the quest for romance and riches, for power and privilege, and, most important, for a way out of the woods back to the safety and security of home. Bringing myths down to earth and inflecting them in human rather than heroic terms, fairy tales put a familiar spin on the stories in the archive of our collective imagination. Think of Tom Thumb, who miniaturizes David's killing of Goliath in the Bible, Odysseus' blinding of the Cyclops in *The Odyssey*, and Siegfried's conquest of the dragon Fafner in Richard Wagner's *Ring of the Nibelung*. Or of Cinderella, who is sister under the skin to Shakespeare's Cordelia and to Charlotte Brontë's Jane Eyre. Fairy tales take us into a reality that is familiar in the double sense of the term—deeply personal and at the same time centered on the family and its conflicts rather than on what is at stake in the world at large.

John Updike reminds us that the fairy tales we read to children today had their origins in a culture of adult storytelling: "They were the television and pornography of their day, the life-lightening trash of preliterate peoples." If we look at the stories in their earliest written forms, we discover preoccupations and ambitions that conform to adult anxieties and desires. Sleeping Beauty may act like a careless, disobedient child when she reaches for the spindle that puts her to sleep, but her real troubles come in the form of a hostile mother-in-law who plans to serve her for dinner with a sauce Robert. "Bluebeard," with its forbidden chamber filled with the corpses of former wives, engages with issues of marital trust, fidelity, and betrayal, showing how marriage is haunted by the threat of murder. "Rumpelstiltskin" charts a woman's narrow escape from a bargain that could cost the life of her first-born. And "Rapunzel" turns on the perilous cravings of a pregnant woman and on the desire to safeguard a girl's virtue by locking her up in a tower.

Fairy tales, once told by peasants around the fireside to distract them from the tedium of domestic chores, were transplanted with great success into the nursery, where they thrive in the form of entertainment and edification for children. These tales, which have come to constitute a powerful cultural legacy passed on from one generation to the next, provide more than gentle pleasures, charming enchantments, and playful delights. They contain much that is "painful and terrifying," as the art historian Kenneth Clark recalled in reminiscing about his childhood encounters with the stories of the Brothers Grimm and Hans Christian Andersen. Arousing dread as well as wonder, fairy tales have, over the centuries, always attracted both enthusiastic advocates, who celebrate their robust charms, and hard-edged critics, who deplore their violence.

Our deepest desires as well as our most profound anxieties enter the folkloric bloodstream and remain in it through stories that find favor with a community of listeners or readers. As repositories of a collective cultural consciousness and unconscious, fairy tales have attracted the attention of psychologists, most notably the renowned child psychologist Bruno Bettelheim. In his landmark study, *The Uses of Enchantment*, Bettelheim argued that fairy tales have a powerful therapeutic value, teaching children that "a struggle against severe difficulties in life is unavoidable." "If one does not shy away," Bettelheim added with great optimism, "but steadfastly meets unexpected and often unjust hardships, one masters all obstacles and at the end emerges victorious."

Over the past decades child psychologists have mobilized fairy tales as powerful therapeutic vehicles for helping children and adults solve their problems by meditating on the dramas staged in them. Each text becomes an enabling device, allowing readers to work through their fears and to purge themselves of hostile feelings and damaging desires. By entering the world of fantasy and imagination, children and adults secure for themselves a safe space where fears can be confronted, mastered, and banished. Beyond that, the real magic of the fairy tale lies in its ability to extract pleasure from pain. In bringing to life the dark figures of our imagination as ogres, witches, cannibals, and giants, fairy tales may stir up dread, but in the end they always supply the pleasure of seeing it vanquished.

Like Bettelheim, the German philosopher Walter Benjamin applauded the feisty determination of fairy-tale heroes and heroines: "The wisest thing—so the fairy tale taught mankind in olden times, and teaches children to this day—is to meet the forces of the mythical world with cunning and with high spirits." If Bettelheim emphasized the value of "struggle" and "mastery" and saw in fairy tales an "experience in moral education," Benjamin reminded us that the morality endorsed in fairy tales is not without complications and complexities. While we may all agree that promoting "high spirits" is a good thing for the child outside the book, we may not necessarily concur that "cunning" is a quality we wish to encourage by displaying its advantages. Early commentators on fairy tales quickly detected that the moral economy of the fairy tale did not necessarily square with the didactic agendas set by parents. The British illustrator George Cruikshank was appalled by the story "Puss in Boots," which seemed to him "a succession of successful falsehoods—a clever lesson in lying!—a system of imposture rewarded by the greatest worldly advantage!" He found Jack's theft of the giant's treasures morally reprehensible and felt obliged to rewrite the story, turning the robbery into a reappropriation of the dead father's fortune. Cruikshank would have reacted similarly to Aladdin, that prototypical fairy-tale hero who is described as "headstrong," as an "incorrigible good-for-nothing," and as a boy who will never amount to anything. Wherever we turn, fairy-tale characters always seem to be lying, cheating, or stealing their way to good fortune.

In stories for children, we have come to desire and expect clear, positive moral direction, along with straightforward messages. The popular success of William Bennett's *Book of Virtues*, a collection of stories chosen for their ability to transmit "timeless and universal" cultural values, reveals just how invested we are in the notion that moral literature can produce good citizens. Bennett is completely at ease with his list of the virtues we all embrace: self-discipline, compassion, responsibility, friendship, work, courage, perseverance, honesty, loyalty, and faith. But he fails to recognize the complexities of reading, the degree to which children often focus on single details, produce idiosyncratic interpretations, or become passionate about vices as well as virtues.

In her memoir *Leaving a Doll's House*, the actress Claire Bloom reminisces about the "sound of Mother's voice as she read to me from Hans Christian Andersen's *The Little Mermaid* and *The Snow Queen*." Although the experience of reading produced "a pleasurable sense of warmth and comfort and safety," Bloom also emphasizes that "these emotionally wrenching tales . . . instilled in me a longing to be overwhelmed by romantic passion and led me in my teens and early twenties to attempt to emulate these self-sacrificing heroines." That Bloom played the tragic, self-effacing heroine not only on stage but in real life becomes clear from the painful account of her many failed romances and marriages. The stories, to be sure, may merely have reinforced what was already part of Bloom's character and disposition, but it is troubling to read her real-life history in light of her strong identification with figures like Andersen's Little Mermaid. Bloom's recollection of childhood reading reminds us that reading may yield warmth and pleasure, but that there can be real consequences to reading without reflecting on the effect of what is on the page.

The Book of Virtues, like many anthologies of stories "for children," endorses a kind of mindless reading that fails to interrogate the cultural values embedded in stories written once upon a time, in a different time and place. In its enunciation of a moral beneath each title, it also insists on reducing every story to a flat one-liner about one virtue or another, failing to take into account Eudora Welty's observation that "there is absolutely everything in great fiction but a clear answer." Even fairy tales, with their naïve sense of justice, their tenacious materialism, their reworking of familiar territory, and their sometimes narrow imaginative range, rarely send unambiguous messages.

This lack of ethical clarity did not present a problem for many of the collectors who put fairy tales between the covers of books. When Charles Perrault published his *Tales of Mother Goose* in 1697, he appended at least one moral, sometimes two. Yet those morals often did not square with the events in the story and sometimes offered nothing more than an opportunity for random social commentary and digressions on character. The explicit behavioral directives added by Perrault and others also have a tendency to misfire when they are aimed at children. It did not take Rousseau to discover that when you observe children learning lessons from stories, "you will see that when they are in a position to apply them, they almost always do so in a way opposite to the author's intention." Nearly every former child has learned this lesson through self-observation or through personal experience with children.

Do we, then, abandon the notion of finding moral guidance in fairy tales? Is reading reduced to an activity that yields nothing but aesthetic delight or pure pleasure? If fairy tales do not provide us with the tidy morals and messages for which we sometimes long, they still present us with opportunities to think about the anxieties and desires to which the tale gives shape, to reflect on and discuss the values encapsulated in the narrative, and to contemplate the perils and possibilities opened up by the story.

Today we recognize that fairy tales are as much about conflict and violence as about enchantment and happily-ever-after endings. When we read "Cinderella," we are fascinated more by her trials and tribulations at the hearth than by her social elevation. We spend more time thinking about the life-threatening chant of the giant in "Jack and the Beanstalk" than about Jack's acquisition of wealth. And Hansel and Gretel's encounter with the seemingly magnanimous witch in the woods haunts our imagination long after we have put the story down.

Through the medium of stories, adults can talk with children about what matters in their lives, about issues ranging from fear of abandonment and death to fantasies of revenge and triumphs that lead to happily-ever-after endings. While looking at pictures, reading episodes, and turning pages, adults and children can engage in what the cultural critic Ellen Handler-Spitz calls "conversational reading," dialogues that meditate on the story's effects and offer guidance for thinking about similar matters in the real world. This kind of reading can take many different turns: earnest, playful, meditative, didactic, empathetic, or intellectual.

In her recollections of reading "Little Red Riding Hood" with her grandmother, Angela Carter gives us one such scene of reading fairy tales: "My maternal grandmother used to say, 'Lift up the latch and walk in,' when she told it to me when I was a child; and at the conclusion, when the wolf jumps on Little Red Riding Hood and gobbles her up, my grandmother used to pretend to eat me, which made me squeak and gibber with excited pleasure." Carter's account of her experience with "Little Red Riding Hood" reveals the degree to which the meaning of a tale is generated in its performance. This scene of reading—with its cathartic pleasures—tells us more about what the story means than the "timeless truths" that were enunciated by Charles Perrault in his moral to the first literary version of the tale.

Luciano Pavarotti, by contrast, had a very different experience with "Little Red Riding Hood." "In my house," he recalls, "when I was a little boy, it was my grandfather who told the stories. He was wonderful. He told violent, mysterious tales that enchanted me. . . . My favorite one was *Little Red Riding Hood*. I identified with Little Red Riding Hood. I had the same fears as she. I didn't want her to die. I dreaded her death—or what we think death is." Charles Dickens had an even more powerful sentiment about the girl in this story. Little Red Riding Hood was his "first love": "I felt that if I could have married Little Red Riding Hood, I should have known perfect bliss."

Each of these three readers responded in very different ways to a story that we are accustomed to considering as a cautionary tale warning about the dangers of straying from the path. Often it is the experience of reading out loud or retelling that produces the most powerful resonances and responses. Since the stories in this collection were once part of an oral tradition and since they are meant to be read aloud and revised, I have sought to recapture the rhythms of oral storytelling in my translations, using phrasing, diction, and pacing that reminds us that these stories were once broadcast, spoken out loud to an audience of young and old.

It is the readers of these fairy tales who will reinvigorate them, making them hiss and crackle with narrative energy with each retelling. Hans Christian Andersen, according to his friend Edvard Collin, had a special way of breathing new life into fairy tales:

> Whether the tale was his own or someone else's, the way of telling it was completely his own, and so lively that the children were thrilled. He, too, enjoyed giving his humor free rein, his speaking was without stop, richly adorned with the figures of speech well known to children, and with gestures to match the situation. Even the driest sentence came to life. He did not say, "The children got into the carriage and then drove away," but "They got into the carriage—'goodbye, Dad! Goodbye, Mum!'—the whip cracked smack! smack! and away they went, come on! gee up!"

Reading these stories in the fashion of Andersen is a way of reclaiming them, turning them into *our* cultural stories by inflecting them in new ways and in some cases rescripting what happened "once upon a time."

The fairy tales in this volume did not require editorial interventions in an earlier age, precisely because they were brought up to date by their tellers and tailored to the cultural context in which they were told. In presenting the "classic" versions of the tales, this volume is offering foundational texts that may not necessarily be completely transparent to readers today. They offer the basis for retelling, but in many cases they will call out for parental intervention. The background material on each fairy tale anchors the story in its historical context, revealing the textual peculiarities and ideological twists and turns taken over time at different cultural sites. Knowing that Cinderella lives happily ever after with her stepsisters in some versions of her story and that doves are summoned to peck out the eyes of the stepsisters in others is something that parents will want to know when they read "Cinderella" to their children. That Little Red Riding Hood outwits the wolf in some versions of her story will be an important point to bear in mind when reading Perrault's version of the story, in which the girl is devoured by the wolf. Understanding something about how Bluebeard's wife is sometimes censured for her curiosity and sometimes praised for her resourcefulness will help adults reflect on how to talk about this story with a child.

The annotations to the stories are intended to enrich the reading experience, providing cues for points in the story where adult and child can contemplate alternative possibilities, improvise new directions, or imagine different endings. These notes draw attention to moments at which adult and child can engage with issues raised, sometimes simply indulging in the pleasures of the narrative, but sometimes also thinking about the values endorsed in the story and questioning whether the plot has to take the particular turn that it does in the printed version.

The illustrations for *The Annotated Classic Fairy Tales* have been drawn largely from the image repertoire of nineteenth-century artists, contemporaries of the collectors and editors of the great national anthologies of fairy tales. Arthur Rackham, Gustave Doré, Edmund Dulac, Walter Crane, Edward Burne-Jones, George Cruikshank, and others produced illustrations that provide not only visual pleasure but also powerful commentaries on the tales, interrupting the flow of the story at critical moments and offering opportunities for further reflection and interpretation. For many of us, the most memorable encounters with fairy tales came in the form of illustrated books. Those volumes, as Walter Benjamin points out, always had "one saving grace: their illustration." The pictures in those anthologies escaped the kind of censorship and bowdlerization to which the texts were often subjected. "They eluded the control of philanthropic theories and quickly, behind the backs of the pedagogues, children and artists came together."

The Annotated Classic Fairy Tales seeks to reclaim a powerful cultural legacy, creating a storytelling archive for children and adults. While the fairy tales have been drawn from a variety of cultures, they constitute a canon that has gained nearly universal currency in the Western world and that has remained remarkably stable over the centuries. Even those unfamiliar with the details of "The Frog Prince" or "The Little Match Girl" have some sense of what these stories are about and how the salient points in them (attraction and repulsion in the one, compassion in the other) are mobilized in everyday discourse to underscore an argument or to embellish a point. This volume collects the stories that we all think we know—even when we are unable to retell them—providing also the texts and historical contexts that we often do not have firmly in mind.

Disseminated across a wide variety of media, ranging from opera and drama to cinema and advertising, fairy tales have become a vital part of our cultural capital. What keeps them alive and pulsing with vitality and variety is exactly what keeps life pulsing: anxieties, fears, desires, romance, passion, and love. Like our ancestors, who listened to these stories at the fireside, in taverns, and in spinning rooms, we remain transfixed by stories about wicked stepmothers, bloodthirsty ogres, sibling rivals, and fairy godmothers. For us, too, the stories are irresistible, for they offer opportunities to talk, to negotiate, to deliberate, to chatter, and to prattle on endlessly as did the old wives from whom the stories are thought to derive. And from the tangle of that talk and chitchat, we begin to define our own values, desires, appetites, and aspirations, creating identities that will allow us to produce happily-ever-after endings for ourselves and for our children.

—MARIA TATAR
Cambridge, Massachusetts

ACKNOWLEDGMENTS

L ike the fairy tales once told around the fireside, this book is a collaboration that has drawn on many different voices. It also required the labors of many hands, and I am grateful to students, colleagues, librarians, friends, and family for their generous support, encouragement, and assistance over the years.

Bob Weil at Norton brought this project to life and remained intellectually engaged with it right to the end. Jason Baskin patiently guided the manuscript through the complications of the production process, expertly navigating the editorial waters. For breathtaking precision in copyediting, I am grateful to Otto Sonntag.

Without the rich resources of Houghton Library, this volume would have been far less vibrant and colorful, and I am grateful to the capable staff members there, both in the reading room and in imaging services.

This book is dedicated to my children, who rekindled my interest in fairy tales and reminded me how powerfully and deeply stories nurture imagination, spirit, and passion.

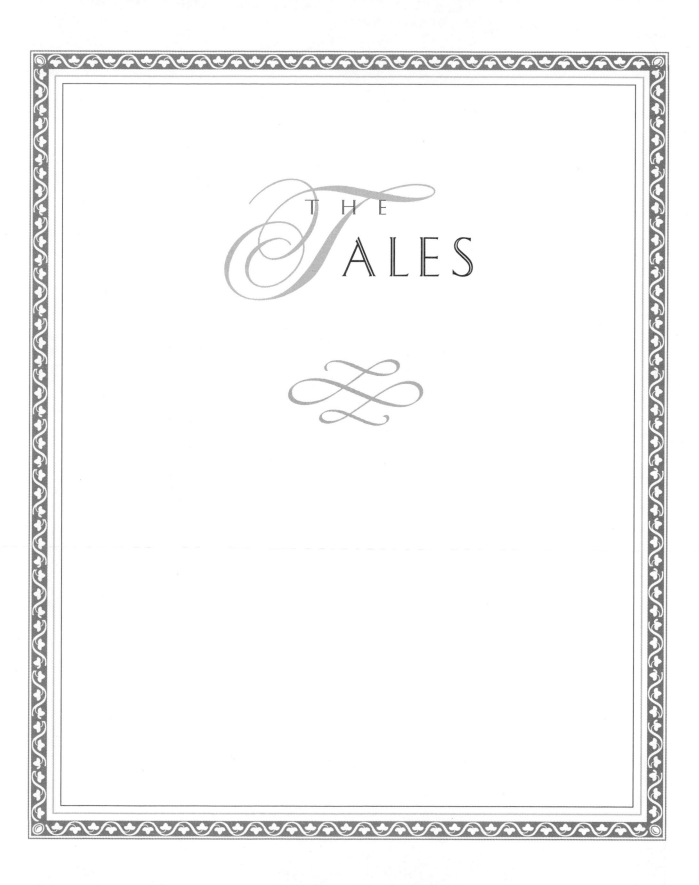

THE TALES

SCENES OF STORYTELLING

CHARLES PERRAULT,
Tales of Mother Goose
(*Contes de ma Mère l'Oye*), 1695

The frontispiece to the manuscript of Perrault's collection takes us to the fireside. As the warmest spot in the house, it was the perfect site for carrying out household chores (in this case, spinning) and telling tales. The cat, the door with the keyhole, and the spindle all prefigure what is to come in the volume: "Puss in Boots," "Bluebeard," and "Sleeping Beauty." The three children appear to be of a higher social class than this Mother Goose, who is both spinner and raconteur.

CHARLES PERRAULT,
Tales of Mother Goose
(*Contes de ma Mère l'Oye*), 1697

The frontispiece for the first printed edition of Perrault's fairy tales.

JOSEPH HIGHMORE,
Pamela Tells a Nursery Tale, 1744

The famous protagonist of Samuel Richardson's novel recites a story to her attentive charges. Gathered near the fireside, the young women sew and amuse themselves and the children with nursery tales.

GEORGE CRUIKSHANK,
"The Droll Story," 1823

For *German Popular Stories,* the first British translation of the Grimms' fairy tales, George Cruikshank produced a fireside scene in which an audience varied in age finds amusement in the stories read from a volume of tales.

GEORGE CRUIKSHANK,
"Vignette to the second series of German Popular Stories," 1823

A hearth, a spinning wheel, a contented cat, and a granny telling stories to attentive children come to serve as the standard features of storytelling scenes. Note that Cruikshank's old woman is still telling the stories rather than reading them out loud from a book.

LOUIS-LÉOPOLD BOILLY,
And the Ogre Ate Him
(Et l'ogre l'a mangé), 1824

With book on her lap, a somber granny tells about the triumph of evil. Her story, a cautionary tale that takes a disciplinary turn, is unusual in suggesting that the ogre triumphs over the protagonist. Her listeners are stunned, dismayed, and silenced.

DANIEL MACLISE,
A Winter Night's Tale, 1867

A crone imparts her wisdom through storytelling. The shadow cast on the screen and the thoughtful expressions on the faces of her listeners suggest a dark, admonitory side to the story. The entire family seems to take part in this evening activity. The spinning wheel is present, but this is clearly not a peasant family.

LUDWIG RICHTER,
"Die Spinnstube," 1857

Adults and children listen to this male storyteller spin his yarns while they work. The frontispiece for a collection of German fairy tales, this illustration suggests that there was a gendered division of labor in the spinning room.

LUDWIG RICHTER,
"Fairy Tales," 1857

A benevolent granny tells stories in an outdoor setting. The sentimental turn is revealed
in the decorative flourishes and idealized natural setting, which suggests that fairy tales
represent the poetry of nature.

HENRY F. DARBY,
The Reverend John Atwood and His Family, 1845

This family of eight, immersed in the reading of bibles, is reminiscent of the Smallweed family, described by Dickens in *Bleak House:* "The house of Smallweed . . . has discarded all amusements, discountenanced all story-books, fairy tales, fictions, and fables, and banished all levities whatsoever. Hence the gratifying fact, that it has had no child born to it, and that the complete little men and women whom it has produced, have been observed to bear a likeness to old monkeys with something depressing on their minds."

ARTHUR RACKHAM,
"Andersen's Fairy Tales," 1932

In this frontispiece to a collection of Andersen's tales, Rackham suggests that the Danish author had a personal charm and playful appeal that he lacked in real life. Andersen cuts silhouettes of characters from his fairy tales for a youthful admirer.

GUSTAVE DORÉ, 1861

Puss in Boots, Little Red Riding Hood, and other fairy-tale characters sit on the spine of a book containing their adventures.

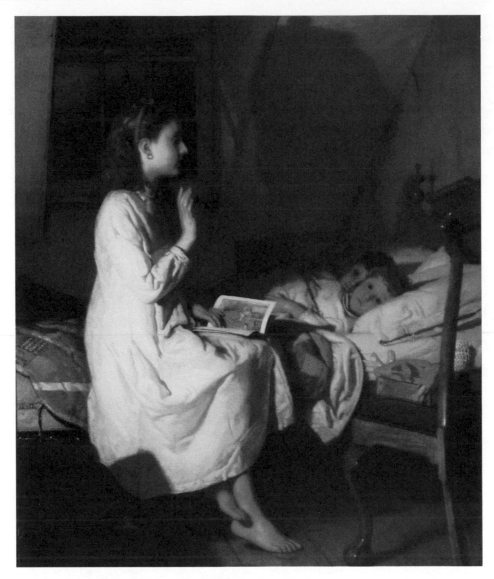

SEYMOUR JOSEPH GUY,
The Story of Golden Locks, 1870

The terrified children tucked in bed have just heard about the arrival of the bears.

JESSIE WILLCOX SMITH,
Rainy Day with Dream Blocks, 1908

Mother and daughter enjoy a quiet moment, reading together in a scene that captures our contemporary notion of parent-child bonding through stories.

I

LITTLE RED RIDING HOOD[1]

Jacob and Wilhelm Grimm

Charles Perrault published the first literary adaptation of "Little Red Riding Hood" in 1697, but few parents choose to read that version of the tale to their children, for it ends with the "wicked wolf" throwing himself on Little Red Riding Hood and gobbling her up. In the Grimms' version, the young girl and her grandmother are rescued by a huntsman, who dispatches the wolf after performing a caesarian section with a pair of scissors.

"Little Red Riding Hood" has a revealing history. Early versions of her story, told around the fireside or in taverns, show a shrewd young heroine who does not need to rely on hunters to escape the wolf and to find her way back home. In "The Story of Grandmother," an oral version of the tale recorded in France at the end of the nineteenth century, Little Red Riding Hood performs a striptease before the wolf, then ends the litany of questions about the wolf's body parts by asking if she can go outside to relieve herself. The wolf is outwitted by Little Red

1. *Little Red Riding Hood.* The French and German titles for the story—"Le Petit Chaperon rouge" and "Rotkäppchen"—suggest caps rather than hoods. Psychoanalytic critics have made much of the color red, equating it with sin, passion, blood, and thereby suggesting a certain complicity on the part of Red Riding Hood in her seduction. But these views have been rebutted by folklorists and historians, who point out that the color red was first introduced in Perrault's literary version of the tale.

From Jacob and Wilhelm Grimm, "Rotkäppchen," in *Kinder- und Hausmärchen*, 7th ed. (Berlin: Dieterich, 1857; first published, Berlin: Realschulbuchhandlung, 1812).

Riding Hood, who is more resourceful trickster than naïve young girl.

Both Perrault and the Grimms worked hard to excise the ribald grotesqueries of the original peasant tales (in some versions, Little Red Riding Hood eats the wolf's leftovers, tasting the "meat" and "wine" in her grandmother's pantry). They rescripted the events to produce a cautionary tale that accommodates a variety of messages about vanity and idleness. Perrault's Little Red Riding Hood has a "good time" gathering nuts, chasing butterflies, and picking flowers, and it is not by chance that she falls into the hands of a savage predator. The Grimms' "Little Red Riding Hood" (literally "Little Red Cap") also erased all traces of the erotic playfulness of oral versions and placed the action in the service of teaching lessons to the child inside and outside the book.

Critics of this story have played fast and loose with its elements, displaying boundless confidence in their interpretive pronouncements. To be sure, the tale itself, by depicting a conflict between a weak, vulnerable protagonist and a large, powerful antagonist, lends itself to a certain interpretive elasticity. But the multiplicity of interpretations does not inspire confidence, with some critics reading the story as a parable of rape, others as a parable of man-hating, still others as a blueprint for female development.

"Little Red Riding Hood" taps into many childhood anxieties, but especially into one that psychoanalysts call the dread of being devoured. While Perrault's story and the Grimms' tale may take too violent a turn for some children, for others those same stories will end with a squeal of delight and a cry for more. And for those who are irritated by Little Red Riding Hood's failure to perceive that the creature lying in her grandmother's bed is a wolf, James Thurber's "The Little Girl and the Wolf" and Roald Dahl's "Little Red Riding Hood and the Wolf" are healthy tonics to Perrault and the Grimms. In Thurber's version, we learn that a wolf does not look any more like your grandmother than the Metro-Goldwyn lion looks like Calvin Coolidge, and we watch the girl take an automatic out of her basket and shoot the wolf dead. "It is not so easy to fool little girls nowadays as it used to be," Thurber concludes in the *moral appended to the tale. And Dahl's Little Red Riding Hood "whips a pistol from her knickers" and, in a matter of weeks, sports a "lovely furry wolf skin coat."*

Cinematic adaptations move in many different directions, from Neil Jordan's The Company of Wolves *(1984), based on a Little Red Riding Hood story by the British novelist Angela Carter, to Matthew Bright's* Freeway *(1996), but they unfailingly explore the erotic dimensions of the story.*

For this first fairy tale, I have selected the Grimms' version for annotation, but included two variant forms in appendix 1 to demonstrate the different inflections, both oral and literary, to the tale. "The Story of Grandmother" is based on an oral tale recorded in nineteenth-century France. Perrault's "Little Red Riding Hood," which appeared at the end of the seventeenth century, gives us a literary version of a tale that was widely disseminated in the oral storytelling culture of the time.

ONCE UPON A TIME there was a charming little girl. Everyone who set eyes on her adored her. The person who loved her most of all was her grandmother, and she was always giving her presents. Once she made her a little hood of red velvet. It was so becoming that the girl wanted to wear it all the time, and so she came to be called Little Red Riding Hood.

One day, the girl's mother said to her: "Little Red Riding Hood, here are some cakes and a bottle of wine.[2] Take them to your grandmother. She's ill and feels weak, and they will make her strong. You'd better start off now, before it gets too hot, and when you're out in the woods, look straight ahead of you like a good little girl and don't stray from the path.[3] Otherwise you'll fall and break the bottle, and then there'll be nothing for Grandmother. And when you walk into her parlor, don't forget to say

2. *cakes and a bottle of wine.* In Perrault's version, Little Red Riding Hood takes some cakes and a pot of butter to her grandmother. Trina Schart Hyman's illustrations for *Little Red Riding Hood* depict a red-nosed, alcoholic grandmother. Recent modern rescriptings, such as Lois Lowry's *Number the Stars*, use the girl's function as courier to construct a heroic figure who saves lives by making it through the woods with her basket of food.

3. *when you're out in the woods, look straight ahead of you like a good little girl and don't stray from the path.* The Grimms added this warning, along with the behavioral imperatives that follow. Acutely aware that their collection of fairy tales would model behavior for children, they looked for opportunities to encode the stories with morals, messages, and lessons in etiquette.

MAXFIELD PARRISH,
"Little Red Riding Hood," 1897

With her wide, flowing cape and white ribbons, the figure of Little Red Riding Hood creates a decorative effect for an image used as a poster. The rigid symmetry of the girl's costume creates the effect of a prim and proper Little Red Riding Hood.

WARWICK GOBLE,
"Little Red Riding Hood," 1923

Little Red Riding Hood is not sure what to make of the predator who eyes her as a tasty morsel. Ears perked and tongue hanging out, this wolf may not seem ferocious, but he is ready to pounce.

ARTHUR RACKHAM,
"Little Red Riding Hood," 1909

In a barren landscape with spooky trees and no hint of flowers on the path, an unwary Little Red Riding Hood gives a lean and hungry wolf directions to Grandmother's house.

4. *the wolf.* The predator in this story is unusual, for he is a real beast rather than a cannibalistic ogre or witch. Folklorists have suggested that the story of Little Red Riding Hood may have originated relatively late (in the Middle Ages) as a cautionary tale warning children about the dangers of the forest. Wild animals, sinister men, and the hybrid figure of the werewolf were thought to menace the safety of children with powerful immediacy. In seventeenth-century Germany, shortly after the Thirty Years' War, fear of wolves and hysteria about werewolves reached especially high levels. The wolf, with his predatory nature, is frequently seen as a metaphor for sexually seductive men.

good morning, and don't go poking around in all the corners of the house."

"I'll do just as you say," Little Red Riding Hood promised her mother.

Grandmother lived deep in the woods, about half an hour's walk from the village. No sooner had Little Red Riding Hood set foot in the forest than she met the wolf.[4] Little Red Riding Hood had no idea what a wicked beast he was, and so she wasn't in the least afraid of him.

"Good morning, Little Red Riding Hood," the wolf said.

"Thank you kindly, Mr. Wolf," she replied.

"Where are you headed so early this morning, Little Red Riding Hood?"

"To Grandmother's house," she replied.

"What's that tucked under your apron?"

"Some cakes and wine. Yesterday we baked, and

JESSIE WILLCOX SMITH,
"Little Red Riding Hood," 1919

The wolf's red tongue blends in with the hue of Red Riding Hood's cloak. Putting her best foot forward (like the wolf), the girl looks with some trepidation at the sharp canines, which are too close for comfort.

HARRY CLARKE,
"Little Red Riding Hood," 1922

"He asked her whither she was going." A cautious Little Red Riding Hood carries an umbrella with her as she walks on a paved path through the woods. The wolf, impressed by the girl's fashion sense, observes her with bared teeth and blue eyes.

MARGARET EVANS PRICE,
"Little Red Riding Hood," 1921

Red Riding Hood meets up with a wolf, who listens attentively to what she has to say. The outskirts of the village are still visible from the edge of the woods, where the two meet.

Grandmother, who is ill and feeling weak, needs something to make her better," she replied.

"Where is your grandmother's house, Little Red Riding Hood?"

"It's a good quarter of an hour's walk into the woods, right under the three big oak trees. You must know the place from the hazel hedges around it," said Little Red Riding Hood.

The wolf thought to himself: "That tender young thing will make a nice dainty snack! She'll taste even better than the old woman. If you're really crafty, you'll get them both."

The wolf walked alongside Little Red Riding Hood for a while. Then he said: "Little Red Riding Hood, have you

ANONYMOUS,
"Little Red Riding Hood"

Little Red Riding Hood has strayed from the path and is picking flowers when she encounters a wolf with a hang-dog look.

ANONYMOUS,
"Little Red Riding Hood"

One of the few Red Riding Hood figures in somewhat formal attire, this girl sports a red hat but no cape or cloak. The long-legged wolf eyes her as a tasty morsel.

GUSTAVE DORÉ,
"Little Red Riding Hood," 1861

The wolf and Little Red Riding Hood gaze at one another, each attempting to fathom what is on the mind of the other. Note how the lines of the wolf's body conform to the tree trunk, how his tail and rear haunches face the viewer, and how he peers down at the girl, who seems to be pointing the way to Grandmother's house.

noticed the beautiful flowers all around? Why don't you stay and look at them for a while? I don't think you've even heard how sweetly the birds are singing. You're acting as if you were on the way to school, when it's so much fun out here in the woods."

Little Red Riding Hood looked with eyes wide open and noticed how the sunbeams were dancing in the trees. She caught sight of the beautiful flowers all around and thought: "If you bring Grandmother a fresh bouquet, she'll be overjoyed. It's still so early in the morning that I'm sure to get there in plenty of time."

Little Red Riding Hood left the path and ran off into the woods looking for flowers. As soon as she had picked one, she caught sight of an even more beautiful one somewhere else and went after it. And so she went ever deeper into the woods.

The wolf ran straight to Grandmother's house and knocked at the door.

"Who's there?"

"Little Red Riding Hood. I've brought some cakes and wine. Open the door."

"Just raise the latch," Grandmother called out. "I'm too weak to get out of bed."

GUSTAVE DORÉ,
"Little Red Riding Hood," 1861

The cat scurries under the bed, and Grandma, whose glasses and snuffbox slide down the bedcovers, becomes the victim of the wolf.

The wolf raised the latch, and the door swung wide open. Without saying a word, he went straight to Grandmother's bed and gobbled her right up. Then he put on her clothes and her nightcap, lay down in her bed, and drew the curtains.

Meanwhile, Little Red Riding Hood was running around looking for flowers. When she had so many in her arms that she couldn't carry any more, she suddenly remembered Grandmother and got back on the path leading to her house. She was surprised to find the door open,

GUSTAVE DORÉ,
"Little Red Riding Hood," 1861

It seems to be dawning on Little Red Riding Hood that the large nightcap cannot conceal the identity of the figure wearing it. Yet she does not look at all startled and makes no effort to bolt from the bed.

ARTHUR RACKHAM,
"Little Red Riding Hood," 1909

Little Red Riding Hood's cloak builds a powerful contrast to the dark patterns of "Granny's" sheet, blanket, and curtain. The sharp teeth are in clear evidence when Red Riding Hood draws the floral curtain.

ARTHUR RACKHAM,
"Little Red Riding Hood," 1930

The wolf, with nightcap and spectacles, looks quite benign as Little Red Riding Hood approaches with her basket and flowers. The paws, with their long claws, betray the fact that this wolf is up to no good.

5. *"Oh, Grandmother, what big ears you have!"* In the classic dialogue between girl and wolf, Little Red Riding Hood invokes the sense of hearing, sight, feeling, and taste, leaving out the sense of smell. The inventory of body parts was no doubt expanded by folk raconteurs, who took advantage of opportunities for ribald humor. A parallel dialogue in oral versions of the tale provides an inventory of Little Red Riding Hood's clothes, which she removes and discards one by one.

and when she stepped into the house, she had such a strange feeling that she thought: "Oh, my goodness, I'm usually so glad to be at Grandmother's house, but today I feel really uncomfortable."

Little Red Riding Hood called out a hello, but there was no reply. Then she went over to the bed and pulled back the curtains. Grandmother was lying there with her nightcap pulled down over her face. She looked very strange.

"Oh, Grandmother, what big ears you have!"**5**

"The better to hear you with."

"Oh, Grandmother, what big eyes you have!"

"The better to see you with."

"Oh, Grandmother, what big hands you have!"

"The better to grab you with!"

"Oh, Grandmother, what a big, scary mouth you have!"

"The better to eat you with!"

LITTLE RED RIDING HOOD

ANONYMOUS,
"Little Red Riding Hood," 1865

This Little Red Riding Hood is clearly aware that the creature in Grandmother's bed is not a human being. Since this is an illustration for Perrault's version of the tale, we know that the girl is doomed.

ROSA PETHERICK,
"Little Red Riding Hood"

The naïve girl seems baffled but not at all terrified of the creature in Grandmother's bed. Note that one of the flowers has dropped on the floor as she ponders the furry face under the nightcap.

No sooner had the wolf said these words than he leaped out of bed and gobbled up poor Little Red Riding Hood.[6]

Once the wolf had stilled his appetite, he lay back down in the bed, fell asleep, and began to snore very loudly. A huntsman[7] happened to be passing by the house just then and thought: "How loudly the old woman is snoring! I'd better check to see if anything's wrong." He walked into the house and, when he reached the bed, he realized that a wolf was lying in it.

"I've found you at last, you old sinner," he said. "I've been after you for a long time now."

He pulled out his musket and was about to take aim when he realized that the wolf might have eaten Grandmother and that he could still save her. Instead of firing, he took out a pair of scissors and began cutting open the

6. *he leaped out of bed and gobbled up poor Little Red Riding Hood.* Many critics have viewed this scene as a symbolic death, followed by rebirth, once Little Red Riding Hood is released from the belly of the beast. The connection with biblical and mythical figures (most notably Jonah) is self-evident, though Little Red Riding Hood has also been interpreted as a figure that symbolizes the sun, engulfed by the night and reemerging at dawn. More recently, the swallowing whole of the grandmother and the girl has been seen as a symbolic double rape.

7. *A huntsman.* Note that the male figures in the story are either predators or rescuers. The huntsman has been seen as representing

EUGÈNE FEYEN,
"Little Red Riding Hood," 1846

An ailing Granny appears to be enjoying small talk with a well-coiffed Little Red Riding Hood. Teeth and paws signal that this wolf, masquerading as an invalid, can turn at any moment into a murderous predator. The quiet formality of the tableau stands in stark contrast to the violence that will follow.

patriarchal protection for the two women, who are unable to fend for themselves. In oral versions, the girl in the story does not need to rely on a huntsman passing by grandmother's house.

8. *began cutting open the belly of the sleeping wolf.* Freud and others read this scene as an allusion to the birth process. The wolf, as the poet Anne Sexton wryly notes, undergoes "a kind of caesarian section." One psychoanalytic critic views the wolf as suffering from pregnancy envy.

9. *fetched some large stones and filled the wolf's belly with them.* The stones have been read as

ARPAD SCHMIDHAMMER,
"Little Red Riding Hood"

Flowers and basket are scattered on the ground when the ferocious wolf attacks Little Red Riding Hood. This scene adorned a German book of fairy tales for children.

belly of the sleeping wolf.[8] After making a few cuts, he caught sight of a red cap. He made a few more cuts, and a girl leaped out, crying: "Oh, I was so terrified! It was so dark in the belly of the wolf."

Although she could barely breathe, the aged grandmother also found her way back out of the belly. Little Red Riding Hood quickly fetched some large stones and filled the wolf's belly with them.[9] When the wolf awoke, he tried to race off, but the stones were so heavy that his legs collapsed, and he fell down dead.

Little Red Riding Hood, her grandmother, and the huntsman were elated. The huntsman skinned the wolf and took the pelt home with him. Grandmother ate the cakes and drank the wine that Little Red Riding Hood had brought her and recovered her health. Little Red Riding Hood said to herself: "Never again will you stray from the path and go into the woods, when your mother has forbidden it."

THERE IS A story about another time that Little Red Riding Hood met a wolf on the way to Grandmother's house, while she was bringing her some cakes. The wolf tried to get her to stray from the path, but Little Red Riding Hood was on her guard and kept right on going. She told her grandmother that she had met a wolf and that he had greeted her. But he had looked at her in such an evil way that "If we hadn't been out in the open, he would have gobbled me right up."

"Well then," said Grandmother. "We'll just lock the door so he can't get in."

A little while later the wolf knocked at the door and called out: "Open the door, Grandmother. It's Little Red Riding Hood, and I'm bringing you some cakes."

The two kept completely quiet and refused to open the door. Then old Graybeard circled the house a few times and jumped up on the roof. He was planning on waiting until Little Red Riding Hood went home. Then he was going to creep after her and gobble her up in the dark. But Grandmother figured out what was on his mind. There was a big stone trough in front of the house. Grandmother said to the child: "Here's a bucket, Little Red Riding Hood. Yesterday I cooked some sausages in it. Take the water in which they were boiled and pour it into the trough."

Little Red Riding Hood kept taking water to the trough until it was completely full. The smell from those sausages reached the wolf's nostrils. His neck was stretched out so far from sniffing and looking around that he lost his balance and began to slide down the roof. He slid right down into the trough and was drowned. Little Red Riding Hood walked home cheerfully, and no one ever did her any harm.

a sign of sterility, but they are more likely an appropriate retaliation for the incorporation of Little Red Riding Hood and her grandmother.

2

CINDERELLA,
OR THE LITTLE GLASS SLIPPER[1]

Charles Perrault

1. *the little glass slipper.* For many years scholars debated the issue of whether the slipper was made of *vair* (an obsolete word for "fur") or *verre* ("glass"). Folklorists have now discredited the view that the slipper was made of fur and endorse the notion that the slipper has a magical quality to it and is made of glass.

Yeh-hsien, Cendrillon, Aschenputtel, Rashin Coatie, Mossy Coat, Katie Woodencloak, Cenerentola: these are just a few of Cinderella's folkloric cousins. If Cinderella has been reinvented by nearly every known culture, her story is also perpetually rewritten within any given culture. Working Girl with Melanie Griffith, Pretty Woman with Julia Roberts, and Ever After with Drew Barrymore: these films offer striking evidence that we continue to recycle the story to manage our cultural anxieties and conflicts about courtship and marriage. Few fairy tales have enjoyed the rich literary, cinematic, and musical afterlife of "Cinderella."

The first Cinderella we know was named Yeh-hsien, and her story was recorded around A.D. 850 by Tuan Ch'eng-shih. Yeh-hsien wears a dress made of kingfisher feathers and tiny shoes made of gold. She triumphs over her stepmother and stepsister, who are killed by flying stones. Like Western Cinderellas, Yeh-hsien is a humble creature, who discharges the

From Charles Perrault, "Cendrillon ou la petite pantoufle de verre," in *Histoires ou contes du temps passé, avec des moralités* (Paris: Barbin, 1697).

household chores and is subjected to humiliating treatment at the hands of her stepmother and stepsister. Her salvation appears in the form of a ten-foot-long fish who provides her with gold, pearls, dresses, and food. The Cinderellas who follow in Yeh-hsien's footsteps all find their salvation in the form of magical donors. In the Grimms' "Aschenputtel," a tree showers Cinderella with gifts; in Perrault's "Cendrillon," a fairy godmother provides a coach, footmen, and beautiful garments; in the Scottish Rashin Coatie, a little red calf produces a dress.

The enduring appeal of "Cinderella" derives not only from the rags-to-riches trajectory of the tale's heroine but also from the way in which the story engages with classic family conflicts ranging from sibling rivalry to sexual jealousies. Cinderella's father may not have much of a part in this story, but the role of the (step)mother and (step)sisters is writ large. If Cinderella's biological mother is dead, her spirit reappears as the magic donor who provides the heroine with the gifts she needs to make a splendid appearance at the ball. With the good mother dead, the evil mother takes over—alive and active— undermining Cinderella in every possible fashion, yet unable to hinder her ultimate triumph. In this splitting of the mother into two polar opposites, psychologists have seen a mechanism for helping children work through the conflicts created as they begin to mature and separate from their primary caretakers. The image of the good mother is preserved in all her nurturing glory, even as feelings of helplessness and resentment are given expression through the figure of the predatory wicked stepmother.

Fairy tales place a premium on surfaces, and Cinderella's beauty, along with her magnificent attire, singles her out as the fairest in the land. Through labor and good looks, Cinderella works her way up the social ladder of success. If the story in its older versions does not capture the dynamics of courtship and romance in today's world, it remains a source of fascination in its documentation of fantasies about love and marriage in an earlier time. Perrault's version of 1697 from Tales of Mother Goose is among the first full literary elaborations of the story. It was followed by the more violent version recorded in 1812 *by the Brothers Grimm. The Grimms delight in describing the blood in the shoes of the stepsisters, who try to slice off their heels and toes in order to get a perfect fit. The German version also gives us a far less compassionate Cinderella, one who does not forgive her stepsisters but invites them to her wedding, where doves peck out their eyes.*

2. *the menial household chores.* Cinderella is always the household drudge, a creature who not only has to discharge domestic chores but whose true beauty is concealed by soot, dust, and cinders. That she is always hardworking and kind points to the way in which character can create powerfully attractive figures. Rodgers and Hammerstein asked a central question in their musical *Cinderella* (1957): "Do I love you because you're beautiful, or are you beautiful because I love you?"

3. *with mirrors so tall that you could see yourself reflected in them from head to toe.* Vanity ranks high among the cardinal sins of fairy-tale figures. Snow White's stepmother is always consulting the mirror, and Cinderella's stepsisters repeatedly look in the mirror to admire themselves. Floor-length mirrors were a real extravagance in Perrault's day, and there is something almost magical associated with being able to see your image from head to toe.

THERE ONCE LIVED a gentleman who, when he married for the second time, took for his wife the most vain and haughty woman imaginable. She had two daughters who shared her bad temperament and were just like her. The husband, however, had a young daughter whose kindness and sweet temper were unrivaled. The girl took after her mother, who had been the finest person you can imagine.

As soon as the wedding was over, the stepmother began to display her true colors. She could not tolerate the young child, whose many good qualities made her own daughters appear all the more hateful. She ordered the girl to carry out all the menial household chores.[2] It was she who had to wash the dishes and scrub the stairs, who cleaned the rooms of the mistress and her daughters. She herself slept on a wretched bed of straw in a garret, while her sisters occupied rooms with inlaid floors, with beds done up in the latest style, and with mirrors so tall that you could see yourself reflected in them from head to toe.[3]

The poor child endured everything with patience. She didn't dare complain to her father, who would have scolded her, for he was completely under the thumb of his wife. Whenever she finished her chores, she would go over to a corner by the chimney and sit down among the cinders and ashes. And so everyone started calling her Cindertail. But the younger of the two sisters, who was not quite as vicious as the older girl, began calling her

Cinderella. The stepsisters dressed in magnificent clothes, yet Cinderella looked a thousand times prettier, even in her shabby apparel.

One day the son of the king was hosting a ball to which he had invited all the notables in the land. The two young ladies were included in the invitation, for they had attained a certain social prominence. They were thrilled to be going and were busy choosing the most flattering clothes and headdresses. This meant more work for Cinderella, for she was the one who had to iron her sisters' linen and who set their ruffles. All day long the two talked of nothing but clothes.

"I think I'll wear that red velvet dress with the English trimming," said the older sister.

ARTHUR RACKHAM,
"Cinderella," 1919

Cinderella gazes with longing out the window from her garret in the attic. A barefoot princess, she has a girlish charm that bodes well for her move from rags to riches. The frame that turns her image into a work of art contains playful allusions to the animals that are to serve as her servants. Beneath her, the two outlandishly dressed stepsisters dance a jig with their ludicrous suitors, while her footmen await their magical transformation.

ALBERT HENSCHEL,
"Cinderella," 1863

This German Cinderella serenely watches as birds sort the grains for her. The heroine may be poor, but she clearly keeps a tidy household and manages to dress herself in more than rags.

HARRY CLARKE,
"Cinderella," 1922

"Anyone else but Cinderella would have given them unflattering hairdos." The stepsisters, with their hideous hairdos and dresses, admire themselves in mirrors and allow themselves to be attended by a Cinderella wearing a patched, but elegant, skirt. Creatures of excess, they are surrounded by too much of almost everything.

RIE CRAMER,
"Cinderella," early 20th century

This Dutch Cinderella is physically overwhelmed by her stepsisters, almost doubles of each other, who primp and fuss while the heroine attends to their needs. Note that vanity is associated with aristocratic bearing, while Cinderella is presented as a modest young woman, willing to humble herself before her domineering stepsisters.

"I only have my usual petticoat to wear, but I'll make up for that with a gold-flowered shawl and my diamond necklace, which is far from ordinary."

The sisters sent for the best hairdresser around to put up their hair in two rows of curls, and they bought beauty marks from the finest makeup artist. They summoned Cinderella to ask her opinion, for they knew she had excellent taste. She gave them the best possible advice and even volunteered to do their hair, an offer that was gladly accepted. While Cinderella was working on them, the sisters asked: "Cinderella, wouldn't you like to go to the ball?"

"Alas, dear ladies! You're just making fun of me. That's not a place where I could be seen."

WANDA GÁG,
"Cinderella," 1936

In a composition that has a wonderfully unified design, the American Gág presents a youthful Cinderella who delights in the gift of a cloak from the tree planted at her mother's grave. This Cinderella seems carefree and relaxed in comparison with her counterparts drawn by European artists.

WANDA GÁG,
"Cinderella," 1936

In a wonderful dig at the pompous stepsisters, Gág presents two women who, with flowers and arrows in their headdresses, appear singularly unattractive. Whatever efforts these two matronly women channel into finery, they only intensify their unsightliness, which becomes evident not merely in their facial expressions but in the pudgy hands of the one and the gnarled fingers of the other.

"You're right, everyone would have a good laugh if they saw Cinderella going to the ball."

Anyone else but Cinderella would have given them unflattering hairdos, but Cinderella was good-natured, and she put their hair up perfectly. The two sisters were so excited that they were unable to eat a thing for two days. They tore nearly a dozen laces while trying to make their waists as small as possible, and they spent nearly all their time in front of the mirror. At last the happy day arrived. They set off for the ball, and Cinderella followed them with her eyes as long as possible. When they were out of sight, she began to cry. Her godmother, who saw that she was in tears, asked what was wrong.[4] "I should so like to

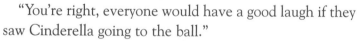

4. *Her godmother, who saw that she was in tears, asked what was wrong.* Cinderella usually finds in nature the help she needs. A fish, a calf, or a tree comes to her rescue. Perrault, by contrast, created a fairy godmother, whose importance is underscored, tongue in cheek, through the second moral to the tale. Disney's *Cinderella*, based on Perrault's version, enlarges the role of the fairy godmother and uses her to create comic relief.

5. *if you're good.* Perrault, who was heavily invested in the idea that fairy tales reward virtue, made a point of underscoring the heroine's kindness and sweet disposition. His tale is encoded with numerous behavioral imperatives, revealing the degree to which children are the implied audience for his story.

6. *"I'll go and see if there's a rat in the rattrap."* The Disney version of "Cinderella" substitutes a horse and a dog for the rat and the lizards of Perrault's story.

. . . I should so like to . . . ." Cinderella was sobbing so hard that she could not finish the sentence.

The godmother, who was a fairy, said to her: "You really want to go to the ball, don't you?"

"With all my heart," Cinderella said, sighing deeply.

"Well, if you're good,**5** I'll make sure you get there."

The fairy godmother went up to her room and said: "Go down into the garden and bring me a pumpkin."

Cinderella picked out the most splendid pumpkin in the garden and brought it back to her godmother. She had no idea how it was going to get her to the ball. Her godmother scooped out the pumpkin, leaving nothing but the rind. When she tapped it with her wand, it was instantly transformed into a beautiful coach, covered with fine gold. Next she went over to look into her mousetrap, where she found six mice who were still alive. She told Cinderella to lift the door of the trap just a bit. As each mouse ran out, she tapped it with her wand, and it was instantly transformed into a fine horse. That made a magnificent team of six handsome, mouse-gray, dappled horses. The godmother was at a loss for a coachman, but Cinderella said: "I'll go and see if there's a rat in the rattrap.**6** We may be able to turn him into a coachman."

"You're right," said the godmother. "Go take a look."

Cinderella brought the trap over to her, and there were three huge rats in it. The fairy picked out the one with the fullest beard. When she tapped it with her wand, it turned into a portly coachman with the most handsome mustache imaginable. Then the godmother said to Cinderella: "Go down to the garden, and you'll find some lizards behind the watering pot. Bring them up to me."

As soon as she brought them up the stairs, the godmother turned them into six footmen, who stationed themselves at once on the back of the coach in their braided liveries and perched there as if they had been doing nothing but that all their lives.

The fairy godmother then said to Cinderella: "Well, you finally have something that will take you to the ball. Aren't you happy?"

"Yes, but do I have to go as I am, in these shabby clothes?" The fairy godmother waved her magic wand, and Cinderella's clothes were instantly transformed into garments of gold and silver, encrusted with jewels.[7] Then she gave her a pair of glass slippers, the most beautiful ever seen.

Cinderella was finally ready for the ball, and she climbed into the coach. Her godmother told her how important it was that she return by midnight, warning her that if she stayed just one moment longer, her carriage

7. *garments of gold and silver, encrusted with jewels.* If Cinderella finds help by turning to nature, she wears a dress that is associated with the realm of artifice. Gold and silver are spun into fine threads, and jewels often cover her garment. The dress contributes powerfully to the radiant appearance she makes at the ball.

ARTHUR RACKHAM,
"Cinderella," 1933

Rackham's original caption to this image for Perrault's version of "Cinderella" reads: "Now, Cinderella, you may go; but remember . . ." The contrast in the physical appearance of fairy-tale heroine and fairy godmother could hardly be more striking and is further intensified by the fact that both faces appear in profile. Rackham's fairy godmother may have a smile on her face, but her witch's hat, along with the reminder that there will be real consequences to a late return, suggests that she is not purely benevolent. With diaphanous evening wear that blends with the ivory and rose hues of her skin, and with one hand coyly lifting her skirts to reveal a slipper peaking out from under them, Cinderella seems a model of playful feminine beauty. The awkward positioning of her arms suggests that the effect achieved is not without effort.

EDMUND DULAC,
"Cinderella," 1929

EDMUND DULAC,
"Cinderella," 1929

EDMUND DULAC,
"Cinderella," 1929

"They sent for the best hairdresser to arrange their hair." The vanity of the stepsisters is emphasized through the art of the hairdresser, who prepares elaborate coiffures for the young women. The omnipresence of mirrors, with one positioned before the stepsister with her hairdresser, the other reflecting the robes of the second young woman, further underscores the importance of surface appearances for Cinderella's rivals. Excess in hairstyle, dress, and perfume is the signature of their style.

"And her godmother pointed to the finest of all with her wand." With a wave of her magic wand, Cinderella's godmother chooses the pumpkin destined to become a coach. A luminous figure whose dress lights up the scene more powerfully than the stars in the skies, this godmother promises salvation for the lowly heroine dressed in carefully patched skirts. The light in the cottage window adds a touch of warmth, even if the space within is the site for Cinderella's oppression.

"She was driven away, beside herself with joy." Cinderella seems to float rather than ride on the trail of fog leading to the castle. Lit up by a full moon, the carriage, horse, coachman, and footmen glow in the dark. Contained within the miniature space of the carriage, Cinderella's beauty remains secret until she emerges from her hiding place to attend the ball in her regal splendor.

would turn back into a pumpkin, the horses would become mice, and the footmen lizards, and her clothes would return to their former state. Cinderella promised her godmother that she would leave by midnight. She set out for the ball, overwhelmed with joy.

As soon as the prince learned that a grand princess had just arrived and that no one knew her, he went out to welcome her. He offered his arm to help her out of the coach and escorted her to the hall where the company had

EDMUND DULAC,
"Cinderella," 1929

EDMUND DULAC,
"Cinderella," 1929

EDMUND DULAC,
"Cinderella," 1929

"The King's son led her through the gardens, where the guests drew apart and gazed in wonder at her loveliness." The palace in the background forms a strong contrast to the humble cottage where Cinderella lives. The assembled company is struck by the stunning beauty of the mysterious young woman who has appeared at the ball in a radiant costume. The servant boy continues to show up in the pictures to add a touch of the exotic and distinctly dark that stands in opposition to the luminous whiteness of the guests.

"Whereupon she instantly desired her partner to lead her to the KING and QUEEN." It is a quarter to twelve, and Cinderella does not have much time to make her getaway before the transformation takes place. The prince kisses the hand of the woman with whom he has fallen in love, little realizing that her request to meet the king and queen are nothing but a pretext for getting away.

"She made her escape as lightly as a deer." Starry skies, lights in the castle, the marble staircase, and Cinderella's apron illuminate a scene in which Dulac once again uses blues and whites to display a mastery of nocturnal scenes. Unstoppable, especially now that she is wearing her rags and unencumbered by the ballroom dress, Cinderella is in a kind of natural state that is the antithesis of the seemingly aristocratic young woman at the ball.

assembled. Suddenly everyone fell silent. No one was dancing, and the violins stopped playing, because everyone was so absorbed in contemplating the great beauty of the unknown lady who had just entered. There was nothing but a confusion of voices. "Oh, how beautiful she is!" The king himself, as old as he was, could not take his eyes off the princess and whispered to the queen that it had been a long time since he had seen such a beautiful and charming person. All the ladies were carefully inspecting

EDMUND DULAC,
"Cinderella," 1929

"The Prime Minister was kept very busy during the next few weeks." The courtly pomp of the prime minister and his assistant appears ludicrous in the context of the two cottages, which are in a natural state of disarray. The cock strutting before the prime minister makes a mockery of an aristocratic bearing. Still, as we know from the face in the window, the visit has evoked some curiosity.

HARRY CLARKE,
"Cinderella," 1922

"Cinderella and her Prince." As the clock strikes twelve, Cinderella has an anxious look on her face, realizing that she must release herself from the grip of the prince and get back to the coach within a matter of seconds.

Cinderella's headdress and clothing so that they could try to find the same beautiful fabrics and hire able hands to make what she was wearing.

The prince conducted Cinderella to the place of honor and asked if she would dance with him. She danced with such grace that everyone admired her even more. There was a sumptuous dinner, but the prince was not able to eat a thing, because he couldn't take his eyes off her. Cinderella went to sit with her sisters and paid them a thousand compliments. She shared with them the oranges and lemons that the prince had given her. The sisters were astonished, for they did not recognize her at all. While Cinderella was talking with them, she heard the clock sound a quarter to twelve. She bowed low to the company and departed as quickly as possible.

As soon as she came back, Cinderella went to look for

her godmother. After thanking her, she said that she was hoping to go to the ball again, for the prince had invited her to return the next day. While she was telling her godmother about everything that had happened at the ball, the two sisters started knocking at the door. Cinderella went to open it.

"You stayed out really late!" Cinderella said, yawning, rubbing her eyes, and stretching as if she had just gotten up. In reality she had not had the slightest desire to sleep since the time that the two had left. "If you had gone to the ball," one of the sisters said to her, "you would not have found it boring. A beautiful princess was there, more beautiful than you can imagine, and she paid us a thousand compliments. She even gave us some oranges and lemons."

Cinderella felt overjoyed when she heard those words. She asked the name of the princess, but her stepsisters said that no one knew who she was and that even the prince was baffled. He would give anything in the world to know her name. Cinderella smiled and said: "Was she really beautiful? Dear God, how lucky you are! Won't I ever have a chance to see her? Alas! Mademoiselle Javotte, would you lend me that yellow dress, the one that you wear every day?"

"Of course," said Mademoiselle Javotte. "That's a great idea! Lend my dress to a dirty little Cindertail like you. I would be a fool to do something like that!" Cinderella was not surprised by that answer, and in fact she was pleased, since she would have been terribly embarrassed if her sister had been willing to lend the dress.

The following day the sisters went to the ball, and so did Cinderella, but this time she was dressed even more magnificently than before. The prince never left her side and whispered sweet things in her ear all night long. The young lady was enjoying herself so much that she completely forgot her godmother's advice. She thought it was still eleven o'clock when she suddenly realized that the clock was beginning to strike twelve. She rose and fled as gracefully as a deer. The prince followed her, but he was unable to catch up with her. One of the glass slippers fell off Cinderella's foot, and the prince picked it up very carefully.

When Cinderella reached home, she was out of breath. The coach was gone, there were no footmen, and she was dressed in shabby clothes. Nothing remained of her magnificent attire except for one of the little slippers, the mate to the one she had dropped. The guards at the palace gates were asked if they had seen a princess leaving the ball. They said that they had not seen anyone leave except a girl who was poorly dressed and who looked more like a peasant than a lady.

WARWICK GOBLE,
"Cinderella," 1923

The original caption reads: "The only remnant of her past magnificence being one of her little glass slippers." Goble's Cinderella admires the perfect fit of the one remaining slipper. The rat, lizard, and pumpkin in the foreground are all that is left of her magnificent carriage, coachman, and footmen. Broom and spinning wheel are reminders of the domestic duties that bind Cinderella to the hearth, and the patched skirt is an emblem of her destitute state in the household. The white slipper nearly glows in its contrast to the dreary realities of Cinderella's life.

MAXFIELD PARRISH,
Enchantment, 1914

Produced for a calendar advertising General Electric–Edison
Mazda Lamps, this painting, entitled *Enchantment,* illustrates
the spectacular allure of Parrish's commercial art. Cinderella,
the quintessential fairy-tale heroine, is captured in a moment
of dreamy meditation, contemplating the entrance she will
make at the ball. The characteristically vibrant blue background, the decorative flowers, and the statuesque beauty of
Cinderella combine to cast a spell of enchantment on the
viewer.

When the two sisters returned from the ball, Cinderella
asked whether they had enjoyed themselves as much as
the first time and whether the beautiful lady had been
present. They said that she had been there, but had fled
when the clock struck twelve. She had been in such a
rush that she had dropped one of the glass slippers, the
prettiest shoe in the world. The prince had picked it up,
and for the rest of the night he did nothing but stare at it.
They were sure that he was very much in love with the
person to whom the slipper belonged.

The sisters spoke the truth, for a few days later the
prince proclaimed, with a flourish of trumpets, that he was
going to marry the woman whose foot fit the slipper. His

ARTHUR RACKHAM,
"Cinderella," 1919

Decorative borders adorn the silhouettes of Cinderella and the messenger sent by the prince. Accompanied by a Moor servant, the messenger tips his hat and extends the slipper that will elevate Cinderella from her humble condition at the hearth, complete with broom and cat, to the rank of royalty. The statue on the mantelpiece prefigures her new destiny.

ANONYMOUS,
"Cinderella," 1865

Many illustrators, like this one, focus on the moment in the story at which the shoe is fitted to Cinderella's foot. When the drudge in the kitchen unexpectedly turns out to have a dainty foot that fits the glass slipper, those surrounding Cinderella cannot conceal their wonder and astonishment.

JESSIE WILLCOX SMITH,
"Cinderella," 1911

This latter-day Cinderella is assisted with her boots by a young Prince Charming.

men began by trying the shoe on princesses, then on duchesses, then on everyone at court, but in vain. The shoe was brought to the house of the two sisters, who each did her best to get her foot into the shoe, but neither succeeded. Cinderella, who was watching them, recognized her slipper and said, smiling: "Let me see if it will fit me." The sisters burst out laughing and made fun of her. But the gentleman who had been entrusted with the slipper looked intently at Cinderella and, finding that she was very beautiful, said that it was acceptable and that he was under orders to have everyone try on the slipper.

The gentleman asked Cinderella to sit down. He brought the slipper to her foot and saw that it fit perfectly, like a wax mold. The two sisters were filled with astonishment, and even more so when Cinderella pulled another little slipper from her pocket and put it on her foot. Just then, the fairy godmother arrived, and, tapping her wand, she made Cinderella's garments more magnificent than ever before.

The two sisters realized that Cinderella was the beautiful woman they had seen at the ball. They threw themselves at her feet, begging her forgiveness for treating her so badly and for making her suffer. Cinderella helped them get up, kissed them, and said that she was willing to forgive them with all her heart. She hoped that they would love her always. Dressed in dazzling clothes, she was escorted to the castle of the prince. He found her more beautiful than ever, and a few days later they were married. Cinderella, who was as kind as she was beautiful, let the two sisters live in the palace and had them married, on the very same day, to two noblemen at the court.

MORAL

The beauty of a woman is a rare treasure.
To admire it is always a pleasure.
But what they call real grace
Is priceless and wins any race.

That's what the fairy in this tale
Taught Cinderella without fail,
Here's how she could become a queen
Teaching lessons, yet staying serene.

Beauties: that gift is worth more than a dress.
It'll win a man's heart; it will truly impress.
Grace is a gift that the fairies confer:
Ask anyone at all; it's what we prefer.

Surely it's a benefit
To show real courage and have some wit,
To have good sense and breeding too
And whatever else comes out of the blue.
But none of this will help you out,
If you wish to shine and gad about.
Without the help of godparents
Your life will never have great events.

3

HANSEL AND GRETEL[1]

Jacob and Wilhelm Grimm

1. *Hansel and Gretel.* This tale was originally known as "Little Brother and Little Sister." The Grimms note similarities to Perrault's "Tom Thumb," in which a woodcutter and his wife abandon their seven sons in the woods.

"Hansel and Gretel" is a story that celebrates the triumph of children over hostile and predatory adults. Addressing anxieties about starvation, abandonment, and being devoured, it shows two young siblings joining forces to defeat monsters at home and in the woods. Folklorists refer to this and other stories pitting young, powerless protagonists against cruel brutes as "The Children and the Ogre." A child or a group of children innocently enter the abode of an ogre, wicked witch, giant, or other type of villain, succeed in turning the tables on a bloodthirsty antagonist, and flee, often with material goods in the form of jewels or gold.

Sibling solidarity is so rare in fairy tales (think of the sisters in "Cinderella") that "Hansel and Gretel" provides a unique opportunity for displaying its advantages. While Hansel takes the lead at the beginning of the tale, soothing Gretel's fears and using his wits to find the way back home, Gretel outsmarts the witch, tricking her into entering the oven. The siblings in the

From Jacob and Wilhelm Grimm, "Hänsel und Gretel," in *Kinder- und Hausmärchen*, 7th ed. (Berlin: Dieterich, 1857; first published, Berlin: Realschulbuchhandlung, 1812).

Grimms' version of "The Children and the Ogre" may be somewhat pious for modern sensibilities, but they were youthful insurgents by nineteenth-century standards, eavesdropping on their parents' nighttime conversations, deploying a ruse to get back home, greedily feasting on the house of the witch, and running off with the witch's jewels after Gretel pushes her into the oven. Determined to find a way back home, Hansel and Gretel survive what children fear more than anything else: abandonment by parents and exposure to predators.

In Engelbert Humperdinck's 1893 operatic version of the story, the children, who are sent into the woods to collect berries as a punishment for neglecting their chores, end up liberating themselves and also lifting the spell that transformed many other children into gingerbread. A happy ending reunites the children with both parents.

AT THE EDGE of a great forest, there once lived a poor woodcutter with his wife and two children.[2] The little boy was called Hansel, and the girl was named Gretel. There was never much to eat in their home, and once, during a famine, the woodcutter could no longer put bread on the table. At night he lay in bed worrying, tossing and turning in his despair. With a sigh, he turned to his wife and said: "What is going to happen to us? How can we take care of our poor little children when the two of us don't have enough to eat?"

"Listen to me," his wife replied. "Tomorrow, at the crack of dawn, let's take the children out into the deepest part of the forest. We can make a fire for them and give them each a crust of bread. Then we'll go about our work, leaving them all by themselves. They'll never find their way back home, and we'll be rid of them."

"Oh, no," her husband said. "I can't do that. Who would have the heart to leave those children all alone in

2. *a poor woodcutter with his wife and two children.* In early versions of the tale, the woodcutter and his wife are the biological parents of the children. By the fourth edition of the *Nursery and Household Tales* in 1840, the Grimms had turned the "wife" into a "stepmother" and made her the real villain of the piece. Whereas the father shares the blame for abandoning the children in the woods in early versions of the tales (as in Perrault's "Tom Thumb"), in later versions he protests against the actions of his wife, even if without success.

the woods when wild beasts are sure to find them and tear them to pieces?"

"You fool," she replied. "Then all four of us will starve to death. You might as well start sanding the boards for our coffins."

The wife didn't give her husband a moment of peace until he consented to her plan. "But still, I feel sorry for the poor children," he said.

The children had also not been able to sleep, because they were starving, and they heard everything that their stepmother had told their father. Gretel wept inconsolably and said to Hansel: "Well, now we're done for."

"Be quiet, Gretel," said Hansel, "and stop worrying. I'll figure out something."

After the old folks had fallen asleep, Hansel got up, put on his little jacket, opened the bottom half of the Dutch door, and slipped outside. The moon was shining brightly, and the white pebbles in front of the house were glittering like silver coins. Hansel stooped down and put as many as would fit into his jacket pocket. Then he went back to Gretel and said: "Don't worry, little sister. Just go to sleep. God will not forsake us." And he went back to bed.

At daybreak, just before the sun had risen, the wife came in and woke the two children up. "Get up, you lazy-bones, we're going to go into the forest to get some wood."

The wife gave each child a crust of bread and said: "Here's something for lunch. But don't eat it before then, because you're not getting anything else."

Gretel put the bread in her apron, because Hansel had the pebbles in his jacket pocket. Together they all set out on the path into the forest. After they had walked for a little while, Hansel stopped and looked back in the direction of the house, and every so often he did it again. His father said: "Hansel, why are you always stopping and staring? Watch out, and don't forget what your legs were made for."

"Oh, Father," said Hansel. "I'm looking back at my white kitten, which is sitting up on the roof trying to say good-bye to me."

WANDA GÁG,
"Hansel and Gretel," 1936

The evil stepmother leads the way into the woods, while the woodcutter father of the siblings follows. Hansel strews crumbs on the path, while Gretel trudges forward with provisions tucked in her arms.

The woman said: "You fool, that's not your kitten. Those are the rays of the sun, shining on the chimney."

But Hansel had not been looking at a kitten. He had been taking the shiny pebbles from his pocket and dropping them on the ground.

When they got to the middle of the forest, the father said: "Go gather some wood, children. I'll build a fire so that you won't get cold."

Hansel and Gretel gathered a little pile of brushwood and lit it. When the flames were high enough, the woman said: "Lie down by the fire, children, and try to get some rest. We're going back into the forest to chop some wood. When we're done, we'll come back to get you."

Hansel and Gretel sat by the fire. At noontime they ate their crusts of bread. Since they could hear the sounds of an ax, they were sure that their father was nearby. But it wasn't an ax that they heard, it was a branch that their father had fastened to a dead tree, and the wind was banging it back and forth. They had been sitting there for such a long time that finally their eyes closed from exhaustion, and they fell fast asleep. When they awoke, it was pitch dark. Gretel began crying and said: "How will we ever get out of the woods!"

Hansel comforted her: "Just wait until the moon comes out. Then we will find our way back."

And when the moon had come out, Hansel took his sister by the hand and followed the pebbles, which were shimmering like newly minted coins and pointing the way back home for them. They walked all night long and got to their father's house just as day was breaking. They knocked at the door, and when the woman opened and saw that it was Hansel and Gretel, she said: "You wicked children! Why were you sleeping so long in the woods? We thought you were never going to come back."

WANDA GÁG,
"Hansel and Gretel," 1936

Hansel and Gretel make their way through woods that are adorned with a variety of decorative trees. Gretel nearly molds herself to her brother, who leads the way.

The father was overjoyed, for he had been very upset about abandoning the children in the forest.

A while later, every square inch of the country was stricken by famine, and one night the children could hear what the mother was saying to their father after they had gone to bed: "We've eaten everything up again. All that's left is half a loaf of bread, and when that's gone, we're finished. The children have to go. This time we'll take them deeper into the forest so that they can't find a way out. Otherwise there's no hope for us."

All this weighed heavily on the husband's heart, and he thought: "It would be better if you shared the last crumb of bread with the children." But the woman would not listen to anything he said. She did nothing but scold and find fault. In for a penny, in for a pound, and since he had given in the first time, he also had to give in a second time.

The children were still awake and heard the entire conversation. When their parents had fallen asleep, Hansel got up and wanted to go out and pick up some pebbles as he had done before, but the woman had locked the door, and Hansel couldn't get out. Hansel comforted his sister and said: "Don't cry, Gretel. Just get some sleep. The good Lord will protect us."**3**

Early the next morning the woman came and woke the children up. They each got a crust of bread, this time even smaller than last time. On the way into the woods, Hansel crushed the bread in his pocket and would stop from time to time to scatter crumbs on the ground.

"Hansel, why are you stopping and staring?" asked the father. "Keep on walking."

"I'm looking at my little dove, the one sitting on the roof and trying to say good-bye to me," Hansel replied.

"You fool," said the woman. "That isn't your little dove. Those are the rays of the morning sun shining on the chimney."

Little by little, Hansel had scattered all the crumbs on the path.

The woman took the children deeper into the forest, to a place where they had never ever been before. Once again a large fire was built, and the mother said: "Don't move from there, children. If you get tired, you can sleep for a while. We're going to go into the forest to chop some wood. In the evening, when we're done, we'll come to get you."

It was noontime, and Gretel shared her bread with Hansel, who had scattered bits of his bread on the path.

3. *The good Lord will protect us.* This reference, along with other religious references, was added to the second edition of the tales by the Grimms.

WANDA GÁG,
"Hansel and Gretel," 1936

In a clearing the children discover the quaint and charming house of gingerbread, where a cat guards the front door. Only the arched back of the cat offers a signal that there might be anything sinister behind the door.

KAY NIELSEN,
"Hansel and Gretel," 1914

The cottage in the woods appears like a green oasis in the midst of a terrifying tangle of trees. Hansel and Gretel, holding hands to illustrate their solidarity, have found a haven that is closer to their proportions than the vast woods in the background.

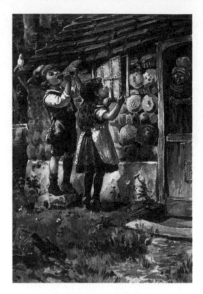

ANONYMOUS,
"Hansel and Gretel"

A nearsighted witch peers out the door, while Gretel helps herself to sugary window panes and Hansel bites into a slice of bread. The raven in the foreground has an ominous-looking bone in its beak.

Then they fell asleep. The evening went by, but no one came to get the poor children. They awoke when it was pitch-dark, and Hansel comforted his sister by saying: "Just wait, Gretel, until the moon comes out. Then we will be able to see the crumbs of bread I strewed on the path. They will point the way home for us."

When the moon came out, they started out for home, but they couldn't find the crumbs, because the many thousands of birds flying around in the forest and across the fields had eaten them. Hansel said to Gretel: "We'll find the way back." But they couldn't find it. They walked all night long and then the next day from early in the morning until late at night. They just couldn't find their way out of the woods, and they got more and more hungry, for they had nothing to eat but a few berries scattered

ARTHUR RACKHAM,
"Hansel and Gretel," 1909

Hansel and Gretel cautiously approach a witch who, with her crutches, bent back, and bulbous nose, hovers over the children as a threatening presence. A barefoot Hansel takes the lead, while Gretel stands in her brother's shadow.

ARTHUR RACKHAM,
"Hansel and Gretel"

Hansel and Gretel are caught in the act, nibbling on the roof and windows of the witch's house. Here the pointed hat, the gnarled fingers, the oversized feet, and the large nose of the inhabitant startle the children, who are not at all reassured by the smile on the witch's face.

JESSIE WILLCOX SMITH,
"Hansel and Gretel," 1919

Hansel drops what he has ripped from the roof when the witch appears at the door. Like many of her counterparts, this witch is hunched over, with gnarled hands and a large nose.

on the ground. When they got so tired that their legs would no longer carry them, they lay down under a tree and fell asleep.

Three days had passed since they had left their father's house. They started walking again, but they just got deeper and deeper into the woods. If they didn't get help soon, they were sure to perish. At noontime they saw a beautiful bird, white as snow, perched on a branch. It was singing so sweetly that they stopped to listen to it. When it had finished its song, it flapped its wings and flew on ahead of them. They followed the bird until they arrived at a little house, and the bird perched right up on the roof. When they got closer to the house, they realized that it was made of bread, and that the roof was made of cake and the windows of sparkling sugar.[4]

4. *sparkling sugar.* Bruno Bettelheim claims that "Hansel and Gretel" is a story about the oral greed of children. In his view, the tale enacts childhood feelings of hostility to the omnipotent mother, who, in her role as supreme provider, is always also the withholder of nourishment. By the end of the story, the children have mastered their "oral anxieties" and learned that "wishful thinking has to be replaced by intelligent action." By implying that the children in the story are "greedy," Bettelheim produces a one-sided interpretation that exonerates the adults and suggests that the real source of evil in the story is nothing more than an alter ego of the children.

HERMANN VOGEL,
"Hansel and Gretel," 1894

The nearsighted witch peers out from her porch to find Hansel and Gretel nibbling at her house. A snake in the foreground suggests a connection with the story of Adam and Eve's temptation, with the children succumbing to the desire for forbidden gingerbread. The vignette in the frame gives us the bleak prehistory of the two siblings, lost in the woods.

LUDWIG RICHTER,
"Hansel and Gretel," 1842

This early illustration for the Grimms' tale set the tone for later depictions of the witch. The two siblings clutch each other for dear life when they are caught partaking of the house. Vignettes beneath the scene show other moments in the tale, including the flight of the siblings and the reunion with their father.

LUDWIG RICHTER,
"Hansel and Gretel," 1842

A rather benign-looking witch greets the children at the door of her cottage. As in many of the German scenes, the avian creatures who devoured the bread crumbs scattered by Hansel hover around and over the house.

"Let's see how it tastes," said Hansel. "May the Lord bless our meal. I'll try a piece of the roof, Gretel, and you can try the window. That's sure to be sweet." Hansel reached up and broke off a small piece of the roof to see what it tasted like. Gretel went over to the windowpane and nibbled on it. Suddenly a gentle voice called from inside:

"Nibble, nibble, where's the mouse?
Who's that nibbling at my house?"

The children replied:

"The wind so mild,
The heavenly child."

They continued eating, without being in the least distracted. Hansel, who liked the taste of the roof, tore off a big piece of it, and Gretel knocked out an entire windowpane and sat down on the ground to savor it. Suddenly the door opened, and a woman as old as the hills,[5] leaning on a crutch, hobbled out. Hansel and Gretel were so terrified that they dropped everything in their hands. The old woman wagged her head and said: "Well, dear little children. How in the world did you get here? Just come right in, and you can stay with me. You will come to no harm in my house."

She took them by the hand and led them into her little house. A fine meal of milk and pancakes, with sugar, apples, and nuts was set before them. A little later, two beautiful little beds were made up for them with white sheets. Hansel and Gretel lay down in them and felt as if they were in heaven.

The old woman had only pretended to be kind. She was really a wicked witch, who waylaid little children and had built the house of bread just to get them inside. As soon

5. *a woman as old as the hills.* The term "wicked witch" was not used in the first version of the story, nor was there much elaboration of the witch's physical appearance. Witches are not common in the Grimms' collection, but the witch from this story has taken on a representative importance.

GEORGE SOPER,
"Hansel and Gretel," 1915

Standing before her house of bread, the witch leans on two sticks as she reproaches a Dutch Hansel and Gretel for eating parts of the roof and window of her house.

as a child fell into her hands, she killed it, cooked it, and ate it. That meant a day of real feasting for her. Witches have red eyes and can't see very far, but, like animals, they do have a keen sense of smell and they can always tell when a human being is around. When Hansel and Gretel got near her, she laughed fiendishly and hissed: "They're mine! This time they won't get away!" Early in the morning, before the children were up, she got out of bed and gazed at the two of them sleeping so peacefully with their soft red cheeks. And she muttered quietly to herself: "They will make a tasty little morsel."

She grabbed Hansel with her scrawny arm, took him to a little shed, and closed the barred door on him. Hansel could cry with all his might, it didn't do him any good. Then she went back to Gretel, shook her until she was awake, and shouted: "Get up, lazy bones. Go get some water and cook your brother something tasty. He's staying outside in the shed until he's put on some weight. When he's nice and fat, I'll eat him up."

Gretel began crying as loud as she could, but it did no good at all. She had to do whatever the wicked witch told her. The finest food was cooked for poor Hansel, and Gretel got nothing but crab shells. Every morning the old woman would slink over to the little shed and shout: "Hansel, hold out your finger so that I can tell if you're plump enough."

Hansel would stick a little bone through the bars, and the old woman, who had poor eyesight, believed that it was Hansel's finger and couldn't figure out why he wasn't putting on weight. When four weeks had gone by and Hansel was still as scrawny as ever, she lost her patience and decided that she couldn't wait any longer. "Hey there, Gretel," she shouted at the girl. "Go get some water and be quick about it. I don't care whether Hansel's lean or plump. Tomorrow I'm going to butcher him, and then I'll cook him."

The poor little sister sobbed with grief, and tears flowed down her cheeks. "Dear God, help us!" she cried out. "If

ARTHUR RACKHAM,
"Hansel and Gretel," 1909

"Hansel would stick a little bone through the bars, and the old woman, who had poor eyesight, believed that it was Hansel's finger and couldn't figure out why he wasn't putting on weight." Helpless in his cage, Hansel still uses his wits to outsmart the old woman.

HERMANN VOGEL,
"Hansel and Gretel," 1894

With her familiars, a cat and a crow, the witch becomes impatient to fatten up Hansel and to place him into the large cauldron, above which appear her most recent prey.

only the wild animals in the forest had eaten us up, at least then we would have died together."

"Spare me your blubbering!" the old woman said. "Nothing can help you now."

Early in the morning, Gretel had to go fill the kettle with water and light the fire. "First we'll do some baking," the old woman said. "I've already heated up the oven and kneaded the dough."

She pushed poor Gretel over to the oven, from which flames were leaping. "Crawl in," said the witch, "and see if it's hot enough to slide the bread in."

The witch was planning to shut the door as soon as

6. *the godless witch burned to death in a horrible way.* The punishment of the witch has been read as a portent of the horrors of the Third Reich. That the witch is often represented as a figure with stereotypical Jewish traits, particularly in twentieth-century illustrations, makes this scene all the more ominous. In her rewriting of "Hansel and Gretel," the poet Anne Sexton refers to the abandonment of the children as a "final solution."

7. *Like a bird fleeing its cage.* Birds figure prominently in this story, first eating the bread crumbs sprinkled on the path by Hansel, then leading the children to the witch's house, and finally carrying the two across the water. As representatives of nature, they ensure that the children remain in the woods, yet also provide the means for escape.

8. *put what he could into his pockets.* Like Jack in "Jack and the Beanstalk," Hansel and Gretel feel no qualms about appropriating the riches of the witch and taking the jewels back home to their father. The "perfect happiness" of the ending is brought about in part by the acquisition of material wealth, which guarantees that the father and children will live happily ever after.

Gretel got into the oven. Then she was going to bake her and eat her up too. But Gretel saw what was on her mind and said: "I don't know how to get in there. How will I manage it?"

"Silly goose," the old woman said. "There's enough room. Just look, I can even get in," and she scrambled over to the oven and stuck her head in it. Gretel gave her a big shove that sent her sprawling. Then she shut the iron door and bolted it. Phew! The witch began screech-

'Stupid goose!' cried the Witch. 'The opening is big enough; you can see that I could get into it myself.'

ARTHUR RACKHAM,
"Hansel and Gretel," 1909

The witch stands before the oven as Gretel contemplates the possibilities for action.

ing dreadfully. But Gretel ran off, and the godless witch burned to death in a horrible way.[6]

Gretel ran straight to Hansel, opened the door to the little shed, and shouted: "Hansel, we're saved! The old witch is dead."

Like a bird fleeing its cage,[7] Hansel flew out the door as soon as it opened. How thrilled they were: they hugged and kissed and jumped up and down for joy! Since there was nothing more to fear, they went right into the witch's house. In every corner there were chests filled with pearls and jewels. "These are even better than pebbles," said Hansel and put what he could into his pockets.[8]

Gretel said, "I'll take something home too," and she filled up her little apron.

"Let's get going right now," said Hansel. "We have to get out of this witch's forest."

After walking for several hours, they reached a large body of water. "We won't be able to get across," said Hansel. "There's not a bridge in sight."

"There aren't any boats around either," Gretel said, "but here comes a white duck. She will help us cross, if I ask." She shouted:

> "Help us, help us, little duck
> The two of us ran out of luck.
> Nary a bridge, neither far nor wide,
> Help us, give us both a ride."

The duck came paddling over. Hansel got on its back and told his sister to sit down next to him. "No," said Gretel, "that would be too heavy a load for the little duck. She can take us over one at a time."

That's just what the good little creature did. When they were brought safely to the other side and had walked along for some time, the woods began to look more and more familiar. Finally they could see their father's house in the distance. They began running, and they raced right into their house, throwing their arms around their father. The man had not had a happy hour since the day that he had abandoned his children in the forest. His wife had died.[9] Gretel emptied her apron, and pearls and jewels rolled all over the floor. Hansel reached into his pockets and pulled out one handful of jewels after another. Their worries were over, and they lived together in perfect happiness.

My fairy tale is done.[10] See the mouse run. Whoever catches it gets to make a great big fur hat out of it.

9. *His wife had died.* No explanation is offered for the death of the stepmother. That she is dead suggests some kind of inner identity between her and the wicked witch. While the stepmother at home was intent on starving the children, providing neither food nor nurturing care, the witch in the forest initially appears to be a splendidly bountiful figure, offering the children a sumptuous repast and comfortable beds. Yet she represents an intensification of the maternal evil at home, for she feeds the children only in order to fatten them up for her next meal.

10. *My fairy tale is done.* Storytellers often ended their tales with whimsical touches, frequently in verse and with a request for monetary contributions embedded in the verses.

4

BEAUTY AND THE BEAST

Jeanne-Marie Leprince de Beaumont

Virtually every culture knows the story of Beauty and Beast and the differences the two figures must resolve in order to be joined in wedlock. "Beauty and the Beast" has been celebrated as the quintessential story of romantic love, demonstrating its power to transcend physical appearances. But in many ways it is also a plot rich in opportunities for expressing a woman's anxieties about marriage, and it may at one time have circulated as a story that steadied the fears of young women facing arranged marriages to older men. In cultures where arranged marriages were the rule, it was a tale that could brace women for an alliance that required them to efface their own desires or to favor the desire for wealth over other considerations.

"Cupid and Psyche," the earliest known version of "Beauty and the Beast," appeared in the second century A.D. in The Transformations of Lucian, Otherwise Known as the Golden Ass, written in Latin by the distinguished rhetorician

From Jeanne-Marie Leprince de Beaumont, "La Belle et la bête," in *Le Magasin des enfants* (London: Haberkorn, 1757).

Apuleius of Madaura. Told by a "drunken and half-demented" woman to a young bride abducted by bandits on her wedding day, it is described as a fairy tale designed to console the distraught captive. But in "Cupid and Psyche" the "beast" is only rumored to be a beast, and Psyche, the tale's heroine, resolves the romantic conflict not by showing compassion but by carrying out a series of tasks. Still, it seems evident that most Anglo-American and European versions of the tale either derived from or were contaminated in some way by Apuleius's story about the complexities of romantic love.

The version of "Beauty and the Beast" best known to Anglo-American audiences was penned in 1756 by Madame de Beaumont (Jeanne-Marie Leprince de Beaumont) for publication in a magazine designed for girls and young women and translated into English three years later. Showing signs that it is intended as a vehicle for instructing children about the value of good manners, good breeding, and good behavior, this "Beauty and the Beast" concludes with a flurry of commendations and condemnations. Beauty has "preferred virtue to looks" and has "many virtues," and she enters a marriage "founded on virtue." Her two sisters, by contrast, have hearts "filled with envy and malice" and are turned into statues that symbolize their cold, hard essence.

Beauty's virtues, as her name and her story make clear, stem from her attractive appearance and her sterling character. After discovering that Beast is prepared to accept a daughter in place of the father, she declares her good fortune, for she will have "the pleasure of saving" her father and proving "feelings of tenderness for him." To be sure, not every "Beauty" is so willing a victim. The heroine of the Norwegian "East of the Sun and West of the Moon" (included in this volume as tale 14), for example, has to be talked into marrying the beast (a white bear) by her father. But many beauties are not only willing to sacrifice themselves for their fathers but are also prepared to marry a beast out of pity for his condition. Madame de Beaumont's Beauty comes to a conclusion that few would embrace wholeheartedly today as a recipe for a successful marriage. Claiming that neither "good looks" nor "great intelligence" are what count, Beauty disavows the passion of romantic love and asserts that feelings of "respect, friendship, and gratitude" suffice for a good marriage.

"Beauty and the Beast" remains a powerful story for meditating on what we value in a marriage partner. Rooted in a culture where arranged marriages were often the norm, Madame de Beaumont's tale endorses obedience, self-denial, and a form of love based on gratitude rather than passion for women even as it gives us a Beast who clearly appreciates physical perfection in addition to kindness and compassion. But those very values can be challenged in a variety of ways as the story is read. Can we imagine, as Chaucer did in the Wife of Bath's tale, a story that could be called "Handsome and the Beast"? Why is Beauty physically perfect while Beast can remain a perfect marriage partner despite his looks? Why does the story end by subverting its own terms when it turns both marriage partners into figures of physical perfection? Does Beauty feel any disappointment after Beast's transformation, as she does in Jean Cocteau's cinematic version, made in France right after World War II?

Just as oral versions from earlier centuries took advantage of the comic possibilities of stories in which girls are betrothed to pigs, hedgehogs, snakes, frogs, or donkeys, so modern retellings capitalize on the rich opportunities for social satire and irony. Today we produce stories that celebrate the superiority of beasts over humans, with "happy endings" marked by the transformation of the tale's "Beauty" into a noble beast. In works ranging from Jon Scieszka's Frog Prince Continued to Angela Carter's The Tiger's Bride, we see a profound ideological shift revealing that humans are the real beasts in need of redemption.

1. *a wealthy merchant.* Note that the fairy tale puts the reader in a social milieu different from that of the customary village, forest, or castle of fairy tales. "Beauty and the Beast" reflects the presence of an emerging bourgeoisie in pre-revolutionary France, one that functions in a moral, social, and financial economy very different from that of feudal times.

ONCE UPON A TIME there was a wealthy merchant[1] who lived with his six children, three boys and three girls. Since he was a man of intelligence and good sense, he spared no expense in educating his children and hiring all kinds of tutors for them. His daughters were all very beautiful, but everyone fell in love with the youngest. When she was a small child, people used to call her "Little Beauty." The name "Beauty" stuck, and it was no surprise that the two older girls grew jealous of their sister.

The youngest of the three daughters was not only more beautiful than her sisters; she was also far more charming. The two older sisters were vain and proud just because they came from a wealthy family. They tried to act like ladies of the court and paid no attention at all to other girls from merchant families. They chose to spend their time solely with people of rank. Every day they went to balls, to the theater, and to the park, and they made fun of their younger sister for spending most of her time reading good books.[2]

Since the girls were known to be very wealthy, many prominent merchants sought their hands in marriage. But the two older sisters vowed that they would never marry unless they found a duke or, at the very least, a count. Beauty (remember, this was the name of the youngest daughter) very politely thanked all those who proposed to her and told them that she was still too young for marriage. She was hoping to stay by her father's side for a few more years to come.

One day, out of the blue, the merchant lost his entire fortune, and he was left with nothing but a small country house quite far from town. With tears in his eyes, he told his children that they would have to stay in that house from now on and live like peasants in order to make ends meet. The two older daughters vowed that they would not leave town and insisted that they had many admirers who would be more than happy to marry them, even though they had lost their fortune. But these fine young ladies were wrong. Their admirers had lost interest in them now that they were poor. And since they had always been disliked for their arrogance, everyone said: "Those two girls don't deserve our sympathy. It's reassuring to see that

2. *reading good books.* It is unusual for fairy-tale characters to advance themselves by reading. Most are relegated to menial tasks at home, or they set out on journeys into the world.

3. *Her two sisters, on the other hand, were dreadfully bored.* Beauty compares favorably in every way with her two sisters. As in most fairy-tale trios of same-sex siblings, the youngest, as underdog, is superior to the two older siblings. Beauty combines good looks with a powerful work ethic, impeccable manners, and compassion.

4. *not only made Beauty do all the housework.* Like Cinderella, Beauty is an innocent young heroine, persecuted by sibling rivals.

pride takes a fall. Let them play the ladies while tending sheep." Everyone was also saying: "As for Beauty, her misfortune is distressing. She's such a kind girl! She speaks with such compassion to the poor. And she is so sweet and sincere."

There were a number of gentlemen who would have been happy to marry Beauty even though she didn't have a penny. She told them that she could not bring herself to abandon her father in his anguish and that she was planning to accompany him to the country in order to console him and to help him with his work. Poor Beauty was upset at the loss of the family fortune, but she just said to herself: "No matter how much I cry, my tears won't bring back our fortune. I will try to be happy without it."

When the merchant and his three sons arrived at the country house, they began working the land. Beauty got up every day at four in the morning and started cleaning the house and making breakfast for the family. It was hard for her at first, because she was not accustomed to working like a servant. By the end of two months, however, she had become stronger, and the hard work improved her health. After finishing her housework, she would read a book or sing some songs while spinning. Her two sisters, on the other hand, were dreadfully bored.[3] They would get up at ten in the morning, take walks all day long, and talk endlessly about the beautiful clothes they used to wear.

"Look at our sister," they said to each other. "She's such a simpleton and so dim-witted that she seems perfectly satisfied with her miserable lot."

The good merchant did not agree with his two daughters. He knew that Beauty stood out from the crowd in a way that her sisters did not. He admired his daughter's many virtues, especially her patience. The sisters not only made Beauty do all the housework;[4] they also insulted her whenever they had the chance.

The family had lived an entire year in seclusion when the merchant received a letter informing him that a ship containing his merchandise had just arrived safely in its home port. The news made the two older sisters giddy with joy, for they were sure that they would finally be able to leave the countryside, which they found terribly dull. When they saw that their father was about to go on a trip, they begged him to bring back dresses, furs, laces, and all kinds of trinkets. Beauty did not ask for anything, because she was sure that the profits from the ship would not suffice to buy everything her sisters wanted.

"Don't you want me to buy anything for you?" her father asked.

"You are kind to think of me," Beauty replied. "Perhaps you could bring me a rose,**5** for they do not grow here."

It was not that Beauty was really anxious to have a rose, but she didn't want to make her sisters look bad. They, in turn, would have said that she was not asking for anything in order to make herself look good.

The good merchant left home, but when he arrived at the port, he found that there were legal problems with his merchandise. After much aggravation, he set off for home as impoverished as ever. He had only thirty miles left before him and was already feeling revived by the prospect of seeing his children again when he arrived at the edge of a deep forest and realized that he was lost. A snowstorm was raging, and the wind was so strong that twice he was knocked off his horse. When night fell, he was sure that he was going to die either of hunger or of the cold or, worse yet, that the wolves howling in the distance would attack and devour him.

All of a sudden he saw a bright light at the end of a long row of trees. The light seemed very distant. As he walked toward it, he realized that it was coming from an immense castle that was completely lit up. The merchant thanked God for sending help, and he made his way quickly toward the castle. He was surprised to find that no one was in the courtyard. His horse sauntered over toward a large, open stable and found some hay and oats there. The poor animal, near starvation, began eating with a voracious appetite. The merchant tied the horse up in the stable and began walking toward the castle. There was not a soul

5. *Perhaps you could bring me a rose.* The "modest choice" of the youngest sister often stirs up trouble in fairy tales. The plot of Shakespeare's *King Lear*, with its three daughters—two arrogant and one modest— is fueled by similar circumstances.

in sight. When he entered the great hall, he found a warm fire and a table laden with food, but with just a single place setting. Since he was soaked to the bone from the rain and snow, he went over to the fire to get dry. He thought: "The master of the house and his servants will not be offended by the liberties I am taking. No doubt someone will be back soon."

He waited a long time. When the clock struck eleven and there was still no one in sight, he could not control the pangs of hunger he was feeling, and, trembling all over, he took a chicken and made short work of it in just two bites. He also drank several glasses of wine, and, feeling somewhat emboldened, he left the great hall and crossed many large, magnificently furnished apartments. Finally he found a room with a good bed in it. Since it was past midnight and he was exhausted, he decided to shut the door and go to sleep.

When he woke up the next day, it was already ten in the morning. He was greatly surprised to find clean clothes in place of the ones that had been completely soaked by the rain. He thought: "This palace must belong to a good fairy who has taken pity on me."

He looked out the window and noticed that it was no longer snowing. Before his eyes a magnificent vista of gardens and flowers unfolded. He returned to the great hall where he had dined the night before and found a small table with a cup of hot chocolate on it. "Thank you, Madame Fairy," he said out loud, "for being so kind as to remember my breakfast."

After finishing his hot chocolate, the good man left to find his horse. Passing beneath a magnificent arbor of roses, he remembered that Beauty had asked him for a rose, and he picked one from a branch that had many flowers on it. All of a sudden he heard a loud noise and saw a beast coming toward him. It looked so dreadful that he nearly fainted.

"You are very ungrateful," the beast said in a ferocious voice. "I have saved your life by giving you shelter in my castle, and you repay me by stealing my roses, which I love

LANCELOT SPEED,
"Beauty and the Beast," 1913

Beauty's father, given an oriental look with his cloak, turban, and slippers, cowers before an upright beast whose magnificent castle, complete with domes and minarets, looms large in the background. The modest possessions of the merchant, wrapped in a large scarf, contrast sharply with the vastness of Beast's holdings.

W. HEATH ROBINSON,
"Beauty and the Beast," 1921

Although the lower half of Beast appears close to human form, his upper parts present a ferocious appearance. Poised to attack when he discovers an intruder on his property, this Beast remains to be tamed.

ARTHUR RACKHAM,
"Beauty and the Beast," 1909

Beauty's father is caught red-handed by the Beast, whose elaborate robe cannot conceal his true beastliness. The bower of roses also fails to mask the sinister black and white trees and sky in the background.

more than anything in the world. You will have to pay for your offense. I'm going to give you exactly a quarter of an hour to say your prayers."

The merchant fell to his knees and, hands clasped, pleaded with the beast: "My Liege, forgive me. I did not think I would be offending you by picking a flower for my daughter, who asked me to bring her back a rose or two."

"I am not called 'My Liege,'" said the monster. "My name is Beast, and I don't like flattery. I prefer that people say what they think. So don't try to change my mind with your compliments. But you mentioned something about daughters. I am prepared to forgive you if one of your daughters consents to die in your place. Don't argue with me. Just go. If your daughters refuse to die for you, swear that you will return in three days."

EDMUND DULAC,
"Beauty and the Beast," 1910

"After she had done her work, [she] would sing and play." Dulac's Beauty, with her musical talents, is introduced as a raven-haired young woman who banishes loneliness through music. The rich blues and pinks of Beauty's clothing are repeated in the landscape, which, in its somewhat desolate state, mirrors her feelings.

EDMUND DULAC,
"Beauty and the Beast," 1910

"He had been fasting for more than twenty-four hours, and lost no time in falling to." Beauty's father sits in regal splendor, feasting on the magnificent banquet before him. The picture is idyllic, but the one claw foot left exposed by the tablecloth is a powerful omen that all is not as serene as it seems.

EDMUND DULAC,
"Beauty and the Beast," 1910

"The good merchant let drop the rose and flung himself on his knees." Beast, a grotesque hybrid animal with the paws of a lion, inspires fear in the merchant. Note the orientalizing touch in the turban and slippers worn by Beast and by Beauty's father.

The good man was not about to sacrifice one of his daughters to this hideous monster, but he thought: "At least I will have the chance to embrace my children one last time."

The merchant swore that he would return, and Beast told him that he could leave whenever he wanted. "But I don't want you to go empty-handed," he added. "Return to the room in which you slept. There you will find a large, empty chest. You can fill it up with whatever you like, and I will have it delivered to your door at home."

The beast withdrew, and the good man thought: "If I have to die, I will at least die with the reassurance of leaving something for my poor children to live on."

The merchant returned to the room where he had

EDMUND DULAC,
"Beauty and the Beast," 1910

EDMUND DULAC,
"Beauty and the Beast," 1910

EDMUND DULAC,
"Beauty and the Beast," 1910

"Soon they caught sight of the castle in the distance." Despite her humble mount, Beauty appears regal in the icy landscape before which Beast's castle is situated. She stoically prepares herself to cross the threshold from the safe, yet snowy, climes of home territory to the perils of the castle. That Beast lives in an enchanted palace is suggested by the verdant landscape surrounding the castle.

"These no sooner saw BEAUTY than they began to scream and chatter." With the castle brilliantly lit up in the background, Beauty appears to stand on cobblestones that bleed into a fog connecting to the castle. Even the exotic birds of Beast's realm are attracted to Beauty's loveliness, and they gather around her to crown her beauty and to exchange views about her radiance.

"'Ah! what a fright you have given me!' she murmured." Beauty ministers to the lovestruck Beast, who has been pining away for his beloved. This final illustration reprises the first in the series, which featured Beauty alone, and it prefigures a happy ending in which the two have become a couple.

slept. He filled the great chest described by Beast with the many gold pieces he discovered in his room. He went to the stable, found his horse, and left the palace with a sense of sadness equal to the joy he had felt on entering it. His horse instinctively followed one of the paths in the forest, and, in just a few hours, the good man arrived at his little house. His children gathered around him, but instead of responding to their caresses, the merchant burst into tears as he was gazing at them. In his hand he was holding the branch of roses he had brought for Beauty. He gave it to her and said: "Beauty, take these roses. They have cost your poor father dearly."

The merchant then told his family about the dreadful events that had befallen him. Upon hearing his tale, the two sisters uttered cries of distress and made insulting remarks about Beauty, who was not crying at all. "See what the pride of this little creature has brought down on us!" they said. "Why didn't she ask for fine clothes the way we did? No, she wanted to get all the attention. Now she's going to be the cause of Father's death, and she's not even shedding any tears."

"That would be quite pointless," Beauty replied. "Why should I shed a tear about Father when he is not going to die? Since the monster is willing to accept one of his daughters, I am prepared to offer myself to appease his fury. I feel fortunate that I can make this sacrifice, since I will have the pleasure of saving Father and proving my feelings of tenderness for him."

"No, dear Sister," said her three brothers. "You will not die. We will find this monster, and if we can't slay him, we are prepared to die trying."

"Don't count on that, children," said the merchant. "The beast's power is so great that I don't have the least hope of killing him. I am moved by the goodness of Beauty's heart, but I refuse to let her risk her life. I'm old, and I don't have many years left. I will only lose a few years of my life, and I don't regret losing them for your sake, my dear children."

"Rest assured, Father," said Beauty, "that you will not go to the palace without me. You can't stop me from following you. I may be young, but I am not fiercely attached to life, and I would rather be devoured by that monster than die of grief from losing you."

There was no arguing with Beauty. She was determined to go to the palace. Her sisters were delighted, for Beauty's virtues had long filled them with envy. The merchant had been so preoccupied by the bleak prospect of losing his daughter that he had forgotten all about the chest filled with gold that he had brought back. When he retired to his room to get some sleep, he was stunned to find it beside his bed. He decided not to tell his children that he had become rich, for his daughters would then want to return to town, and he was determined to die in the country. He did confide his secret to Beauty, who told him that several gentlemen had come during his absence and that two of them were hoping to marry her sisters. Beauty pleaded with her father to let them marry. She was so kind that she still loved her sisters with all her heart[6] and forgave them the evil they had done her.

When Beauty set out with her father, the two cruel sisters rubbed their eyes with an onion in order to draw tears. The brothers, however, cried real tears, as did the merchant. Only Beauty did not cry at all, because she did not want to make everyone even sadder.

The horse got on the road to the palace, and, when night fell, they could see that Beast's residence was all lit up. The horse went on its own over to the stable, and the good man went with his daughter into the hall, where there was a magnificently set table with two place settings. The merchant did not have the stomach for supper, but Beauty, forcing herself to appear calm, sat down and served her father. "You see, Father," she said while forcing a laugh, "the beast wants to fatten me up before eating me, since he paid so dearly for me."

After finishing supper, they heard a loud noise, and the merchant tearfully bid adieu to his poor daughter, for he knew that the beast was approaching. Beauty could not help shuddering at the sight of this horrible figure, but she tried as hard as she could to stay calm. The monster asked her if she had come of her own free will, and, trembling, she said that she had.

"You are very kind," said Beast, "and I am very grateful to you. As for you, my good man, get out of here by tomorrow morning and don't think of coming back here ever again. Good-bye, Beauty."

"Good-bye, Beast," she replied, and suddenly the monster vanished.

"Oh, my daughter!" cried the merchant, embracing Beauty. "I'm half dead with fear. Believe me, you have to let me stay with you," he said.

6. *she still loved her sisters with all her heart.* Like some Cinderellas (Perrrault's, to cite one example), Beauty is willing to forgive her sisters, no matter how wickedly they behave. Beauties and Cinderellas in oral folktales tend to be less forgiving.

7. *The good deed you have done in saving your father's life will not go unrewarded.* In fairy tales, virtue is never its own reward. Good deeds are settled in gold, or through ascension to a throne.

"No, Father," Beauty said firmly. "You must be on your way tomorrow morning and leave me to the mercy of heaven. Perhaps heaven will take pity on me after all."

Beauty and her father went to bed thinking that they would not be able to sleep all night long, but they had hardly gotten into their beds when they nodded off. While she was asleep, Beauty saw a woman who told her: "Your kindness brings me great satisfaction, Beauty. The good deed you have done in saving your father's life will not go unrewarded."**7**

Upon awakening, Beauty recounted this dream to her father. While it comforted him a little, it did not prevent him from sobbing when he had to separate from his dear daughter. After he had left, Beauty sat down in the great hall and began to cry as well. But since she was courageous, she put herself in God's hands and resolved not to complain about her fate for the short time she had left to live.

Convinced that Beast was planning to devour her that very evening, Beauty decided to walk around the grounds and to explore the castle while awaiting her fate. She could not help admiring the castle's beauty, and who can imagine her surprise when she found a door upon which was written: "Beauty's Room." She opened the door right away and was dazzled by the radiant beauty of the chamber. She was especially impressed by a huge bookcase, a harpsichord, and various music books. "Someone is hoping I won't get bored!" she said softly. Then she realized: "If I had only one hour left to live, no one would have made such a fuss about my room." This thought lifted her spirits.

Beauty opened the bookcase and saw a book, on the cover of which was written in golden letters: "Your wish is our command. Here you are queen and mistress."

"Alas," she sighed. "I wish only to see my poor father again and to know what he is doing now."

Beauty had spoken these words to herself, so you can imagine how surprised she was when she looked into a large mirror and saw her father arriving home with a dejected look on his face. Her sisters were going out to meet him, and, despite the faces they were making in order to act as if they were upset, they were visibly happy to have lost their sister. A moment later everything in the mirror vanished. Beauty could not help thinking that Beast was very obliging and that she really had nothing to fear from him.

At noon Beauty found the table set, and, during her meal, she listened to an excellent concert, even though she could not see a soul in her room. That evening, as she was about to sit down at the table, she could hear Beast making noises, and she could not help trembling with fear.

"Beauty," the monster said, "will you let me watch you dine?"**8**

"You are my master," Beauty replied, shuddering.

"No, you are the only mistress here," replied Beast. "If I start to bother you, tell me to go away, and I will leave at once. Tell me, don't you find me very ugly?"

"Yes, I do," said Beauty. "I don't know how to tell lies. But I do think that you are very kind."

"You are right," said the monster. "But in addition to being ugly, I also lack intelligence. I know very well that I am nothing but a beast."

"You can't be a beast," replied Beauty, "if you know that you lack intelligence. A fool never believes himself to be stupid."

"Go ahead and eat, Beauty," said the monster, "and try not to get bored in this house, for everything here is yours, and I would be distressed if you were to become unhappy."

"You are very kind," said Beauty. "I swear to you that I am completely pleased with your tender heart. When I think of it, you no longer seem ugly to me."

"Oh, of course," Beast replied. "I have a tender heart, but I am still a monster."

"There are certainly many men more monstrous than you," said Beauty. "I like you better, even with your looks, than men who hide false, corrupt, and ungrateful hearts behind charming manners."

"If I were intelligent," said Beast, "I would pay you a

8. *"Beauty," the monster said, "will you let me watch you dine?"* The extended dialogue that follows points to the literary nature of this version of "Beauty and the Beast." Note also the way in which the dialogue takes an uncharacteristic philosophical turn in reflecting on matters of appearances and essences. The embedded sermon on kindness and intelligence is also not typical for fairy tales.

)

fine compliment to thank you. But I am so stupid that all I can say is that I am very much obliged."

Beauty ate supper with a good appetite. She no longer dreaded the monster, but she thought that she would die of fright when he said: "Beauty, would you be my wife?"

It took her a moment to get to the point of being able to answer. She was afraid to provoke the monster by refusing him. Trembling, she said to him: "No, Beast."

At that moment the poor monster began to sigh deeply, and he made such a frightful whistling sound that it echoed throughout the palace. Beauty regained her composure, however, because Beast, turning to look at her from time to time, left the room and bid her adieu in a sad voice. Finding herself alone, Beauty began to feel compassion for poor Beast. "Alas," she said, "it's too bad he's so ugly, for he's really very kind."

The next three months passed for Beauty in great tranquillity. Every evening, Beast paid her a visit and, while she was dining, entertained her with good plain talk, though not with what the world would call wit. Each day Beauty discovered new qualities in the monster. Since she was meeting him on a daily basis, she grew accustomed to his ugly appearance, and, far from fearing his arrival, she would check her watch to see if it was nine o'clock yet. Beast never failed to appear at that hour. There was only one thing that still bothered Beauty. Before leaving, the monster would always ask her if she wanted to be his wife, and he seemed deeply wounded when she refused.

One day, Beauty said: "You are putting me in an awkward position, Beast. I would like to be able to marry you, but I am far too honest to allow you to believe that that could ever happen. I will always be your friend. Try to be satisfied with friendship."

"I will have to," Beast replied. "I don't flatter myself, and I know that I'm horrible looking, but I do love you very much. However, I am very happy that you want to stay here. Promise me that you will never leave."

Beauty blushed when she heard those words. In her mirror she could see that her father was feeling sick at heart for having lost her. She had been hoping to see him again. "I can promise you that I will never leave you," she said to Beast. "But right now I feel a longing so powerful to see my father that I would die of grief if you were to deny me this wish."

"I would rather die than cause you pain," said Beast. "I will send you back to your father. But if you stay there, your poor beast will die of grief."

"No," Beauty said, bursting into tears. "I love you too much to be the cause of your death. I promise to return in a week. You have allowed me to discover that my sisters are married and that my brothers have left to serve in the army. Father is living all by himself. Let me stay with him for just a week."

"You will be there tomorrow morning," said Beast. "But don't forget your promise. In order to get back here, all you have to do is put your ring on the table before you go to sleep. Good-bye, Beauty."

Beast sighed deeply in his characteristic way after speaking, and Beauty went to bed feeling very sad to see him so downcast. The next morning, on waking up, she was in her father's house. She pulled a cord at the side of her bed, and a bell summoned a servant, who uttered a loud cry upon seeing her. The good man of the house came running when he heard the cry, and he almost fainted dead away when he set eyes on his beloved daughter. The two held on to each other for over a quarter of an hour. After the first wave of excitement subsided, Beauty realized that she didn't have any clothes to wear. But the servant told her that she had just discovered in the room next to hers a huge trunk full of silk dresses embroidered with gold and encrusted with diamonds. Beauty silently thanked Beast for his thoughtfulness. She took the least extravagant of the dresses and told the servants to lock up the others, for she wanted to make a present of them to her sisters. Hardly had she spoken these words when the chest disappeared. As soon as her father told her that Beast probably wanted her to keep everything for herself, the dresses and the chest reappeared on the spot.

9. *Let's try to keep Beauty here for more than a week.* Note that the sisters are blamed for Beauty's failure to keep her promise to Beast. As in "Cupid and Psyche," the responsibility for an act of disobedience is attributed to the sisters rather than to the actual agent of transgression.

While Beauty was getting dressed, the two sisters learned about her return home and rushed to the scene with their husbands. Both sisters were very unhappy. The older one had married a remarkably handsome gentleman, but he was so enamored of his own looks that he spent all day in front of the mirror. The other one had married a man of great intelligence, but he used his wit only to enrage everybody, first and foremost his wife. Beauty's sisters were ready to die when they saw her dressed like a princess and more beautiful than the bright day. In vain Beauty tried to shower them with attention, but they felt mortified and nothing could diminish their jealousy, which only intensified when Beauty told them how happy she was. The two women, filled with envy, walked out to the garden so that they could weep to their heart's content. They both asked themselves: "Why should that little monster enjoy greater happiness than we do? Aren't we more charming than she is?"

"Sister dear," the older one said, "I have an idea. Let's try to keep Beauty here for more than a week.**9** Her stupid beast will be furious when he sees that she has broken her promise, and maybe he'll eat her up."

"You're right," the other one replied. "We'll make it work by showering her with affection and acting as if we're delighted to have her here."

After conspiring with each other, the two wicked creatures returned to Beauty's room and were so affectionate to her that she nearly wept for joy. When a week had gone by, the two sisters started tearing out their hair and acting so upset that Beauty promised to stay a few days longer. At the same time, she felt terrible about the grief she was causing poor Beast, whom she loved with all her heart and whom she missed deeply. On the tenth night spent at her father's house, she dreamed that she was in a garden of the palace when she noticed Beast, half dead, lying in the grass and reproaching her for her ingratitude.

Beauty woke up with a start and began weeping. "It's dreadful of me to cause heartache to someone who did so much to please me," she said. "Is it his fault that he's ugly and lacks intelligence? He is kind. That's worth more than anything else. Why haven't I wanted to marry him? I would be happier with him than my sisters are with their husbands. It is neither good looks nor great intelligence that makes a woman happy with her husband, but character, virtue, and kindness. Beast has all those qualities. I may not be in love with him, but I feel respect, friendship, and gratitude toward him. If I make him unhappy, my lack of gratitude will make me feel terrible for the rest of my life."

With these words, Beauty got up, wrote her father a short note to explain why she was leaving, put her ring on the table, and went back to bed. She had hardly gotten into bed when she fell sound asleep. And when she awoke in the morning, she was overjoyed to find herself in Beast's palace. She dressed up in magnificent clothes just to please him and spent the day feeling bored to death, waiting for the clock to strike nine. But nothing happened when the clock struck nine. Beast was nowhere to be seen.

Beauty feared that she might have caused Beast's death. She ran to look for him in every room of the castle, sobbing loudly. In a state of despair, she searched everywhere for him. Then she remembered her dream and ran into the garden, toward the canal where she had seen Beast in her sleep. Poor Beast was stretched out on the ground unconscious, and she was sure that he was dead. Feeling no dread about the way he looked, she flung herself on him and, realizing that his heart was still beating, ran to get some water from the canal and threw it on him. Beast opened his eyes and said to Beauty: "You forgot your promise. The thought of having lost you made me decide to starve myself to death. Now I will die happy, for I have the pleasure of seeing you one last time."

"No, dear Beast, you will not die," said Beauty. "You will live and become my husband. From this moment on, I give you my hand in marriage, and I swear that I will belong only to you. Alas, I thought that I felt only friendship for you, but the anguish I am feeling makes me realize that I can't live without you."

ANONYMOUS,
"Beauty and the Beast:
or a Rough Outside with a Gentle
Heart," 1811

Despite the differences in their physical representations, Beauty and Beast share a wide-eyed determination to forge ahead. Difficult to identify, this Beast is all animal, without a trace of a human feature.

ELEANOR VERE BOYLE,
"Beauty and the Beast," 1875

The hybrid beast embraced by Beauty blends into the natural landscape, while Beauty herself, with her bright robes, appears as a powerful visual presence. Despite the tusks and powerful paws, Beast appears to be a gentle creature, eager for Beauty's human ministrations.

ARTHUR RACKHAM,
"Beauty and the Beast," 1915

Looking rather like a bat without wings, this Beast, tears in his eyes, attracts Beauty's pity. More whimsically suited and proportioned than most Beasts, Rackham's creature stirs compassion but also provides a measure of comic relief to the story.

10. *A wicked fairy condemned me to remain in that form.* Few versions of the story explain why the spell was cast on the prince. In some versions the prince's arrogance or failure to show charity to an old woman leads to his enchantment.

Scarcely had Beauty uttered these words when the castle became radiant with light. Fireworks and music signaled a celebration. But these were mere distractions for Beauty. She turned back to look at her dear beast, whose perilous condition made her tremble with fear. You can imagine her surprise when she discovered that Beast had disappeared and that a young prince more handsome than the day was bright was lying at her feet, thanking her for having broken the magic spell cast on him.

Even though she was worried about the prince, she could not keep herself from asking about Beast. "You see him at your feet," the prince said. "A wicked fairy condemned me to remain in that form[10] until a beautiful girl would consent to marry me. She prohibited me from revealing my intelligence. You were the only person in the world kind enough to be touched by the goodness of my character. Even by offering you a crown, I still can't repay you for what you have done."

Beauty was pleasantly surprised, and she gave the handsome prince her hand so that he could stand up. Together they went to the castle, and Beauty was nearly overcome with joy when she found her father and her entire family in the large hall. The beautiful lady who had appeared to her in a dream had transported them to the castle.

"Beauty," said the lady, who was a grand fairy, "come and accept the reward for your wise choice. You preferred virtue to looks and intelligence, and so you deserve to see those qualities united in a single person. You will become a noble queen, and I hope that sitting on a throne will not damage your many virtues. As for you, my dear ladies," the fairy continued, addressing Beauty's two sisters, "I know your hearts and all the malice that is in them. I am going to turn you into two statues, but you will keep your awareness beneath the stone that envelops you. You will be taken to the entrance of your sister's palace, and I can think of no better punishment for you than to witness her

WARWICK GOBLE,
"Beauty and the Beast," 1923

Beauty is overcome by pity at the sight of a disconsolate Beast, whose princely body cannot compensate for a horse-like head.

happiness. You will not return to your natural state until you acknowledge your faults. I fear that you may have to remain statues forever. You can correct pride, anger, gluttony, and laziness. But you need a miracle to transform a heart filled with malice and envy."

The fairy waved her wand, and everyone there was transported to the great hall of the prince's kingdom, where the subjects were elated by his return. The prince married Beauty, who lived with him for a long time in perfect happiness, for their marriage was founded on virtue.

5

SNOW WHITE[1]

Jacob and Wilhelm Grimm

Walt Disney's Snow White and the Seven Dwarfs *(1937) has so overshadowed other versions of the story that it is easy to forget that the tale is widely disseminated across a variety of cultures. The heroine may ingest a poisoned apple in her cinematic incarnation, but in Italy she is just as likely to fall victim to a toxic comb, a contaminated cake, or a suffocating braid. Disney's queen, who demands Snow White's heart from the huntsman who takes her into the woods, seems restrained by comparison with the Grimms' evil queen, who orders the huntsman to return with the girl's lungs and liver, both of which she plans to eat after boiling them in salt water. In Spain the queen is even more bloodthirsty, asking for a bottle of blood stoppered with the girl's toe. In Italy she instructs the huntsman to return with the girl's intestines and her blood-soaked shirt. Disney's film has made much of Snow White's coffin being made of glass, but in other versions of the tale that cof-*

1. *Snow White.* Only the Grimms' version of the story alludes to the heroine's complexion in her name. Sneewittchen, Snow White's name in German, is a diminutive form and could be literally translated as Little Snow White.

From Jacob and Wilhelm Grimm, "Sneewittchen," in *Kinder- und Hausmärchen*, 7th ed. (Berlin: Dieterich, 1857; first published, Berlin: Realschulbuchhandlung, 1812).

fin is made of gold, silver, or lead, or is jewel encrusted. While it is often displayed on a mountaintop, it can also be set adrift on a river, placed under a tree, hung from the rafters, or locked in a room and surrounded with candles.

"Snow White" may vary tremendously from culture to culture in its details, but it has an easily identifiable, stable core in the conflict between mother and daughter. In many versions of the tale, the evil queen is the girl's biological mother, not a stepmother. (The Grimms, in an effort to preserve the sanctity of motherhood, were forever turning biological mothers into stepmothers.) The struggle between Snow White and the wicked queen so dominates the psychological landscape of this fairy tale that Sandra Gilbert and Susan Gubar, in a landmark book of feminist literary criticism, proposed renaming the story "Snow White and Her Wicked Stepmother." In The Madwoman in the Attic, they describe how the Grimms' story stages a contest between the "angel-woman" and the "monster-woman" of Western culture. For them the motor of the "Snow White" plot is driven by the relationship between two women, "the one fair, young, pale, the other just as fair, but older, fiercer; the one a daughter, the other a mother; the one sweet, ignorant, passive, the other both artful and active; the one a sort of angel, the other an undeniable witch."

Gilbert and Gubar, rather than reading the story as an oedipal plot in which mother and daughter become sexual rivals for approval from the father (incarnated as the voice in the mirror), suggest that the tale mirrors our cultural division of femininity into two components, one that is writ large in our most popular version of the tale. In Disney's Snow White and the Seven Dwarfs, we find these two components fiercely polarized in a murderously jealous and forbiddingly cold woman on the one hand and an innocently sweet girl accomplished in the art of good housekeeping on the other. Yet the Disney film also positions the evil queen as the figure of gripping narrative energy and makes Snow White so dull that she requires a supporting cast of seven to enliven her scenes. Ultimately it is the stepmother's disruptive, disturbing, and divisive presence that invests the film with a degree of fascination that has facilitated *its widespread circulation and that has allowed it to take such powerful hold in our own culture.*

Children reading this story are unlikely to make the interpretive moves described above. For them, this will be the story of a mother-daughter conflict, which, according to Bruno Bettelheim, offers cathartic pleasures in its lurid punishment of the jealous queen. Once again, as in "Cinderella," the good mother is dead, and in this story the only real assistance she offers is in her legacy of beauty. Snow White must contend with a villain doubly incarnated as beautiful, proud, and evil queen and as ugly, sinister, and wicked witch. Small wonder that she is reduced to a role of pure passivity, a "dumb bunny," as the poet Anne Sexton put it. In its validation of murderous hatred as a "natural" affect in the relationship between daughter and (step)mother and its promotion of youth, beauty, and hard work, "Snow White" is not without problematic dimensions, yet it has remained one of our most powerful cultural stories. In 1997 Michael Cohn drew out the dark, gothic elements of the story in his Grimm Brothers' Snow White, starring Sigourney Weaver.

ONCE UPON A TIME in the middle of winter, when snowflakes the size of feathers were falling from the sky, a queen was sitting and sewing by a window with an ebony frame. While she was sewing, she looked out at the snow and pricked her finger with a needle. Three drops of blood fell onto the snow. The red looked so beautiful against the white snow that she thought: "If only I had a child as white as snow, as red as blood, and as black as the wood of the window frame."[2] Soon afterward she gave birth to a little girl who was white as snow, red as blood, and black as ebony, and she was called Snow White. The queen died after the child was born.[3]

2. *as black as the wood of the window frame.* Sandra M. Gilbert and Susan Gubar see the mother as a figure trapped by the ebony frame, just as the second queen is later trapped by the magic mirror. While the mother is confined indoors, sewing, the second queen is mobile and wily, but locked in a state of narcissistic desire. Note that one queen looks through a transparent surface, whereas the other is captivated by an opaque surface that reflects her own image back to her. That Snow White is put on aesthetic display in a glass coffin seems to refer back to both the window and the looking glass.

3. *The queen died after the child was born.* The Grimms added the prefatory episode about Snow White's birth and about her mother's death to later editions of their collection. In

ARTHUR RACKHAM,
"Snow White and the Seven Dwarfs," 1909

The proud queen looks into the mirror that is perched on an anthropomorphized stand.

the 1810 manuscript version of "Snow White," there is only one queen, and she is both Snow White's biological mother and persecutor.

4. *Who's the fairest one of all?* The voice in the mirror may be viewed as a judgmental voice, representing the missing, absent father or patriarchy in general, which places a premium on beauty. But that voice could also be an echo of the queen's own self-assessment, one that is, to be sure, informed by cultural norms about physical appearances.

A year later, her husband, the king, married another woman. She was a beautiful lady, but proud and overbearing, and she could not bear the thought that anyone might be more beautiful than she was. She owned a magic mirror, and whenever she stood in front of it to look at herself, she would say:

> "Mirror, mirror, on the wall,
> Who's the fairest one of all?"**4**

The mirror would always reply:

> "You, O Queen, are the fairest of all."

Then she was happy, for she knew that the mirror always spoke the truth.

Snow White was growing up, and with each passing day

she became more beautiful. When she reached the age of seven,[5] she had become as beautiful as the bright day and more beautiful than the queen herself. One day the queen asked the mirror:

"Mirror, mirror, on the wall,
Who's the fairest one of all?"

The mirror replied:

"My Queen, you may be the fairest here,
But Snow White is a thousand times more fair."

When the queen heard these words, she began to tremble, and her face turned green with envy. From that moment on, she hated Snow White,[6] and whenever she set eyes on her, her heart turned cold like a stone. Envy and pride grew like weeds in her heart. By day or by night, she never knew a moment's peace.

One day she summoned a huntsman and said: "Take the child out into the forest. I don't want to lay eyes on her ever again. Bring me her lungs and her liver as proof that you have killed her."

The huntsman obeyed and took the girl out into the woods, but just as he was taking out his hunting knife and about to take aim at her innocent heart, she began weeping and pleading with him. "Alas, dear huntsman, spare my life. I promise to run into the woods and never return."

Snow White was so beautiful that the huntsman took pity on her and said: "Just run off, you poor child."

"The wild animals will devour you before long," he thought. He felt as if a great weight had been lifted from his heart, for at least he would not have to kill the girl. Just then, a young boar ran in front of him, and the huntsman stabbed it to death. He removed the lungs and liver and brought them to the queen as proof that he had murdered the child. The cook was told to boil them in brine, and the wicked woman ate them up,[7] thinking that she had eaten Snow White's lungs and liver.

5. *When she reached the age of seven.* In earlier centuries, especially before the onset of public education, childhood was of a much shorter duration, with the child integrated into the adult world of work even before the onset of puberty. Still, Snow White's youth is difficult to square with the fact that she marries at the end of the story, particularly since there are no markers of aging. Most illustrations for the story depict her as an adolescent or young adult approaching an age suitable for marriage.

6. *she hated Snow White.* The tale turns on the (sexual) rivalry between stepmother and daughter, with Snow White positioned as the classic "innocent persecuted heroine" of fairy tales. "Snow White" has been read as a story that plots the trajectory of "normal" female maturation (in symbolic terms) and maps a case study of maternal jealousy in its most pathological form.

7. *the wicked woman ate them up.* Like the witches and ogres of folklore, the queen engages in cannibalistic acts, hoping that by incorporating her stepdaughter, she will also acquire her beauty.

THEODOR HOSEMANN,
"Snow White and the Seven Dwarfs,"
1847

On bended knees, Snow White, clad in a white dress, entreats the hunter to spare her life. With sword drawn, the courtly hunter is overcome by feelings of compassion and stops himself from harming the girl.

GEORGE SOPER,
"Snow White and the Seven Dwarfs,"
1915

Snow White, draped in red, entreats a hunter, preparing to use his spear, to show mercy. Although diminutive in size, this Snow White is more like a small woman than a young girl. Almost stage-like in its composition, this scene has a certain formal, theatrical quality to it.

FRANZ JÜTTNER,
"Snow White and the Seven Dwarfs,"
1905

Wolves lurk in the forest as Snow White searches for shelter. The unusual combination of russets, tans, and browns gives the scene a muted quality that is absent from most artistic renderings of Snow White lost in the forest.

8. *Everything in the house was tiny and indescribably dainty and spotless.* Unlike Disney's seven dwarfs, these men are models of tidiness whose home provides a cozy haven. Like Hansel and Gretel, Snow White finds shelter in the woods, and she also is subjected to another threat in her new home.

The poor child was left all alone in the vast forest. She was so frightened that she looked at all the leaves on the trees and had no idea where to turn. She started running and raced over sharp stones and through thorn bushes. Wild beasts darted past her at times, but they did her no harm. She ran as far as her legs would carry her. When night fell, she discovered a little cottage and went inside to rest. Everything in the house was tiny and indescribably dainty and spotless.[8] There was a little table, with seven little plates on a white cloth. Each little plate had a little spoon, seven little knives and forks, and seven little cups. Against the wall were seven little beds in a row, each made up with sheets as white as snow. Snow White was so hungry and so thirsty that she ate a few vegetables and some bread from each little plate and drank a drop of wine from each little cup. She didn't want to take everything away from one of the places. Later she was so tired that she tried out the beds, but they did not seem to be the right size. The first one was too long, the second too short, but the seventh one was just right,[9] and she stayed in it. Then she said her prayers and fell fast asleep.

It was completely dark outside when the owners of the cottage returned. They were seven dwarfs who spent their days in the mountains,[10] mining ore and digging for minerals. They lit their seven little lanterns, and when the

ARTHUR RACKHAM,
"Snow White and the Seven Dwarfs," 1909

Weighed down by complex equipment, the dwarfs wind their way home.

cottage brightened up, they saw that someone had been there, for not everything was as they had left it.

The first dwarf asked: "Who's been sitting in my little chair?"

The second one asked: "Who's been eating from my little plate?"

The third asked: "Who's been eating my little loaf of bread?"

9. *but the seventh one was just right.* Like Goldilocks, Snow White tries out different possibilities and finds the bed that is just right for her, in this case a signal that she has found an appropriate refuge.

10. *seven dwarfs who spent their days in the mountains.* Associated with earth, the dwarfs are hardworking creatures who lead an existence on the social periphery, yet who show compassionate hospitality to the orphaned girl. Unlike Disney's dwarfs, the Grimms' dwarfs are not differentiated from each other. Their diminutive stature makes them sexually unthreatening, even as their sevenfold admiration for Snow White's beauty magnifies her attractiveness.

The fourth asked: "Who's been eating from my little plate of vegetables?"

The fifth asked: "Who's been using my little fork?"

The sixth asked: "Who's been using my little knife to cut?"

The seventh asked: "Who's been drinking from my little cup?"

The first dwarf turned around and saw that his sheets were wrinkled and said: "Who climbed into my little bed?"

The others came running and each shouted: "Someone's been sleeping in my bed too."

When the seventh dwarf looked in his little bed, he saw Snow White lying there, fast asleep. He shouted to the others, who came running and who were so stunned that

WARWICK GOBLE,
"Snow White and the Seven Dwarfs," 1923

Surrounded by the seven dwarfs, who seem both pleased and bewildered by her presence, Snow White discusses the opportunities for coexistence. The bedding and furniture give the scene a contemporary look.

they all raised their seven little lanterns to let light shine on Snow White.

"My goodness, my goodness!" they all exclaimed. "What a beautiful child!"

The dwarfs were so delighted to see her that they decided not to wake her up and to let her keep sleeping in her little bed. The seventh dwarf slept for one hour with each of his companions until the night was over.

In the morning Snow White woke up. When she saw the dwarfs, she was frightened, but they were friendly and asked: "What's your name?"

"My name is Snow White," she replied.

"How did you get to our house?" asked the dwarfs.

Snow White told them how her stepmother had tried to kill her and how the huntsman had spared her life. She had run all day long until she had arrived at their cottage.

The dwarfs told her: "If you will keep house for us,[11] cook, make the beds, wash, sew, knit, and keep everything neat and tidy, then you can stay with us, and we'll give you everything you need."

"Yes, with pleasure," Snow White replied, and she stayed with them.

Snow White kept house for the dwarfs. In the morning they would go up to the mountains in search of minerals and gold. In the evening they would return, and dinner had to be ready for them. Since the girl was by herself during the day, the good dwarfs gave her a strong warning: "Beware of your stepmother. She'll know soon enough that you're here. Don't let anyone in the house."

After the queen had finished eating what she thought were Snow White's lungs and liver, she was sure that she was once again the fairest of all in the land. She went up to the mirror and said:

> "Mirror, mirror, on the wall,
> Who's the fairest of them all?"

The mirror replied:

> "Here you're the fairest, my dear Queen,
> But Little Snow White, who plans to stay
> With the seven dwarfs so far away,
> Is now the fairest ever seen."

When the queen heard these words she was horrified, for she knew that the mirror never told a lie. She realized

11. *If you will keep house for us.* In carrying out domestic chores, Snow White moves into a new developmental stage, demonstrating her ability to engage in labor and to carry out the terms of a contract. No longer a child, she is preparing herself for the state of matrimony.

12. *she came up with a plan.* Susan M. Gilbert and Sandra Gubar try to move against the grain of conventional interpretations, which focus on the queen as the source of evil. They view the queen as the consummate "plotter, a plot-maker, a schemer, a witch, an artist" and as a woman who is "witty, wily, and self-absorbed as all artists traditionally are." It is the queen who becomes the center of narrative energy, advancing the action and providing powerfully attractive twists and turns to the plot.

13. *The old woman laced her up so quickly and so tightly that Snow White's breath was cut off.* Snow White's attraction to staylaces and combs, along with the fact that she is easily duped, has been seen as a sign of her immaturity. But Snow White seems to be less "dumb bunny" than innocent child who falls victim to the stepmother's duplicity. The stepmother traps Snow White by donning disguises and by mimicking nurturing behavior.

that the huntsman must have deceived her and that Snow White was still alive. She thought long and hard about how she could get rid of Snow White. Unless she herself was the fairest in the land, she would never be able to feel anything but envy. Finally, she came up with a plan.[12] By staining her face and dressing up as an old peddler woman, she made herself completely unrecognizable. In that disguise she traveled beyond the seven hills to the home of the seven dwarfs. Then she knocked on the door and called out: "Pretty wares for a good price."

Snow White peeked out the window and said: "Good day, old woman. What do you have for sale?"

"Nice things, pretty things," she replied. "Staylaces in all kinds of colors," and she took out a silk lace woven of many colors.

"I can let this good woman in," Snow White thought, and she unbolted the door and bought the pretty lace.

"Oh, my child, what a sight you are. Come, let me lace you up properly."

Snow White wasn't the least bit suspicious. She stood in front of the old woman and let her put on the new lace. The old woman laced her up so quickly and so tightly that Snow White's breath was cut off,[13] and she fell down as if dead.

"So much for being the fairest of them all," the old woman said as she hurried away.

Not much later, in the evening, the seven dwarfs came home. When they saw their beloved Snow White lying on the ground, they were horrified. She wasn't moving at all, and they were sure she was dead. They lifted her up, and when they saw that she had been laced too tightly, they cut the staylace in two. Snow White began to breathe, and little by little she came back to life. When the dwarfs heard what had happened, they said: "The old peddler woman was none other than the wicked queen. Be on your guard, and don't let anyone in unless we're at home."

When the wicked woman returned home, she went to the mirror and asked:

"Mirror, mirror, on the wall,
Who's the fairest of them all?"

The mirror replied as usual:

"Here you're the fairest, my dear Queen,
But Little Snow White, who plans to stay
With the seven dwarfs so far away,
Is now the fairest ever seen."

When the queen heard those words, the blood froze in her veins. She was horrified, for she knew that Snow White was still alive. "But this time," she said, "I will dream up something that will destroy you."

Using all the witchcraft in her power, she made a poisoned comb. She then changed her clothes and disguised herself once more as an old woman. Again she traveled beyond the seven hills to the home of the seven dwarfs, knocked on the door, and called out: "Pretty wares at a good price."

Snow White peeked out the window and said: "Go away, I can't let anyone in."

"But you can at least take a look," said the old woman, and she took out a poisoned comb and held it up in the air. The child liked it so much that she was completely fooled and opened the door. When they had agreed on a price, the old woman said: "Now I'll give your hair a good combing."

Poor Snow White suspected nothing and let the woman go ahead, but no sooner had the comb touched her hair than the poison took effect, and the girl fell senseless to the ground.

"There, my beauty," said the wicked woman. "Now you're finished." And she rushed away.

Fortunately, the dwarfs were on their way home, for it was almost nighttime. When they saw Snow White lying on the ground as if she were dead, they suspected the stepmother right away. When they examined her, they

14. *white with red cheeks.* Note that the physical description of the apple coincides with the description of Snow White. Ever since the Garden of Eden, apples have been invested with powerful symbolic significance.

discovered the poisoned comb. As soon as they pulled it out, Snow White came back to life and told them what had happened. Again they warned her to be on her guard and not to open the door to anyone.

At home the queen stood in front of the mirror and said:

> "Mirror, mirror, on the wall,
> Who's the fairest of them all?"

The mirror answered as before:

> "Here you're the fairest, my dear Queen,
> But Little Snow White, who plans to stay
> With the seven dwarfs so far away,
> Is now the fairest ever seen."

When the queen heard the words spoken by the mirror, she began trembling with rage. "Snow White must die!" she cried out. "Even if it costs me my life."

The queen went into a remote, hidden chamber in which no one ever set foot and made an apple full of poison. On the outside it looked beautiful—white with red cheeks**14**—and if you saw it, you craved it. But if you took the tiniest bite, you would die. When the apple was finished, the queen stained her face again, dressed up as a peasant woman, and traveled beyond the seven hills to the home of the seven dwarfs.

The old woman knocked at the door, and Snow White stuck her head out the window to say: "I can't let anyone in. The seven dwarfs won't allow it."

"That's all right," the peasant woman replied. "I'll get rid of my apples soon enough. Here, I'll give you one."

"No," said Snow White. "I'm not supposed to take anything."

"Are you afraid that it's poisoned?" asked the old woman. "Here, I'll cut the apple in two. You eat the red part, I'll eat the white."

The apple had been made so craftily that only the red

GUSTAV TENGGREN,
"Snow White and the Seven Dwarfs," 1923

The witch bites into the apple to prove that it is safe for Snow White to eat. Setting and costumes, with their subdued beiges and browns, create an effect more realistic than that of most fairy-tale illustrations.

part of it had poison. Snow White felt a craving for the beautiful apple, and when she saw that the peasant woman was taking a bite, she could no longer resist. She put her hand out the window and took the poisoned half. But no sooner had she taken a bite than she fell to the ground dead. The queen stared at her with savage eyes and burst out laughing: "White as snow, red as blood, black as ebony![15] This time the dwarfs won't be able to bring you back to life!"

At home she asked the mirror:

> "Mirror, mirror, on the wall,
> Who's the fairest of them all?"

And finally it replied:

15. *"White as snow, red as blood, black as ebony!"* The stepmother's invocation of the first queen's fantasy about her child points to the underlying identity of the biological mother and the evil queen. Fairy tales often split the maternal figure into two components: a good, dead mother and a mobile, malicious stepmother. Children are thereby able to preserve a positive image of the mother even as they indulge in fantasies about maternal evil.

ARTHUR RACKHAM,
"Snow White and the Seven Dwarfs,"
1909

The seven dwarfs try in vain to revive a catatonic Snow White.

KAY NIELSEN,
"Snow White and the Seven Dwarfs,"
1914

Preserved in a glass coffin, Snow White has the pallor and look of death. The seven dwarfs keep guard in a setting that places the coffin on display.

MAXFIELD PARRISH,
"Snow White and the Seven Dwarfs,"
1912

Standing guard over the catatonic Snow White, the dwarf exudes power and determination in his stark verticality. The horizontal Snow White nearly blends in with the craggy landscape, although the sheet wrapped around her coffin produces a stunning draped contrast to the rocks.

"O Queen, you are the fairest in the land."

The queen's envious heart was finally at peace, as much as an envious heart can be.

When the dwarfs returned home in the evening, they found Snow White lying on the ground. Not a breath of air was coming from her lips. She was dead. They lifted her up and looked around for something that might be poisonous. They unlaced her, combed her hair, washed her with water and wine, but it was all in vain. The dear child was gone, and nothing could bring her back. After placing her on a bier, all seven of them sat down around it and mourned Snow White. They wept for three days.

They were about to bury her, but she still looked like a living person with beautiful red cheeks.

The dwarfs said: "We can't possibly put her into the dark ground." And so they had a transparent glass coffin made that allowed Snow White to be seen from all sides. They put her in it, wrote her name on it in golden letters,[16] and added that she was the daughter of a king. They brought the coffin up to the top of a mountain, and one of them always remained by it to keep vigil. Animals also came to mourn Snow White, first an owl, then a raven, and finally a dove.

Snow White lay in the coffin for a long, long time. But she did not decay and looked just as if she were sleeping, for she was still white as snow, red as blood, and had hair as black as ebony.

One day the son of a king was traveling through the forest and came to the cottage of the dwarfs. He was hoping to spend the night there. When he went to the top of the mountain, he saw the coffin with beautiful Snow White lying in it, and he read the words written in gold letters. Then he said to the dwarfs: "Let me have the coffin. I will give you whatever you want for it."

The dwarfs replied: "We wouldn't sell it for all the gold in the world."

He said: "Make me a present of it, for I can't live without seeing Snow White. I will honor and cherish her as if she were my beloved."

The good dwarfs took pity when they heard those words, and they gave him the coffin. The prince ordered his servants to put the coffin on their shoulders and to carry it away. It happened that they stumbled over a shrub, and the jolt freed the poisonous piece of apple lodged in Snow White's throat.[17] She came back to life. "Good heavens, where am I?" she cried out.

The prince was thrilled and said: "You will stay with me," and he told her what had happened. "I love you more than anything else on earth," he said. "Come with me to my father's castle. You shall be my bride." Snow

16. *wrote her name on it in golden letters.* Snow White becomes an object that is put on aesthetic display. Like the title of a painting in a museum, her name is written in golden letters, and she becomes something of a tourist attraction.

17. *the jolt freed the poisonous piece of apple lodged in Snow White's throat.* This accidental awakening stands in sharp contrast to the kiss (borrowed from "Sleeping Beauty") that awakens Snow White in Disney's animated film version. Although the prince has shown his devotion to Snow White, it is ultimately by sheer chance that Snow White comes back to life.

18. *red-hot iron shoes.* In the Disney film version, the queen is pursued to the edge of a cliff and falls to her death. The Grimms' queen is subjected to a painful and humiliating death, one that puts her on display in the same way that Snow White was exhibited as the consummate beautiful woman. Note, however, that the queen's tortured dance stands in sharp contrast to Snow White's immobilization in the coffin. The queen is presented as a cowardly figure, who shows no sign of repentance, unlike some fairy-tale villains (the father in "Hansel and Gretel," for example), who regret their evil ways.

White had tender feelings for him, and she departed with him. The marriage was celebrated with great splendor.

Snow White's wicked stepmother had also been invited to the wedding feast. She put on beautiful clothes, stepped up to the mirror, and said:

"Mirror, mirror, on the wall,
Who's the fairest of them all?"

The mirror replied:

"My Queen, you may be the fairest here,
But the young queen is a thousand times more fair."

The wicked woman let out a curse, and she was so paralyzed with fear that she didn't know what to do. At first she didn't want to go to the wedding feast. But she never had a moment's peace after that and had to go see the young queen. When she entered, Snow White recognized her right away. The queen was so terrified that she just stood there and couldn't budge an inch. Iron slippers had already been heated up for her over a fire of coals. They were brought in with tongs and set up right in front of her. She had to put on the red-hot iron shoes[18] and dance in them until she dropped to the ground dead.

6

SLEEPING BEAUTY[1]

Jacob and Wilhelm Grimm

The Grimms' story of Sleeping Beauty is considered a truncated version of Giambattista Basile's "Sun, Moon, and Talia" (1636) and Charles Perrault's "Sleeping Beauty in the Wood" (1697). In Basile's story Talia (whose name derives from the Greek word Thaleia, meaning "the blossoming one") gets a tiny piece of flax under her fingernail and falls down dead. The king who discovers Talia in an abandoned castle is already married, but he is so overcome with desire for her that he "plucks from her the fruits of love" while she is still asleep. Talia is awakened from her deep sleep when one of the two infants to which she gives birth, exactly nine months after the king's visit, sucks the piece of flax from her finger. When the king's wife learns about Talia and her two children, Sun and Moon, she orders their deaths, but she herself perishes in the fire she prepares for Talia, and the others live happily ever after.

Perrault's "Sleeping Beauty in the Wood" is awakened when

1. *Sleeping Beauty.* The Grimms' title, "Dornröschen," is sometimes translated literally as "Little Briar Rose." Perrault's French title is "The Beauty in the Sleeping Forest." The theme of a person slumbering or hibernating until the time is ripe for awakening appears in many folktales and legends. Snow White lies in her glass coffin; Brunhilde, surrounded by a wall of fire, is awakened by a kiss in Richard Wagner's nineteenth-century opera *Siegfried*; Frederick Barbarossa slumbers in his mountain retreat, awakening every hundred years to see if Germany needs his help as a leader.

From Jacob and Wilhelm Grimm, "Dornröschen," in *Kinder- und Hausmärchen*, 7th ed. (Berlin: Dieterich, 1857; first published, Berlin: Realschulbuchhandlung, 1812).

a prince kneels before her, and the two carry on a love affair that produces a daughter named Aurora and a son named Day. Although the prince marries Sleeping Beauty, he is soon summoned to battle and entrusts his wife and children to the care of his mother, who is descended from a "race of ogres." The mother's cannibalistic inclinations get the better of her, but a compassionate steward spares the lives of mother and children, substituting animals for the humans. In the end the queen, caught by her son in the act of trying to do away with his family, flings herself headfirst into a vat filled with "toads, vipers, adders, and serpents."

The Grimms' "Sleeping Beauty" has a narrative integrity that has made it more appealing than Basile's story and Perrault's tale, at least to audiences in the United States. The second phase of action in the Italian and the French versions features postmarital conflicts that, according to some folklorists, constitute separate narratives. It is not at all unusual for the tellers of tales to splice stories together to produce a narrative that charts premarital conflicts as well as what happens in the not so happily-ever-after.

The quintessential female heroine of fairy tales, Sleeping Beauty is the fabled passive princess who awaits liberation from a prince. Deprived of agency, she resembles the catatonic Snow White, who can do nothing more than lie in wait for Prince Charming. Yet this cliché about fairy-tale heroines overlooks the many clever and resourceful girls and women who are able to liberate themselves from danger. Anthologies by Kathleen Ragan, Angela Carter, Alison Lurie, and Ethel Johnston Phelps have resurrected older stories about strong, courageous, and resilient heroines who rescue themselves and others, thus providing weighty evidence that not all princesses wait passively for Prince Charming.

LONG, LONG AGO there lived a king and a queen. Day after day they would say to each other: "Oh, if only we could have a child!"[2] But nothing ever happened. One day, while the queen was bathing, a frog crawled out of the water, crept ashore, and said to her: "Your wish shall be fulfilled. Before a year goes by, you will give birth to a daughter."

The frog's prediction came true,[3] and the queen gave birth to a girl who was so beautiful that the king was beside himself with joy and arranged a great feast. He invited relatives, friends, and acquaintances, and he also sent for the wise women of the kingdom, for he hoped that they would be kind and generous toward his child. There were thirteen wise women in all, but since the king had only twelve golden plates for them to dine on, one of the women had to stay home.

The feast was celebrated with great splendor, and when it drew to a close, the wise women bestowed their magic gifts on the girl.[4] One conferred virtue on her, a second gave her beauty, a third wealth, and on it went until the girl had everything in the world you could ever want. Just as the eleventh woman was presenting her gift, the thirteenth in the group appeared out of nowhere. She had not been invited, and now she wanted her revenge.[5] Without looking at anyone or saying a word to a soul there, she cried out in a loud voice: "When the daughter of the king turns fifteen, she will prick her finger on a spindle and fall down dead." And without saying another word, she turned her back on everyone and left the hall.

Everyone was horrified, but just then the twelfth in the group of women stood up. There was still one wish left to make for the girl, and, although the wise woman could not lift the evil spell, she could make it less severe. And so she said: "The king's daughter shall not die, but she will fall into a deep sleep lasting one hundred years." The

2. *"Oh, if only we could have a child!"* The inability to conceive often leads fairy-tale couples to make reckless promises or to strike outlandish bargains. In "Sleeping Beauty," the parents' lack of foresight appears only at the festivities celebrating the birth of a daughter.

3. *The frog's prediction came true.* In the Grimms' first version of the story, a crab makes the prophecy, hence the hazards of reading too much into the fact that a frog makes the prediction about the birth of a child and is therefore a symbol of fertility in fairy tales.

4. *the wise women bestowed their magic gifts on the girl.* In Perrault's version and in the Grimms' early version, fairies provide the gifts. The gifts promise to turn the Grimms' Sleeping Beauty into an "ideal" woman—virtuous, beautiful, and wealthy. In Perrault's version the girl is given beauty, an angelic disposition, grace, the ability to dance perfectly, the voice of a nightingale, and the ability to play instruments.

5. *She had not been invited, and now she wanted her revenge.* The resentment of the slighted wise woman calls to mind the wrath of Eris, goddess of discord, who, when not invited to the wedding feast of Peleus and Thetis, exacted her revenge by throwing the notorious Apple of Discord, marked with the words "For the Fairest," among the assembled wedded guests. The elaborate debates and negotiations over the Apple of Discord led, eventually, to the Trojan War.

EDMUND DULAC,
"Sleeping Beauty," 1912

"Her head nodded with spite and old age together, as she bent over the cradle." The wicked fairy, who looks more like an angry granny than a disgruntled fairy, prepares to put a curse on the princess, as horrified parents and courtiers look on helplessly.

EDMUND DULAC,
"Sleeping Beauty," 1912

"'I am spinning pretty one,' answered the old woman, who did not know who she was." Up in the tower room, an overdressed Sleeping Beauty is fascinated by the spinning paraphernalia she discovers and by the old woman's subversive activity.

EDMUND DULAC,
"Sleeping Beauty," 1912

"They grew until nothing but the tops of the castle towers could be seen." A laborer with a boy surveys the impenetrable foliage surrounding the castle. The instrument he carries seems powerless to pierce the thick forest surrounding the castle.

6. *a little door with a rusty old key in its lock.* Note that Sleeping Beauty's curiosity, her desire to see what is behind the door and her fascination with the spindle, gets her into trouble. By contrast, the prince is rewarded for his curiosity, which takes the form of the desire to find the fabled castle in which Sleeping Beauty slumbers.

king, who wanted to do everything possible to guard his dear child from misfortune, sent out an order that every spindle in the entire kingdom was to be burned to ashes.

As for the girl, all the wishes made by the wise women came true, for she was so beautiful, kind, charming, and sensible that everyone who set eyes on her grew to love her. On the exact day that she turned fifteen, the king and the queen were not at home, and the girl was left at home all alone. She wandered around in the castle, poking her head into one room after another, and eventually she came to the foot of an old tower. After climbing up a narrow winding staircase in the tower, she ended up in front of a little door with a rusty old key in its lock.[6] As she turned the key, the door swung open to reveal a tiny little room. An old woman was in it with her spindle, busily spinning flax.

EDMUND DULAC,
"Sleeping Beauty," 1912

"The ruddy faces of the switzers told him that they were no worse than asleep." The military musicians and palace guard have been so frozen in their positions that, but for their skin color, they resemble the statue towering above them. The reds and blues are uncharacteristic of Dulac's pastel palettes.

EDMUND DULAC,
"Sleeping Beauty," 1912

"And there, on a bed the curtains of which were drawn wide, he beheld the loveliest vision he had ever seen." Dulac's princess reclines on her bed, with cherubim floating above her. A cat sleeps on Dulac's signature cushion with tassels.

GUSTAVE DORÉ,
"Sleeping Beauty in the Wood," 1861

A curious Sleeping Beauty reaches her hand out to touch the spindle that will put her to sleep. The bird perched on the chair suggests a sinister moment in this scene of domestic tranquility. The door in the background connects this scene with the opening of a forbidden door in Perrault's "Bluebeard." Note also the unusual position of the cat, a figure connected to curiosity, crouched in such a way as to draw attention to the door.

"Good afternoon, granny," said the princess. "What are you doing here?"

"I'm spinning flax,"[7] the old woman replied, and she nodded to the girl.

"What is that thing bobbing about so oddly?" asked the girl, and she put her hand on the spindle, for she too wanted to spin. The magic spell began to take effect at once, for she had pricked her finger on the spindle.[8]

Right after touching the tip of the spindle, the girl collapsed on a nearby bed and fell into a deep sleep. Her slumber spread throughout the castle.[9] The king and the queen, who had just returned home and were entering the great hall, fell asleep, and the entire court with them.

7. *"I'm spinning flax."* The spindle or distaff is associated with the Fates, who "spin" or measure out the span of life. Spinning is also an activity that fostered female storytelling, and the spinning of flax often crossed over from the storytelling context into the story itself. The German term for spinning has a secondary meaning associated with fantasizing and building castles in the air. As standard symbols for female domesticity, the spindle and distaff were sometimes carried before the bride in wedding processions of an earlier age. The Grimms' *German Mythology* points out the powerful connection between spindles and domesticity.

GUSTAVE DORÉ,
"Sleeping Beauty in the Wood," 1861

The prince is given directions to the castle in which Sleeping Beauty slumbers. The dominance of the vegetation makes the castle appear inaccessible to the tiny figure anchored in a craggy landscape. While others hunt and gather, the prince goes in search of adventure.

GUSTAVE DORÉ,
"Sleeping Beauty in the Wood," 1861

The prince from Perrault's "Sleeping Beauty in the Wood" marches under a dark arch of trees toward the steps of the castle. The light at the entrance to the castle reveals a figure asleep on the stairs, a male counterpart and precursor to Sleeping Beauty.

GUSTAVE DORÉ,
"Sleeping Beauty in the Wood," 1861

The prince passes the figures of sleeping dogs, horses, and courtiers, all of whom were stopped in their tracks when the princess pricked her finger on the only spindle in the kingdom. Vines have grown over some of the figures.

8. *she had pricked her finger on the spindle.* The story of Sleeping Beauty has been thought to map female sexual maturation, with the touching of the spindle representing the onset of puberty, a kind of sexual awakening that leads to a passive, introspective period of latency.

9. *Her slumber spread throughout the castle.* The whimsical elaboration that follows this statement was added by the Grimms to the first edition of their collection.

The horses went to sleep in the stables, the dogs in the courtyard, the doves on the roof, and the flies on the wall. Even the fire flickering in the hearth died down and fell asleep. The roast stopped sizzling, and the cook, who was about to pull the hair of the kitchen boy because he had done something stupid, let him go and fell asleep. The wind also died down so that not a leaf was stirring on the trees outside the castle.

Soon a hedge of briars began to grow all around the castle. Every year it grew higher, until one day it surrounded the entire castle. It had grown so thick that you could not even see the banner on the turret of the castle. Throughout the land, stories circulated about the beautiful Briar Rose, for that was the name given to the slumbering princess. From time to time a prince would try to force his way through the hedge to get to the castle. But no one ever succeeded, because the briars clasped each other as

GUSTAVE DORÉ,
"Sleeping Beauty in the Wood," 1861

"The prince walked along a little farther, over to the great hall, where he saw the entire court fast asleep, with the king and the queen sleeping right next to their thrones." The prince makes his way through the rooms of the castle to the chamber of Sleeping Beauty. On his way, he encounters an eerie scene in which a lavish repast, halted by the spell, lies in ruins, crisscrossed by gigantic spiderwebs.

GUSTAVE DORÉ,
"Sleeping Beauty in the Wood," 1861

The prince rushes toward Sleeping Beauty, whose "radiant beauty" is described as having "an almost unearthly luster" in Perrault's version of the tale. How she was transported from the chamber in the tower to her bedroom is unclear. The "bower" in which she sleeps combines elaborate architectural detail with lush natural growth.

if they were holding hands, and the young men who tried got caught in them and couldn't pry themselves loose. They died an agonizing death.**10**

After many, many years had passed, another prince appeared in the land. He heard an old man talking about a briar hedge that was said to conceal a castle, where a fabulously beautiful princess named Briar Rose had been sleeping for a hundred years, along with the king, the queen, and the entire court. The old man had learned from his grandfather that many other princes had tried to make their way through the briar hedge, but they had gotten caught on the briars and died horrible deaths. The young man said: "I am not afraid. I am going to find that castle so that I can see the beautiful Briar Rose." The kind old man did his best to discourage the prince, but he refused to listen.

It so happened that the term of one hundred years had

10. *They died an agonizing death.* Wilhelm Grimm added descriptions of the death throes of the suitors to the first printed edition of the tales.

EDWARD BURNE-JONES,
"Briar Rose," 1870–90

Entitled *The Briar Wood*, this painting shows the prince preparing to hack his way through the woods in which lie the dead, but physically preserved, princes who were unsuccessful in their quest.

EDWARD BURNE-JONES,
"Briar Rose," 1870–90

In *The Garden Court*, the servant girls have fallen asleep over the loom and on tables. Their delicate hands, bare feet, and perfect visages stand out from the architectural background covered with flowering briars.

EDWARD BURNE-JONES,
"Briar Rose," 1870–90

The Council Chamber shows the slumbering monarch and his courtiers, along with the briar branches pushing their way into the palace.

EDWARD BURNE-JONES,
"Briar Rose," 1870–90

The Rose Bower displays Sleeping Beauty as an icon of aesthetic perfection. Surrounded by sleeping figures, she lies in a richly decorated setting in which the briars figure as ornaments rather than perils.

11. *They opened to make a path for him.* This prince does not have to kill any giants or slay any dragons in order to win his bride. His timing is, however, impeccable, illustrating how good fortune often trumps heroic feats in fairy tales.

just ended, and the day on which Briar Rose was to awaken had arrived. When the prince approached the briar hedge, he found nothing but big, beautiful flowers. They opened to make a path for him[11] and let him pass unharmed; then they closed behind him to form a hedge.

In the courtyard, the horses and the spotted hounds were lying in the same place fast asleep, and the doves

WARWICK GOBLE,
"Sleeping Beauty," 1923

Sleeping Beauty appears as if on display, with draperies behind her, a canopy above her, and a richly embroidered blanket covering her. The prince is about to wake her up by kneeling before her, while a small dog watches with anticipation in the foreground.

MAXFIELD PARRISH,
"Sleeping Beauty," 1912

For the cover of *Collier's* magazine, Parrish produced a sensuous Sleeping Beauty, draped across a staircase topped by classical columns. The two ladies-in-waiting, with their floral wreaths, contribute to the extraordinary compositional balance of the painting. Fusing the classical with the gothic, Parrish produces an eerily beautiful tableau.

were roosting with their little heads tucked under their wings. The prince made his way into the castle and saw how the flies were fast asleep on the walls. The cook was still in the kitchen, with his hand up in the air as if he were about to grab the kitchen boy, and the maid was still sitting at a table with a black hen that she was about to pluck.

The prince walked along a little farther, over to the great hall, where he saw the entire court fast asleep, with the king and the queen sleeping right next to their thrones. He continued on his way, and everything was so quiet that he could hear his own breath. Finally he got to the tower, and he opened up the door to the little room in which Briar Rose was sleeping. There she lay, so beautiful that he could not take his eyes off her, and he bent down to kiss her.

No sooner had the prince touched Briar Rose's lips

12. *No sooner had the prince touched Briar Rose's lips than she woke up.* In Perrault's version Sleeping Beauty is awakened when the prince drops to his knees. Many versions of "The Frog King" now end in the manner of "Sleeping Beauty," with the princess kissing the frog (and thereby transforming him into a prince) rather than hurling him against the wall.

than she woke up,[12] opened her eyes, and smiled sweetly at him. They went down the stairs together. The king, the queen, and the entire court had awoken, and they were all staring at each other in amazement. The horses in the courtyard stood up and shook themselves. The hounds jumped to their feet and wagged their tails. The doves pulled their heads out from under their wings, looked around, and flew off into the fields. The flies began crawling on the walls. The fire in the kitchen flickered, flared up, and began cooking the food again. The roast started to sizzle. The cook slapped the boy so hard that he let out a screech. The maid finished plucking the hen.

The wedding of Briar Rose and the prince was celebrated in great splendor, and the two lived out their days in happiness.

7

RAPUNZEL[1]

Jacob and Wilhelm Grimm

The story of a girl locked in a tower sounds a powerful chord in cultures that cloister young women in convents, isolating them or segregating them from the male population. "The Maiden in the Tower," as "Rapunzel" is known to folklorists, has been thought to be based on the legend of Saint Barbara, who was locked by her father in a tower. In The Book of the City of Ladies (1405), Christine de Pisan relates how Barbara's father shut her up in a tower for refusing marriage offers. But the story of Rapunzel seems rooted in a more general cultural tendency to "lock daughters up" and protect them from roving young men.

"Rapunzel" unfolds in two acts, the first beginning with man, wife, and the desired rapunzel, which is forbidden and secured through a transgressive act (climbing over a wall). In the second phase of action, the child Rapunzel is kept in a tower forbidden to others. When the enchantress discovers the

[1] *rapunzel.* The critic Joyce Thomas points out that rapunzel, or rampion, is an autogamous plant, one that can fertilize itself. Furthermore, it has a column that splits in two if not fertilized, and "the halves will curl like braids or coils on a maiden's head, and this will bring the female stigmatic tissue into contact with the male pollen on the exterior surface of the column." Most versions of the story give the girl the name of a savory herb.

From Jacob and Wilhelm Grimm, "Rapunzel," in *Kinder- und Haus-märchen,* 7th ed. (Berlin: Dieterich, 1857; first published, Berlin: Real-schulbuchhandlung, 1812).

prince's transgression (scaling the wall of a tower), she punishes once again, this time with blindness. The conclusion reunites the separated partners, restores the prince's sight, and liquidates the forbidden desires that launched the narrative.

In "Rapunzel," as in "Rumpelstiltskin" and "Beauty and the Beast," an adult barters a child to secure personal welfare or safety. This uneven exchange is presented in matter-of-fact terms, never interrogated or challenged in any way by the characters. It is, to be sure, a sign of desperation as well as a move that raises the stakes of the plot in a powerful way. Whereas the parents at the start of the story barter away the child in almost cavalier fashion, Mother Gothel figures as the consummate overprotective parent, isolating Rapunzel from human contact and keeping her prisoner in a tower that lacks both stairs and an exit. In the final tableau of the story, the power of love and compassion triumphs, and Rapunzel lives happily ever after with the prince and their twins. In some versions, as in the French "Godchild of the Fairy in the Tower," things end badly when the fairy turns the Rapunzel figure into a frog and curses the prince with a pig's snout. Much turns on the character of the maternal figure in the tale, who is presented as a wicked witch in some versions of the tale and as a benevolent guardian in other versions. Rapunzel's departure from the tower can be seen, depending on the character of the enchantress, as an act of clever resourcefulness or as an act of deep betrayal.

The first literary version of "The Maiden in the Tower" appeared in Giambattista Basile's Pentamerone (1636). The name of Basile's heroine, Petrosinella, is derived from the word for parsley. While the Grimms' "Rapunzel" moves in a dark register, with the heroine's exile and the blinding of the prince, Basile's version of the tale is sprightly, with humorous twists and bawdy turns. When the prince enters the tower, for example, he and Petrosinella at once become lovers: "Jumping in from the window into the room, he sated his desire, and ate of that sweet parsley sauce of love."

The Grimms based their "Rapunzel" on an eighteenth-century literary version by Friedrich Schulz, who in turn had borrowed from a French literary fairy tale published by Charlotte-Rose Caumont de La Force. Thus their "Rapunzel" is a hybrid form, drawing elements from different cultures and social milieus.

Like many fairy-tale characters, Rapunzel has given her name to a syndrome, which Margaret Atwood defines in her analysis of the tale's characters: "Rapunzel, the main character; the wicked witch who has imprisoned her, usually her mother . . . ; the tower she's imprisoned in—the attitudes of the society, symbolized usually by her house and children . . . ; and the Rescuer, a handsome prince of little substantiality. . . . [I]n the Rapunzel Syndrome the Rescuer is not much help." The best thing Rapunzel can do, according to Atwood, is to "learn how to cope." And cope she does, first in the wilderness with her twins and then when she encounters her beloved and restores his sight.

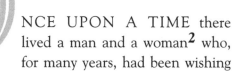

ONCE UPON A TIME there lived a man and a woman[2] who, for many years, had been wishing for a child, but with no success. One day the woman began to feel that God was going to grant their wish. In the back of the house in which they lived, there was a little window that looked out onto a splendid garden, full of beautiful flowers and vegetables. A high wall surrounded the garden,[3] and no one dared enter it, because it belonged to a powerful enchantress, who was feared by everyone around. One day the woman was looking out her window into the garden. Her eye lit on one patch in particular, which was planted with the finest rapunzel, a kind of lettuce. It looked so fresh and green that she was seized with a craving for it and just had to get some for her next meal. From day to day her appetite grew, and she began to waste away because she knew she would never get any of it. When her husband saw how pale and

2. *Once upon a time there lived a man and a woman.* That the story will center on procreation becomes evident from its opening line.

3. *A high wall surrounded the garden.* Note that the garden, like the tower, is a forbidden site and that both are enclosures for "rapunzel."

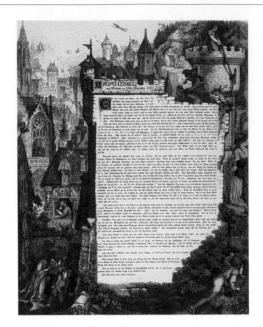

OTTO SPECKTER,
"Rapunzel," 1857

Illustrated pages offering both text and images were popular in nineteenth-century Germany. As the story is read, the reader can consult images showing the father caught by the enchantress in the garden, Rapunzel lowering her braid, the prince's punishment at the hands of the enchantress, and the reunion of Rapunzel and the prince.

wretched she had become, he asked: "What is the matter, dear wife?"

"If I don't get some of that rapunzel from the garden behind our house, I'm going to die," she replied.

Her husband loved her dearly and thought: "Rather than let your wife die, you will go get some of that rapunzel, no matter what the price."

As night was falling, he climbed over the wall into the garden of the enchantress, hastily pulled up a handful of rapunzel, and brought it back to his wife. She made a salad out of it right away and devoured it with a ravenous appetite. The rapunzel tasted so good, so very good, that the next day her craving for it increased threefold. The only way the man could settle his wife down was to go back to the garden for more.

ARTHUR RACKHAM,
"Rapunzel," 1916

The enchantress startles the man in search of rapunzel for his wife. A hideous hag with a scowl on her face, she reaches out a gnarled hand to stop the intruder. The propped-up trees in the garden suggest that the enchantress is a woman invested in proper growth for what lies under her supervision.

As night was falling, he returned, but after he climbed over the wall, he had an awful fright, for there was the enchantress,[4] standing right in front of him. "How dare you sneak into my garden and take my rapunzel like a common thief?" she said with an angry look. "This isn't going to turn out well for you."

"Oh, please," he replied, "show some mercy for my deed, for I did it only because I had to. My wife got a look at your rapunzel from our window. Her craving for it was so great that she said she would die if I couldn't get it for her."

The enchantress relented in her anger and said to the man: "If what you said is true, then I'm going to let you take as much rapunzel as you want back with you. But on one condition: You must hand over the child after your wife gives birth.[5] I will take care of it like a mother, and it will not want for anything."

In his fright the man agreed to everything. When it came time for the delivery, the enchantress appeared right away, gave the child the name Rapunzel, and whisked her away.

4. *enchantress.* The Grimms initially described the proprietor of the garden as a "fairy," then changed her to an "enchantress." Some translations of the story into English change the enchantress to a "witch."

5. *You must hand over the child after your wife gives birth.* Many cultures have legends about child-stealing witches or demons, who hover around pregnant women, waiting for the opportunity to snatch an infant.

WANDA GÁG,
"*Rapunzel,*" 1936

Bent over with age, the enchantress watches as Rapunzel releases her hair, which takes the form of a fish tail. How she will manage to climb up the braids is not entirely clear.

OTTO UBBELOHDE,
"*Rapunzel,*" 1907

The enchantress watches as Rapunzel lets down her hair from a tower that is somewhat less daunting in its appearance than those in other illustrations.

ARTHUR RACKHAM,
"*Rapunzel,*" 1917

Rapunzel dutifully lets down her golden hair for the enchantress, who nimbly climbs up the ladder with bare feet. The briars in the foreground suggest a connection with the story of Sleeping Beauty, also known as Briar Rose.

6. *a tiny little window.* This window resembles the window that looks down into the garden of the enchantress.

7. *as beautiful as spun gold.* Rapunzel's hair is a sign of her fairness, in the double sense of the term. In fairy tales golden hair is a marker of ethical goodness as well as aesthetic appeal.

Rapunzel was the most beautiful child on earth. When she was twelve years old, the enchantress took her into the forest and locked her up in a tower that had neither stairs nor a door. At the very top of the tower was a tiny little window.⁶ Whenever the enchantress wanted to get in, she stood at the foot of the tower and called out:

"Rapunzel, Rapunzel,
Let your hair down."

Rapunzel had long hair, as fine and as beautiful as spun gold.⁷ Whenever she heard the voice of the enchantress, she would undo her braids, fasten them to a window latch, and let them fall twenty ells down, right to the ground. The enchantress would then climb up on them to get inside.

A few years later it so happened that the son of a king was riding through the forest. He passed right by the tower and heard a voice so lovely that he stopped to listen. It was Rapunzel, who, all alone in the tower, was passing the time of day by singing sweet melodies to herself. The prince was hoping to go up to see her, and he searched around for a door to the tower, yet there was none. He rode home, but Rapunzel's voice had stirred his heart so powerfully that he went out into the forest every day to hear her. Once when he was hiding behind a tree, he saw the enchantress come to the tower and heard her call up:

> "Rapunzel, Rapunzel,
> Let your hair down."

HEINRICH LEFLER,
"Rapunzel," 1905

Yarn-like golden tresses are the center of attention in this portrait of Rapunzel as she lets down her hair. The trees, with their light-brown foliage, repeat in muted form the colors of the tower and the girl's hair. A gargoyle is positioned to ward off intruders. The elaborate border, with its stern owls gazing straight out at the viewer, underscore the theme of supervision in the story.

8. *Mother Gothel.* The term is a generic one in Germany, designating a woman who serves as godmother.

Rapunzel let down her braids, and the enchantress climbed up to her.

"If that is the ladder by which you climb up to the top of the tower, then I'd like to try my luck at it too," the prince thought. The next day, when it was just starting to get dark, the prince went up to the tower and called out:

"Rapunzel, Rapunzel,
Let your hair down."

The braids fell right down, and the prince climbed up on them.

ERNST LIEBERMANN,
"Rapunzel," 1922

Rapunzel is frightened by the appearance of a young man in place of the enchantress. Her comfortable bed, rich draperies, graceful clothing, and ornate mirror create a sensual atmosphere in her wooded retreat.

At first Rapunzel was terrified when she saw a man coming in through the window, especially since she had never seen one before. But the prince started talking with her in a kind way and told her that he had been so moved by her voice that he could not rest easy until he had set eyes on her. Soon Rapunzel was no longer afraid, and when the prince, who was young and handsome, asked her if she wanted to marry him, she thought to herself: "He will like me better than old Mother Gothel."**8** And so she accepted, put her hand in his, and said: "I want to go away from here with you, but I can't figure out how to get out of this tower. Every time you come to visit, bring a skein of silk with you, and I will braid a ladder from the silk. When it's finished, I'll climb down and you can take me with you on horseback."

The two agreed that he would come visit her every evening, for the old woman was there in the daytime. The enchantress didn't notice a thing until one day Rapunzel said to her: "Tell me, Mother Gothel, why are you so much harder to pull up than the young prince?[9] He gets up here in a twinkling."

"Wicked child!" shouted the enchantress. "What have you done? I thought I had shut you off from the rest of the world, but you betrayed me."

Flying into a rage, she seized Rapunzel's beautiful hair, wound the braids around her left hand and grabbed a pair of scissors with her right. Snip, snap went the scissors and the beautiful tresses fell to the floor. The enchantress was so hard-hearted that she took poor Rapunzel to a wilderness, where she had to live in a miserable, wretched state.

On the very day she had sent Rapunzel away, the enchantress fastened the severed braids to the window latch, and when the prince came and called out:

"Rapunzel, Rapunzel,
Let your hair down,"

she let down the hair.

The prince climbed up, but instead of his precious Rapunzel, the enchantress was waiting for him with an angry, poisonous look in her eye. "Ha!" she shouted triumphantly. "You want to come get your darling little wife,[10] but the beautiful bird is no longer sitting in the nest, singing her songs. The cat caught her, and before she's done, she's going to scratch out your eyes too. Rapunzel is lost to you forever. You will never see her again."

The prince was beside himself with grief, and in his despair he jumped from the top of the tower. He was still

9. *"Tell me, Mother Gothel, why are you so much harder to pull up than the young prince."* In the first version of the Grimms' *Nursery and Household Tales*, Rapunzel asks the enchantress why her clothes are getting so tight and don't fit any longer. The allusion to the fact that the daily meetings with the prince in the tower have led to pregnancy was considered inappropriate for children.

10. *wife.* Rapunzel becomes a "wife" because the Grimms did not want to suggest that Rapunzel's twins were born out of wedlock.

KAY NIELSEN,
"Rapunzel," 1922

A monstrous enchantress with wild locks and a misshapen nose wields the scissors she will use to cut off Rapunzel's long braid. The coil of braided hair resembles a snake as it winds itself around the feet of the enchantress. The power of this illustration derives in part from the stunning contrast between the simple, flowing lines of the girl's dress and the angular grotesqueries of the enchantress's body.

alive, but his eyes were scratched out by the bramble patch into which he had fallen. He wandered around in the forest, unable to see anything. Roots and berries were the only thing he could find to eat, and he spent his time weeping and wailing over the loss of his dear wife.

The prince wandered around in misery for many years and finally reached the wilderness where Rapunzel was just barely managing to survive with the twins—a boy and a girl—to whom she had given birth. The prince heard a voice that sounded familiar to him, and so he followed it. When he came within sight of the person singing, Rapunzel recognized him. She threw her arms around him and wept. Two of those tears dropped into the prince's eyes, and suddenly he could see as before, with clear eyes.

The prince went back to his kingdom with Rapunzel, and there was great rejoicing. They lived in happiness and good cheer for many, many years.

8

THE FROG KING, OR IRON HEINRICH[1]

Jacob and Wilhelm Grimm

This story, the first in the Grimms' Nursery and Household Tales, bears a distinct family resemblance to "Beauty and the Beast." Like Beauty, the princess is obliged to accept an animal suitor, but she finds herself relentlessly repulsed by the beast who helped her out when she needed a favor. Despite her father's double admonition to accept the frog as her "companion" ("If you make a promise, you have to keep it," and "You shouldn't scorn someone who helped you when you were in trouble."), the princess balks at the idea of allowing a frog into her bed. She flies into a rage and hurls the erotically ambitious frog against the wall: "Now you'll get your rest, you disgusting frog."

Bruno Bettelheim has read "The Frog King" as a compressed version of the maturation process, with the princess navigating a path between the pleasure principle (represented by her play) and the dictates of the superego (represented by the father's commands). His reading helps to understand why

1. *Iron Heinrich.* The tale seems to be a hybrid form, combining a story about an animal groom with a tale about a loyal servant. Iron Heinrich gets his name from the hoops of steel that keep his heart from bursting while his master remains under a spell.

From Jacob and Wilhelm Grimm, "Der Froschkönig, oder der eiserne Heinrich," in *Kinder- und Hausmärchen*, 7th ed. (Berlin: Dieterich, 1857; first published, Berlin: Realschulbuchhandlung, 1812).

the tale has such a powerful combination of erotic and didactic elements. In the end the princess does not overcome her disgust and kiss the frog (as in some versions disseminated in the United States) but asserts herself and expresses her true feelings: "To be able to love, a person first has to become able to feel; even if the feelings are negative, that is better than not feeling." Rather than showing how compassion and subordination lead to true love, as in "Beauty and the Beast," "The Frog King" endorses an act of defiance and an expression of genuine feeling. The princess may have failed to keep a promise, but she has been able to set limits for her importunate suitor, and this, above all, redeems him.

I**N THE OLDEN DAYS,** when you could still wish for things, there lived a king whose daughters were all beautiful. The youngest was so beautiful that even the sun, which had seen so much, was filled with wonder when it shone upon her face.

There was a deep, dark forest near the king's castle, and in that forest, beneath an old linden tree, was a spring. When the weather turned really hot, the king's daughter would go out into the woods and sit down at the edge of the cool spring. And if she got bored, she would take out her golden ball, throw it up in the air, and catch it. That was her favorite activity.

One day it so happened that the golden ball didn't land in the princess's hands when she reached up to catch it, but fell down on the ground and rolled right into the water. The princess followed the ball with her eyes, but it disappeared, and the spring was so deep that you couldn't even see the bottom. The princess began to shed tears, and she wept louder and louder, unable to stop herself. A voice interrupted her crying and called out: "What's

ARTHUR RACKHAM,
"The Frog King, or Iron Heinrich,"
1913

The princess can barely contain her disgust as she extends her arm to recover the golden ball retrieved by the frog. The large tree trunks looming in the background suggest a sense of isolation, far from the security of the palace and court, in this wooded setting.

OTTO UBBELOHDE,
"The Frog King, or Iron Heinrich,"
1907

The princess seems intrigued by the amphibian that promises to help her by retrieving her golden ball. The frog, emerging from a spring with a headstone bearing a patriarchal visage, seems to show some empathy for the princess's loss.

MAXFIELD PARRISH,
"The Enchanted Prince," 1934

The princess and the frog prince face one another, each gazing directly into the eyes of the other. The forest behind the two, with its unusual lighting and majestic intricacies, gives us a classic Parrish landscape.

going on, Princess? Stones would be moved to tears if they could hear you."

She turned around to figure out where the voice was coming from[2] and saw a frog, which had stuck its big old ugly head out of the water.

"Oh, it's you, you old splasher," she said. "I'm in tears because my golden ball has fallen into the spring."

"Be quiet and stop crying," said the frog. "I can probably help you, but what will you give me if I fetch your little toy?"

"Anything you want, dear frog," she said. "My dresses,

2. *She turned around to figure out where the voice was coming from.* Critics frequently underscore the phallic nature of the frog. Julius Heuscher notes, "The innocent young girl's fear of and repugnance toward the male genitals and the transformation of this disgust into happiness and sanctioned matrimony can hardly be symbolized better than by this transformation of the frog into a prince." Frogs are also animals that undergo transformations, existing in one form when young, in another when mature.

3. *"My dresses, my pearls and my jewels, even the golden crown I'm wearing."* In "Rumpelstiltskin," the miller's daughter similarly tries to satisfy the demands of the helper with material possessions.

my pearls and my jewels, even the golden crown I'm wearing."**3**

The frog said: "I don't want your dresses, your pearls and jewels, or your golden crown. But if you promise to cherish me and let me be your companion and playmate, and let me sit beside you at the table and eat from your little golden plate, drink from your little cup, and sleep in your little bed, if you promise me all that, I will dive down into the spring and bring back your golden ball."

"Oh, yes," she said. "I'll give you anything you want as long as you get that ball back for me." But all the while she was thinking: "What nonsense that stupid frog is talking! He's down there in the water croaking away with all the other frogs. How could anyone want him as a companion?"

Once the frog had gotten her word, he put his head in the water and dove down into the spring. After a while he came paddling back with the ball in his mouth, and he tossed it on the grass. When the princess saw her beautiful toy in front of her, she was overjoyed. She picked it up and ran off with it.

"Wait for me," the frog cried out. "Take me with you. I can't run the way you do."

He croaked as loudly as he could, but it did him no good at all. The princess paid no attention, hurried home as fast as her legs would carry her, and quickly forgot about the poor frog, who had to crawl back down into the spring.

The next day, the princess sat down to dinner with the king and some courtiers and was eating dinner on her little golden plate when something came crawling up the marble staircase, splish, splash, splish, splash. When it reached the top of the stairs, it knocked at the door and called out: "Princess, youngest princess, let me in!"

The princess ran to the door to see who was there. When she opened it, she saw the frog standing right before her. Terrified, she slammed the door as hard as she could and went back to the table. The king could see that her heart was pounding and said: "My child, what are you afraid of? Is there some kind of giant at the door coming to get you?"

"Oh, no," she replied. "It wasn't a giant, but it was a disgusting frog."

"What does a frog want with you?"

"Oh, Father dear, yesterday when I was playing by the spring, my little golden ball fell into the water. And because I was crying so hard, the frog got it for me, and because he insisted, I promised that he could become my companion. I never thought that he would be able to leave the water. Now he's outside and wants to come in and see me."

Just then there was a second knock at the door, and a voice cried out:

> Princess, Youngest Princess,[4]
> Let me in.
> Did you forget
> Yesterday's promise
> Down by the chilly waters?
> Princess, Youngest Princess,
> Let me in.

The king declared: "If you make a promise, you have to keep it.[5] Just go and let him in."

The princess went and opened the door. The frog hopped into the room and followed close on her heels until she reached her chair. Then he sat down and cried out: "Lift me up and put me next to you."

The princess hesitated, but the king ordered her to obey. Once the frog was up on the chair, he wanted to get on the table, and once he was there, he said: "Push your little golden plate closer to me so that we can eat together."

The princess did as he told her, but it was obvious that she was not happy about it. The frog had enjoyed his meal, but for her almost every bite stuck in her throat. Finally he said: "I've had enough to eat, and I'm tired.

4. *Princess, Youngest Princess.* In this version of the story, as in others, the frog speaks in verse. Compare the Scottish "Well at the World's End":

> *"Open the door, my hinny, my hart,*
> *Open the door, my ain wee thing.*
> *And mind the words that you and I spak*
> *Down in the meadow, at the well-spring."*

5. *"If you make a promise, you have to keep it."* The Grimms added maxims like this one to strengthen the moral backbone of the tale.

ANNE ANDERSON,
"The Frog King, or Iron Heinrich," 1930

An unwelcome guest, the frog helps himself to the food on the princess's plate, while the king and servants ponder the unusual situation.

6. *threw him with all her might against the wall.* Some variants of the Grimms' tale feature a princess who admits the frog to her chamber despite his revolting appearance, but most give us a princess who is perfectly capable of committing acts rivaling the cold-blooded violence of dashing a creature against a wall. In Scottish and Gaelic versions of "The Frog King," the princess beheads her suitor, and a Polish variant replaces the frog with a snake and recounts in lavish detail how the princess tears it in two. A more tame Lithuanian text requires the burning of the snake's skin before the prince is freed from his reptilian state. Deeds of passion as much as acts of compassion have the power to disenchant. Although the princess of "The Frog King" is self-absorbed, ungrateful, and cruel, in the end she does as well for herself as modest, obedient, and charitable Beauty.

Carry me up to your room and turn down the silken covers on your little bed."

The princess began to weep, and she was afraid of the clammy frog. She didn't dare touch him, and now he was going to sleep in her beautiful, clean bed. The king grew angry and said: "You shouldn't scorn someone who helped you when you were in trouble."

The princess picked up the frog with two fingers, carried him up to her room, and put him in a corner. While she was lying in bed, he came crawling over and said: "I'm tired and want to sleep as much as you do. Lift me up into your bed, or I'll tell your father."

The princess became really annoyed, picked up the frog, and threw him with all her might against the wall.**6** "Now you'll get your rest, you disgusting frog!"

When the frog fell to the ground, he was no longer a

ARTHUR RACKHAM,
"The Frog King, or Iron Heinrich,"
1909

A horrified princess carries the frog
upstairs to her bedroom.

FERNANDE BIEGLER,
"The Frog King, or Iron Heinrich,"
1921

On tiptoes, with a coverlet pulled
over her body to hide her naked-
ness, the redheaded princess is horrified to discover a frog at the foot of
her bed. The crown on the frog's
head, suggesting that he might be
more than he seems, does not seem
to reassure her.

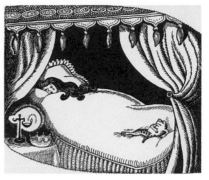

WANDA GÁG,
"The Frog King, or Iron Heinrich,"
1936

A tearful princess considers her
next move, as the frog reclines comfortably at the end of her coverlet.
The crown resting on the night-
stand is the only sign that this little
girl is anything more than an ordinary child.

frog but a prince with beautiful, bright eyes. At her
father's bidding, he became her dear companion and husband. He told her that a wicked witch had cast a spell on
him[7] and that the princess alone could release him from
the spring. The next day they planned to set out together
for his kingdom.

The two fell asleep and, in the morning, after the sun
had woken them, a coach drove up. It was drawn by eight
white horses in golden harnesses, with white ostrich
feathers on their heads. At the back of the coach stood
Faithful Heinrich,[8] the servant of the young prince. Faithful Heinrich had been so saddened by the transformation
of his master into a frog that three hoops had been placed
around his chest to keep his heart from bursting with pain
and sorrow. Now the coach had arrived to take the young
prince back to his kingdom, and Faithful Heinrich lifted
the two of them into the carriage and took his place in the
rear. He was elated by the transformation. When they had
covered a good distance, the prince heard a cracking

7. *a wicked witch had cast a spell on him.* The
cause of the transformation is not elaborated
in any variants of the tale.

8. *At the back of the coach stood Faithful Heinrich.* The cracking of the three iron bands
around Heinrich's chest externalizes the
sense of liberation felt by all the characters.
The name Heinrich, as the Grimms point
out, has a representative quality, suggesting
solidity and decency.

noise behind him, as if something had broken. He turned around and cried out:

> "Heinrich, the coach is falling apart!"
> "No, My Lord, it's not the coach,
> But a hoop from round my heart,
> Which was in sheer pain,
> When you were down in the spring,
> Living there as a frog."

Two more times the prince heard the cracking noise, and he was sure that the coach was falling apart. But it was only the sound of the hoops breaking from around Faithful Heinrich's chest, for his master had been set free and was happy.

9

RUMPELSTILTSKIN

Jacob and Wilhelm Grimm

Rumpelstiltskin goes by many names. Titeliture, Purzinigele, Batzibitzili, Panzimanzi, and Whuppity Stoorie are just a few of his sobriquets. Whether he makes an appearance as Ricdin-Ricdon in a French tale or as Tom Tit Tot in a British tale, his essence and function remain much the same. Not so with the tale's heroine. Although she is almost always a young girl of humble origins, her other attributes and abilities change dramatically from one tale to the next. In some versions of the story, she is hopelessly lazy and often gluttonous to boot; in others she is a hard worker, a diligent daughter who can spin heaps upon heaps of straw or who can spin straw into gold, even without the assistance of a helper. In one of the versions of "Rumpelstiltskin" recorded by the Grimms, for example, the heroine needs help because she is "cursed" with the gift of spinning flax to gold, unable to produce "a single flaxen thread."

What makes "Rumpelstiltskin" particularly troubling for those who seek moral guidance for children in fairy tales is the

From Jacob and Wilhelm Grimm, "Rumpelstilzchen," in *Kinder- und Hausmärchen*, 7th ed. (Berlin: Dieterich, 1857; first published, Berlin: Realschulbuchhandlung, 1812).

way in which its plot turns on deception and greed. The miller tricks the king into thinking that his daughter can spin straw into gold; the miller's daughter misleads the king; the king marries because he lusts after gold. Finally, the queen not only dodges the terms of the contract drawn up with Rumpelstiltskin but also engages in a cruel game of playing dumb as she rehearses various names before pronouncing the one that will release her from a dreadful pact made in a moment of desperation. The cast of characters is neither clever, resourceful, nor quick-witted. To the contrary, all seem rash, irresponsible, and recklessly opportunistic. And the queen's only real triumph seems to be the identification of "The Name of the Helper," as the story is known to folklorists.

"Rumpelstiltskin" is almost universally known in cultures that depended on spinning for the garments the people wore. Spinning, according to the German philosopher Walter Benjamin, who wrote an essay about old-fashioned storytelling, produces more than textiles—it is also the breeding ground for texts, creating the endless stretch of time that demands relief through storytelling. "Rumpelstiltskin" shows us how the straw of domestic labor can be transformed into the gold that captures the heart of a king. It is a tale that thematizes the labor that gives birth to storytelling, suggesting in turn that there is an even exchange between the life-giving labors of the queen and the life-saving labors of the diminutive gnome. Spinning straw to gold, Rumpelstiltskin is less demonic helper than agent of transformation, a figure who becomes heroic in his power to save life and to demonstrate compassion. Is it any wonder that many versions of his story show him as a sprightly figure who hightails it out of the palace on a spoon rather than as a vicious gnome who tears himself in two when his name is discovered?

NCE UPON A TIME there lived a miller. He was very poor, but he had a beautiful daughter. One day it happened that the miller was given an audience with the king, and, in order to appear as a person of some importance,[1] he said to him: "I have a daughter who can spin straw into gold."

"Now there's a talent worth having," the king said to the miller. "If your daughter is as clever as you say she is, bring her to my palace tomorrow. I will put her to the test."

1. *in order to appear as a person of some importance.* Boasting about a child is what generally sets the plot of Rumpelstiltskin stories in motion. The exaggerated claims of an ambitious parent lead to a crisis for the child.

EUGEN NEUREUTHER,
"Rumpelstiltskin," 1878

Many nineteenth-century illustrators produced multiple scenes from a fairy tale on a single page. These composite illustrations, by providing visual cues for the plot, create the opportunity for reviving oral storytelling, even when the text was included next to the images.

ARTHUR RACKHAM,
"Rumpelstiltskin," 1918

Bent over with age and with a tail
that hints at diabolical origins,
Rumpelstiltskin appears both wiz-
ened and wizard-like.

ARTHUR RACKHAM,
"Rumpelstiltskin," 1909

Sword in hand, this Rumpelstiltskin
seems less diabolical than sullen.

When the girl arrived at the palace, he put her into a
room full of straw, gave her a spinning wheel and a spindle, and said: "Get to work right away. If you don't manage to spin this straw into gold by tomorrow morning,
then you shall die." And the king locked the door after he
went out and left her all alone inside.

The poor miller's daughter sat there in the room and
had no idea what to do. She didn't have a clue about how
to spin straw into gold. She felt so miserable that she
started crying. Suddenly the door opened, and a tiny little
man walked right in and said: "Good evening, Little Miss
Miller Girl. Why are you sobbing so hard?"

"Oh, dear," the girl answered. "I'm supposed to spin that straw into gold, and I have no idea how it's done."

The little man asked: "What will you give me if I do it for you?"

"My necklace," the girl replied.

The little man took the necklace, sat down at the spinning wheel, and whirr, whirr, whirr, the wheel spun three times, and the bobbin was full. Then he put another bundle of straw up and whirr, whirr, whirr, the wheel spun three times, and the second bobbin was full. He worked on until dawn, and by that time the straw had been spun and all the bobbins were full of gold.

At the crack of dawn, the king made his way to the room. When he saw all that gold, he was astonished and filled with joy, but now he lusted more than ever for that precious metal. He ordered the miller's daughter to go to a much larger room, one that was also filled with straw, and he told her that if she valued her life she would spin it all into gold by dawn. The girl had no idea what to do, and she began to cry. The door opened, as before, and the tiny little man reappeared and asked: "What will you give me if I spin the straw into gold for you?"

"I'll give you the ring on my finger," the girl replied. The little man took the ring, began to whirl the wheel around, and, by dawn, had spun all of the straw into glittering gold. The king was pleased beyond measure at the sight of the gold, but his greed was still not satisfied. This time he ordered the miller's daughter to go into an even larger room filled with straw and said: "You have to spin this into gold in one night. If you succeed, you will become my wife."

"She may just be a miller's daughter," he thought, "but I could never find a richer wife if I were to search for one the world over."

When the girl was all by herself, the tiny little man appeared for the third time and asked: "What will you give me if I spin the straw for you again?"

"I have nothing left to give you," the girl replied.

"Then promise to give me your first child, after you become queen."[2]

2. *"Then promise to give me your first child, after you become queen."* Escalating demands are typical of fairy-tale helpers. They ask for something trivial to start with, then move to something that is beyond the norm of an economy of bartering. The helper or donor quickly moves into the role of villain.

3. *"I prefer a living creature to all the treasures in the world."* Rumpelstiltskin's desire for something "living" links him with demonic creatures who make pacts with mortals in order to secure living creatures. At the heart of all versions of "Rumpelstiltskin" is the contract made between an innocent young girl and a devilish creature, a misshapen gnome of questionable origins who is probably one of the least attractive of fairy-tale figures. Yet Rumpelstiltskin comes off rather well in a world where fathers tell brazen lies about their daughters, marriages are based on greed, and young women agree to give up a firstborn child. He works hard to hold up his end of the bargain made with the miller's daughter, shows genuine compassion when the queen regrets the agreement into which she has entered, and is prepared to add an escape clause to their contract even though he stands to gain nothing from it.

4. *"If by then you can guess my name, you can keep your child."* Rumpelstiltskin's challenge to the queen reminds us of the power of names and how the name taboo came about. In ancient religions, naming the gods compelled them to respond to worshipers, hence the taboo against invoking their names. Knowing the name of your antagonist represents a form of control, a way of containing the power of the adversary. Since names are a vital part of personal identity, revealing your name can be dangerous. In numerous myths and folktales, there is a prohibition against asking the name of the beloved, and violation of the taboo often leads to flight or transformation into an animal. In Puccini's opera *Turandot* (1926) the Chinese princess named in the title is challenged to identify the name of the man who has solved her riddles.

"Who knows what may happen before that?" thought the miller's daughter. Since she was desperate to find a way out, she promised the little man what he had demanded, and, once again, he set to work and spun the straw into gold.

When the king returned in the morning and found everything as he wished it to be, he made the wedding arrangements, and the beautiful miller's daughter became a queen.

A year later the miller's daughter gave birth to a beautiful child. She had forgotten all about the little man, but one day he suddenly appeared in her room and said: "Give me what you promised."

The queen was horrified, and she offered the little man the entire wealth of the kingdom if only he would let her keep the child. But the little man replied: "I prefer a living creature to all the treasures in the world."[3] The queen's tears and sobs were so heartrending that the little man took pity on her. "I will give you three days," he declared. "If by then you can guess my name, you can keep your child."[4]

All night long the queen racked her brains, thinking of all the names she had ever heard. She dispatched a messenger to inquire throughout the land if there were any names she had forgotten. When the little man returned the next day, she began with Casper, Melchior, and Balthasar and recited every single name she had ever heard. But at each one the little man said: "That's not my name."

The next day she sent the messenger out to inquire about the names of all the people in the neighborhood, and she tried out the most unusual and bizarre names on the little man: "Do you happen to be called Ribfiend or Muttonchops or Spindleshanks?" But each time he replied: "That's not my name."

On the third day the messenger returned and said: "I couldn't find a single new name, but when I rounded a bend in the forest at the foot of a huge mountain, a place so remote that the foxes and hares bid each other goodnight,

ARTHUR RACKHAM,
"Rumpelstiltskin," 1909

Rumpelstiltskin parades triumphantly around a fire, confident that the queen will not divine his name.

I came across a little hut. A fire was burning right in front of the hut, and a really strange little man was dancing around the fire, hopping on one foot and chanting:

> 'Tomorrow I brew, today I bake,
> Soon the child is mine to take.
> Oh what luck to win this game,
> Rumpelstiltskin is my name.'"

You can imagine how happy the queen was to hear that name. The little man returned and asked: "Well, Your Majesty, who am I?"

The Queen replied: "Is your name Conrad?"

"No, it's not."

"Is your name Harry?"

"No, it's not."

George Cruikshank,
"Rumpelstiltskin," 1823

Rumpelstiltskin is about to tear himself in two, while courtiers look on in amusement. Note how the gnome appears diabolical through his dress, hat, cane, and scowl.

Kay Nielsen,
"Rumpelstiltskin," 1925

An enraged Rumpelstiltskin, dressed in vibrant red, begins to tear himself in two. The serenity of the courtiers, expressed in the perfect symmetries of the composition, is disrupted by the mad gnome.

"Could your name possibly be Rumpelstiltskin?"

"The Devil told you that, the Devil told you!" the little man screamed, and in his rage he stamped his right foot so hard that it went into the ground right up to his waist. Then in his fury he seized his left foot with both hands and tore himself in two.

10

JACK AND THE BEANSTALK[1]

Joseph Jacobs

*The quintessential British folktale, "Jack and the Beanstalk"
replays a conflict familiar from the stories of Odysseus and the
Cyclops, David and Goliath, Tom Thumb and the ogre. The
weak, but shrewd, Jack manages to defeat a dim-witted giant,
acquire his wealth, and return home triumphant. While this
story is widely disseminated in England and its former
colonies, it had few analogues in other lands, though it has now
taken root in many cultures. No single authoritative text for
"Jack and the Beanstalk" has evolved to establish itself as the
master narrative from which all other variants derive. Instead,
there are a number of competing literary versions that draw, in
varying degrees, from oral sources.*

*The adventures of Jack were first recorded by Benjamin
Tabart in 1807 as* The History of Jack and the Bean-Stalk.
*Tabart no doubt relied on oral versions in circulation at the
time, though he claimed to base his tale on an "original manuscript." What is particularly striking about Tabart's Jack is his*

1. *beanstalk.* There are many myths and legends of a giant plant rooted on earth that
leads to an upper realm. In South America
the world-tree serves as a bridge between the
two worlds; in Norse mythology there is
Yggdrasil, the world-tree that stretches up
into heaven and sends its roots down to hell;
and Buddha relies on the Bodhi tree. The
beanstalk has a certain whimsical inventive-
ness, for beanstalks are notoriously unstable
and usually require staking to remain
propped up.

From Joseph Jacobs, "Jack and the Beanstalk," *English Fairy Tales*
(London: David Nutt, 1890).

evolution from an "indolent, careless, and extravagant" boy into a son who is both "dutiful and obedient." Instead of marrying a princess and ascending to a throne, Jack lives with his mother "a great many years, and continued to be always happy."

Tabart's Jack becomes an exemplary character, a role model for children listening to his story. He is not at all a master thief who makes off with the giant's possessions but a dispossessed boy who is recovering what by rights belonged to him. From a fairy, Jack learns that his father was swindled and murdered by the giant up in the beanstalk and that he was destined to avenge his father's death. A powerful moral overlay turns what was once probably a tale of high adventure and shrewd maneuvering into a morally edifying story.

When Joseph Jacobs began compiling stories for his anthology English Fairy Tales, he dismissed Tabart's "History of Jack and the Bean-Stalk" as "very poor" and reconstructed the version he recalled from childhood. Drawing on the memory of a tale told by his childhood nursemaid in Australia around 1860, Jacobs produced a story that is relatively free of the moralizing impulse that permeates Tabart's story. The British folklorist Katherine Briggs has referred to Jacobs's version as the "original," but it is in fact simply one of many efforts to recapture the spirit of the oral versions in widespread circulation during the nineteenth century.

In the southern Appalachian mountains, Jack has become a popular hero, a trickster figure who lives by his wits, with the difference that the American Jack steals guns, knives, and coverlets rather than gold, hens that lay golden eggs, and self-playing harps. A 1952 film adaptation of "Jack and the Beanstalk" stars Bud Abbott and Lou Costello, with Costello playing Jack, an adult "problem child."

THERE WAS ONCE upon a time a poor widow who had an only son named Jack, and a cow named Milky-white.[2] And all they had to live on was the milk the cow gave every morning, which they carried to the market and sold. But one morning Milky-white gave no milk, and they didn't know what to do.

MAXFIELD PARRISH,
"Ferry's Seeds," 1923

A fey Jack is about to plant the magic beans in this advertisement for Ferry's seeds.

"What shall we do, what shall we do?" said the widow, wringing her hands.

"Cheer up, mother, I'll go and get work somewhere," said Jack.

"We've tried that before, and nobody would take you,"[3] said his mother. "We must sell Milky-white and with the money start shop, or something."

"All right, mother," says Jack. "It's market day today,

2. *Milky-white.* That Milky-white ceases to give milk has been seen by psychologists as a marker for the end of infancy, a time when the child must begin to separate from the mother. It is perhaps no coincidence that Jack leaves home just when the cow goes dry.

3. *"We've tried that before, and nobody would take you."* Jack, like Aladdin before him, is the prototype of the undeserving hero who succeeds in living happily ever after. Aladdin is described as an "incorrigible good-for-nothing" who refuses to learn a trade and drives his father to an early death. In Tabart's version of the tale, Jack is "indolent, careless, and extravagant" and brings his mother to "beggary and ruin."

ARTHUR RACKHAM,
"Jack and the Beanstalk," 1933

A quaint fellow offers the naïve Jack a handful of beans for the cow tethered at the end of the rope he is holding.

ARTHUR RACKHAM,
"Jack and the Beanstalk," 1918

Jack inspects the beans that he has been offered in exchange for his cow. He and the bargain hunter are seen in profile, while Milky-white, the cow, looks straight ahead at the observer.

4. *sharp as a needle.* Folktales are usually devoid of irony, but this judgment is clearly intended to emphasize Jack's gullibility and to set the stage for the foolish bargain he makes. Contrary to conventional wisdom, which identifies fairy-tale heroes as active, handsome, and cunning, Jack and his folkloric cousins are decidedly unworldly figures, innocent, silly, and guileless. Yet Jack (like most simpletons, numbskulls, and noodles) slips into the role of a cunning trickster. In fairy tales, character traits shift almost imperceptibly into their opposites as the plot unfolds.

and I'll soon sell Milky-white, and then we'll see what we can do."

So he took the cow's halter in his hand, and off he started. He hadn't gone far when he met a funny-looking old man, who said to him: "Good morning, Jack."

"Good morning to you," said Jack, and wondered how he knew his name.

"Well, Jack, and where are you off to?" said the man.

"I'm going to market to sell our cow here."

"Oh, you look the proper sort of chap to sell cows," said the man. "I wonder if you know how many beans make five."

"Two in each hand and one in your mouth," says Jack, as sharp as a needle.[4]

"Right you are," says the man, "and here they are, the very beans themselves," he went on, pulling out of his pocket a number of strange looking beans. "As you are so sharp," says he, "I don't mind doing a swap with you— your cow for these beans."

"Go along," says Jack, "wouldn't you like it?"

"Ah! You don't know what these beans are," said the man. "If you plant them overnight, by morning they grow right up to the sky."

"Really," said Jack. "You don't say so."

"Yes, that is so, and if it doesn't turn out to be true you can have your cow back."

"Right," says Jack and hands him over Milky-white's halter and pockets the beans.

Back goes Jack home, and as he hadn't gone very far it wasn't dusk by the time he got to his door.

"Back already, Jack?" said his mother. "I see you haven't got Milky-white, so you've sold her. How much did you get for her?"

"You'll never guess, mother," says Jack.

"No, you don't say so. Good boy! Five pounds, ten, fifteen, no, it can't be twenty."

"I told you you couldn't guess. What do you say to these beans? They're magical, plant them overnight and—."

"What!" says Jack's mother. "Have you been such a fool, such a dolt, such an idiot, as to give away my Milky-white, the best milker in the parish, and prime beef to boot, for a set of paltry beans? Take that! Take that! Take that! And as for your precious beans here, they go out of the window. And now off with you to bed. Not a sup shall you drink, and not a bit shall you swallow this very night."

So Jack went upstairs to his little room in the attic, and sad and sorry he was, to be sure, as much for mother's sake, as for the loss of his supper.

At last he dropped off to sleep.

When he woke up, the room looked so funny. The sun was shining into part of it, and yet all the rest was quite dark and shady. So Jack jumped up and dressed himself and went to the window. And what do you think he saw? Why, the beans his mother had thrown out of the window into the garden had sprung up into a big beanstalk, which went up and up and up till it reached the sky. So the man spoke truth after all.

The beanstalk grew up quite close past Jack's window, so all he had to do was to open it and give a jump on to the beanstalk, which ran up just like a big ladder.[5] So Jack climbed and he climbed and he climbed and he climbed and he climbed and he climbed and he climbed till at last

5. *like a big ladder.* Like Jacob's ladder in the Old Testament, the beanstalk connects earth with an upper realm, though the ogre's domain is pagan and perilous.

6. *great big tall woman.* Jacobs objected to the fairy that Jack first meets on his way to the giant's castle: "The object [of the fairy's account] was to prevent the tale from becoming an encouragement to theft! I have had greater confidence in my young friends, and have deleted the fairy who did not exist in the tale as told to me." Some oral tales suggest that the giant stole his wealth from Jack's father, but most, like Jacobs's version, eliminate the fairy and show Jack's first encounter as a meeting with the ogre's wife.

7. *My man is an ogre.* Jack's biological father does not appear in the tale. Like fairy tales that split the mother into a good, dead biological mother and a vigorous, evil stepmother, "Jack and the Beanstalk" can be seen as dividing the father into a benevolent, dead father and a powerful, cannibalistic father.

8. *the ogre's wife was not half so bad after all.* A metrical rendering of the story published in 1807 under the title *The History of Mother Twaddle, and the Marvelous Atchievments* [sic] *of Her Son Jack* turns the giant's servant into Jack's ally, whom he marries after decapitating the giant. Most versions of the tale show the ogre's wife as a protective figure who tries to shield Jack from the cannibalistic assaults of her husband.

9. *Fee-fi-fo-fum.* The rhyme appears in variant forms, most notably when it is recited in *King Lear* as "Fie, foh, and fume, I smell the blood of a Brittish man." The verse was first uttered by the two-headed Welsh giant Thunderdel: "Fee, fau, fum, / I smell the blood of an *English* man, / Be he alive, or be he dead, I'll grind his bones to make my bread."

he reached the sky. And when he got there he found a long broad road going as straight as a dart. So he walked along and he walked along and he walked along till he came to a great big tall house, and on the doorstep there was a great big tall woman.

"Good morning, mum," says Jack, quite polite-like. "Could you be so kind as to give me some breakfast?" For he hadn't had anything to eat, you know, the night before and was as hungry as a hunter.

"It's breakfast you want, is it?" says the great big tall woman.[6] "It's breakfast you'll be if you don't move off from here. My man is an ogre[7] and there's nothing he likes better than boys broiled on toast. You'd better be moving on or he'll soon be coming."

"Oh! Please, mum, do give me something to eat, mum. I've had nothing to eat since yesterday morning, really and truly, mum," says Jack. "I may as well be broiled as die of hunger."

Well, the ogre's wife was not half so bad after all.[8] So she took Jack into the kitchen, and gave him a hunk of bread and cheese and a jug of milk. But Jack hadn't half finished these when thump! thump! thump! the whole house began to tremble with the noise of someone coming.

"Goodness gracious me! It's my old man," said the ogre's wife. "What on earth shall I do? Come along quick and jump in here." And she bundled Jack into the oven just as the ogre came in.

He was a big one, to be sure. At his belt he had three calves strung up by the heels, and he unhooked them and threw them down on the table and said: "Here, wife, broil me a couple of these for breakfast. Ah! What's this I smell?

Fee-fi-fo-fum,[9]
I smell the blood of an Englishman,
Be he alive, or be he dead
I'll have his bones to grind my bread."

"Nonsense, dear," said his wife. "You're dreaming. Or perhaps you smell the scraps of the little boy you liked so

MAXFIELD PARRISH,
"Jack and the Giant," 1908

A defiant Jack stands in the palm of the ogre, whose smile betrays his contempt for this diminutive fellow. The oil painting appeared on the cover of *Collier's National Weekly Magazine* in 1910.

much for yesterday's dinner. Here, you go and have a wash and tidy up,[10] and by the time you come back, your breakfast will be ready for you."

So off the ogre went, and Jack was just going to jump out of the oven and run away when the woman told him not to. "Wait till he's asleep," says she. "He always has a doze after breakfast."

Well, the ogre had his breakfast, and after that he goes to a big chest and takes out of it a couple of bags of gold,[11] and down he sits and counts till at last his head begins to nod and he began to snore till the whole house shook again.

Then Jack crept out on tiptoe from his oven, and as he was passing the ogre he took one of the bags of gold under his arm, and off he pelters till he came to the beanstalk, and then he threw down the bag of gold, which, of course, fell

10. *have a wash and tidy up.* The monsters of fairy tales and children's literature are often doubles of the protagonist, representing the uncivilized self with all its unrestrained impulses. The giant is somewhat like a big baby, who is treated by his wife like an unruly child.

11. *gold.* Jack usually takes gold, a hen that lays golden eggs, and a harp that plays itself, but some variants show him stealing a crown, jewelry, a gun, or a light. In a Blue Ridge Mountain version, Jack steals a rifle, a skinning knife, and a coverlet tricked out with golden bells. The last object usually sings, plays music, or calls out in some way to awaken the giant.

MAXFIELD PARRISH,
"Giant with Jack at His Feet," 1904

The giant's primitive club contrasts as powerfully with Jack's delicate sword as the giant himself with Jack. The cover illustration for *Poems of Childhood* reveals the beauty and strength of youth.

12. *to try his luck once more.* Jack has been seen as a capitalist risk taker who has the kind of entrepreneurial energy required in the new economies developing in the British Empire. His expropriation of the "uncivilized" giant has been read as an allegory of colonialist enterprises.

ANONYMOUS,
"Jack and the Beanstalk"

While the ogre is sleeping, Jack slips over to the table to grab one of the bags of money.

into his mother's garden, and then he climbed down and climbed down till at last he got home and told his mother and showed her the gold and said: "Well, mother, wasn't I right about the beans? They are really magical, you see."

So they lived on the bag of gold for some time, but at last they came to the end of it, and Jack made up his mind to try his luck once more**12** at the top of the beanstalk. So, one fine morning he rose up early, and got on to the beanstalk, and he climbed and he climbed and he climbed and he climbed and he climbed and he climbed till at last he came out on to the road again and up to the great big tall house he had been to before. There, sure enough, was the great big tall woman a-standing on the doorstep.

"Good morning, mum," says Jack, as bold as brass. "Could you be so good as to give me something to eat?"

"Go away, my boy," said the big tall woman, "or else my man will eat you up for breakfast. But aren't you the youngster who came here once before? Do you know, that very day my man missed one of his bags of gold?"

"That's strange, mum," said Jack. "I dare say I could tell you something about that, but I'm so hungry I can't speak till I've had something to eat."

Well, the big tall woman was so curious that she took him in and gave him something to eat. But he had scarcely begun munching it as slowly as he could when thump! thump! they heard the giant's footstep, and his wife hid Jack away in the oven.

All happened as it did before. In came the ogre as he did before, said:

> "Fee-fi-fo-fum,
> I smell the blood of an Englishman,
> Be he alive, or be he dead
> I'll have his bones to grind my bread,"

and had his breakfast of three broiled oxen. Then he said: "Wife, bring me the hen that lays the golden eggs." So she brought it, and the ogre said: "Lay," and it laid an egg all

ARTHUR RACKHAM,
"Jack and the Beanstalk," 1933

The ogre's wife warns Jack to keep still, but he cannot resist poking his head out from the oven to watch while the ogre looks with satisfaction at the golden egg laid by his hen.

ANONYMOUS,
"Jack and the Beanstalk"

Jack peers out from his hiding place to watch as the ogre looks at the hen that lays golden eggs.

WARWICK GOBLE,
"Jack and the Beanstalk," 1923

Jack makes a graceful descent down the beanstalk with the hen that lays golden eggs. Bean pods and blossoms create a dramatic decorative effect.

of gold. And then the ogre began to nod his head, and to snore till the house shook.

Then Jack crept out of the oven on tiptoe and caught hold of the golden hen, and was off before you could say "Jack Robinson." But this time the hen gave a cackle which woke the ogre, and just as Jack got out of the house, he heard him calling: "Wife, wife, what have you done with my golden hen?"

And the wife said: "Why, my dear?"

But that was all Jack heard, for he rushed off to the beanstalk and climbed down like a house on fire. And when he got home he showed his mother the wonderful hen, and said "Lay" to it; and it laid a golden egg every time he said "Lay."

Well, Jack was not content, and it wasn't very long

before he determined to have another try at his luck up there at the top of the beanstalk. So one fine morning, he rose up early, and got on to the beanstalk, and he climbed and he climbed and he climbed and he climbed till he got to the top. But this time he knew better than to go straight to the ogre's house. And when he got near it, he waited behind a bush till he saw the ogre's wife come out with a pail to get some water, and then he crept into the house and got into the copper.**13** He hadn't been there long when he heard thump! thump! thump! as before, and in came the ogre and his wife.

> "Fee-fi-fo-fum,
> I smell the blood of an Englishman,
> Be he alive, or be he dead
> I'll have his bones to grind my bread,"

cried out the ogre. "I smell him, wife, I smell him."

"Do you, my dearie?" says the ogre's wife. "Then, if it's that little rogue that stole your gold and the hen that laid

ARTHUR RACKHAM,
"Jack and the Beanstalk," 1918

With three cows dangling from his belt already, this ogre, who towers over his wife, sniffs the air and senses that there is even more to eat in the kitchen. Rackham's mastery in the art of drawing hands and feet becomes particularly evident in his rendition of the ogre.

13. *copper.* A copper is a large kettle used for cooling or to boil laundry.

the golden eggs he's sure to have got into the oven." And they both rushed to the oven. But Jack wasn't there, luckily, and the ogre's wife said: "There you are again with your fee-fi-fo-fum. Why, of course, it's the boy you caught last night that I've just broiled for your breakfast. How forgetful I am, and how careless you are not to know the difference between live and dead after all these years."

So the ogre sat down to the breakfast and ate it, but every now and then he would mutter: "Well, I could have sworn—" and he'd get up and search the larder and the cupboards and everything, only, luckily, he didn't think of the copper.

After breakfast was over, the ogre called out: "Wife, wife, bring me my golden harp." So she brought it and put it on the table before him. Then he said: "Sing!" and the golden harp sang most beautifully. And it went on singing till the ogre fell asleep, and commenced to snore like thunder.

Then Jack lifted up the copper lid very quietly and got down like a mouse and crept on hands and knees till he came to the table, when up he crawled, caught hold of the golden harp and dashed with it towards the door. But the harp called out quite loud: "Master! Master!" and the ogre woke up just in time to see Jack running off with his harp.

Jack ran as fast as he could, and the ogre came rushing after, and would soon have caught him only Jack had a start and dodged him a bit and knew where he was going. When he got to the beanstalk the ogre was not more than twenty yards away when suddenly he saw Jack disappear, and when he came to the end of the road he saw Jack underneath climbing down for dear life. Well, the ogre didn't like trusting himself to such a ladder, and he stood and waited, so Jack got another start. But just then the harp cried out: "Master! Master!" and the ogre swung himself down on to the beanstalk, which shook with his weight. Down climbs Jack, and after him climbed the ogre. By this time Jack had climbed down and climbed

ANONYMOUS,
"Jack and the Beanstalk"

Axe still in hand, Jack shows his mother what happened to the ogre once the beanstalk was chopped down. The good fairy hovering over Jack appears in some versions of the tale to inform Jack that the ogre appropriated his father's wealth and that he is fully entitled to recover it, even by theft.

ARTHUR RACKHAM,
"Jack and the Beanstalk," 1913

The axe used by Jack to chop down the beanstalk goes flying through the air as the ogre tumbles down from his kingdom, feet first. Note that the decorative frame reprises the beanstalk motif and adds a touch of whimsy with the talking heads.

down and climbed down till he was very nearly home. So he called out: "Mother! Mother! bring me an axe, bring me an axe." And his mother came rushing out with the axe in her hand, but when she came to the beanstalk she stood stock still with fright, for there she saw the ogre with his legs just through the clouds.

But Jack jumped down and got hold of the axe and gave a chop at the beanstalk which cut it half in two. The ogre felt the beanstalk shake and quiver, so he stopped to see what was the matter. Then Jack gave another chop with the axe, and the beanstalk was cut in two and began

14. *married a great princess.* Jack often lives happily ever after with his mother, as in Tabart's version, but Jacobs felt obliged to end with fairy-tale nuptials.

to topple over. Then the ogre fell down and broke his crown, and the beanstalk came toppling after.

Then Jack showed his mother the golden harp, and what with showing that and selling the golden eggs, Jack and his mother became very rich, and he married a great princess,**14** and they lived happily ever after.

11

BLUEBEARD[1]

Charles Perrault

Known as Silver Nose in Italy and as the Lord of the Underworld in Greece, the French Bluebeard has many folkloric cousins. The blue in his beard tips the reader off to his exotic, otherworldly nature. This is a man who is justifiably spurned as a husband, despite his wealth and power. With its raised sabers, forbidden chambers, corpses hanging from hooks, and bloody floors, "Bluebeard" is the stuff of horror. And although it has a happy ending (the heroine marries a "worthy man" who banishes the memory of her first marriage), it is more a cautionary tale about marriage than a celebration of marital bliss. Perrault takes us beyond "happily ever after," into a post-marital nightmare.

Cultural historians have pointed out that Perrault's "Bluebeard" may be based on fact, that it broadcasts the misdeeds of various noblemen, among them Cunmar of Brittany and Gilles de Rais. But neither Cunmar the Accursed, who decapitated his pregnant wife Triphine, nor Gilles de Rais, the mar-

1. *Bluebeard.* Beards were not fashionable in Perrault's time, and Bluebeard's monstrous growth of a shadowy color marked him as an outsider and libertine. The exotic beard inspired a number of interpretations that cast Bluebeard in the role of oriental tyrant. Edmund Dulac's illustrations set the tale in the Orient, with Bluebeard sporting a turban, while his wife lounges with other women in what appears to be a harem. Many authors who took up the story set the tale in the East and gave the wife the name Fatima.

From Charles Perrault, "La Barbe bleue," in *Histoires ou contes du temps passé, avec des moralités* (Paris: Barbin, 1697).

shal of France who was hanged in 1440 for murdering hundreds of children, present themselves as compelling models for Bluebeard. This French aristocrat remains a construction of collective fantasy, a figure firmly anchored in the realm of folklore.

The Bluebeard story has traditionally been seen as turning on the curiosity of the wife, who can never "resist" the temptation to look into the chamber forbidden to her. Perrault, too, presents Bluebeard's wife as a figure who suffers from an excess of desire for knowledge, a woman who makes the near-fatal mistake of disobeying her husband. In his moral to the story, Perrault aligns the intellectual curiosity of Bluebeard's wife with the sexual curiosity of women in general, thus hinting that his protagonist is very much a daughter of Eve. By underscoring the heroine's kinship with certain literary, biblical, and mythical figures (most notably Psyche, Eve, and Pandora), Perrault gives us a tale that willfully undermines a robust folkloric tradition in which the heroine is a resourceful agent of her own salvation. Rather than celebrating the courage and wisdom of Bluebeard's wife in discovering the dreadful truth about her husband's murderous deeds, Perrault and many other tellers of the tale disparage her unruly act of insubordination.

"Bluebeard," with its focus on postmarital conflicts, serves as a reminder that fairy tales and folktales were rooted in an adult culture. These stories were told around the fireside and in the kitchen to lighten the labors of those living in an earlier age. They encapsulate collective truths—the wisdom of the ages—about romance, courtship, marriage, divorce, and death, and they are passed on from one generation to the next. Gossip and gospel truth, gossip as gospel truth, these stories, often referred to now as old wives' tales, represent a buried narrative tradition, one that flowed largely through oral tributaries as women's speech until it was appropriated by editors and collectors who channeled it into a print culture.

THERE ONCE LIVED a man who owned owned grand houses, both in the town and in the country. His dinner services were of gold and silver, his chairs fitted with fine tapestries, his coaches covered with gold. But this man also had the misfortune of having a blue beard. The beard made him look so ugly and frightening that women and girls alike fled when they set eyes on him.

A respected woman who lived nearby had two daughters who were real beauties. The man asked for the hand of one, but he left it up to the mother to choose which of the two he would marry. Neither of the two girls wanted to accept the proposal, and they passed the offer back and forth between them, for neither one could bring herself to

EDMUND DULAC,
"Bluebeard," 1910

"They were rowed to the sound of music on the waters of their host's private canal." In this orientalized illustration for Perrault's French story, Bluebeard's wife, with her richly textured layers of clothing, enters a gondola filled with sumptuous pillows. Bluebeard's realm is marked by voluptuous beauty and sensual delights.

EDMUND DULAC,
"Bluebeard," 1910

"They overran the house without loss of time." Looking more like a harem than a party of young women at a French country manor, Bluebeard's wife and her guests take pleasure in the luxuries of the castle. The soft, sensual flow of the fabrics suggests a state of quiet languor rather than an active overrunning of the household.

EDMUND DULAC,
"Bluebeard," 1910

"And then, in a room, hung the bodies of seven dead women." Amid the somber beauty of the castle, Bluebeard's wife stops short in horror as she contemplates the corpses of her husband's dead wives. The dark room, illuminated by the light from behind the door, contains the evidence of Bluebeard's crimes.

EDMUND DULAC,
"Bluebeard," 1910

"You SHALL go in and take your place among the ladies you saw there." With keys scattered on the ground as a signal of his outrage, a massively proportioned Bluebeard with an oversized turban is determined to add this eighth wife to the collection in his chamber of horrors.

marry a man with a blue beard. That the man had already married several women added to their sense of revulsion. No one knew what had become of the previous wives.

In order to strike up a friendship with the family, Bluebeard threw a party for the two girls and their mother, along with three or four of their closest friends and a few young men who lived near one of his country houses. The festivities lasted an entire week. Every day there were parties—hunting, fishing, dancing, and dining. The guests were so busy cavorting and carousing that they never slept a wink. Everything went so well that the younger of the two sisters began to think that the beard of the lord of the manor was not so blue after all and that he was in fact a fine fellow. As soon as they got back to town, the two celebrated their marriage.

EDMUND DULAC,
"Bluebeard," 1910

EDMUND DULAC,
"Bluebeard," 1910

EDMUND DULAC,
"Bluebeard," 1910

"The unhappy FATIMA cried up to her: — 'Anne, Sister Anne, do you see anyone coming?'" Leaning over the railing, Bluebeard's wife seems only mildly desperate in the hope that her sister, up in the tower, will catch sight of the brothers who were planning to visit on that day. While Bluebeard's wife is given an Arabic name, Sister Anne retains her European Christian name.

"Then BLUBEARD roared out so terribly that he made the whole house tremble." Wielding a scimitar, Bluebeard orders his wife downstairs for her execution. The dry leaves on the branches, which repeat the color of Bluebeard's robes, magnify the sense of desolation at the site where the wife is to be murdered.

"They overtook him as he reached the steps of the main porch." With bloodied swords, the brothers of Bluebeard's wife chase the husband, who has lost his turban, down the steps and slay him.

After a month had gone by, Bluebeard told his wife that he had to go on a trip to take care of some urgent business in the provinces. He would be away for at least six weeks. He urged his wife to enjoy herself while he was away. If she liked, she could invite her close friends to go out to the country house. Anything to keep her in good spirits.

He gave his wife a ring with keys on it and said: "These are the keys to the two large storerooms where I keep my gold and silver. Here are the ones to the caskets where I store my jewels. And finally, this is the master key to all the rooms in my mansion. As for this particular key, it opens the small room at the end of the long gallery on the ground floor. Open anything you want. Go anywhere you

GUSTAVE DORÉ,
"Bluebeard," 1861

Bluebeard offers his wife the key to the forbidden chamber, admonishing her, with uplifted finger, not to use it. The wife's attraction to the forbidden object is readily apparent, and her eyes are riveted on it, as if by magic. Even Bluebeard's bulging eyes are unable to distract her from the object he puts into her hands.

HARRY CLARKE,
"Bluebeard," 1922

"This man had the misfortune to have a blue beard." Clarke's red-headed Bluebeard cuts an interesting figure with his striped hose and lavender waistcoat. An aesthete and dandy, this Bluebeard presents himself as a man who is comfortable in the solitude of his palatial domain.

KAY NIELSEN,
"Bluebeard," 1930

Kay Nielsen's sinister Bluebeard has a flowing beard and walks with an imposing cane. His coquettish wife seems unaware of the perils that await her when she takes the key to the forbidden chamber.

wish. But I absolutely forbid you to enter that little room, and if you open it so much as a crack, nothing will protect you from my wrath."

The wife promised to follow exactly the orders given by her husband. Bluebeard gave his wife a farewell kiss, got into the carriage, and set off on his journey.

Friends and neighbors of the young bride were so impatient to see the splendors of the house that they did not even wait for an invitation before coming to call. They had not dared to visit while the husband was at home, because they were so frightened of his blue beard. They lost no time exploring the rooms, closets, and wardrobes, each of which was more splendid and sumptuous than the last. Then they went upstairs to the storerooms, and they could not find words to describe the beauty of the numerous tapestries, beds, sofas, cabinets, stands, and tables. There were looking glasses in which you could see yourself from head to toe. Some mirrors had frames of glass, others were painted silver or lacquered, but all of them were finer and more magnificent than any that anyone had ever seen.

The guests were envious of their friend's good fortune, and they praised everything they saw in the house. But the wife was unable to enjoy any of these riches, because she was anxious to get into that room on the ground floor. She was so tormented by her curiosity[2] that, without stopping to think about how rude it was to leave her friends, she raced down the staircase so fast that more than once she was afraid she was going to break her neck. When she reached the door to the room, she stopped for a moment to think about how her husband had forbidden her to enter the room, and she imagined what might happen to her if she were to disobey him. But the temptation was too great. She was unable to resist, and, trembling, she took the little key and opened the door.

At first she could not see anything, for the windows were shuttered. After a few minutes it dawned on her that the floor was sticky with clotted blood and, worse yet, the pools of blood reflected the corpses of a number of women hanging from the walls (these were all the women Bluebeard had married[3] and then murdered one after another).

The wife thought that she was going to die of fright, and the key to the room, which she was about to pull out of the lock, dropped from her hand. After regaining her senses, she picked up the key, locked the door, and went back up to her bedroom to pull herself together. But her nerves were too frayed for her to recover completely. When she noticed that the key to the room was stained with blood,[4] she wiped it two or three times, but the blood would not go away. She tried to rinse it off and scrubbed it with sand and grit as well. But the bloodstain would not

2. *tormented by her curiosity.* In Perrault's version of the story, as in many others, the curiosity of Bluebeard's wife is seen in a negative light. Many nineteenth-century dramatizations of the story bore subtitles such as "The Consequences of Curiosity" or "The Hazards of Female Curiosity." Note that in this story the wife's curiosity is so powerful that it nearly causes her to break her neck.

3. *all the women Bluebeard had married.* Bluebeard's wives are usually seven in number, which, like three, is a popular figure in folklore. Interrogating the number in this story inevitably leads to the question of why the chamber was forbidden to the first wife. Films from the 1940s revived the Bluebeard story, showing the hazards of marrying men with a past. See, for example, Fritz Lang's *Secret beyond the Door*, Alfred Hitchcock's *Notorious*, and George Cukor's *Gaslight*.

4. *the key to the room was stained with blood.* Folklorists describe this motif as "blood-stained key as sign of disobedience," ignoring the fact that the blood is a telltale sign that you should not be trusting your husband. Perrault's key is "enchanted," and, like the eggs, flowers, and straws that come to be stained with blood in other versions of "Bluebeard," it resists attempts to remove stains.

ARTHUR RACKHAM,
"Bluebeard," 1919

A young oriental maiden with European features, Bluebeard's wife
appears both wary and eager as she
tests the key and is about to open
the door forbidden to her. That
door, in contrast to the other ornate
openings, is constructed as an ordinary wooden door.

ANONYMOUS,
"Bluebeard"

"The young wife turns the forbidden
key / And, horror of horrors! what
does she see? / The luckless victims of
Bluebeard's crime, / But she herself is
rescued in time." This diminutive figure from a picture book published in
the United States, suggests that the
lesson about disobedience applies to
children as well as to women.

go away, because the key was enchanted and there was no
way to remove the blood from it. When you got the stain
off one side of the key, it came back on the other.

That evening Bluebeard came back from his journey
unexpectedly and reported that he had received letters on
the way informing him that the urgent business matters
calling him away had been settled to his satisfaction. His
wife did everything she could to make it appear that she
was delighted with his early return. The following day he
asked for the ring of keys, and she returned them, but with
a hand shaking so badly that he guessed right away what
had happened.

OTTO BRAUSEWETTER,
"Bluebeard," 1865

Bluebeard's wife recoils in horror when she sees the mutilated bodies of her husband's previous wives in a tub. An ax leaning against the tub gives us the murder weapon. Note how the keys still dangle from the waist of Bluebeard's wife.

HERMANN VOGEL,
"Bluebeard," 1887

Bluebeard's wife drops the key to the forbidden chamber in shock, and it falls on the bloodied floor, leaving a telltale stain as a sign of transgression. The corpses of the wives, hung from the wall as if on display, suggest that Bluebeard is a master in the art of murder. The chopping block and ax in the foreground reveal the scene of the crimes.

"Why isn't that key to the little room here with the others?" he asked.

"I must have left it upstairs on my dressing table," she replied.

"Don't forget to bring it right back to me," Bluebeard told her.

She made one excuse after another, but finally she had to bring him the key. Bluebeard inspected it, then said to his wife: "How did blood get on this key?"

"I have no idea," the poor woman replied, and she turned pale as death.

"You have no idea," Bluebeard said. "But I've got an

5. *give me just a moment to say my prayers.* Using her wits, Bluebeard's wife uses prayers as a pretext for delaying her execution. In some oral versions of the story recorded by folklorists, the wife sends a talking parrot or dog back home to fetch help.

6. *to see if our brothers are on the way here.* Note that the brothers rescue their sister and return her to her original family. "Bluebeard" is unique in the way that it begins with marriage and moves the protagonist back to her first family, a reversal of the conventional trajectory of fairy-tale heroes and heroines. How and when Sister Anne gets to the castle is not clear.

idea. You tried to get into that little room. Well, madam, now that you have opened it, you can walk right in and take your place beside the ladies whom you saw there."

The woman threw herself at her husband's feet, weeping and begging forgiveness, with every sign that she felt genuine regret for disobeying him. This beauty in distress would have melted a heart of stone, but Bluebeard's heart was harder than stone.

"Madam, you must die," he declared. "Your time has come."

"Since I must die," she replied, gazing at him, her eyes filled with tears, "give me just a moment to say my prayers."**5**

"I will give you a quarter of an hour," Bluebeard replied, "but not a second longer."

When the wife was alone, she called for her sister and said to her: "Sister Anne"—for that was her name—"I beg you, go to the top of the tower to see if our brothers are on the way here.**6** They promised that they were coming to visit today. If you catch sight of them, send them a signal to speed up."

Sister Anne climbed to the top of the tower, and, from time to time, the poor woman cried out to her: "Anne, Sister Anne, can you see anyone coming?"

Sister Anne replied: "I see nothing but the sun shining and the green grass growing."

In the meantime Bluebeard picked up an enormous saber and shouted as loud as he could up to his wife: "Come down here at once, or I'll go up there!"

"Just give me one more second, I beg you," his wife replied and then she whispered loudly: "Anne, Sister Anne, do you see anyone heading this way?"

"I see a great big cloud of dust heading in this direction," replied Sister Anne.

"Is it our brothers?"

"No, oh no, Sister dear, it's just a flock of sheep."

"Are you coming down here or not?" Bluebeard roared.

"Just one more second," his wife replied, and then she

called out: "Anne, Sister Anne, do you see anyone heading this way?"

"I see two horsemen heading this way, but they're still so far away," she replied. A moment later she called out: "Thank God, it must be our brothers. I'll send them a signal to hurry up."

Bluebeard roared so loudly that the entire house shook. His poor wife came downstairs in tears, her hair disheveled. She threw herself at her husband's feet.

"That won't do you any good," said Bluebeard. "Prepare to die." Taking her by the hair with one hand and raising his saber with the other, he was getting ready to

ANONYMOUS,
"Bluebeard," 1865

A savage and enraged Bluebeard seizes his wife by the wrist and prepares to murder her with his sword. In the background the two brothers pass through an arch and rush to reach their sister before it is too late.

chop off her head. The poor woman turned to him and, with dimmed eyes, begged him to stop and to give her a moment to prepare for her death.

"No, no," Bluebeard said. "Prepare to meet your maker." And lifting his arm . . . .

Just then there was a pounding at the gate so loud that Bluebeard stopped in his tracks. The gate was opened. Two men on horseback, swords in hand, galloped in, heading straight for Bluebeard, who realized that the

7. *The rest she used to marry herself to a very worthy man.* Technically, one can speak of a happy ending to this particular tale, despite the hair-raising events in the story. Note that Bluebeard's wife is more successful in marriage when she brings a hefty dowry to it than when she marries for wealth. The story may have served as a cautionary fable to young women against marrying wealthy men with a past.

men—one a dragoon, the other a musketeer—must be his wife's brothers. He fled at once, hoping to escape, but the two brothers showed no mercy and closed in on him before he could get to the stairs. They ran their swords through him and left him for dead. Bluebeard's wife was almost as lifeless as her husband. She barely had the strength to rise and embrace her brothers.

It turned out that Bluebeard had left no heirs, and so his wife was able to take possession of his entire fortune. She used some of it to marry her sister, Anne, to a young

ARTHUR RACKHAM,
"Bluebeard," 1919

Rackham's silhouette provides a fascinating cross section of Bluebeard's palace, with the husband demanding that the wife descend to her execution, the wife straining to learn whether her brothers are on the way, and Sister Anne surveying the horizon for the brothers.

gentleman who was deeply in love with her. And some of it went to buying commissions for her two brothers. The rest she used to marry herself to a very worthy man,[7] who helped her banish the memory of the terrible days she had spent with Bluebeard.

MORAL

Curiosity, with its many charms,
Can stir up serious regrets;
Thousand of examples turn up every day.
Women give in, but it's a fleeting pleasure;
Once satisfied, it ceases to be.
And always it proves very costly.

SECOND MORAL

Take the time to stop and think,
And to ponder this grim little story.
You surely know that this tale
Took place many years ago.
No longer are husbands so terrible,
Demanding the impossible,
Acting unhappy and jealous.
They toe the line with their wives.
And no matter what color their beards,
It's not hard to tell who is in charge.

12

THE JUNIPER TREE[1]

Philipp Otto Runge[2]

1. *juniper tree.* The juniper has a rich folkloric tradition, but it is not especially pertinent to the tree in this tale. The oil, ashes, berries, leaves, and bark are used in many cultures for healing purposes, and it is the therapeutic power of the tree that seems to make it a natural choice as the resting place for the boy. In Russia the juniper tree is a birch; in England it is a rose tree.

2. *Philipp Otto Runge.* The version of the story published in the Grimms' collection came from the pen of the Romantic artist Philipp Otto Runge (1777–1810). A master of ornamental detail and decorative art, Runge sent the Grimms a highly stylized narrative that used dialect to convey the impression of "artless" narration. Runge's version of the story is the only one that weds the biological mother so closely to nature—once she becomes fertile and conceives, she is turned into a virtual prisoner of nature, subject to its laws of growth and decay. An elaborate duet

With its lurid descriptions of decapitation and cannibalism, "The Juniper Tree" (also known as "My Mother Slew Me; My Father Ate Me") is probably the most shocking of all fairy tales. In most versions the central character is a boy, yet occasionally, as in the British story "The Rose Tree," a girl undergoes the transformation into a bird. The scenes of the boy's beheading by the mother and consumption by the father did not deter P. L. Travers, the British author of Mary Poppins, *from describing the tale as "beautiful," nor did they keep J. R. R. Tolkien from referring to the "beauty and horror" of the story, with its "exquisite and tragic beginning."*

The "beauty" of "The Juniper Tree" probably turns less on its aesthetic appeal than on its engagement with anxieties that fascinate us in their evocation of sheer dread. In the stepmother we find a figure who represents maternal power run mad, an incarnation of a natural force so cruel and inexorable that it

From Jacob and Wilhelm Grimm, "Von dem Machandelboom," in *Kinder- und Hausmärchen*, 7th ed. (Berlin: Dieterich, 1857; first published, Berlin: Realschulbuchhandlung, 1812).

heightens the weakness and helplessness of the children. In the Grimms' version, the boy is transformed back to human form and reunited with his father and sister to live in a motherless household. But in some versions, as in the Scottish "Pippety Pew," the boy remains a bird, while "the Goodman and his daughter lived happy and died happy."

Although the poignancy of the opening paragraph in "The Juniper Tree" is unsettled by the complexities of the biological mother's associations with nature and death, it still stands in sharp contrast to the horrors of the tale's main events, events engineered largely by the (step)mother. The biological mother is presented as a "natural" foil to the stepmother, who represents self-consciousness and artifice in its most dreaded and dreadful form. The co-presence of birth and death is inscribed in the first scene, then doubled and repeated as rebirth and murder in the body of the tale.

"The Juniper Tree" eliminates both biological mother and stepmother in the end, giving us a tableau in which brother, sister, and father are seated at a table, dining. This is the same "happily ever after" we know from "Hansel and Gretel" and countless other fairy tales. "The Juniper Tree" seems to enact the process of growing away from the mother, who in our culture represents dependence and domesticity, and turning to the father, who, by virtue of his traditional absence from early child-rearing, comes to signify autonomy. By crushing the mother and joining the father, the children "successfully" negotiate the path from dependence to autonomy. It is important to bear in mind that versions of this tale and others are sacred only as cultural documents mapping the developmental routes of another era. Enough has changed and is changing since Runge recorded this tale for us to begin producing variants on this cultural story, which demonizes mothers in a powerful way and represents fathers as passive and detached.

coordinates the rhythms of the child's gestation period with nature's seasonal changes.

3. *as many as two thousand years ago.* The specification of an era is unusual in fairy tales. The figure of two thousand years anchors the tale in biblical times and suggests a connection with the origins of Christianity. In light of the boy's death and resurrection, the date has a special significance.

4. *they had no children.* This fairy tale, like so many others, begins with "lack" and moves to the liquidation of the lack, which in turn produces a new motor to the plot, in this case the death of the biological mother. Like many fairy-tale couples, this one is childless, and, rather than just wishing for a child, the two pray. Many couples make desperate wishes that lead to the birth of some type of animal—a hedgehog, for example, in the Grimms' story "Hans My Hedgehog."

5. *peeling an apple under the tree.* The apple reappears as the object of desire that leads to the boy's death. Note also the connection with the apple that is used to tempt and poison Snow White.

6. *as red as blood and as white as snow.* The story resembles "Snow White" in many ways, especially because its plot turns on the conflict between stepmother and child. But note that in this case it is a little boy whose lips are as red as blood and whose skin is as white as snow. Most versions of this particular tale type do not include the background story about the death of the biological mother.

7. *A month went by, and the snow melted.* In the paragraph that follows, the parallels drawn between the seasons and the woman's gestation period are elaborated in a man-

A LONG TIME AGO, as many as two thousand years ago,[3] there was a rich man who had a beautiful and pious wife. They loved each other dearly, but they had no children,[4] even though they longed to have them. Day and night the wife prayed for a child, but still they had none.

In front of the house there was a garden, and in the garden there grew a juniper tree. Once, in the wintertime, the wife was peeling an apple under the tree,[5] and while she was peeling it, she cut her finger. Blood dripped on the snow. "Ah," said the woman, and she sighed deeply. "If only I had a child as red as blood and as white as snow!"[6] After she said that, she began to feel better, for she had a feeling that something would come of it. And she went back into the house.

A month went by, and the snow melted.[7] Two months passed, and everything had become green. Three months went by, and flowers were sprouting from the ground. Four months passed, and all the trees in the woods were growing tall, with their green branches intertwining. The woods echoed with the song of birds, and blossoms were falling from the trees. And so the fifth month went by. And when the woman sat under the juniper tree, her heart leaped for joy because the tree was so fragrant. She fell to her knees and was beside herself with happiness. When the sixth month had passed, the fruit grew large and firm, and she became very quiet. In the seventh month she picked the berries from the juniper tree and gorged herself on them until she became miserable and ill. After the eighth month went by, she called her husband and, in tears, said to him: "If I die, bury me under the juniper tree." After that she felt better and was calm until the ninth month had passed. Then she bore a child as white as snow and as red as blood. When she saw the child, she was so happy that she died of joy.**8**

The woman's husband buried her under the juniper tree, and he wept day after day. After a while he felt better, but he still cried from time to time. Eventually he stopped, and then he took a second wife.

The man had a daughter with his second wife. The child from the first marriage had been a little boy, as red as blood and as white as snow. Whenever the woman looked at her daughter, she felt love for her, but whenever she looked at the little boy, she felt sick at heart. It seemed that no matter where he went he was always in the way, and she kept wondering how she could make sure that her daughter eventually inherited everything.**9** The devil got hold of her so that she began to hate the little boy, and she slapped him around and pinched him here and cuffed him there. The poor child lived in terror, and when he came home from school, he had no peace at all.

One day the woman went into the pantry. Her little daughter followed her and asked: "Mother, will you give me an apple?"

"All right, my child," said the woman, and she gave her a beautiful apple from a chest that had a big heavy lid with a sharp iron lock on it.

"Mother," asked the little girl, "Can Brother have one too?"

The woman was irritated, but she said: "Yes, he can have one when he gets back from school."

When the woman looked out the window and saw the boy walking home, it was as if the devil had taken hold of her,**10** and she snatched the apple out of her daughter's hand and said: "You can't have one before your brother." Then she tossed the apple into the chest and shut it.

The little boy walked in the door, and the devil got her to whisper sweetly to him and say: "My son, would you like an apple?" But she gave him a look filled with hate.

"Mother," said the little boy, "What a scary look! Yes, give me an apple."

nered style more characteristic of fiction than of fairy tales. Runge was no doubt hoping to create a poetic effect with the descriptions of nature.

8. *she was so happy that she died of joy.* Many historians have pointed out that the high rate of mortality in childbirth may have motivated the prominence of stepmothers in fairy tales. Like Cinderella and Snow White, the little boy in this story suffers under the cruel regime of his stepmother.

9. *make sure that her daughter eventually inherited everything.* The inheritance issue creates friction even today in many blended families. In "The Juniper Tree" anxiety about dividing the patrimony is spelled out as a key factor in motivating the stepmother's hatred of the boy.

10. *it was as if the devil had taken hold of her.* The presence of the devil as a motivating force suggests that the teller of this tale was influenced by religious beliefs. Note that the stepmother's duplicity is connected with a diabolical force that incarnates the spirit of division and divisiveness.

LUDWIG RICHTER,
"The Juniper Tree," 1857

With grim determination, the stepmother slams the lid of the chest on the boy and beheads him. The sun streaming in the window suggests that she will not be able to conceal her crimes.

When the little boy bent down, the devil prompted her, and *bam*! She slammed the lid down so hard that the boy's head flew off and fell into the chest with the apples. Then she was overcome with fear and thought: "How am I going to get out of this?" She went to her room and took a white kerchief from her dresser drawer. She put the boy's head back on his neck and tied the scarf around it so that you couldn't tell that anything was wrong. Then she sat him down on a chair in front of the door and put an apple in his hand.

Later on Little Marlene came into the kitchen to see her mother, who was standing by the fire, madly stirring a pot of hot water. "Mother," said Little Marlene, "Brother is sitting by the door and looks pale. He has an apple in his hand, and when I asked him to give me the apple, he wouldn't answer. It was very scary."

"Go back to him," the mother said, "and if he doesn't give you an answer, slap his face."

Little Marlene went back to him and said: "Brother, give me the apple."

Her brother wouldn't answer. So Marlene gave him a slap, and his head went flying off. She was so terrified that she began to howl and weep. Then she ran to her mother and said: "Mother, I've knocked Brother's head right off!" And she was crying so hard that she couldn't stop.

"Little Marlene," said her mother, "what a dreadful thing you've done! But don't breathe a word to a soul, for there's nothing we can do. We'll cook him up in a stew."

The mother then took the little boy and chopped him up.[11] She put the pieces into a pot and cooked them up into a stew. Little Marlene stood by the fire and wept so hard that the stew didn't need any salt at all because of her tears.

When the father came home, he sat down at the table and said: "Where's my son?"

The mother brought in a huge dish of stew, and Little Marlene was weeping so hard that she couldn't stop.

11. *The mother then took the little boy and chopped him up.* The stepmother's serving up of the boy in a stew is reminiscent of the Greek myth in which Atreus prepares a banquet for his enemy Thyestes, who unknowingly feasts on his own sons. Her deed is also reminiscent of dismemberment scenes in other fairy tales (most notably Perrault's "Bluebeard" and the Grimms' "Fitcher's Bird"). The powerful resurrection scene at the end forges a connection with the dismemberment of the Egyptian god Osiris as well as of the Greek poet Orpheus, who is torn to pieces by the maenads.

HERMANN VOGEL,
"The Juniper Tree," 1893

"'Mother,' said Little Marlene, 'Brother is sitting by the door and looks pale. He has an apple in his hand, and when I asked him to give me the apple, he wouldn't answer. It was very scary.'" Little Marlene ponders her brother's condition, wondering why he is so pale. The scarf tied around his neck conceals the stepmother's crime.

KAY NIELSEN,
"The Juniper Tree," 1925

"A mist arose from the tree, and in the middle of the mist a flame was burning, and from the flame a beautiful bird emerged and began singing gloriously." Little Marlene watches in awe as the bird, of the same hue as her dress, emerges from the flame.

WARWICK GOBLE,
"The Juniper Tree," 1923

The bird, whose feathers match the hues of his half sister's cap and dress, emerges in all his glory from the flame in the tree. The bird's plumage, the girl's hair, and the tree's branches create a dramatic effect linking the girl with the bird.

"Where's my son?" the father asked again.

"Oh," said the mother, "he went off to the country to visit his mother's great-uncle. He is planning to stay there a while."

"What's he going to do there? He didn't even say good-bye to me."

"Well, he really wanted to go, and he asked if he could stay for six weeks. They'll take good care of him."

"Oh, that makes me so sad," said the husband. "It's not right. He should have said good-bye."

Then he began eating and said: "Little Marlene, why are you crying? Your brother will be back soon." And he said: "Oh, dear wife, this stew tastes so good! Give me some more."

The more the father ate, the more he wanted. "Give me some more," he said. "No one else can have any of it. Somehow I feel as if it's all for me."

The father kept eating, and he threw the bones under the table until he had finished everything. Meanwhile, Little Marlene went to her dresser and got her best silk kerchief. She picked up all the bones from beneath the table, tied them up in her silk kerchief, and carried them outside. She began weeping bitter tears. She put the bones down in the green grass under the juniper tree. After she had put them down, she suddenly felt much better and stopped crying. The juniper tree began stirring. Its branches parted and came back together again as though it were clapping its hands for joy. A mist arose from the tree, and in the middle of the mist a flame was burning, and from the flame a beautiful bird emerged**12** and began singing gloriously. It soared up in the air, and then vanished. The tree was as it had been before, but the kerchief with the bones was gone. Little Marlene felt so happy and relieved because it seemed as if her brother were still alive. She returned home feeling happy and sat down at the table to eat.

Meanwhile, the bird flew away, perched on the roof of a goldsmith's house, and began singing:

> "My mother, she slew me,
> My father, he ate me,
> My sister, Little Marlene,
> Gathered up my bones,
> Tied them up in silk,
> And put them under the juniper tree.
> Tweet, tweet, what a fine bird I am!"

The goldsmith was sitting in his shop, making a chain of gold. He heard the bird singing on his roof, and he found its song very beautiful. He got up and, while walking across the threshold, lost a slipper. Still, he kept right

12. *a beautiful bird emerged.* The boy's transformation resonates with the many mythological metamorphoses from human to bird (Procne and Philomela) but is also linked to the powerful role of birds in the Grimms' fairy tales. In "Cinderella," to cite just one example, the heroine takes refuge in a dovecote, is helped with her chores by birds, and witnesses the blinding of her stepsisters by doves.

on going out into the middle of the street with only one sock and one slipper on. He was also wearing his apron, and in one hand he had the golden chain, in the other his tongs. The sun was shining brightly on the street. He stopped to look at the bird and said: "Bird, you sing so beautifully. Sing me that song again."

"No," said the bird. "I never sing a second time for nothing. Give me that golden chain, and I'll sing for you again."

"Here," said the goldsmith. "Here's the golden chain. Now sing that song again."

The bird came swooping down. Grasping the golden chain in its right claw, it perched in front of the goldsmith and began singing:

> "My mother, she slew me,
> My father, he ate me,
> My sister, Little Marlene,
> Gathered up my bones,
> Tied them up in silk,
> And put them under the juniper tree.
> Tweet, tweet, what a fine bird I am!"

Then the bird flew off to a shoemaker's house, perched on the roof and sang:

> "My mother, she slew me,
> My father, he ate me,
> My sister, Little Marlene,
> Gathered up my bones,
> Tied them up in silk,
> And put them under the juniper tree.
> Tweet, tweet, what a fine bird I am!"

When the shoemaker heard the song, he ran out the door in his shirtsleeves and looked up at the roof. He had to put his hand over his eyes to keep the sun from blinding him. "Bird," he said, "You sing so beautifully." Then he called into the house: "Wife, come out here for a moment.

There's a bird up there. See it? How beautifully it is singing!"

The shoemaker called his daughter and her children, his apprentices, the hired hand, and the maid. They all came running out into the street to look at the bird and to admire its beauty. It had red and green feathers, and around its neck was a band of pure gold, and the eyes in its head sparkled like stars.

"Bird," said the shoemaker, "sing that song again."

"No," said the bird, "I never sing a second time for nothing. You have to give me something."

"Wife," said the man, "go up to the attic. On the top shelf you'll find a pair of red shoes. Get them for me."

His wife went and got the shoes.

"Here," said the man. "Now sing that song again."

The bird came swooping down. Taking the shoes in its left claw, it flew back up on the roof and sang:

> "My mother, she slew me,
> My father, he ate me,
> My sister, Little Marlene,
> Gathered up my bones,
> Tied them up in silk,
> And put them under the juniper tree.
> Tweet, tweet, what a fine bird I am!"

When the bird had finished the song, it flew away. It had the chain in its right claw and the shoes in its left, and it flew far away to a mill. The mill went "Clickety-clack, clickety-clack, clickety-clack." Inside the mill sat twenty of the miller's men, hewing a stone, "Hick hack hick hack hick hack." And the mill kept going "Clickety-clack, clickety-clack, clickety-clack." And so the bird went and perched on a linden tree outside the mill and sang:

> "My mother, she slew me . . ."

And one of the men stopped working.

"My father, he ate me . . ."

And two more stopped working and listened,

"My sister, Little Marlene . . ."

Then four men stopped working.

"Gathered up my bones,
Tied them up in silk,"

Now only eight were still hewing,

"And put them under . . ."

now only five,

". . . the juniper tree."

now only one.

"Tweet, tweet, what a fine bird I am!"

The last one stopped to listen to the final words. "Bird," he said, "you sing so beautifully! Let me hear the whole thing too. Sing that song again."

"I never sing the second time for nothing. If you give me the millstone, I'll sing the song again."

"If it belonged to me alone," he said, "I would give it to you."

"If the bird sings again," the others said, "it can have the millstone."

Then the bird swooped down, and the miller's men, all twenty of them, set the beam to and raised up the stone. "Heave-ho-hup, heave-ho-hup, heave-ho-hup." And the bird stuck its neck through the hole, put the stone on as if it were a collar, flew back to the tree, and sang:

"My mother, she slew me,
My father, he ate me,
My sister, Little Marlene,
Gathered up my bones,
Tied them up in silk,
And put them under the juniper tree.
Tweet, tweet, what a fine bird I am!"

When the bird had finished its song, it spread its wings. In its right claw was the chain, in its left claw the shoes, and around its neck was the millstone. Then it flew away, far away to the house of its father.

The father, mother, and Little Marlene were sitting at the table in the parlor, and the father said: "How happy I am! My heart feels so light."

"Not me," said the mother. "I feel frightened, as if a big storm were brewing."

Meanwhile, Little Marlene just sat there weeping. The bird flew up, and, when it landed on the roof, the father said: "How happy I'm feeling. And outside the sun is shining so brightly! I feel as if I'm about to see an old friend again."

"I don't," said the woman. "I'm so scared that my teeth are chattering, and I feel as if there's fire running through my veins."

She tore at her bodice to loosen it, while Little Marlene sat there weeping. She held her apron up to her eyes and wept so hard that it was completely soaked with tears. The bird swooped down to the juniper tree, perched on a branch, and sang:

"My mother, she slew me . . ."

The mother stopped up her ears and closed her eyes, for she didn't want to see or hear anything, but the roaring in her ears was like the wildest possible storm, and her eyes burned and flashed like lightning.

"My father, he ate me . . ."

"Oh, Mother," said the man, "there's a beautiful bird out there, and it's singing so gloriously. The sun is shining so warmly, and the air smells like cinnamon."

"My sister, Little Marlene . . ."

Little Marlene put her head in her lap and just kept crying and crying. But the husband said: "I'm going outside. I've got to see this bird close up."

"Oh, don't go," said the wife. "It feels as if the whole house is shaking and about to go up in flames!"

But the husband went out and looked at the bird.

"Gathered up my bones,
Tied them up in silk,
And put them under the juniper tree.
Tweet, tweet, what a fine bird I am!"

After finishing its song, the bird dropped the golden chain, and it fell right around the man's neck, hanging perfectly. He went inside and said: "Just look at that fine bird out there! It gave me this beautiful golden chain, almost as beautiful as it is."

The woman was so terrified that she fell right down on the floor, and the cap she was wearing came off her head. And once again the bird sang:

"My mother, she slew me . . ."

"Oh, if only I were a thousand feet under the ground so that I wouldn't have to listen to this!"

"My father, he ate me . . ."

Then the woman fell down again as if dead.

"My sister, Little Marlene . . ."

"Oh," said Little Marlene. "I want to go outside and see if the bird will give me something too." And she went out.

> "Gathered up my bones,
> Tied them up in silk . . ."

And the bird tossed her the shoes.

> "And put them under the juniper tree.
> Tweet, tweet, what a fine bird I am!"

Little Marlene felt lighthearted and happy. She put on the new red shoes and came dancing and skipping into the house.

"Oh," Little Marlene said, "I was so sad when I went out, and now I feel so cheerful. What a fine bird that is out there. It gave me a pair of red shoes."

The woman jumped to her feet, and her hair stood straight on end like tongues of flame. "It's as if the world is coming to an end. If I go outside, maybe I'll feel better too."

The woman went over to the door and, *bam!* the bird dropped the millstone on her head[13] and crushed her to death. The father and Little Marlene heard the crash and went outside. Smoke, flames, and fire were rising up from the spot, and when they vanished, Little Brother was back, standing right there. He took his father and Little Marlene by the hand, and the three of them were overcome with joy. Then they went back in the house, sat down at the table, and dined.[14]

13. *the bird dropped the millstone on her head.* Many critics have associated the millstone that crushes the stepmother with a biblical millstone that drowns those who injure the young and the innocent: "Whoever receives one such child in my name receives me; but whoever causes one of these little ones who believe in me to sin, it would be better for him to have a great millstone fastened around his neck and to be drowned in the depth of the sea" (Matthew 18:5–6).

14. *sat down at the table, and dined.* The trio at the end partakes of a meal, almost as if it were a sacrament, recalling the sacrilege of the stew served up to the father. Yet here the dining ritual renews and restores the new family.

VASILISA THE FAIR[1]

Alexander Afanasev

1. *Vasilisa the Fair.* Unlike Snow White, Cinderella, or Sleeping Beauty, the Russian Vasilisa has a double mission: bringing light back to the household and finding her tsar. She solves the domestic problems by carrying out tasks rather than suffering in silence. And she earns her final reward by demonstrating her domestic skills. Vasilisa is the generic name for a heroine who appears in multiple Russian tales and who rises from humble origins to a royal rank.

A powerful Russian hybrid of "Cinderella" and "Hansel and Gretel," Alexander Afanasev's story of a girl who is persecuted by her stepmother and who dwells in the hut of a cannibalistic witch traces the heroine's rise from rags to riches. A double victim, Vasilisa is persecuted at the house of her father by a cruel stepmother, then exposed to the threats of an ogress eager to turn her into her next meal. Vasilisa finds aid and comfort in the form of a doll, who helps her carry out the impossible tasks posed by the evil stepmother and wicked witch. The doll, a "blessing" from her mother, is both competent alter ego and magical helper, providing and performing where there is need. Unlike Jack in the story "Jack and the Beanstalk," who takes possession of a giant's treasure by using his wits, Vasilisa, the peasant bride, gets her reward by carrying out household chores—sweeping the yard, cleaning a hut, cooking dinner, washing linen, and sorting grain. She becomes a consummate

From A. N. Afanasev, "Vasilisa Prekrasnaia," in *Narodnye russkie skazki* (Russian Fairy Tales) (Moscow: A. Semena, 1855–63).

spinner and seamstress, who wins the heart of a tsar with her beautiful fabrics and handicraft.

The story of Vasilisa reflects the cultural values of an earlier age, of a time in which excellence in the household crafts was treasured as highly as beauty. But Vasilisa is more than spinner and seamstress. She also nurtures the doll given to her by her mother, understanding that she must sacrifice some of her own needs in order to benefit from her advice and help. As a figure who brings light (in the form of fire) back to her home, Vasilisa becomes a cultural heroine who restores order and creates the conditions for a real home. In the end she works hard to promote a happy ending that includes not only herself and the tsar but also her father and the woman who sheltered her.

ONCE UPON A TIME there lived a merchant in a faraway kingdom. Although he had been married twelve years, he had only one child, and she was called Vasilisa the Fair. When Vasilisa was eight years old, her mother fell ill. She called her daughter to her side, took a doll out from under her coverlet, and gave it to the girl, saying: "Listen, Vasilisushka. Pay attention to my last words, and remember what I say. I'm dying, and all I can leave you is my maternal blessing with this doll.[2] Keep the doll with you wherever you go, but don't show her to anyone. If you get into trouble, just give her some food and ask her advice. After she has eaten, she will tell you what to do." The mother kissed her daughter farewell and died.

Following his wife's death, the merchant mourned her in proper fashion and then began to think about remarrying. He was a handsome man and had no difficulty finding a bride, but he liked a certain widow best. This widow had two daughters of her own, who were almost the same age as Vasilisa, and the merchant thought she would make

2. *my maternal blessing with this doll.* Whereas Cinderella and her folkloric cousins usually receive assistance from nature (trees, fish, brooks) or from a fairy godmother, Vasilisa is given a cultural artifact, a figure that can be seen as a miniaturized version of herself or as a symbolic form of her mother. While the doll protects and helps Vasilisa, it is also something to be nurtured and cared for, thus strengthening the fact of her own agency in escaping from villainy at home.

IVAN BILIBIN,
"Vasilisa the Fair," 1900

Baba Yaga, in silhouette as she erases her traces with a broom, roams the moonlit forests, searching for tasty children to eat. Bilibin, using the triptych form capped by an onion-shaped dome, turns the Russian fairy-tale figure into a sacred, if also somewhat sinister, cultural icon.

3. *her stepmother and stepsisters were jealous of her beauty.* Like Cinderella and Snow White, Vasilisa suffers because of her unrivaled beauty. In Russian tales the stepmother and stepsisters hope that work and harsh weather will destroy the girl's beauty. In European tales spinning is often the activity that is seen as deforming, and it is telling that that activity is assigned to Vasilisa.

4. *Some days Vasilisa did not eat anything at all.* The doll's help comes with a cost. Vasilisa must nourish the doll, the spirit of her mother as well as an alter ego, and must sacrifice in order to empower it.

a good housekeeper and mother. And so he married her, but he was wrong, for she did not turn out to be a good mother for his Vasilisa.

Vasilisa was the fairest girl in the entire village, and her stepmother and stepsisters were jealous of her beauty.[3] They tormented her by giving her all kinds of work to do, hoping that she would grow bony from toil and weather-beaten from exposure to the wind and the sun. And indeed, her life was miserable. But she bore it all without complaint and became lovelier with every passing day, while the stepmother and her daughters, who sat around all day doing nothing, grew thin and ugly as a result of spitefulness.

How did all this come about? Things would have been different without the doll. Without her aid the girl could never have managed all the work. Some days Vasilisa did not eat anything at all.[4] She would wait until everyone was in bed in the evening and then lock herself in the room where she slept. Giving her doll a tasty morsel, she would say: "Eat this, little doll, and listen to my troubles. I live in my father's house, but I'm deprived of joy. That stepmother of mine is going to be the death of me. Tell me how I should live and what I should do." First the doll would eat, and then she gave Vasilisa advice and comforted her in her woe. And in the morning she would take care of all the chores, while Vasilisa rested in the shade and picked flowers. The doll weeded the flowerbeds, watered the cabbages, went to the well, and fired the stove. The doll even showed Vasilisa an herb that would protect her against sunburn.[5] Thanks to the doll, Vasilisa's life was easy.

The years passed, and Vasilisa grew up, reaching the age of marriage. All the young men in the village wanted to marry her, and they never so much as cast a glance at the stepmother's daughters. The stepmother grew to hate Vasilisa more than ever. To all the suitors she declared: "I will not give the youngest in marriage before the elder ones." Then she vented her anger on Vasilisa with cruel blows.

One day Vasilisa's father had to go on a long journey[6] in order to trade in distant lands. The stepmother moved to another house near the edge of a deep forest. In the glade of that forest was a hut, and in the hut lived Baba Yaga.[7] She never allowed anyone to come near her and ate human beings just as if they were chickens. The merchant's wife hated Vasilisa so much that, at the new house, she would send her stepdaughter into the woods for one thing or another. But Vasilisa always returned home safe and sound. Her doll showed her the way and kept her well clear of Baba Yaga's hut.

One evening in autumn the stepmother gave each of the girls a task. She told the oldest to make lace, the second to knit stockings, and Vasilisa was supposed to spin. Then she snuffed out all the candles in the house except for the one in the room where the girls were working. For a while the girls carried out their tasks quietly. Then the candle began to smoke. One of the stepsisters took a pair of scissors and pretended to trim the wick, but instead, following her mother's orders, she snuffed it out, as if by accident.

"What on earth should we do now?" said the stepsisters. "There's no light in the house, and we haven't even come close to finishing our tasks. Someone must run to Baba Yaga to get some fire."

5. *an herb that would protect her against sunburn.* Vasilisa's chief attribute is her "fairness," and the sun represents the greatest threat to her beauty. For this reason the stepsisters try to force her to work outdoors, where the wind and sun can spoil her perfect complexion.

6. *Vasilisa's father had to go on a long journey.* The father's journey takes him away from home, leaving Vasilisa unprotected against the animosity between (step)mother and daughter. It is that relationship which is at stake in this story. Absent fathers are almost the rule in stories about stepmothers and their stepdaughters.

7. *in the hut lived Baba Yaga.* Baba Yaga, also known as the bony-legged one, is a monstrous, cannibalistic hag in Slavic folklore. An ogress who prefers children to adults, she lives in a hut on chicken legs in a clearing in the forest. Skulls sit on the posts of the picket fence surrounding the house. Baba Yaga rides through the air on a mortar and uses a pestle as her oar, as she sweeps her traces with a broom. She is described as having fangs that are like the blades of a knife, and her eyes turn people into stone. When she sees a victim, she lets her jaw drop and swallows the person whole. Her blue hooked nose touches the ceiling when she lies down in her little hut. While she poses a powerful threat to figures in fairy tales, she also becomes an unwitting helper and ally, providing whatever it is that the fairy-tale hero or heroine lacks.

8. *Suddenly another horseman galloped past her. His face was black.* The three horsemen, representing the times of day, also bear a resemblance to the Four Horsemen of the Apocalypse. The horseman in black is a death figure, one said to accompany Baba Yaga on her travels.

"I'm not going," said the girl who was making lace. "I can see by the light of my pins."

"I'm not going," said the girl who was knitting stockings. "I can see by the light of my knitting needles."

"That means you have to go," they both shouted to their stepsister. "Get going! Go and see your friend Baba Yaga!" And they pushed Vasilisa out of the room.

Vasilisa went into her own little room, laid out the supper she had prepared for her doll, and said: "There, dolly, eat and help me in my need. They want me to go to Baba Yaga for fire, and she will eat me up." The doll ate her supper. Her eyes glowed like two candles. "Don't be afraid, Vasilisushka," she said. "Go where they send you. Only be sure to take me with you. If I'm in your pocket, Baba Yaga can't hurt you."

Vasilisa got ready to go, put the doll in her pocket, and crossed herself before setting out for the deep forest. She trembled with fear as she walked through the woods. Suddenly a horseman galloped past her. His face was white, he was dressed in white, and he was riding a white horse with white reins and stirrups. After that it began to grow light.

Vasilisa walked deeper into the forest, and a second horseman galloped past her. His face was red, he was dressed in red, and he was riding a red horse. Then the sun began to rise.

Vasilisa walked all night and all day long. Late on the second evening she arrived in the clearing where Baba Yaga's hut was standing. The fence around it was made of human bones. Skulls with empty eye sockets stared down from the posts. The gate was made from the bones of human legs; the bolts were made from human hands; and the lock was a jaw with sharp teeth. Vasilisa was terrified and stood rooted to the spot. Suddenly another horseman galloped past her. His face was black,**8** he was dressed in black, and he was riding a black horse. He galloped up to Baba Yaga's door and vanished, as though the earth had swallowed him up. Then it was night. But it wasn't dark for long. The eyes on all the skulls on the fence began to gleam, and the clearing grew bright as day. Vasilisa shud-

IVAN BILIBIN,
"Vasilisa the Fair," 1900

Vasilisa encounters the white horseman, a symbol of the dawn, as she makes her way into a wood filled with birches. The red-eyed ravens framing the scene hint at peril. Birds of ill-omen, ravens traditionally signal death and pestilence, though in Russian epic they are symbols of the enemy.

IVAN BILIBIN,
"Vasilisa the Fair," 1900

The red horseman gallops through the forest while Vasilisa, outside the picture, watches. This horseman represents the rising sun, and he carries a torch of fire, bringing light into the woods. The frame is decorated with clover, a symbol of the Trinity used to ward off spells and witchcraft. Despite his menacing appearance, the red horseman, bringing fire and light, clearly has a salutary power.

dered with fright. She wanted to run away, but didn't know which way to turn.

A dreadful noise sounded in the woods. The trees creaked and groaned. The dead leaves rustled and crunched. Baba Yaga appeared, flying in a mortar, prodding it with her pestle, and sweeping her traces with a broom. She rode up to the gate, stopped, and sniffed the air around her. "Foo, Foo! This place smells of a Russian girl![9] Who's there?"

Vasilisa went up to the old witch and, trembling with fear, bowed down low and said: "It is I, Granny. My stepsisters sent me to get some light."

"Very well," said Baba Yaga. "I know your sisters all

9. *"Foo, Foo! This place smells of a Russian girl!"* Baba Yaga's words are reminiscent of the giant's chant in "Jack and the Beanstalk," thus reinforcing the notion that Vasilisa is the female counterpart to the British Jack. Note the importance of nourishment in the tale: Baba Yaga wants to consume Vasilisa, while Vasilisa has to feed her doll. And Vasilisa must fetch fire, the substance that turns the raw into the cooked.

IVAN BILIBIN,
"Vasilisa the Fair," 1900

As the sun sinks in the background, the black horseman, representing night and death, saunters into Baba Yaga's yard. A powerful ally of the Russian witch, he is framed by hybrid creatures akin to the Greek harpies, monsters with destructive powers.

right. But before I give you fire you must stay and work for me. If you don't, I'll have you for dinner!" Then she turned to the gate and shouted: "Slide back, my strong bolts! Open up, my wide gates!" The gates opened, and Baba Yaga rode in with a shrill whistle. Vasilisa followed her, and then everything closed up again.

Baba Yaga went into the hut, stretched herself out on a bench, and said to Vasilisa: "I'm hungry. Bring me whatever's in the oven!" Vasilisa lit a taper from the skulls on the fence and began serving Baba Yaga the food from the oven. There was enough to feed ten people. She brought kvass, mead, beer, and wine from the cellar. The old woman ate and drank everything put before her, leaving for Vasilisa only a little bowl of cabbage soup, a crust of bread, and a scrap of pork.

Baba Yaga got ready for bed and said: "Tomorrow, after I leave, see to it that you sweep the yard, clean the hut, cook supper, wash the linen, and go to the corn bin and sort out a bushel of wheat. And if you haven't finished by the time I get back, I'll eat you up!" After giving the orders, Baba Yaga began snoring. Vasilisa took her doll out of her pocket and placed Baba Yaga's leftovers before it. Then she burst out crying and said: "There, doll, have some food and help me out! Baba Yaga has given me impossible tasks and has threatened to eat me up if I don't take care of everything. Help me." The doll replied: "Don't be afraid, Vasilisa the Fair! Eat your supper, say your prayers, and go to sleep. Mornings are wiser than evenings."

Vasilisa got up early. Baba Yaga was already up and about. When Vasilisa looked out the window, she saw that the lights in the skulls' eyes were fading. Then the white horseman galloped by, and it was daybreak. Baba Yaga went out into the yard and gave a whistle. Her mortar, pestle, and broom appeared. The red horseman flashed by, and the sun rose. Baba Yaga sat down in her mortar, prodded it on with her pestle, and swept over her traces with the broom.

IVAN BILIBIN,
"Vasilisa the Fair," 1900

Broomstick in one hand, mortar in the other, Baba Yaga, her white hair blowing in the breeze, is a menacing presence. Unlike the witches of German folklore, she is not bent over with age, but rigid with rage, and there is no mistaking her for a kind old granny figure.

Vasilisa was alone, and she looked around Baba Yaga's hut. She had never seen so many things to do in her life and couldn't figure out where to begin. But lo and behold, all the work was done. The doll was picking out the last bits of chaff from the wheat. "You've saved me!" Vasilisa said to her doll. "If it weren't for you, I would have been gobbled up tonight."

"All you have to do now is prepare supper," said the doll as it climbed back into her pocket. "Cook it with God's blessing, and then get some rest so that you'll stay strong."

Toward evening Vasilisa set the table and waited for Baba Yaga. It grew dark, and when the black horseman galloped by, it was night. The only light came from the skulls on the fence. The trees creaked and groaned; the dry leaves crackled and crunched. Baba Yaga was on her way. Vasilisa went out to meet her. "Is everything done?" asked Baba Yaga. "See for yourself, Granny," Vasilisa replied.

Baba Yaga went all around the hut. She was annoyed that there was nothing to complain about, and said: "Well done." Then she shouted: "My faithful servants, my dear friends, grind the wheat!" Three pairs of hands appeared. They took the wheat and whisked it away. Baba Yaga ate her fill, made ready to sleep, and again gave Vasilisa her tasks. "Tomorrow," she ordered, "do just what you did today. Then take the poppy seeds out of the bin and get rid of the dust, speck by speck. Someone threw dust into the bins just to annoy me." Baba Yaga turned over and began to snore.

Vasilisa began to feed her doll. The doll ate everything in front of her, and repeated just what she had said the day before: "Pray to God and go to sleep. Mornings are wiser than evenings. Everything will get done, Vasilisushka."

The next morning Baba Yaga rode off again in her mortar. With the help of her doll, Vasilisa finished the housework in no time at all. The old witch returned in the evening, looked everything over, and cried out: "My faithful servants, my dear friends, press the oil from these poppy seeds." Three pairs of hands appeared, took the bin of poppy seeds, and whisked it away. Baba Yaga sat down to dine. Vasilisa stood silently next to her while she ate. "Why don't you talk to me?" Baba Yaga asked. "You stand there as though you were mute."

"I did not dare speak," said Vasilisa, "but if you'll give me permission, there is something I'd like to ask."

"Ask away!" said Baba Yaga. "But be careful. Not every question has a good answer. If you know too much, you will soon grow old."

"Oh, Granny, I only want to ask you about some things I saw on the way here. When I was on my way over here, a horseman with a white face, riding a white horse, and dressed in white overtook me. Who was he?"

"That was the bright day," Baba Yaga replied.

"Then another horseman overtook me. He had a red face, was riding a red horse, and was dressed in red. Who was he?"

"He is my red sun," Baba Yaga replied.

"Then who was the black horseman I met at your gate, Granny?"

"He is my dark night. The three of them are my faithful servants."

Vasilisa remembered the three pairs of hands, but kept her mouth shut. "Don't you want to ask about anything else?" Baba Yaga said.

"No, Granny, that's enough. You were the one who said that the more you know, the sooner you grow old."

"You are wise," Baba Yaga said, "to ask only about things you saw outside my house, not inside it. I don't like to have my dirty linen aired in public, and if people get too curious, I eat them up. And now I have a question for you. How did you get all that work done so fast?"

"I was helped by my mother's blessing," said Vasilisa.

"Oh, so that's how you did it!" Baba Yaga shrieked. "Get out of here, blessed daughter!**10** I don't want any blessed ones in my house." She dragged Vasilisa out of the room and pushed her out through the gate. Then she took one of the skulls with blazing eyes from the fence, stuck it on the end of a stick, and gave it to the girl, saying:

10. *blessed daughter.* The tale mingles pagan with Christian elements, showing how the sacred can exorcise the profane. But it also shows how the power of the good mother, incarnated in the doll, is able to defeat the bad mother, who threatens Vasilisa's welfare.

"Here's fire for your stepsisters. Take it. That's what you came here for, isn't it?"

Vasilisa ran home, using the fire from the skull to light the path. At dawn the fire went out, and by evening she

IVAN BILIBIN,
"Vasilisa the Fair," 1900

Vasilisa has succeeded in acquiring fire. Leaving Baba Yaga's hut, which rests on chicken legs and is surrounded by a fence topped by skulls, she brings fire back home.

reached the house. As she was approaching the gate, she was about to throw the skull away, thinking that her stepsisters surely already had fire, when she heard a muffled voice coming from the skull: "Don't throw me away. Take me to your stepmother." She looked at the stepmother's house and, seeing that there was no light in the window, decided to enter with her skull. For the first time the stepmother and stepsisters received her kindly. They told her that since she had left, they had had no fire at all in the house. They had been unable to produce a flame themselves. They had tried to bring one back from the neighbors, but it went out as soon as they crossed the threshold.

"Perhaps your fire will last," said the stepmother. Vasilisa carried the skull in. Its eyes began to stare at the step-mother and two sisters. It burned them. They tried to hide, but the eyes followed them wherever they went. By morning they had turned into three heaps of ashes on the floor. Only Vasilisa remained untouched by the fire.

Vasilisa buried the skull in the garden, locked up the house, and went to the nearest town. An old woman without children[11] gave her shelter, and there she lived, waiting for her father's return. One day she said to the woman, "I am weary of sitting here with nothing to do, Granny. Buy me the best flax you can find. Then at least I'll get some spinning done."

The old woman bought some of the best flax around, and Vasilisa set to work. She spun as fast as lightning, and her threads were even and fine as hair. She spun a great deal of yarn. It was time to start weaving it, but there were no combs fine enough for Vasilisa's yarn, and no one was willing to make one. Vasilisa asked her doll for help. The doll said: "Bring me an old comb, an old shuttle, and a horse's mane. I will make a loom for you." Vasilisa did as the doll said, went to sleep, and found a wonderful loom waiting for her the next morning.

By the end of the winter the linen was woven. It was so fine that you could pass it through the eye of a needle. In the spring, the linen was bleached, and Vasilisa said to the old woman: "Granny, sell this linen and keep the money for yourself."

The old woman looked at the cloth and gasped. "No, my child! No one can wear linen like this except the tsar. I shall take it to the palace."

The old woman went to the tsar's palace[12] and began walking back and forth beneath the windows. The tsar saw her and asked: "What do you want, Granny?"

"Your Majesty," she answered, "I have brought some rare merchandise. I don't want to show it to anyone but you."

The tsar ordered the old lady to appear before him, and when he saw the linen, he gazed at it in amazement. "What do you want for it?" he asked.

11. *An old woman without children.* The crone in this final episode represents another surrogate mother, one who brings Vasilisa's skills as a spinner and seamstress to the attention of the tsar. The host of maternal figures and maternal substitutes strengthens the argument that "Vasilisa the Fair" is about the empowerment of the daughter through the mother.

12. *The old woman went to the tsar's palace.* Since we are in Russia, the tsar replaces the kings and princes of European folklore.

IVAN BILIBIN,
"Vasilisa the Fair," 1900

"When the tsar saw Vasilisa the Fair,
he fell head over heels in love with
her." The tsar and his entourage
visit Vasilisa and the old woman
who helped her.

IVAN BILIBIN,
"Vasilisa the Fair," 1900

In this final decorative flourish to the
story of Vasilisa, the daisy, symbol of
fidelity, mingles with thistles and
clover, used to ward off evil spirits.

"I can't put a price on it, Little Father Tsar! It's a gift."
The tsar thanked her and loaded her down with presents.

The tsar ordered shirts made from the linen. He had
them cut, but no one could find a seamstress who was
willing to sew them. Finally, he summoned the old woman
and said: "You were able to spin and weave this linen. You
must be able to sew it into shirts for me."

"I was not the one who spun and wove this linen, Your
Majesty," said the old woman. "This is the work of a girl
to whom I gave shelter."

"Well then, let her sew the shirts," the tsar ordered.

The old woman returned home and told Vasilisa everything. "I knew all along that I would have to do this
work," Vasilisa told her. Vasilisa locked herself in her room
and began sewing. She worked without stopping and soon
a dozen shirts were ready.

The old woman took the shirts to the tsar. Vasilisa
washed up, combed her hair, dressed in her finest clothes,
and sat down by the window to see what would happen.
She saw one of the tsar's servants enter the courtyard.
The messenger came into the room and said: "His Majesty
wishes to meet the seamstress who made his shirts and
wants to reward her with his own hands."

Vasilisa appeared before the tsar. When the tsar saw Vasilisa the Fair, he fell head over heels in love with her. "No, my beauty," he said. "I shall never part from you. You will be my wife."

The tsar took Vasilisa by her white hands and sat her down next to him. The wedding was celebrated at once. Soon afterward Vasilisa's father returned.[13] He was overjoyed with her good fortune and went to live in his daughter's house. Vasilisa took the old woman into her home as well and carried the doll in her pocket until the day she died.

13. *Soon afterward Vasilisa's father returned.* As in "Hansel and Gretel" and "The Juniper Tree," the heroine is reunited with her father. Her good mother remains buried, though she could be said to survive in the form of the doll. The happy ending reveals Vasilisa's full evolution into a woman so caring and compassionate that she takes in all those who provided her with help.

14

EAST OF THE SUN AND WEST OF THE MOON[1]

Peter Christen Asbjørnsen and Jørgen Moe

1. *east of the sun and west of the moon.* The geographical location suggests an otherworldly realm, a mysterious region apart from everyday reality, especially since the sun rises in the east.

This Norwegian tale was first published in English in a volume entitled Fairy Tales of All Nations *(1849). A variant of "Beauty and the Beast," it was inspired by "Cupid and Psyche," a story that appeared in Apuleius's* Golden Ass, *written in Latin during the second century* A.D. *"East of the Sun and West of the Moon" has its origins in Scandinavian countries, but has also enjoyed widespread popularity in Anglo-American cultures. Unlike the French "Beauty and the Beast," this tale includes a coda in which the daughter has to undertake a journey, outwit a rival, and demonstrate her domestic worthiness.*

From Peter Christen Asbjørnsen and Jørgen Moe, *Østenfor sol og vestenfor måne, Norske Folkeeventyr* (Oslo: Christiania, 1841–52). Translated by George Webbe Dasent (1859), revised by Maria Tatar.

ONCE UPON A TIME there lived a poor peasant who had so many children that he did not have enough food or clothing for them. They were all pretty children, but the prettiest was the youngest daughter, who was so lovely that there was no end to her beauty.[2]

One Thursday evening late in the fall,[3] the weather was stormy, and it was dreadfully dark outside. The rain was falling so hard and the wind was blowing so fiercely that the walls of the cottage shook. Everyone was sitting

2. *there was no end to her beauty.* In many fairy tales the beauty of one of the daughters holds the promise of relieving the economic distress of a family.

3. *One Thursday evening late in the fall.* The teller of this tale offers a temporal specificity that is unusual for fairy tales. Rather than relying on the familiar formula of the first paragraph, "once upon a time," he adds precise details about the time of day and season.

EDMUND DULAC,
The Dreamer of Dreams, 1915

Inspired by fairy-tale fantasies like "East of the Sun and West of the Moon," Dulac explores the alliance between a princess and two immense, but seemingly tame, white bears.

4. *three taps.* Three and seven are privileged numbers in fairy tales, which give us three sons, three bears, three tasks, and, in this case, three taps on the windowpane.

5. *"Will you give me your youngest daughter in marriage?"* Ogres and animal suitors always seek the youngest of three daughters, perhaps because, in an earlier age, the youngest daughter in a family was, in all likelihood, the most attractive. The older sisters still around had generally not been successful, for one reason or another, in making a match.

6. *kept on telling her about how rich they would be.* The father's callous alacrity to marry his daughter to a monster reveals the degree to which marriage is connected to economic opportunity in many of the old tales. But it is also the event that sets in motion a plot with a happily-ever-after ending. While Beauty's father is reluctant to turn his daughter over to Beast, most fathers willingly part with their daughters for the sake of economic gain.

7. *until they came to a mountain.* That the castle is in a mountain suggests a kinship between this story and tales about men trapped in wilderness caves and mountain caverns. Kingdoms are often concealed in mountains in myths and folktales. Venus was said to lure her suitors into a palace hidden in a mountain, and Peer Gynt spends time in the hall of the mountain king. For those living in the countryside near mountains, the wooded terrain of the mountains possessed powerfully mysterious qualities.

8. *A table was already laid.* The castle, with its rich appointments and invisible hands, is reminiscent of the palace in "Beauty and the Beast."

around the fire busy with one thing or another. Then all at once there were three taps[4] at the window. The father went out to see what was the matter. When he got outside, he saw a great big white bear.

"Good evening to you," said the white bear.

"Same to you," said the man.

"Will you give me your youngest daughter in marriage?[5] If you do, I'll make you as rich as you are now poor," said the bear.

Well, the man thought it would not be a bad idea to be rich, but he thought he should talk with his daughter first. So he went back inside and told everyone about the great white bear outside, who had promised to make them all rich if he could only marry the youngest daughter.

The girl said "No!" outright. Nothing could persuade her to say anything else. The man went out and arranged for the white bear to come the following Thursday evening to get an answer. In the meantime he talked with his daughter and kept on telling her about how rich they would be[6] and how well off she herself would be. At last she agreed to it. And so she washed and mended her rags, and she made herself up as smart as she could. It didn't take long to prepare for the trip, for her packing didn't give her much trouble.

The next Thursday evening the white bear came to fetch her. She climbed on his back with her bundle, and off they went. After they had been on the road a good stretch, the white bear asked: "Aren't you afraid?"

No, she wasn't.

"Just hold on tight to my shaggy coat, and you'll have nothing to fear," said the bear.

The two rode a long, long way, until they came to a mountain.[7] The white bear knocked on its face, and a door opened. The two walked into a castle, where there were many rooms, all lit up and gleaming with silver and gold. A table was already laid,[8] and it was all as grand as grand could be. The white bear gave her a silver bell. If she ever wanted anything, all she had to do was ring the bell, and she would get it at once.

KAY NIELSEN,
"East of the Sun and West of the Moon," 1914

Turning her head back toward home, the heroine remains powerless to change her destiny. A diminutive figure, she makes her way through the barren Nordic landscape on the back of her betrothed.

Well, after she had something to eat and drink, it was late in the evening. She felt sleepy from the long journey and decided to go to bed. And so she picked up the bell to ring it. As soon as it was in her hand, she found herself in a chamber, with a bed that was as white as you can imagine, with silken pillows and curtains, and gold fringe. Everything in the room was gold or silver. After she went to bed and put out the light, a man came and lay down beside her.[9] It was the white bear, who cast off his pelt during the night. She was never able to set eyes on him, because he never came in until after she had put out the light, and he was up and about before the sun rose.

The girl was feeling content for a while, but soon she turned silent and sorrowful. All day long she was alone, and she longed to go home to visit her father and mother

9. *a man came and lay down beside her.* In Apuleius's "Cupid and Psyche," Cupid enters Psyche's bedroom after dark and departs before sunrise. Fairy-tale women seem to be unusually tolerant of the hedgehogs, pigs, snakes, and other beasts that steal into their rooms at night, perhaps because the animals usually manage to make the transformation into a human form before getting between the sheets.

10. *talk to your mother only when others are around to hear.* In "Cupid and Psyche," Psyche's sisters are the source of treachery. In this story the mother, who still has a deep attachment to her daughter and who was not complicit in persuading the daughter to go off with the white bear, imperils the daughter's relationship with her beloved. The mother represents the powerful attachment to home felt by young women who enter the state of matrimony, particularly in cases of arranged marriages.

11. *I have no idea what else she said.* The voice of the raconteur or storyteller often intervenes to comment on behavior or to react to an event.

and her brothers and sisters. One day, when the white bear asked what was ailing her, she said that she was feeling lonely and bored and that she wanted to go home to see her father and mother and her brothers and sisters. She felt sad because she hadn't been able to visit them.

"Well, well," said the bear. "Perhaps we can find a cure for that. But you must promise me that you will talk to your mother only when others are around to hear.**10** Never talk to her alone. She will try to take you by the hand and persuade you to go into another room with her. But if you do that, you will bring a curse down on both of us."

One Sunday the white bear came to see her and said that he was ready to take her to see her father and mother. Off they went, with her sitting on his back. They traveled far and wide. At last they came to a grand house, and she saw her brothers and sisters running around outside it. It was a joy to see how pretty everything was.

"Your father and mother live here now," the white bear said. "Don't forget what I told you, or we'll both have bad luck."

No, heaven forbid, she would not forget. After they reached the house, the white bear turned around and left.

The girl went in to see her father and mother, and there was no end to the joy everyone felt. How could they thank her for what she had done for the family. Now they had everything they could possibly want, and it was fine as could be. They were all curious to find out where she was living and how she was managing.

Well, she told them, living where she did was very comfortable. She had everything she could desire. I have no idea what else she said,**11** but it's unlikely that she told anyone the full story. That afternoon, after dining, everything happened exactly as the white bear had predicted. The girl's mother wanted to talk with her alone in her bedroom. But she remembered what the white bear had told her and refused to go upstairs. "What we have to talk about can keep," she said, and she put her mother off. But somehow, the mother got to her at last, and the girl had to tell her the whole story. She told her mother how, every night, when she went to bed, a man came into her room as soon as the light was out. She had never set eyes on him, because he was always up and about by the time the sun rose. She felt terribly sad, because she really wanted to have a look at him, especially since she was by herself all day long, and things got really dreary and lonesome.

"Oh dear," her mother said. "You may be sleeping with a troll or someone like that!" I'll give you some good advice about how to get a look at him. Take this candle stub and hide it in your garments. When he's asleep, you can light it, but just don't drop any tallow on him."[12]

Yes, she took the candle and hid it in her garments, and that evening the white bear returned and took her away.

12. *just don't drop any tallow on him.* Whenever a prohibition is issued in a fairy tale, we know that the next scene will display its violation. In "Cupid and Psyche," it is the heroine's sisters who urge her to take a good look at her nocturnal visitor and who bring about the separation of the two lovers.

KAY NIELSEN,
"East of the Sun and West of the Moon," 1914

Unable to restrain herself, the heroine lights a candle so that she can see the face of the man who comes to her bed every night. Three drops of tallow fall on the prince's shirt, and he awakens to discover that the heroine has disobeyed his command. Here the prince takes his leave and is about to return to the kingdom of the stepmother who bewitched him. The decorative richness of clothing, floor, wallpaper, curtain, bed, and door create an extraordinarily delicate compositional balance.

When they had gone a short distance, the white bear asked if everything had happened as he had foretold. She couldn't deny that it had. "Beware," he said. "If you follow your mother's advice, you will bring a curse down on us, and we'll both be done for." No, by no means!

When the girl arrived home, she went to bed, and everything happened as it had before. A man came and lay down beside her. But in the middle of the night, after making sure that he was fast asleep, she got up and lit the candle. She let the flame shine on him and saw that he was the most handsome prince you could imagine. She fell so deeply in love with him that she thought she wouldn't be able to go on living unless she could give him a kiss

KAY NIELSEN,
"East of the Sun and West of the Moon," 1914

"The next morning, when she awoke, both the prince and the castle were gone, and she was lying on a little green patch, in the midst of a dark, gloomy forest. By her side lay the same bundle of rags she had brought with her from home." A tiny figure dwarfed by the massive trunks of the trees in the forest, the heroine weeps in despair. Note the presence of a sinuous tree trunk in this and in the first of Nielsen's illustrations for the story.

right then and there.[13] And so she did, but when she kissed him, three drops of hot tallow fell on his shirt, and he woke up.

"What have you done?" he cried out. "Now you have brought a curse down on both of us. If you had just waited a year, I would have been set free! The woman who is my stepmother bewitched me,[14] so that I am a white bear by day, and a man by night. But now all ties between us are sundered. I must leave you and go find her. She lives in a castle east of the sun and west of the moon. A princess lives there, too, with a nose three ells long,[15] and she is the woman I must now wed."

The girl wept and bemoaned her fate, but that didn't help at all. The prince had to leave. She asked if she could accompany him. No, she could not. "Then tell me how to get there," she said. "Surely I can at least search for you." Yes, she could do that, but there was no road that led to the place where he was going. It lay east of the sun and west of the moon, and she would never be able to figure out how to get there.

The next morning, when she awoke, both the prince and the castle were gone, and she was lying on a little green patch, in the midst of a dark, gloomy forest. By her side lay the same bundle of rags she had brought with her from home.

After rubbing the sleep out of her eyes and weeping until she was worn out, she set out on her way, walking day after day until she got to a high cliff. An old woman was sitting nearby,[16] playing with a golden apple, tossing it up in the air. The girl asked if she knew how to find a prince who was living with his stepmother in a castle east of the sun and west of the moon and who was supposed to marry a princess with a nose three ells long.

"How do you know about him?" asked the old woman. "Maybe you are the girl destined for him." Yes, she was. "Well, well, it's you then, is it?" said the old woman. "All I know is that he lives in a castle east of the sun and west of the moon, and that you'll get there too late or never. But I'll lend you my horse, and you can ride him to my

13. *unless she could give him a kiss right then and there.* This scene gives us a reversal of the gender roles in "Sleeping Beauty." Here a young woman awakens a sleeping prince with a kiss, but instead of returning her love, as Sleeping Beauty does for the prince, this prince must flee.

14. *The woman who is my stepmother bewitched me.* Few versions of this tale reveal the motivation for the enchantment of the prince. That he takes on a beastly form has been read by psychologists as a way of enacting for children the "beastliness" of sex.

15. *with a nose three ells long.* An older measurement, an ell is about forty-five inches. The exaggerated length of the nose reveals just how repulsive this alternative marriage appears to the prince.

16. *An old woman was sitting nearby.* The encounters with three old women are followed by the encounters with the four winds. The women serve as donors, giving the girl gifts that will enable her to win the prince, while the winds transport her to the unreachable destination. Heroines of folktales are often the recipients of domestic items made out of gold, tokens of the way in which the ordinary can take on the quality of the extraordinary. In nature the girl finds the sustenance and support that she was deprived of at home.

17. *the house of the east wind.* There are many origin stories about the establishment of winds in the four corners of the earth. The winds here represent varying degrees of strength, but in many myths they represent different colors. The Apache people, for example, have black, blue, yellow, and white winds. Winds sometimes come into conflict with each other, but in this story they seem to act in concert as a relay team for the heroine.

closest neighbor. Maybe she'll be able to help you. And when you get there just swat the horse under his left ear and tell him to go back home. You're also welcome to take this golden apple with you."

The girl got on the horse and rode for a long, long time. She reached another cliff, near which sat another old woman. This one had a golden carding comb. The girl asked if she knew the way to the castle that was east of the sun and west of the moon, and she replied, like the first old woman, that she knew nothing about it, except that it was east of the sun and west of the moon. "You'll get there too late or never, but I'll lend you my horse, and you can ride him to my closest neighbor. Maybe she'll be able to help you. And when you get there, just swat the horse under his left ear and tell him to go back home." The old woman gave her the golden carding comb. She might find some use for it, she told her.

The girl got up on the horse, and again she rode for a long, long time. Finally she reached another cliff, near which sat another old woman. This one was spinning with a golden spinning wheel. She asked her, too, if she knew how to find the prince and where the castle was that lay east of the sun and west of the moon. But it was just as before. "Perhaps you are the one destined for the prince?" the old woman said. Yes, she was. But this woman didn't have any better idea of how to reach the castle. She knew it was east of the sun and west of the moon, but that was it. "And you'll get there too late or never; but I'll lend you my horse, and you can ride over to the east wind and ask him. He may know his way around those parts and can blow you over there. When you reach him, just swat the horse under the left ear, and he'll trot home by himself." The old woman gave her the golden spinning wheel. "Maybe you'll find some use for it," the old woman said.

The girl rode many a long day before reaching the house of the east wind,**17** but reach it she did. She asked the east wind if he could tell her the way to the prince who lived east of the sun and west of the moon. Yes, the east wind had often heard tell of the prince and the castle, but he didn't know the way there, for he had never blown that far. "But if you want, I'll go with you to my brother the west wind. Maybe he knows, for he's much more powerful. If you climb on my back, I'll take you there." Yes, she got on his back, and off they went in a blast.

When they reached the house of the west wind, the east wind said that the girl he had brought with him was destined for the prince who lived in the castle east of the sun and west of the moon. She had set out to find him, and he had brought her this far and would be glad to know if the west wind knew how to get to the castle. "No," said the west wind. "I've never blown that far. But if you want, I'll go with you to our brother the south wind, for he's much more powerful than either of us, and he has blown far and wide. Maybe he'll be able to tell you. Climb on my back, and I'll take you to him." Yes, she climbed on his back, and they traveled to the south wind, and I think it didn't take them very long at all.

When they got there, the west wind asked if the south wind knew the way to the castle that lay east of the sun and west of the moon, for the girl with him was destined for the prince who lived there. "Is that so?" said the south wind. "Is she the one? Well, I have visited plenty of places in my time, but I have never yet blown over there. If you want, I'll take you to my brother the north wind; he is the oldest and most powerful of us all. If he doesn't know where it is, you'll never find anyone in the world who will know. Climb on my back, and I'll take you there." Yes, she climbed on his back, and off he went at a good clip.

They did not have to travel far. When they reached the house of the north wind, he was so fierce and cantankerous that he blew cold gusts at them from a long way off. "Blast you both, what do you want?" he roared from afar, and they both felt an icy shiver. "Well," said the south wind, "you don't need to bluster so loudly, for I am your brother, the south wind, and here is the girl who is destined for the prince who lives in the castle that lies east of the sun and west of the moon. She wants to know whether you ever were there and whether you can show her the way, for she wants so much to find the prince again."

"Yes, I know where it is," the north wind said. "Once I blew an aspen leaf over there, but afterward I was so tired that I couldn't blow a single gust for many days. If you really want to go there and aren't afraid to come along with me, I'll take you on my back and see if I can blow you over there." Yes, with all her heart, she wanted to go and had to get there if it was at all possible. And she would not

KAY NIELSEN,
"East of the Sun and West of the Moon," 1914

The north wind puffs himself up and blusters to create storms and floods, but also to mobilize the power to deliver the heroine to the castle that lies east of the sun and west of the moon.

be afraid, no matter how wild the ride. "Very well, then," said the north wind. "But you will have to sleep here tonight, for we need to have an entire day if we are to get there at all."

Early next morning the north wind woke her up. He puffed himself up, blustered around a bit, and made himself so stout and large that he looked a fright. Off they went, high up in the air, as if they could not stop until they reached the end of the world.

Here on earth there was a terrible storm. Acres of forest and many houses were blown down. Ships were wrecked by the hundreds when the storm blew out to sea. The two blew over the ocean—no one can imagine how far they went—and all the while they remained on the ocean. The north wind became more and more weary. Soon he was so out of breath that he barely had a puff left in him. His wings drooped lower and lower until at last he sank so low that the tops of the waves splashed over his heels. "Are you afraid?" asked the north wind. No, she wasn't.

They were not very far from land by now, and the north wind had just enough strength left to toss her up on the shore under the windows of the castle that lay east of the sun and west of the moon. But he was so weak and exhausted that he had to stay there and rest for a number of days before he could go back home again.

The next morning the girl sat down under the castle window and began to play with the golden apple. The first person she saw was the long-nosed princess who was to marry the prince. "What do you want for your golden apple, girl?" said the long-nosed princess, as she opened the window.

"It's not for sale, either for gold or money," said the girl.

"If it's not for sale for gold or money, what is it that you will sell it for? You can name your own price," said the princess.

"Well, you can have it if I can spend the night in the room where the prince sleeps," said the girl whom the north wind had transported. Yes, that could be arranged. So the princess took the golden apple; but when the girl went up to the prince's bedroom that night, she found that he was fast asleep. She called his name and shook him, and she

18. *if she got permission to go to the prince and be with him that night, the princess could have it.* The "true bride" often tricks the "false bride" into letting her spend the night with the prince, or, as in this tale, she bribes her. The impostor bride is always eager to take possession of an object and will sacrifice the prince's welfare for material gain.

19. *some good people who had been staying at the castle.* Although fairy-tale plots are consistently situated in a pagan milieu, they often contain flourishes or nods in the direction of religious pieties. In the original Danish version the good people are referred to as Christians, that is, as men and women of faith who oppose the demonic regime of the trolls.

wept and grieved, but she could not wake him up. The next morning, as the sun was rising, the princess with the long nose walked in and chased her out.

During the day, the girl sat under the castle window and began to card with her golden carding comb, and the same thing happened. The princess asked what she wanted for it. She said it wasn't for sale, either for gold or for money, but if she got permission to go to the prince and be with him that night, the princess could have it.[18] When the girl went to his room, she found that he was fast asleep again. No matter how much she called, and shook, and cried, and prayed, she couldn't get him to respond. At the crack of dawn, the princess with the long nose came and chased her out again.

During the day, the girl sat down outside under the castle window and began to spin with her golden spinning wheel. The princess with the long nose wanted to have it as well. She opened the window and asked what she wanted for it. The girl said, as she had said twice before, that it wasn't for sale, either for gold or for money, but if she could go to the prince who was there and stay with him that night, she would give it to her. Yes, she would be welcome to do that. But now you must know that there were some good people who had been staying at the castle,[19] and while they were sitting in their room, which was next to the prince's, they heard a woman crying, praying, and calling to the prince for two nights in a row. They told the prince about it.

That evening the princess came to the prince's room with a sleeping potion, but the prince only pretended to drink it. He threw it over his shoulder, for he had figured out that it was a sleeping potion. When the girl came in, she found the prince wide-awake, and then she told him the entire story of how she had reached the castle. "Ah," said the prince, "you've come in the nick of time, for tomorrow was to be our wedding day. But now I won't have to marry the long-nose. You are the one woman in the world who can set me free. I'll say that I want to test my bride, to see if she's fit to be my wife. I'll ask her to wash the shirt with the three tallow stains on it. She'll try, for she doesn't know that it was you who dropped the tallow on the shirt and that it may be washed clean only by the one who did it, not by the clever trolls in this place. Then I'll tell her that I will marry only the person who can wash the shirt clean, and I know you can do that."

All night long, they talked of their joy and their love. The next day, when the wedding was about to take place, the prince said: "First of all, I'd like to see what my bride can do."

"Yes!" said the stepmother, in heartfelt fashion.

"Well," said the prince, "I've got a fine shirt that I'd like to wear as my wedding shirt, but somehow or other it got three spots of tallow on it, which I must have washed out. I have sworn to marry the woman who can do that.[20] Anyone who can't isn't worth having."

Well, that was no great challenge, they said, and so they agreed to the bargain. The princess with the long nose began to scrub as hard as she could, but the more she rubbed and scoured, the larger the stains grew. "Ah!" said the old troll woman, her mother, "you don't know how to wash. Let me try it." As soon as she touched the shirt, it was worse than before. Even with all her rubbing, and wringing, and scrubbing, the spots grew larger and darker, and the shirt got ever dingier and uglier. Then all the other trolls began to scrub, but the longer they washed, the darker and uglier the shirt grew, until at last it was as black all over as if it had been up the chimney.

"Ah!" said the prince, "none of you is worth a straw; you don't know how to wash. Why over there, outside, sits a beggar girl. I'll wager that she knows how to wash better than the whole lot of you. Come in, girl!" he shouted. She walked in. "Can you wash this shirt clean, girl?" he asked.

"I'm not sure," she said, "but I think I can." Almost before she had picked it up and dipped it in the water, it was as white as the driven snow, and whiter still. "Yes, you are the girl for me," said the prince.

At that, the old hag flew into such a rage that she burst

20. *I have sworn to marry the woman who can do that.* The contest between the false bride and the true bride often turns on the ability to carry out a domestic chore to perfection— for example, baking a cake, laundering a shirt, or sewing linen.

21. *the whole pack of trolls.* Trolls are supernatural creatures in Scandinavian folklore. Originally giants with great strength but little intelligence, they were later conceived of as dwarfs who inhabited caves and mountains. Often they guard treasures and haunt castles, and it is said that they burst when the sun shines on their faces.

on the spot, and the princess with the long nose right after her, and the whole pack of trolls[21] after her. At least I've never heard a word about them since.

As for the prince and princess, they set free all the good people who had been carried off and shut up there; and they took all the silver and gold with them. And they flitted as far away as possible from the castle that lies east of the sun and west of the moon.

15

MOLLY WHUPPIE

Joseph Jacobs

*Victorian writers for children tended to neglect native tradi-
tions and turned to French and German folklore for their
inspiration. The folklorist Joseph Jacobs collected two volumes
of English fairy tales in 1890 and 1893, hoping to remedy the
absence of a standard work of British folklore. The stories in
his volumes, although widely disseminated in some cases, have
failed to take hold with the power of, say, "Cinderella" or "Little Red Riding Hood."*

*"Molly Whuppie," one of the most compelling stories in
Jacobs's collection, conflates the beginning of "Hansel and
Gretel" with the plot of "Tom Thumb" and casts a girl in the
role of the nimble trickster who turns the tables on her more
powerful adversary. The tale begins tragically, with the abandonment of three children in the woods, and ends in triumph,
as Molly and her two sisters are married to princes. Undertaking three tasks, Molly outwits the giant and his wife and
collects her reward from a king. Molly appears to be without*

From Joseph Jacobs, "Molly Whuppie," *English Fairy Tales* (London:
David Nutt, 1890).

compassion, for she not only dupes the giant repeatedly but also leads him to kill his own offspring and to batter his wife. Her irreverent antics may seem heartless, but they assure her own survival and that of her sisters, enabling all to move from a condition of destitution to one of regal splendor.

1. *left them in a wood.* As in "Hansel and Gretel" and "Tom Thumb," children are taken into the woods and abandoned because there is no food at home. In "Molly Whuppie" both parents conspire to get rid of the children, while in "Hansel and Gretel" an evil stepmother persuades her husband to leave the children in the woods. In "Tom Thumb" it is the father of the children who proposes the plan to his wife, and both carry it out, but only because they cannot bear to see their children die of starvation. All these stories confront and work through primal fears about being abandoned and left to starve, both literally and metaphorically.

ONCE UPON A TIME there was a man and a wife who had too many children, and they could not get meat for them, so they took the three youngest and left them in a wood.[1] They traveled and traveled and could never see a house. It began to be dark, and they were hungry. At last they saw a light and made for it; it turned out to be a house. They knocked at the door, and a woman came to it, who said: "What do you want?" They said: "Please let us in and give us something to eat." The woman said: "I can't do that, as my man is a giant, and he would kill you if he comes home." They begged hard. "Let us stop for a little while," said they, "and we will go away before he comes." So she took them in, and set them down before the fire, and gave them milk and bread; but just as they had begun to eat, a great knock came to the door, and a dreadful voice said:

"Fee, fie, fo, fum,
I smell the blood of some earthly one.

Who have you there, wife?" "Eh," said the wife, "it's three poor lassies cold and hungry, and they will go away. You won't touch 'em man." He said nothing, but ate up a big supper, and ordered them to stay all night. Now he had three lassies of his own, and they were to sleep in the same bed with the three strangers. The youngest of the three strange lassies was called Molly Whuppie, and she was very clever. She noticed that before they went to bed the giant put straw ropes round her neck and her sisters',[2] and round his own lassies' necks, he put gold chains. So Molly took care and did not fall asleep, but waited till she was sure everyone was sleeping sound. Then she slipped out of the bed, and took the straw ropes off her own and her sisters' necks, and took the gold chains off the giant's lassies. She then put the straw ropes on the giant's lassies and the gold on herself and her sisters, and lay down.

And in the middle of the night up rose the giant, armed with a great club, and felt for the necks with the straw. It was dark. He took his own lassies out of the bed on to the floor, and battered them until they were dead, and then lay down again, thinking he had managed finely. Molly thought it time she and her sisters were off and away, so she wakened them and told them to be quiet, and they slipped out of the house.

They all got out safe, and they ran and ran, and never stopped until morning, when they saw a grand house before them. It turned out to be a king's house: so Molly went in, and told her story to the king. He said: "Well, Molly, you are a clever girl, and you have managed well; but, if you would manage better, and go back, and steal the giant's sword that hangs on the back of his bed, I would give your eldest sister my eldest son to marry." Molly said she would try.

So she went back, and managed to slip into the giant's house, and crept in below the bed. The giant came home, and ate up a great supper, and went to bed. Molly waited until he was snoring, and she crept out, and reached over the giant and got down the sword; but just as she got it out over the bed it gave a rattle, and up jumped the giant, and Molly ran out at the door and the sword with her; and she ran, and he ran, till they came to the "Bridge of one hair";[3] and she got over, but he couldn't and he says: "Woe worth you, Molly Whuppie! never you come again."

2. *the giant put straw ropes round her neck and her sisters'.* In "Tom Thumb" the ogre's daughters have golden crowns on their heads, while Tom's brothers wear bonnets. Molly Whuppie's foresight and ingenuity make her kin to the mythical Odysseus, who blinds the giant Polyphemus, and to the biblical David, who slays the giant Goliath. Like so many fairy-tale heroes, she is the underdog who must use her wits to triumph over physical superiority.

3. *"Bridge of one hair."* The Norse gods reached their home by riding over Bifrost, which could not be crossed by giants. By crossing a bridge as fine as a hair, Moslems are said to be able to ascend to heaven. In a Scottish variant of "Molly Whuppie," the heroine plucks a hair from her own head and uses it as a bridge to flee from a giant.

And she says: "Twice yet, carle," quoth she, "I'll come to Spain."**4** So Molly took the sword to the king, and her sister was married to his son.

Well, the king he says: "You've managed well, Molly; but if you would manage better, and steal the purse that lies below the giant's pillow, I would marry your second sister to my second son." And Molly said she would try. So she set out for the giant's house, and slipped in, and hid again below the bed, and waited till the giant had eaten his supper, and was snoring sound asleep. She slipped out and slipped her hand below the pillow, and got out the purse; but just as she was going out the giant wakened, and ran after her; and she ran, and he ran, till they came to the "Bridge of one hair," and she got over, but he couldn't, and he said: "Woe worth you, Molly Whuppie! never you come again." "Once yet, carle," quoth she, "I'll come to Spain." So Molly took the purse to the king, and her second sister was married to the king's second son.

After that the king says to Molly: "Molly, you are a clever girl, but if you would do better yet, and steal the giant's ring that he wears on his finger, I will give you my youngest son for yourself." Molly said she would try. So back she goes to the giant's house, and hides herself below the bed. The giant wasn't long ere he came home, and after he had eaten a great big supper, he went to his bed, and shortly was snoring loud. Molly crept out and reached over the bed, and got hold of the giant's hand, and she pulled and she pulled until she got off the ring; but just as she got it off the giant got up, and gripped her by the hand and he says: "Now I have caught you, Molly Whuppie, and, if I had done as much ill to you as you have done to me, what would you do to me?"

Molly says: "I would put you into a sack, and I'd put the cat inside wi' you, and the dog aside you, and a needle and thread and a shears, and I'd hang you up on the wall, and I'd go to the wood, and choose the thickest stick I could get, and I would come home, and take you down, and beat you till you were dead."

"Well, Molly," says the giant, "I'll just do that to you."

So he gets a sack, and puts Molly into it, and the cat and the dog beside her, and a needle and thread and shears, and hangs her up upon the wall, and goes to the wood to choose a stick.

Molly she sings out: "Oh, if you saw what I see."

"Oh," says the giant's wife, "what do you see, Molly?"

But Molly never said a word but, "Oh, if you saw what I see!"

The giant's wife begged that Molly would take her up into the sack till she would see what Molly saw. So Molly took the shears and cut a hole in the sack, and took out the needle and thread with her, and jumped down and helped the giant's wife up into the sack, and sewed up the hole.

The giant's wife saw nothing, and began to ask to get down again; but Molly never minded, but hid herself at the back of the door. Home came the giant, and a great big tree in his hand, and he took down the sack, and began to batter it.**5** His wife cried, "It's me, man"; but the dog barked and the cat mewed, and he did not know his wife's voice. But Molly came out from the back of the door, and the giant saw her and he after her; and he ran, and she ran, till they came to the "Bridge of one hair," and she got over but he couldn't; and he said, "Woe worth you, Molly Whuppie! never you come again." "Never more, carle," quoth she, "will I come again to Spain."

So Molly took the ring to the king, and she was married to his youngest son, and she never saw the giant again.

5. *he took down the sack, and began to batter it.* "Mutsmag," an Appalachian variant of "Molly Whuppie," is even more violent in its elaboration of the brute force used by the giant. "I'll make your blood run and drip like honey," the giant shouts as he is beating the sack in which he believes he has put Mutsmag. Unlike Molly, Mutsmag is less interested in marriage than in gold. Once she defeats the giant, she gets on her white horse and returns to the king: "He gave her a bag of gold for the horse and another bag for killing that giant. That made three bags of gold Mutsmag had. The last I heard of her, she was getting along very well."

16

THE STORY OF THE THREE LITTLE PIGS

Joseph Jacobs

1. *J. O. Halliwell.* A renowned British collector who sought to preserve stories and rhymes of childhood long before they were dignified with the name of folklore.

The popular story of the three pigs bears a close resemblance to the Grimms' "The Wolf and the Seven Young Kids," although that story takes a different cautionary turn by presenting the kids as falling prey to a wolf by failing to pay attention to their mother's warnings. In the British tale, indolence and lack of foresight are responsible for the deaths of the first two pigs, who build their houses out of materials vulnerable to the destructive puffs of the wolf's breath.

While this story has not entered the folkloric bloodstream with the power of, say, "Little Red Riding Hood" or "Cinderella," it is widely disseminated in Anglo-American cultures and emerged as a key story in Joel Chandler Harris's Tales of Uncle Remus (1880), a collection in which the trickster figure plays a pivotal role. In "The Story of the Pigs," a character named Runt outsmarts Brer Wolf, and in "The Awful Fate of Mr. Wolf," Brer Rabbit turns the tables on Brer Wolf.

From Joseph Jacobs, "The Story of the Three Little Pigs," *English Fairy Tales* (London: David Nutt, 1898), whose source was James Orchard Halliwell's[1] *Nursery Rhymes and Nursery Tales*, published circa 1843.

In 1933 Walt Disney Studios breathed fresh life into the story by releasing The Three Little Pigs, *a "Silly Symphony" cartoon that enjoyed great popular success. The song "Who's Afraid of the Big Bad Wolf" (written for the film by Frank Churchill) led to a reading of the story as a rallying cry against the Depression in particular and economic hard times in general. Disney himself framed the moral: "Wisdom along with courage is enough to defeat big bad wolves of every description and send them slinking away." In 1941 a short version of the silly symphony featured "Thrifty Pig," who built his house of war bonds and managed to thwart a wolf sporting a swastika on his armband.*

Since Disney, "The Three Little Pigs" has been rewritten and reillustrated countless times. Over fifty English versions were in print during the year 2000, some faithful to the Jacobs version, others updated or placed in new cultural contexts. Today we can read about Hawaiian pigs and their conflict with a shark, about Cajun pigs encountering an alligator, or Appalachian pigs getting the better of a fox. We can get the wolf's point of view, as in Jon Scieszka and Lane Smith's True Story of the Three Little Pigs, *which gives the tale a new twist by retelling the story from the vantage point of A. Wolf (Alexander T. Wolf). This amiable chap was in fact just going from door to door trying to borrow a cup of sugar to make a cake for granny. That huffing and puffing and sneezing were simply symptoms of a bad cold. The three pigs have even gone postmodern, appearing in David Wiesner's* Three Pigs *and Bruce Whatley's* Wait! No Paint!—*variants in which the trio is acutely aware that each is nothing more than a literary construct trapped in a text.*

Once upon a time when pigs spoke rhyme
And monkeys chewed tobacco,
And hens took snuff to make them tough,
And ducks went quack, quack, quack, O!

2. *three little pigs.* The prominence of the number three in fairy tales is attested to by stories such as "The Three Wishes," "The Three Billy-Goats Gruff," "The Story of the Three Bears," and "The Three Heads in the Well." This trio, like many trios of siblings, is highly differentiated.

3. *"No, no, by the hair of my chiny chin chin."* Since pigs do not have beards, Joseph Jacobs surmised that the hair on the chin points to a contamination by the Grimms' "The Wolf and the Seven Young Kids." The use of rhyme and repetition within the body of the tale adds a playful quality to the story. Many children memorize these lines quickly and recite them under new circumstances.

THERE WAS AN old sow with three little pigs,[2] and as she had not enough to keep them, she sent them out to seek their fortune. The first that went off met a man with a bundle of straw, and said to him:

"Please, man, give me that straw to build me a house."

Which the man did, and the little pig built a house with it. Presently came along a wolf, and knocked at the door, and said:

"Little pig, little pig, let me come in."

To which the pig answered:

"No, no, by the hair of my chiny chin chin."[3]

The wolf then answered to that:

"Then I'll huff, and I'll puff, and I'll blow your house in."

So he huffed, and he puffed, and he blew his house in, and ate up the little pig.

ARTHUR RACKHAM,
"The Story of the Three Little Pigs," 1918

The wolf seems to have no trouble at all blowing down the house of straw.

The second little pig met a man with a bundle of furze[4] and said:

"Please, man, give me that furze to build a house."

Which the man did, and the pig built his house. Then along came the wolf, and said:

"Little pig, little pig, let me come in."

"No, no, by the hair of my chinny chin chin."

"Then I'll huff, and I'll puff, and I'll blow your house in."

"So he huffed, and he puffed, and he puffed, and he huffed, and at last he blew the house down, and he ate up the little pig.

The third little pig met a man with a load of bricks, and said:

"Please, man, give me those bricks to build a house with."

So the man gave him the bricks, and he built his house

ARTHUR RACKHAM,
"The Story of the Three Little Pigs," 1918

No effort is required to blow down the house of furze.

with them. So the wolf came, as he did to the other little pigs, and said:

"Little pig, little pig, let me come in."

"No, no, by the hair on my chiny chin chin."

"Then I'll huff, and I'll puff, and I'll blow your house in."

Well, he huffed, and he puffed, and he huffed and he puffed, and he puffed and huffed; but he could *not* get the house down. When he found that he could not, with all his huffing and puffing, blow the house down, he said:

4. *furze.* Furze is a spiny shrub, common on wastelands in Europe. Most modern versions replace "furze" with "twigs."

ARTHUR RACKHAM,
"The Story of the Three Little Pigs," 1918

The house of bricks is resistant to the wolf's efforts to demolish it.

"Little pig, I know where there is a nice field of turnips."

"Where?" said the little pig.

"Oh, in Mr. Smith's Home-field, and if you will be ready tomorrow morning I will call for you, and we will go together, and get some for dinner."

"Very well," said the little pig, "I will be ready. What time do you mean to go?"

"Oh, at six o'clock."

Well, the little pig got up at five, and got the turnips before the wolf came (which he did about six), who said:

"Little pig, are you ready?"

The little pig said: "Ready! I have been and come back again, and got a nice potful for dinner."

The wolf felt very angry at this, but thought that he would be up to the little pig somehow or other, so he said, "Little pig, I know where there is a nice apple tree."

"Where?" said the pig.

"Down at Merry Garden," replied the wolf, "and if you will not deceive me I will come for you, at five o'clock tomorrow and get some apples."

Well, the little pig bustled up the next morning at four o'clock, and went off for the apples, hoping to get back before the wolf came; but he had further to go, and had to climb the tree, so that just as he was coming down from it, he saw the wolf coming, which, as you may suppose, frightened him very much. When the wolf came up he said:

"Little pig, what! Are you here before me? Are they nice apples?"

"Yes, very," said the little pig. "I will throw you down one."

And he threw it so far, that, while the wolf was gone to pick it up, the little pig jumped down and ran home. The next day the wolf came again, and said to the little pig:

"Little pig, there is a fair at Shanklin this afternoon. Will you go?"

"Oh yes," said the pig, "I will go. What time shall you be ready?"

"At three," said the wolf. So the little pig went off before the time as usual, and got to the fair, and bought a butter-churn, which he was going home with, when he saw the wolf coming. Then he could not tell what to do. So he got into the churn to hide, and by so doing turned it round, and it rolled down the hill with the pig in it, which frightened the wolf so much, that he ran home without going to the fair. He went to the pig's house, and told him how frightened he had been by a great round thing which came down the hill past him. Then the little pig said:

"Ha, I frightened you, then. I had been to the fair and bought a butter-churn, and when I saw you, I got into it, and rolled down the hill."

Then the wolf was very angry indeed, and declared he *would* eat up the little pig, and that he would get down the chimney after him. When the little pig saw what he was about, he hung on the pot full of water, and made up a blazing fire, and, just as the wolf was coming down, took off the cover, and in fell the wolf; so the little pig put on the cover again in an instant, boiled him up, and ate him for supper,[5] and lived happily ever afterwards.

5. *so the little pig put on the cover again in an instant, boiled him up, and ate him for supper.* The third little pig is something of a trickster figure. Like Little Red Riding Hood in some German versions of her story, he succeeds in outsmarting the wolf, and he ends up turning the predator into dinner.

17

DONKEYSKIN

Charles Perrault

"Cinderella," the story of an innocent beauty persecuted by an evil stepmother, has become our culture's most celebrated fairy-tale heroine, continuing to circulate in a variety of media, ranging from ballets and films to advertisements and plays. While its star continues to rise, its companion piece "Donkeyskin," also known as "The Dress of Gold, of Silver, and of Stars," languishes, unfamiliar to all but the most ardent fairy-tale enthusiasts. If "Cinderella" stories are driven by the anxious sexual jealousy of stepmothers and stepsisters, the plot of "Donkeyskin" is fueled by the sexual desires of fathers, whose unseemly behavior drives their daughters from home.

In tales depicting the social persecution of a girl by her stepmother, the central focus comes to rest on the unbearable family situation produced by a father's remarriage. Cinderella is consigned to the ashes, suffering in silence as she discharges one household task after another. In her story the stepmother becomes a monstrous presence, throwing her stepdaughter into

From Charles Perrault, Griselidis, nouvelle, avec le conte de Peau d'Ane et celui des Souhaits ridicules (Paris: Coignard, 1694).

a river in one version, instructing a hunter to kill her and to recover her lungs and liver for dinner in another, and sending her into a snowstorm wearing nothing but a shift in a third version.

If the heroine of "Cinderella" suffers from an absence of maternal love and affection, the heroine of "Donkeyskin" suffers from an excess of paternal love and affection. In her story mothers and stepmothers are absent, allowing the father to give free rein to the erotic pursuit of his daughter. That our own culture has suppressed the theme of incestuous desire even as it indulges freely in elaborate variations on the theme of maternal malice is not surprising on a number of counts. Since tales such as Perrault's "Donkeyskin" make for troubling reading matter for adults, it hardly seems advisable to put them between the covers of books for children.

Yet, while "Donkeyskin" raises the charged issue of incestuous desire and places the heroine in serious jeopardy, it also furnishes a rare stage for creative action. Unlike Cinderella, who endures humiliation at home and becomes the beneficiary of lavish gifts, the heroine of the so-called Catskin tales is mobile, active, and resourceful. She begins with a strong assertion of will, resistant to the paternal desires that would claim her. Fleeing the household, she moves out into an alien world that requires her to be inventive, energetic, and enterprising if she is to reestablish herself to reclaim her royal rank. To be sure, her resourcefulness is confined largely to sartorial and culinary arts, but these were, after all, the two areas in which women traditionally distinguished themselves. Donkeyskin dazzles with her dress, and she successfully uses her cuisine to draw the prince into romance.

That "Donkeyskin" is disappearing from the fairy-tale canon is perhaps not surprising. The story's critique of paternal authority and its endorsement of filial disobedience turn it into an unlikely candidate for bedtime reading. Perrault's story also traffics in racial stereotypes that can make it unattractive fare for children. Not only is the prince's infatuation linked with the revelation that a desirable "pure, white" surface lies beneath the "dark" soot of Donkeyskin's exterior, but the wedding feast is marked by the presence of Moors, "dark and ugly," who are said to frighten little children.

Still, the story of "Donkeyskin" provides a remarkable opportunity to think through the complexities of the father-daughter relationship and to show how the heroine can make the daring leap from home, striking out on her own to establish a new family.

1. *Master Donkey . . . displayed his two immense ears for everyone to see.* Donkeys play a prominent role in European fairy tales, proverbs, and folklore. The jester's symbolic beasts, they are often associated with brute stupidity, and the two ears become powerful signs of asinine behavior. This donkey, by contrast, becomes the source of endless wealth. Producing gold where dung is expected, it becomes the beastly double of the heroine, who dons its hide to disguise her unearthly beauty.

ONCE UPON A TIME there lived a king who was the most powerful ruler on earth. Gentle in peace and terrifying in war, he had no rivals. Whereas his neighbors feared him, his subjects were perfectly happy. Under his protection, civic virtues and the fine arts flourished everywhere. The king's better half, his faithful companion, was so charming and so beautiful, with a disposition so kind and generous, that he was prouder of being her husband than of being king. From their pure, tender marriage, which was full of affection and pleasure, a girl was born. She had so many virtues that they made up for the lack of additional children.

Everything in the king's palatial, luxurious castle was magnificent, and it was teeming with vast numbers of courtiers and servants. In the stables were steeds large and small, of every description, covered with handsome harnesses, embroidery, and braids of gold. But what surprised everyone who entered the castle was the sight of Master Donkey. He displayed his two immense ears for everyone to see[1] and occupied the most visible place in the palace. This absurdity may surprise you, but once you become aware of the superlative virtues of this creature, you too will agree that he was well worth his keep. Nature had formed him in such a way that, instead of dropping dung, he excreted all kinds of beautiful gold coins, which were gathered from his golden litter every morning when he awoke.

Heaven sometimes tires of letting people enjoy happiness and always mingles the good with the bad, just as it alternates nice weather with rain. One day, out of the blue, a fatal illness attacked the queen and put an end to her blissful existence. Help was summoned from all quarters, but the erudite physicians and charlatans who appeared at her bedside were unable to extinguish the fire started by the fever and fueled by it.

In her dying hour the queen said to her husband the king: "Before I die I want to make one last request of you. If you decide to remarry when I am no longer . . ."

"Oh," said the king, "don't worry about that. Rest assured that I would never in my life consider remarrying."

"I believe you," the queen replied. "Your love and devotion prove that to me. But just to be absolutely certain, I want you to swear that you will pledge your love and remarry only if you find a woman more beautiful,[2] more accomplished, and more wise than I am."

Confidence in her own qualities convinced the queen that the promise, cunningly extracted, was as good as an oath never to marry. The king, his eyes bathed in tears, swore to do as the queen desired. And the queen died in his arms. Never did a king make such a grand display of his emotions. To hear him sobbing both day and night, you would have come to the conclusion that his grief could not possibly last and that he was mourning his deceased wife like a man eager to put the business behind him as quickly as possible.[3]

And indeed, that proved to be the case. After a few months the king wanted to go ahead and choose a new wife. But that was not an easy matter. He had to keep his promise that the new wife would be more charming and attractive than the one who had just been buried. Neither the court with its many beauties, nor the country, nor the city, nor the neighboring kingdom where they were making the rounds could come up with such a woman. Only his own daughter was more beautiful, and she even possessed some qualities that his dead wife had lacked. The king himself noticed this and, burning with a desire that

2. *you will pledge your love and remarry only if you find a woman more beautiful.* The condition set by the queen for remarriage suggests that the mother is in part to blame for the advances made by the father. In some versions of this story, the mother decrees that the king may marry only the woman whose finger fits her own wedding band, and that woman turns out to be the couple's daughter. The queen becomes something of a co-conspirator, though it is still the father who stirs up the trouble in the story.

3. *like a man eager to put the business behind him as quickly as possible.* The touches of irony and stylistic flourishes, along with the verse form of Perrault's original, are signs that this version of the tale has taken a literary turn that has distanced it from its origins in an oral storytelling tradition.

4. *he took it into his head that she should marry him.* The king's passion for his daughter is often rationalized as momentary madness brought on by the death of his spouse. This is part of a pattern that absolves fathers of guilt in Western folklore.

5. *a dress with the colors of the four seasons.* Donkeyskin's attire is connected with celestial bodies (sun, moon, and stars), but also with the heavens and with the seasons. Her gross animal nature in the form of the donkey hide masks a spiritual power with a deep connection to nature.

drove him mad, he took it into his head that she should marry him.[4] He even found a philosopher who agreed that a case could be made for the marriage. But the young princess, saddened by this kind of love, grieved and wept day and night.

With a heart aching from a thousand sorrows, the princess went to find her godmother, who lived some distance away in a remote grotto made of pearls and lavishly adorned with coral. She was an extraordinary fairy, unrivaled in her art. There is no need to tell you what a fairy was in those radiant days, for I am sure that those who love you told you all about them when you were very young.

"I know what has brought you here," the fairy godmother said, looking at the princess. "I understand the depth of sadness in your heart. But with me at your side, there is no need to worry. Nothing can harm you as long as you follow my advice. It is true that your father wants to marry you, and you would be making a fatal mistake if you were to pay any attention to his mad demand. But there is a way of refusing him without defying him. Tell him that, before you are prepared to give him your heart, he must grant you a wish and give you a dress with the colors of the four seasons.[5] No matter how rich and powerful he is and no matter how much he is favored by the heavens, he will never be able to fulfill that request."

Trembling with fear, the young princess went right back to her smitten father, who instantly ordered the most renowned tailors in the land to make, without delay, a dress the color of the sky. If not, they could be assured that he would have them all hanged.

It was not yet dawn of the next day when the desired dress was delivered. The most beautiful blue of the firmament, even when it is encircled with large clouds of gold, is not a deeper azure. Transfixed with joy and with sorrow, the child did not know what to say or how to get around the agreement. The godmother whispered to her: "Ask for a dress more brilliant and less commonplace, one the color of the moon. He will never be able to give it to you."

No sooner had the princess made the request than the king said to his embroiderer: "I want a dress more splendid than the star of the night, and I want it ready without fail in four days."

The elegant dress was ready on the designated day, just as the king had decreed. When the night unfurls its veils in the skies, the moon, whose brilliant voyage makes the stars turn pale, was no more majestic than this dress. The princess admired the wonderful dress and was about to give her consent when, inspired by her godmother, she said to the amorous king: "I can't be satisfied until I have a dress the color of the sun, but one that is even more radiant than the sun."

The king, who loved the princess with a passion beyond compare, summoned a wealthy jeweler and ordered him to make a magnificent garment of gold and diamonds. He told him that if he failed to carry out the work in satisfactory fashion, he would be tortured to death.

The king did not have to go to that trouble, for the industrious worker brought him the precious work of art before the week was over. The dress was so beautiful, vibrant, and radiant that the blond lover of Clymene,[6] who drives his chariot of gold along the arc of the heavens, was not dazzled by a more brilliant light.

These gifts were so confusing to the child that she did not know what to say to her father, the king. Her godmother took her by the hand and whispered in her ear: "You don't have to stay on this lovely path. Are these gifts that you have received really so marvelous when he has a donkey that, as you know, continually fills his coffers with gold coins? Ask him for the hide of that wondrous animal. Unless I'm badly mistaken, you won't get it from him, since it is the sole source of his wealth."

The fairy was very learned, and yet she was unaware that passionate love, provided that it has some hope, takes not the least notice of money or gold. The hide was gallantly bestowed on the child as soon as she asked for it. When it was brought to her, she was filled with horror and complained bitterly about her fate. Her godmother

6. *that the blond lover of Clymene.* The allusion is to Apollo, the Greek god of light and of the sun, who fathered a son named Phaëthon with Clymene. These classical references are additional signs of the literary turn taken by this tale.

7. *The hide of the donkey will be the perfect disguise.* The skin of the donkey turns the heroine into an outcast, but it also affirms her connection to the world of nature and thus empowers her as much as it degrades her. The hide of the donkey is a fur coat or a coat of many different pelts in other versions of the tale.

arrived and explained that as long as she did the right thing, she would not have to be afraid. She should let the king believe that she was completely prepared to take her wedding vows with him, but at the same time she should be preparing a disguise and getting ready to flee all alone to a distant country in order to avoid the evil destiny hovering over her.

"Here's a large trunk," the fairy added. "We'll put all your clothes, your mirror, your toilet articles, your diamonds and rubies into it. I will also give you my wand. If you hold it in your hand, the trunk will remain hidden under the ground and will follow you wherever you go. And if you ever want to open it up, as soon as my wand touches the ground, it will appear right before your eyes. The hide of the donkey will be the perfect disguise[7] to make sure that you are not recognized. Conceal yourself carefully beneath that skin. It is so hideous that no will ever believe that it is covering anything beautiful."

The princess put on her disguise and left the wise fairy while the dew was still in the air. The king, who was just then preparing for his triumphant wedding feast, discovered with dismay that events had taken a bad turn. Every house, road, and avenue was searched forthwith, but it was all in vain. No one could imagine what had become of the princess. A profound, dark sadness spread throughout the land. No more weddings, no more feasts, no more tarts, no more sugarcoated almonds. Most of the ladies of the court were greatly saddened that they were no longer able to attend banquets, but the priest felt the deepest sorrow, for he not only was missing meals but, even worse, found nothing on the offering plate.

In the meantime the child continued on her journey, her face dirtied with mud. She put out a hand to everyone who passed her, trying to find a place to work. But these rude, vulgar people saw someone so disagreeable and unkempt that they were not inclined to pay any attention at all to the dirty little creature, let alone take her in.

And so she journeyed farther and farther, and farther still, until she arrived at a farm where the peasant's wife

ARTHUR RACKHAM,
"Catskin," 1918

A close relative of Donkeyskin, the British Catskin is barefoot and has donned animal furs as she makes her way out into the world with all her possessions wrapped in a cloth. With mountains and a desolate landscape behind her, Catskin faces real challenges as she flees home.

KAY NIELSEN,
"Thousandfurs," 1930

If Donkeyskin puts on the hide of an animal, the Grimms' counterpart to her dons all kinds of rough furs. Here, however, the animal skins cannot hide her radiant beauty, which is illuminated by light with no evident source.

needed a scullery maid who would be agreeable to washing the dishrags and cleaning the trough for the pigs. Donkeyskin was put into a back corner of the kitchen, where the valets, those insolent scoundrels, ridiculed, attacked, and mocked her all the time. They played tricks on her whenever they could, tormenting her at every turn. She became the butt of all their jokes, and they taunted her day and night.

On Sundays she was able to get a little more rest than usual. After finishing her chores early in the morning, she went to her room and closed the door. She cleaned herself up, then opened her chest, and carefully set up a dressing

8. *Did I mention that on that large farm.* The intrusion of the narrator's voice suggests an oral storytelling situation in which the teller improvises and checks facts with his audience. Perhaps because the tale is so constructed, the narrator tries to give signs that he is telling the story spontaneously.

9. *the handsome Cephalus.* A hunter in Greek mythology who was carried away for his beauty by Eos, goddess of the dawn, and who tragically murders his wife, Procris, with a magical javelin that never misses its mark.

10. *he put his eye to the keyhole.* The discovery scene is a typical feature in fairy tales that chart the flight of the protagonist from home and show how heroes and heroines preserve their anonymity until removing the cloak, hat, or other item of apparel that conceals their royal origins.

table for herself, with her little jars on top. Feeling cheerful and pleased with herself, she stood in front of a large mirror and first put on the dress of the moon, then the one from which the fire of the sun burst forth, and finally the beautiful blue dress, which the azure of the heavens could not rival. Her only regret was that there was not enough room on the floor to spread out their long trains. She loved to see herself looking youthful, in ruby and white, a hundred times more elegant than anyone else. This sweet pleasure rejuvenated her from one Sunday to the next.

Did I mention that on that large farm[8] owned by a powerful and regal king, there was also an aviary? Chickens from Barbary, rails, guinea fowls, cormorants, goslings raised on musk, ducks, and thousands of other kinds of exotic birds, each one different from the others, could fill with envy the hearts of ten whole courts.

The king's son frequently went over to that charming place to rest for a while after hunting and to raise a glass with the nobles of the court. Even the handsome Cephalus[9] could not compete with him, with his regal air and his martial bearing, which could fill the proudest battalions with fear. Donkeyskin watched him from a distance with tenderness. She had the confidence to know that, beneath the dirt and rags covering her, she preserved the heart of a princess.

"What a grand manner he has, even though he is dressed casually. How agreeable he is," she said to herself. "The beauty who has won his heart must feel happy! If he honored me with the most modest dress, I would feel myself graced far more than by all the dresses I have here."

One day the young prince was wandering aimlessly from one courtyard to another when he came upon an obscure path where Donkeyskin had set up her humble abode. By chance he put his eye to the keyhole.[10] Since that day happened to be a holiday, Donkeyskin had slipped into elegant clothes, and her magnificent dress, which was made of fine gold and large diamonds, rivaled

GUSTAVE DORÉ,
"Donkeyskin," 1861

The king mourns his dead wife while his courtiers provide advice.

GUSTAVE DORÉ,
"Donkeyskin," 1861

Death stands as a reminder of the king's loss.

GUSTAVE DORÉ,
"Donkeyskin," 1861

Donkeyskin hurries down the staircase, fleeing her palatial residence, lit up by moonlight.

the sun in its pure brightness. The prince looked at her and was at the mercy of his desires. He was so taken with her that he almost lost his breath while gazing at her. No matter what her dress was like, the beauty of her face, her lovely profile, her warm, ivory skin, her fine features, and her fresh youthfulness moved him a hundred times more. But most of all, his heart was captured by a wise and modest reserve that revealed the beauty of her soul.

Three times he was about to push the door open; but each time his arm was arrested by the admiration he felt for this seemingly divine creature. He returned to the palace, where, day and night, he sighed pensively. He didn't want to attend the balls, even though it was the Carnival season.[11] He hated the idea of hunting or of going to the theater. His appetite was gone, and everything felt painful to him. A deep, lethal melancholy was at the root of his ailment.

He made inquiries about the remarkable nymph living in one of the lower courtyards at the end of a squalid alley where you couldn't see a thing, even in broad daylight.

11. *Carnival season.* Carnival takes place immediately before Lent. Also known as Shrovetide, it is celebrated with festive merrymaking.

GUSTAVE DORÉ,
"Donkeyskin," 1861

Pulled by a sheep in a modest cart, Donkeyskin turns around to take one last look at her home.

GUSTAVE DORÉ,
"Donkeyskin," 1861

Donkeyskin keeps company with goats and sheeps, as she removes her animal skin to bathe in the river.

GUSTAVE DORÉ,
"Donkeyskin," 1861

"Guests arrived from every corner of the world and descended on the court in great numbers." Donkeyskin's wedding is celebrated with great pomp and circumstance.

"It's Donkeyskin," he was told. "There's nothing beautiful about her, and she is not at all a nymph. She is called Donkeyskin because of the hide that she wears on her back. She's the ideal remedy for someone in love. Simply put, only wolves are uglier than she is." They spoke in vain, for he never believed them. The traces left by love were so powerfully inscribed in his memory that they could never be erased.

Meanwhile, his mother, the queen, was weeping with anguish, for he was her only child. She urged her son to tell her what was wrong, but it was no use. He moaned, he wept, he sighed, but he wouldn't say a thing except that he wanted Donkeyskin to make him a cake with her own hands. The mother had no idea what her son was talking about.

"Good heavens, Madam," everyone said. "Donkeyskin is nothing but a grubby little fright, uglier and dirtier than the most filthy scullion."

"It doesn't matter," the queen said. "We must satisfy his wish, and that's all that counts." The prince's mother

HARRY CLARKE,
"Donkeyskin," 1922

"By chance he put his eye to the keyhole." Donkeyskin has removed the animal hide that concealed her beauty, and the prince, gazing at her through the keyhole, is enthralled by her beauty. Harry Clarke captures the perverse side to fairy-tale enchantments.

12. *one of her precious rings accidentally fell from her finger into the dough.* Princesses who bake their way to success often "sign" their products with rings from their fingers or with miniature spindles and spinning wheels. These dainty golden objects betray the fact that it is no mere kitchen drudge who has baked up the culinary delight.

loved him so much that she would have given him gold, if he had wanted to dine on that.

Donkeyskin took some flour that she had ground to make her dough as fine as possible and mixed it with salt, butter, and fresh eggs. Then she locked herself up in her room to make the cake as carefully as she could. First she washed her hands, her arms, and her face. Then she put on a silver smock in honor of the work she was about to undertake, and she laced it up.

It is said that she worked a little too hastily and that one of her precious rings accidentally fell from her finger into the dough.[12] But those who are in the know about how this story ends insist that she put it there on purpose. As for me, quite frankly, I believe she did, for I am sure that when the prince stopped at the door to Donkeyskin's room and looked at her through the keyhole, the princess was completely aware of what was happening. In these matters women are so discerning and their eyes are so sharp that you can't look at them for a moment without their knowing it. I have no doubts, and I can give you my word that she felt confident her young admirer would accept the ring with gratitude.

No one had ever kneaded a morsel that was as dainty as the cake baked by Donkeyskin, and the prince thought it tasted so good that, if he had been just a little more hungry, he would have swallowed the ring along with the cake. When he saw the wonderful emerald and the narrow band of gold, which revealed the shape of a finger, he was so moved that he felt incredible joy in his heart. He put the ring by his bedside right away. But his ailment became more serious, and the doctors observed how he was wasting away from day to day. Wise with experience, they used their great scientific erudition to determine that he was lovesick.

People may say bad things about marriage, but it is an excellent remedy for lovesickness. The prince, it was decided, was to marry. He took some time to think about it, then said: "I'll be happy to get married provided that it is to the person whose finger fits this ring."

The queen and the king were greatly surprised by this strange demand, but their son was ailing so badly that they did not dare to refuse. And so a search was undertaken to find the woman who would be elevated to a high rank by the ring, no matter what her ancestry. There was not a woman around who was not prepared to present her finger, and not a one around who was willing to give up the right to try the ring.

Since a rumor had been spreading that you had to have a very slender finger to aspire to marry the prince, every charlatan around, in order to secure his reputation, claimed to possess the secret of making fingers smaller. One woman, following a strange whim, scraped her finger as if it were a radish. Another cut off a small piece of it. A third squeezed it so that it would become smaller. A fourth used a certain kind of liquid to make the skin fall off so that her finger would become smaller. There was not a single trick left untried by women trying to make their fingers fit the ring.[13]

The selection began with young princesses, marquises, and duchesses, but no matter how delicate their fingers were, they were always too large to fit the ring. Countesses, baronesses, and all manner of nobility presented their hands one at a time, but they presented them in vain. Next came the working girls, whose fingers, pretty and slender (for there are many who have well-proportioned hands), seemed almost to fit the ring. But each time the ring, which rejected everyone with equal disdain, was either too small or too large.

Finally they had to summon servants, scullery maids, chambermaids, and peasant girls, in short, all the riffraff whose reddened and blackened hands aspired, no less than the delicate hands, to a happy destiny. Many girls arrived with big, thick fingers, which fit the prince's ring about as well as a rope trying to pass through the eye of a needle.

Everyone believed that the tests were over, for there was no one left but poor Donkeyskin in the corner of the kitchen. But who could believe that the heavens had destined her to rule!

The prince said: "Why not? Let her come here."

Everyone began laughing and shouted out loud: "You mean to say that you are going to let that dirty little fright come in here?"

But when Donkeyskin drew out a little hand as white as ivory and colored by a touch of crimson from under the dark skin and when the destined ring fit her little finger with unmatched precision, the court was in a state of astonishment and shock.

Everyone wanted to take Donkeyskin to the king right away, but she insisted that she wanted some time to change her clothes before appearing in front of her lord and master. If truth be told, everyone was about to burst out laughing because of those clothes. Donkeyskin arrived

13. *to make their fingers fit the ring.* This scene is reminiscent of "Cinderella" and the efforts of the stepsisters to make their feet fit the slipper.

ANONYMOUS,
"Donkeyskin," 1865

"But when Donkeyskin drew out a little hand as white as ivory and colored by a touch of crimson from under the dark skin and when the destined ring fit her little finger with unmatched precision, the court was in a state of astonishment and shock." The lovesick prince is finally able to recover when he finds the right match. As the court watches with amazement, a child sits nearby, with a book on his lap, reading intently—perhaps the story of Donkeyskin.

at the king's chambers and crossed the rooms in her ceremonial robes whose radiant beauty had never before been seen. Her lovely blond hair glittered with diamonds that emitted a bright light with their many rays. Her blue eyes, large and soft, were filled with a proud majesty, but never inflicted pain and gave only pleasure when they looked at you. Her waist was so small and fine that you could encircle it with two hands. Even showing their charms and their divine grace, the women of the court and all their ornaments lost any kind of appeal by comparison.

With all the rejoicing and commotion of those assembled, the good king was beside himself when he saw the charms of his daughter-in-law. The queen was taken with her as well. And the prince, her ardent admirer, succumbed to the sway of his passion when he found his heart filled with a hundred pleasures.

Preparations were made at once for the wedding. The monarch invited all the kings from the surrounding countries, who, radiant in their diverse finery, left their lands to attend the great event. You could see those from the East mounted on huge elephants; and from distant shores came the Moors, who were so dark and ugly that they frightened little children. Guests arrived from every corner of the world and descended on the court in great numbers.

No prince or potentate arrived there with as much splendor as the father of the bride, who, though he had once been in love with her, had since purified the fires that had inflamed his heart. He had purged himself of all lawless desires,[14] and all that was left in his heart of that wicked flame had been transformed into paternal devotion. When he saw his daughter, he said: "May the heavens be blessed for allowing me to see you again, dearest child." With tears of joy in his eyes, he rushed over to embrace her tenderly. Everyone was deeply moved by his happiness, and the future husband of the bride was delighted to learn that he was going to be the son-in-law of such a powerful king. Just then the godmother arrived to tell the whole story, and through her account she succeeded in covering Donkeyskin with glory.

It is not difficult to see that the moral to this story teaches children that it is better to expose yourself to harsh adversity than to neglect your duty. Virtue may sometimes seem ill fated, but it is always crowned with success. Even the most powerful logic is no defense against frenzied love and ardent ecstasy, especially when a lover is prepared to squander his rich treasures. Finally this story shows that pure water and brown bread are enough nourishment for young women, so long as they have beautiful clothes, and that there is no woman on

14. *He had purged himself of all lawless desires.* While stepmothers are often punished for their evil deeds, fathers are almost always excused for their behavior and absolved of guilt. Maternal malice is the cardinal sin that can never be forgiven in fairy tales.

15. *the three beauties of that famous contest.* An allusion to Hera, Athena, and Aphrodite, who were each contestants for the famous Apple of Discord, inscribed with the words "For the most beautiful," thrown by Eris (Discordia) at the wedding feast of Peleus and Thetis. The ensuing disputes over who deserved the apple and title led, eventually, to the Trojan War.

16. *children, mothers, and grandmothers.* The narrator suggests here that the story of Donkeyskin is perpetuated through a storytelling tradition with female raconteurs. The argument has a certain logic, since the story is something of a cautionary tale for young women who have lost their mothers.

earth who does not believe that she is beautiful and who does not see herself as getting the golden apple if she were to be mixed in with the three beauties of that famous contest.[15]

The story of Donkeyskin may be hard to believe, but as long as there are children, mothers, and grandmothers[16] in this world, it will be fondly remembered by all.

18

KATE CRACKERNUTS

Joseph Jacobs

The British folklorist Andrew Lang collected this story on the Orkney Islands, off the north coast of Scotland, and published it in Longman's Magazine in 1889. His colleague Joseph Jacobs subsequently edited it and included it in English Fairy Tales. "Kate Crackernuts" has motifs that connect it with many tales in this volume, but it is most closely related to the Grimms' "The Twelve Dancing Princesses," also known as "The Dancing Shoes" or "The Shoes Danced to Pieces." That story is widely disseminated throughout central Europe, where it appears to have thrived since the seventeenth century. It is included here as an example of a tale close to its oral origins, a story that has not been subjected to much embellishing and homogenizing.

"Kate Crackernuts" belongs to the "do or die" strain of fairy tales. In these tales, a princess is given a task to perform. If she fails, she loses her life; if she succeeds, she wins a prince and a kingdom. With such high stakes, one would expect the heroine

From Joseph Jacobs, "Kate Crackernuts," *English Fairy Tales* (London: David Nutt, 1898).

to show some anxiety about her journey to the green hill, but she possesses an unusual degree of serene confidence throughout her adventures. Although she heals the prince, she never really solves the mystery of his nocturnal wanderings. The green mountain to which he travels is a domain of enchantment that may be related to the Mountain of Venus in the Tannhäuser legend or to other mythological sites dedicated to the gratification of desires. The prince in "The Twelve Dancing Princesses" indulges in sensual pleasures that dissipate his strength, leaving him depleted when he returns home. As in Hans Christian Andersen's "The Red Shoes," pleasure turns to torture once the dancer has lost the power to end the dance.

"Kate Crackernuts" seems to conflate themes from many different stories. It gives us a twist on "The Kind and Unkind Girls" (with one diligent and compassionate, the other lazy and cruel). It also sounds, though fails to develop, the motif of the wicked stepmother. And it gives us a heroine who must disenchant a creature made monstrous by a spell, in this case both her disfigured sister and the ailing prince. Kate's quiet domesticity, the way that she silently gathers nuts to effect a favorable trade and cooks the bird for the prince, proves more powerful than the spells cast by the fairies.

1. *far bonnier.* Bonny in Scottish dialects means "pleasing to the eye" or "pretty."

2. *they loved one another like real sisters.* The tale gives us an unusual instance of solidarity between same-sex siblings.

ONCE UPON A TIME there was a king and a queen, as there have been in many lands. The king had a daughter, Anne, and the queen had one named Kate, but Anne was far bonnier[1] than the queen's daughter, though they loved one another like real sisters.[2] The queen was jealous of the king's daughter being bonnier than her own, and cast about to spoil her beauty. So she took counsel of the hen-wife, who told her to send the lassie to her next morning fasting.

So next morning early, the queen said to Anne, "Go,

my dear, to the hen-wife in the glen, and ask her for some eggs." So Anne set out, but as she passed through the kitchen she saw a crust, and she took and munched it as she went along.

When she came to the hen-wife's, she asked for eggs, as she had been told to do; the hen-wife said to her, "Lift the lid off that pot there and see." The lassie did so, but nothing happened. "Go home to your minnie and tell her to keep her larder door better locked," said the hen-wife. So she went home to the queen and told her what the hen-wife had said. The queen knew from this that the lassie had had something to eat, so she watched the next morning and sent her away fasting; but the princess saw some country-folk picking peas by the roadside, and being very kind she spoke to them and took a handful of the peas, which she ate by the way.

When she came to the hen-wife's, the hen-wife said, "Lift the lid off the pot and you'll see." So Anne lifted the lid, but nothing happened. Then the hen-wife was rare angry and said to Anne, "Tell your minnie the pot won't boil if the fire's away." So Anne went home and told the queen.

The third day the queen goes along with the girl herself to the hen-wife. Now, this time, when Anne lifted the lid off the pot, off falls her own pretty head, and on jumps a sheep's head.

So the queen was now quite satisfied, and went back home.

Her own daughter, Kate, however, took a fine linen cloth and wrapped it round her sister's head[3] and took her by the hand and they both went out to seek their fortune. They went on, and they went on, and they went on, till they came to a castle. Kate knocked at the door and asked for a night's lodging for herself and a sick sister. They went in and found it was a king's castle, who had two sons, and one of them was sickening away to death and no one could find out what ailed him. And the curious thing was that whoever watched him at night was never seen any more. So the king had offered a peck of sil-

3. *took a fine linen cloth and wrapped it round her sister's head.* Kate's action is reminiscent of Little Marlene's efforts to revive her brother in the Grimms' "Juniper Tree."

4. *Kate was a very brave girl.* Like many heroines in the folkloric tradition, Kate does not hesitate to face challenges, even when the risk is great. Once she passes the test of compassion (and she does so with flying colors by undertaking to rescue her sister), she is prepared for the tasks and trials that lie ahead of her.

5. *hid herself behind the door.* Kate, like many a fairy-tale heroine, does not call attention to herself and is able to conceal herself through her discretion.

ver to anyone who would stop up with him. Now Kate was a very brave girl,[4] so she offered to sit up with him.

Till midnight all went well. As twelve o'clock rang, however, the sick prince rose, dressed himself, and slipped downstairs. Kate followed, but he didn't seem to notice her. The prince went to the stable, saddled his horse, called his hound, jumped into the saddle, and Kate leaped lightly up behind him. Away rode the prince and Kate through the greenwood, Kate, as they pass, plucking nuts from the trees and filling her apron with them. They rode on and on till they came to a green hill. The prince here drew bridle and spoke, "Open, open, green hill, and let the young prince in with his horse and his hound," and Kate added, "and his lady behind him."

Immediately the green hill opened, and they passed in. The prince entered a magnificent hall, brightly lighted up, and many beautiful fairies surrounded the prince and led him off to the dance. Meanwhile, Kate, without being noticed, hid herself behind the door.[5] There she saw the prince dancing, and dancing, and dancing, till he could dance no longer and fell upon a couch. Then the fairies would fan him till he could rise again and go on dancing.

At last the cock crew, and the prince made all haste to get on horseback; Kate jumped up behind and home they rode. When the morning sun rose, they came in and found Kate sitting down by the fire and cracking her nuts. Kate said the prince had a good night; but she would not sit up another night unless she was to get a peck of gold. The second night passed as the first had done. The prince got up at midnight and rode away to the green hill and the fairy ball, and Kate went with him, gathering nuts as they rode through the forest. This time she did not watch the prince, for she knew he would dance, and dance, and dance. But she saw a fairy baby playing with a wand, and overheard one of the fairies say: "Three strokes of that wand would make Kate's sick sister as bonnie as ever she was." So Kate rolled nuts to the fairy baby, and rolled nuts till the baby toddled after the nuts and let fall the wand, and Kate took it up and put it in her apron. And at cockcrow, they rode home as before, and the moment Kate got home to her room she rushed and touched Anne three times with the wand, and the nasty sheep's head fell off and she was her own pretty self again. The third night Kate consented to watch, only if she should marry the sick prince. All went on as on the first two nights. This time the fairy baby was playing with a birdie; Kate heard one of the fairies say: "Three bites of that birdie would make the sick prince as well as ever he was." Kate rolled all the nuts she had to the fairy baby till the birdie was dropped, and Kate put it in her apron.

At cockcrow they set off again, but instead of cracking her nuts as she used to do, this time Kate plucked the feathers off and cooked the birdie. Soon there arose a very savory smell. "Oh!" said the sick prince, "I wish I had a bite of that birdie," so Kate gave him a bite of the birdie, and he rose up on his elbow. By and by he cried out again: "Oh, if I had another bite of that birdie!" so Kate gave him another bite, and he sat up on his bed. Then he said again: "Oh! if I had but a third bite of that birdie!" So Kate gave him a third bite, and he rose hale and strong, dressed himself, and sat down by the fire, and when the folk came in next morning they found Kate and the young prince cracking nuts together.[6] Meanwhile his brother had seen Anne and had fallen in love with her, as everybody did who saw her sweet pretty face. So the sick son married the well sister, and the well son married the sick sister, and they all lived happy and died happy, and never drank out of a dry cappy.

6. *they found Kate and the young prince cracking nuts together.* Although the milieu is courtly, the actual details of the story suggest a rustic context, with a couple that finds entertainment by indulging in a snack. In the end the two receive the reward that might be most appealing to peasants—never to drink out of an empty cup ("a dry cappy").

19

MASTER CAT,[1] OR PUSS IN BOOTS

Charles Perrault

1. *Master Cat.* While most western European versions of the tale feature a cat, eastern European variants favor foxes. In India the title hero is a jackal; in the Philippine Islands he is a monkey. Perrault's cat is a male, but in many European analogues the obliging cat is female and sometimes marries the miller's son after she has been disenchanted.

When George Cruikshank, the renowned illustrator of Dickens's novels, took a look at "Puss in Boots," he was appalled at the idea that parents would read the story to their children: "As it stood, the tale was a succession of successful falsehoods—a clever lesson in lying!—a system of imposture rewarded by the greatest worldly advantage!" And indeed, there is little to admire about this cat who threatens, flatters, deceives, and steals in order to install his master as lord of the realm. Puss has been seen as a linguistic virtuoso, a cat who has mastered the fine art of persuasion and rhetoric to acquire power and wealth. A trickster who understands what it takes to succeed, he moves his master from a condition of abject indigence to one of regal splendor, fulfilling his desires even before they are uttered. This Puss does wear the boots, and he stands as the agent elevating the third son to a royal rank.

Although both Giovan Francesco Straparola and Giambattista Basile published versions of "Puss in Boots," neither of

From Charles Perrault, "Le Maître Chat ou le Chat botté," in *Histoires ou contes du temps passé, avec des moralités* (Paris: Barbin, 1697).

their two Italian tales was able to compete successfully with the variant form that appeared in Charles Perrault's Tales of Mother Goose *(1697). Perrault's version attained such prominence that, where it has penetrated, it has altered the shape of older oral versions. Yet for all his near-universal appeal, Perrault's Puss in Boots has been seen as a creature of his time, a cat who models the kind of behavior required to succeed in grand society under Louis XIV in seventeenth-century France. The morals Perrault himself attached to the story either move against the grain of the narrative or are beside the point. The first, declaring that hard work and inge-nuity are preferable to inherited wealth, is belied by the fate of the third son, who neither works hard nor deploys his wits to receive a kingdom. The second moral underscores women's vulnerability to external appearances: fine clothing and youth-ful good looks suffice to win their hearts. What really matters in this story is the use of deception and ingenuity to gain the trappings of a happily-ever-after ending.*

Puss, ever cheery and well-intentioned, seems to transcend his trickery in the end when he installs his master as lord of the realm. If the tale has any real lesson, it has something to do with inspiring respect for those domestic creatures that hunt mice and look out for their masters.

A MILLER LEFT TO his three sons[2] all his worldly possessions: a mill, a don-key, and a cat. The estate was divided up quickly. No one called in a notary or an attorney, for they would have quickly consumed the paltry inheritance. The oldest son got the mill; the second son received the donkey; and the youngest got nothing but the cat.

The youngest son was heartbroken when he saw how little he had inherited. "My brothers can earn an honest living if they decide to join forces," he said. "But as for me,

2. *three sons.* In tales of three sons, the youngest, and often the stupidest, of the three is the one singled out for good fortune. It is the modest, the humble, and often the dispossessed who are elevated to a noble rank.

WARWICK GOBLE,
"Master Cat, or Puss in Boots," 1923

"The oldest son got the mill; the second son received the donkey; and the youngest got nothing but the cat." The youngest son, trying to conceal his disappointment, brings Puss his boots.

3. *pair of boots.* In Perrault's day a fine pair of boots was a sign of distinction, and this male feline creature takes pride in his footwear. Although these are not seven-league boots, they seem to endow their owner with wits and an enterprising spirit. Note that footwear figures importantly in the folklore of many countries. Think of Andersen's red shoes, Cinderella's slipper, or the red-hot iron shoes worn by Snow White's stepmother.

4. *able to catch rats and mice.* The cat's acrobatic skill in catching vermin, the scourge of European cities in earlier times, hints at his resourcefulness and promise.

once I've eaten the cat and made a muff from its skin, I will surely starve to death."

The cat listened to this speech but pretended not to hear it and said in a solemn and earnest manner: "Don't be upset, master. Just get me a pouch and have a pair of boots[3] made up so that I can get through the underbrush easily, and you'll see that you really don't have that bad a deal."

Although the cat's master was not encouraged by this declaration, he had noticed that this cat was able to catch rats and mice[4] by playing clever tricks (hanging upside down by his paws or lying down in flour and playing dead), and so he saw a ray of hope in his miserable situation.

As soon as the cat was given what he had asked for, he brashly pulled on his boots, hung the pouch around his neck, held the strings with his forepaws, and raced over to a warren that housed a large number of rabbits. He put a little clover and lettuce into the pouch, lay down next to

ANONYMOUS,
"Master Cat, or Puss in Boots"

ANONYMOUS,
"Master Cat, or Puss in Boots"

ANONYMOUS,
"Master Cat, or Puss in Boots"

An elegantly shod Puss, complete with collar and bow, makes his way out into the country.

"'Don't be upset, master. Just get me a pouch and have a pair of boots made up so that I can get through the underbrush easily, and you'll see that you really don't have that bad a deal.'" The youngest of three sons, with unmatched shoes and stockings, tries to hide his disappointment that he has inherited nothing but a cat.

"Then he waited for one of the little rabbits, one inexperienced in the ways of the world, to crawl into the sack and try to eat what was in it." The cat, proudly wearing his new boots, lures rabbits into his sack.

it, and played dead. Then he waited for one of the little rabbits, one inexperienced in the ways of the world, to crawl into the sack and try to eat what was in it.

Just as he was stretching out, he scented success: a young rabbit, still wet behind the ears, hopped into the sack. Master Cat pulled the strings in a flash, grabbed the bag, and, without feeling the least pity for his prey,[5] killed it.

Proud of his prize, he raced straight to the king's palace and demanded an audience with him. He was ushered into the chambers of His Majesty, and, upon entering, bowed deeply to the king and said: "I am presenting you with a rabbit from my lord, the Marquis de Carabas (that was the name he had bestowed on his master). He has instructed me to present it to you on his behalf."

"Tell your master that I am grateful to him and that he has given me great pleasure."

5. *without feeling the least pity for his prey.* The cat's mercilessness stands in sharp contrast with the compassion shown by heroes and heroines of fairy tales. Many fairy tales begin with a test of character, requiring the protagonist to share a crust of bread, rescue ants, or help an old woman. Puss in Boots, by contrast, is something of a rogue, who demonstrates his capacity for calculation and cunning by trapping animals.

ANONYMOUS,
"Master Cat, or Puss in Boots"

"While he was in the water, the king drove by, and the cat began to yowl at the top of his lungs: 'Help! Help! My lord, the Marquis de Carabas, is drowning!'" The cat creates an uproar in order to get the attention of the king and his daughter. The compositional similarity to Gustave Doré's rendering of the same scene is remarkable.

ANONYMOUS,
"Master Cat, or Puss in Boots"

"The ogre received him as politely as an ogre can and asked him to sit down." The contrast in size of the two adversaries is especially striking. The ogre is represented as a kind of Goliath, who will be outwitted by Puss.

MAXFIELD PARRISH,
"Master Cat, or Puss in Boots," 1914

"He was ushered into the chambers of His Majesty, and, upon entering, bowed deeply to the king and said: 'I am presenting you with a rabbit from my lord, the Marquis de Carabas.'" Pouch slung over his shoulder, Puss is given an audience with a king who rules over a kingdom of unusually rugged terrain.

Some time later, the cat hid in a field of wheat, keeping his pouch open. When two partridges entered it, he pulled the strings and caught both of them. Then he presented them to the king, just as he had done with the rabbits. The king accepted the two partridges gratefully and gave the cat a small token of his appreciation.

For two to three months, the cat continued presenting the king with game of one kind or another, always "shot by his master." One day, he learned that the king was planning to go on an excursion along the riverbank with his daughter, the most beautiful princess in the world. He said to his master: "If you want to make your fortune, then take my advice. Just go over to the river and take a swim at the spot I will show you. Leave the rest to me."

GUSTAVE DORÉ,
"Master Cat, or Puss in Boots," 1861

Puss summons help for the Marquis de Carabas, who can be seen bathing in the shadows of the trees. Puss sports not only boots, but also a cap with feathers, a belt from which his prey dangles, and a cape decorated with the heads of his victims.

GUSTAVE DORÉ,
"Master Cat, or Puss in Boots," 1861

Peasants follow the orders of Puss in Boots, who threatens them with their lives unless they lie about their master. In the foreground, several peasants offer the viewer a direct view of their backsides.

GUSTAVE DORÉ,
"Master Cat, or Puss in Boots," 1861

Peasants point the way to the palace of the ogre. Puss, lost in the woods and seeking directions, resembles the prince in the story of Sleeping Beauty.

The Marquis de Carabas did as the cat told him, without knowing exactly what good would come of it. While he was in the water, the king drove by, and the cat began to yowl at the top of his lungs: "Help! Help! My lord, the Marquis de Carabas, is drowning!"

At the sound of the yowling, the king stuck his head out the coach window, and when he recognized the cat that had brought him game so many times, he ordered his guards to hurry to the aid of the Marquis de Carabas.

While the guards were rescuing the poor Marquis de Carabas, the cat went up to the royal coach and told the king that thieves had stolen his master's clothing while he was swimming. He had done everything he could by shouting, "Stop the thieves!" but it was no use. In reality, the scoundrel had hidden the clothes under a rock.

The king ordered the officers of the royal wardrobe to fetch one of his finest suits for the Marquis de Carabas. The king paid him a thousand compliments. Since the

GUSTAVE DORÉ,
"Master Cat, or Puss in Boots," 1861

The ogre, whose appetite is voracious and who does not seem to appreciate any diversion from dinner, receives Puss in Boots. On the table can be seen hors d'oeuvres and the main course: a delicate dish of infants along with a dismembered cow.

ANONYMOUS,
"Master Cat, or Puss in Boots," 1865

Wearing an impressive pair of boots, this gigantic cat arches his back and yowls for help with all his might. The evident lack of danger for his master is not obvious to those in the coach. This design seems to reprise Doré's engraving of the same scene.

fine clothes that the marquis was wearing flattered him (he was both handsome and statuesque), the king's daughter found him much to her liking. All the Marquis de Carabas had to do was to cast two or three respectful and somewhat tender glances in her direction to make her fall head over heels in love with him.

The king insisted that the marquis ride in his carriage and accompany them on their excursion. The cat, delighted to see that his plan was succeeding, ran on ahead. When he came across some peasants who were mowing a field, he said: "Listen to me, my good people. If you do not say that the fields you are mowing belong to the Marquis de Carabas, each and everyone of you will be cut into little pieces until you look like chopped meat!"

The king did not fail to ask the mowers whose field they were mowing: "It belongs to our lord, the Marquis de Carabas," they all said in unison, for the cat had frightened them with his threats.

"You have a very substantial inheritance there," the king said to the Marquis de Carabas.

"You can see, Sire, that this field offers an abundant yield every year," the marquis replied.

Master Cat made a point of staying ahead of the coach. When he met some reapers, he said: "Listen to me, my good people. If you do not say that all of this wheat you are reaping belongs to the Marquis de Carabas, you will be cut into little pieces until you look like chopped meat."

The king drove by a moment later and wanted to know who owned the wheat fields in the vicinity. "They belong to the Marquis de Carabas," the mowers all replied, and the king once more expressed his pleasure to the marquis.

Master Cat made a point of staying in front of the coach, and he said the same thing to everyone he met. The king was astonished at the vast amount of property owned by the Marquis de Carabas.

At last Master Cat arrived at a beautiful castle owned by an ogre[6] who was renowned for his wealth. All the

6. *a beautiful castle owned by an ogre.* The castle is sometimes owned by a king, who has the misfortune to be absent at the time of Puss's visit, and who loses his real estate. The ogre is, in this case, the symbolic equivalent of a feudal lord.

ARTHUR RACKHAM,
"Master Cat, or Puss in Boots," 1913

A dapper Puss pulls the bell at the castle door, summoning the ogre to greet his guest.

7. *you have the ability to transform yourself into any animal at all.* Tricking the ogre into using his shape-shifting powers to turn into a creature that can be caught is a motif that appears in many folktales.

lands through which the king had been traveling were in his domain. The cat, who had made a point of finding out who this ogre was and learning the extent of his powers, asked for an audience. He claimed that he could not possibly be so close to his castle without paying his respects.

The ogre received him as politely as an ogre can and asked him to sit down.

"It has been said," the cat stated, "that you have the ability to transform yourself into any animal at all.[7] I'm told that you can, for example, turn yourself into a lion or an elephant."

"It's true," replied the ogre brusquely, "and just to prove it, I will turn into a lion."

The cat was so terrified at seeing a lion before him that he instantly scurried up to the gutters on the roof, not without some pain and peril, for his boots were not made for walking on tiles.

A little later, when the cat saw that the ogre had turned back to his former state, he scampered back down and admitted that he had been terrified.

"It has also been said," the cat declared, "but I can hardly believe it, that you have the power to take the shape of small animals. I've heard, for example, that you can change into a rat or a mouse. I confess that it seems utterly impossible to me."

"Impossible?" the ogre replied. "Take a look."

At that moment, he transformed himself into a mouse, which ran across the floor. As soon as the cat saw it, he pounced on it and ate it up.

Meanwhile, the king, who could see the beautiful castle of the ogre from his coach, was hoping to enter it. The cat heard the sound of the coach rolling over the drawbridge, ran to meet it, and said to the king: "Your Majesty, welcome to the castle of the Marquis de Carabas!"

"What?" the king shouted. "Does this castle also belong to you, Monsieur Marquis? I have never seen anything as beautiful as this courtyard and the buildings surrounding it. Let's go inside, if you please."

The marquis took the hand of the young princess, and

HARRY CLARKE,
"Master Cat, or Puss in Boots," 1922

"The marquis took the hand of the young princess, and they followed the king, who went up the stairs." A proud Puss surveys the success of his project.

they followed the king, who went up the stairs. When they entered the grand hall, they discovered a magnificent repast prepared by the ogre for his friends, who were supposed to see him that very day, but who did not dare enter, knowing that the king was there.

The king was as charmed by the many qualities of the Marquis de Carabas, as was his daughter, who remained head over heels in love with him. Realizing how much wealth he possessed, the king said to him, after having quaffed five or six glasses of wine: "It's up to you whether you want to become my son-in-law or not, Monsieur Marquis."

The marquis, bowing deeply, accepted the honor conferred on him by the king. That very day he married the princess. The cat became a great lord and never again had to run after mice, except when he wanted to amuse himself.

MORAL

However great the benefit
Of inheriting a tidbit
Handed down from father to son.
Young people with industry
Will prefer using ingenuity
Even if the gains are hard-won.

SECOND MORAL

If a miller's son can have success
In winning the heart of a fair princess
And drawing tender gazes from her,
Then watch how his manner, youth, and dress,
Inspire in her tenderness,
They count for something, you'll concur.

20

THE STORY OF THE THREE BEARS

Anonymous

The British poet Robert Southey was the first to record "The Story of the Three Bears" in narrative form, in his anonymous miscellany The Doctor, *which appeared in 1837, the same year that Queen Victoria took the throne. It has been speculated that Southey did not rely on oral sources but instead conflated a Norwegian story about three bears with the scene from the Grimms' "Snow White" in which the heroine enters the cottage of the dwarfs. The little old woman seems to be Southey's own invention.*

A metric rendition penned by Eleanor Mure six years earlier for her four-year-old nephew described the story as a "celebrated nursery tale." In both Southey's version and Mure's, a mannerless old woman is the intruder in the bears' home. A little girl was substituted for the old woman by Joseph Cundall, who edited A Treasury of Pleasure Books *in 1850. The British storyteller Flora Annie Steel turned the girl's name into Goldilocks in her* English Fairy Tales *of 1918, but the girl also went by the names Silver-Hair, Silverlocks, and Goldenlocks.*

From *The Story of the Three Bears* (London: Frederick Warne, 1967).

The relationship among the bears has also changed over time. At first they appear to be a random trio of friends or brothers, but by 1852 they had become a family—mother, father, and baby bear.

Goldilocks has nearly as many endings as she has names. In some versions she runs into the woods; in others she returns home; in still others she vows to be a good girl after her narrow escape. The girl heroines in "The Story of the Three Bears" fare far better than their aged counterparts in the first recorded versions. Southey's old woman is described as a "vagrant" who deserves to be in the house of correction, while Mure's "delinquent" old woman suffers a worse fate:

> On the fire [the bears] threw her, but burn her they couldn't;
> In the water they put her, but drown there she wouldn't;
> They seize her before all the wondering people,
> And chuck her aloft on St. Paul's church-yard steeple.

While the old woman's punishment takes a burlesque turn, her younger successors become part of a cautionary tale intended to teach children lessons about the hazards of wandering off on their own and exploring unfamiliar territory. Like "The Three Little Pigs," this story takes advantage of repetitive formulas to capture the child's attention and to drive home a point about safety and shelter.

For Bruno Bettelheim, "Goldilocks and the Three Bears" fails to encourage children "to pursue the hard labor of solving, one at a time, the problems which growing up presents." Furthermore the story does not end, as fairy tales should, with "any promise of future happiness awaiting those who have mastered their oedipal situation as a child." Despite the story's popularity, it is ultimately a tale that takes an escapist turn and fails to help the child reading it "gain emotional maturity." Bettelheim's reading is perhaps too invested in instrumentalizing fairy tales, that is, in turning them into vehicles that convey messages and set forth behavioral models for the child. While the story may not solve oedipal issues and sibling rivalry as Bettelheim believes that "Cinderella" does, it suggests the importance of respecting property and the consequences of just "trying out" things that do not belong to you.

The version offered here is the standard rewriting that accommodates the figure of Goldilocks. Southey's "The Story of the Three Bears" is included as appendix 2.

ONCE UPON A TIME there were Three Bears who lived together in a house of their own, in a wood. One of them was a Little, Small, Wee Bear; and one was a Middle-sized Bear, and the other was a Great, Huge Bear. They had each a pot for their porridge, a little pot for the Little, Small, Wee Bear; and a middle-sized pot for the Middle Bear, and a great pot for the Great, Huge Bear. And they had each a chair to sit in; a little chair for the Little, Small, Wee Bear, and a middle-sized chair for the Middle Bear and a great chair for the Great, Huge Bear. And they had each a bed to sleep in; a little bed for the Little, Small, Wee Bear; and a middle-sized bed for the Middle Bear; and a great bed for the Great, Huge Bear.

One day, after they had made the porridge for their breakfast and had poured it into their porridge-pots, they walked out into the wood while the porridge was cooling that they might not burn their mouths by beginning too soon to eat it.[1] And while they were walking, a little Girl called Goldilocks came to the house. First she looked in at the window, and then she peeped in at the keyhole; and seeing nobody in the house, she turned the handle of the door. The door was not fastened, because the Bears were good Bears, who did nobody any harm, and never suspected that anybody would harm them. So Goldilocks opened the door, and went in; and well pleased she was when she saw the porridge on the table. If she had been a thoughtful little Girl, she would have waited till the Bears came home, and then, perhaps, they would have asked her to breakfast; for they were good Bears,—a little rough

1. *that they might not burn their mouths by beginning too soon to eat it.* The story, even in its early versions, is encoded with all kinds of comments about appropriate manners. In most versions the bears are models of decorum, while the old lady and Goldilocks are uncouth intruders.

R. ANDRÉ,
"Goldilocks and the Three Bears"

Cutting elegant figures, the three bears set out on a morning stroll, unaware that their house is about to be invaded by an intruder.

R. ANDRÉ,
"Goldilocks and the Three Bears"

After testing the other two containers of porridge, Goldilocks finds the one belonging to the small bear "just right." The small bear's toys, including a stuffed bear, can be seen in the foreground.

or so, as the manner of Bears is, but for all that very good-natured and hospitable. But the porridge looked tempting, and she set about helping herself.

So first she tasted the porridge of the Great, Huge Bear, and that was too hot for her; and she said a bad word about that. And then she tasted the porridge of the Middle Bear, and that was too cold for her; and she said a bad word about that too. And then she went to the porridge of the Little, Small, Wee Bear, and tasted that; and that was neither too hot, nor too cold, but just right; and she liked it so well, that she ate it all up.

Then Goldilocks sat down in the chair of the Great, Huge Bear, and that was too hard for her. And then she sat down in the chair of the Middle Bear, and that was too soft for her. And then she sat down in the chair of the Little, Small, Wee Bear, and that was neither too hard, nor too soft, but just right. So she seated herself in it, and there she sat till the bottom of the chair came out, and down came hers, plump upon the ground.

Then Goldilocks went upstairs into the bedchamber in which the three Bears slept. And first she lay down upon the bed of the Great, Huge Bear; but that was too high at the head for her. And next she lay down upon the bed of the Middle Bear; and that was too high at the foot for her. And then she lay down upon the bed of the Little, Small, Wee Bear; and that was neither too high at the head, nor at the foot, but just right. So she covered herself up comfortably, and lay there till she fell fast asleep.

By this time the Three Bears thought their porridge would be cool enough; so they came home to breakfast. Now Goldilocks had left the spoon of the Great Huge Bear standing in his porridge.

"Somebody has been at my porridge!"

said the Great, Huge Bear, in his great, rough, gruff voice.[2] And when the Middle Bear looked at his, he saw that the spoon was standing in it too.

"Somebody has been at my porridge!"

said the Middle Bear, in his middle voice.

Then the Little, Small, Wee Bear looked at his, and there was the spoon in the porridge-pot, but the porridge was all gone.

"Somebody has been at my porridge, and has eaten it all up!"

said the Little, Small, Wee Bear, in his little, small, wee voice.

Upon this, the Three Bears, seeing that someone had entered their house, and eaten up the Little, Small, Wee Bear's breakfast, began to look about them. Now Goldilocks had not put the hard cushion straight when she rose from the chair of the Great, Huge Bear.

2. *said the Great, Huge Bear, in his great, rough, gruff voice.* Southey used different typefaces and styles to reflect the variations in the voices of the bears. These distinctions ultimately led to the construction of differences in the gender and age of the bears.

"Somebody has been sitting in my chair!"

said the Great, Huge Bear, in his great, rough, gruff voice.

And Goldilocks had squatted down the soft cushion of the Middle Bear.

"Somebody has been sitting in my chair!"

said the Middle Bear, in his middle voice.

And you know what Goldilocks had done to the third chair.

> "Somebody has been sitting in my chair,
> and has sat the bottom of it out!"

said the Little, Small, Wee Bear, in his little, small, wee voice.

Then the Three Bears thought it necessary that they should make further search; so they went upstairs into

ARTHUR RACKHAM,
"The Story of the Three Bears," 1933

The three bears can hardly believe their eyes when they discover that an intruder has tasted their porridge and tried out their chairs. The small bear seems devastated by the sight of his demolished chair.

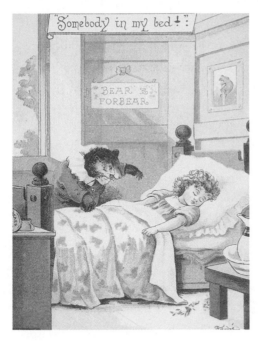

R. ANDRÉ,
"Goldilocks and the Three Bears"

Goldilocks slumbers peacefully in a bedroom tastefully appointed for a small bear, who appears shocked by the discovery of a girl in his bed.

R ANDRÉ,
"Goldilocks and the Three Bears"

This Goldilocks may be saved, but she just barely makes it out the window, and the Great, Huge Bear holds a scrap of dress, indicating just how close a call it was.

their bedchamber. Now Goldilocks had pulled the pillow of the Great, Huge Bear, out of its place.

"Somebody has been lying in my bed!"

said the Great, Huge Bear, in his great, rough, gruff voice.

And Goldilocks had pulled the bolster of the Middle Bear out of its place.

"Somebody has been lying in my bed!"

said the Middle Bear, in his middle voice.

And when the Little, Small, Wee Bear came to look at his bed, there was the bolster in its place; and the pillow in its place upon the bolster; and upon the pillow was the head of Goldilocks—which was not in its place, for she had no business there.[3]

3. *for she had no business there.* While we frame the story today as a tale about finding what is "just right," an earlier age looked on Goldilocks as an intruder, a child unable to control herself when it comes to possessions belonging to others.

"Somebody has been lying in my bed and here she is!"

said the Little, Small, Wee Bear, in his little, small, wee voice.

Goldilocks had heard in her sleep the great, rough, gruff voice of the Great, Huge Bear; but she was so fast asleep that it was no more to her than the roaring of wind, or the rumbling of thunder. And she had heard the middle voice of the Middle Bear, but it was only as if she had heard someone speaking in a dream. But when she heard the little, small, wee voice of the Little, Small, Wee Bear, it was so sharp, and so shrill, that it awakened her at once. Up she started; and when she saw the Three Bears on one side of the bed, she tumbled herself out at the other, and ran to the window. Now the window was open, because the Bears, like good, tidy Bears, as they were, always opened their bedchamber window when they got up in the morning. Out Goldilocks jumped; and ran away as fast as she could run—never looking behind her; and what happened afterwards I cannot tell. But the Three Bears never saw anything more of her.

21

TOM THUMB[1]

Charles Perrault

Like "Hansel and Gretel," "Jack and the Beanstalk," and
"Molly Whuppie," "Tom Thumb" recounts the triumph of the
small and meek over a powerful adversary. Tom Thumb sin-
glehandedly outwits and defeats the ogre and returns home a
hero, rescuing his parents from the poverty that had led them
to turn their children out into the woods.

In the early modern France of Perrault's world, life was a
struggle against poverty, disease, and famine. A woman living
in an earlier age "could not conceive of mastering nature," as
Robert Darnton puts it, "so she conceived as God willed it—
and as Tom Thumb's mother did in 'Le Petit Poucet.'" Additional mouths to feed could mean the difference between
survival and starvation, and child abandonment for economic
reasons, though rare, did occur.

In Perrault's version of the encounter between children and
an ogre, both parents are reluctant to part with their children.
Their discussions on the subject, however, bear a greater

1. *Tom Thumb.* While the name Tom Thumb
suggests British origins to this tale, it seems
preferable to Little Thumbling, a more literal
rendering of the French Petit Poucet. Hop o'
My Thumb is another sobriquet applied to
this hero.

From Charles Perrault, "Le Petit Poucet," in *Histoires ou contes du temps
passé, avec des moralités* (Paris: Barbin, 1697).

resemblance to marital squabbles than to painful struggles to find a way to survive. At times Perrault seems undecided about whether to move in the mode of fairy-tale melodrama or social satire. Tom Thumb, despite his betrayal of the ogre's wife and her hospitality and his theft of the ogre's possession, remains a charming rogue. The coda to the tale relating his fate after the conquest of the ogre reveals Perrault's deep cynicism about the social codes of the era in which he lived.

2. *the youngest was only seven.* Tom Thumb's mother bears children in nearly biblical proportions. Large families were common in seventeenth-century France, especially since the rate of infant mortality was so high.

3. *the underdog in the family.* The youngest of the boys may be the underdog, but he will prove his mettle in the course of the tale.

4. *a year of misfortune.* Robert Darnton has emphasized that Perrault's tales were written down in an era of plagues, famine, and wars, when life was "nasty, brutish, and short."

ONCE UPON A TIME there lived a woodcutter and his wife who had seven children, all boys. The oldest was only ten years old, and the youngest was only seven.[2] Everyone was astonished that the woodcutter had had so many children in so short a time, but his wife didn't waste any time, and she never had fewer than two at a time.

These people were very poor. Having seven children was a great burden, because not one of them was able to earn his own living. To their great distress, the youngest was very sickly and did not speak a word. They mistook for stupidity what was in reality the sign of a kind and generous nature. This youngest boy was very small. At birth he was hardly larger than a thumb, and as a result he was called Tom Thumb. The poor child was the underdog in the family,[3] and he got the blame for everything. All the same, he was the wisest and shrewdest of the brothers, and although he may have spoken little, he listened carefully to everything.

There came a year of misfortune,[4] when famine was so widespread that these poor people resolved to get rid of their children. One evening, after the children had gone to bed, the woodcutter was sitting by the fire with his wife. His heart was heavy with sorrow when he said to her: "It

5. *we can disappear without their noticing it.* In Perrault's story the father takes the initiative in the plan to abandon the children in the woods. His decision is framed as an act of compassion—he cannot bear to watch the children die a slow, painful death.

6. *weeping, went off to bed.* Unlike the stepmother of Hansel and Gretel, the mother of the boys is genuinely disturbed by the turn of events.

GUSTAVE DORÉ,
"Tom Thumb," 1861

Tom Thumb eavesdrops on his parents as they discuss their plan to take the seven children into the woods. Although the woodcutter has managed to lay in a supply of firewood, the empty dish on the floor and the emaciated state of cat and dog are signs of the famine that has come over the land.

must be obvious to you that we can no longer feed our children. I refuse to watch them die of hunger before my very eyes, and I've made up my mind to take them out into the woods tomorrow and to leave them there. It won't be difficult, for collecting firewood will distract them, and we can disappear without their noticing it."**5**

"Oh," cried the woodcutter's wife, "do you mean to say that you have the heart to abandon your own children?" Her husband tried in vain to remind her of their terrible poverty, but she would not give her consent. She was poor, but she was still their mother. In the end, however, when she thought about how distressing it would be to watch them die of hunger, she agreed to the plan and, weeping, went off to bed.**6**

Tom Thumb heard everything that was said. While lying in bed he realized that serious things were being dis-

GUSTAVE DORÉ,
"Tom Thumb," 1861

Tom Thumb goes to the edge of a brook to gather the white pebbles that he will use to mark the route leading back home. A diminutive figure, he appears even smaller against the dense foliage of the forest.

GUSTAVE DORÉ,
"Tom Thumb," 1861

The woodcutter leads the way into the dark forest, while Tom, the seventh and smallest of the children, drops the pebbles that he has been carrying in his pocket to mark the path. Tom is a part of the family line, but he is also singled out as the unique figure who stands in the spotlight.

GUSTAVE DORÉ,
"Tom Thumb," 1861

Tom's weary brothers begin to cry when they realize that they are alone. Tom, confident that he can find the way back home, shows no signs of distress. The dark, forbidding woods offer no consolation.

cussed, and he got up quietly and slipped under his father's stool in order to listen without being seen. He went back to bed, but didn't sleep a wink for the rest of the night, for he was thinking about what to do. In the morning he got up very early and went to the bank of the river. There he filled his pockets with little white pebbles and returned home.

The family set out for the woods, and Tom Thumb did not say a word to his brothers about what he knew. They entered a forest so dense that at ten paces they could not see each other. The woodcutter began his work, and the children started collecting twigs for firewood. The father and mother, seeing them busy at their work, stole gradually away, and then suddenly dashed off along a little side path.

When the children realized that they were all alone, they began to weep and sob with all their might. Tom Thumb let them cry, since he was confident that he would be able to get them back home. On the way, he had dropped the little white pebbles that he had been carrying in his pocket.

"Don't be afraid, brothers," he said to them. "Mother and Father have left us here, but I will take you back home again. Just follow me."

They fell in behind him, and he took them straight home by the same path they had taken into the forest. At first they were afraid to go into the house. Instead, they leaned against the door to hear what their father and mother were saying. Now, the woodcutter and his wife had no sooner reached home than the lord of the manor sent them a sum of ten crowns that he had owed them for a long time and that they had despaired of ever getting. This gave them a new lease on life, for the poor creatures had been dying of hunger.

The woodcutter sent his wife off to the butcher at once,[7] and since it had been such a long time since they had eaten anything, she bought three times more meat than was needed for two people to dine. When they sat down at the table, the woodcutter's wife said: "Alas! Where are our poor children now! They could get a good meal from our leftovers. Mind you, William, it was you who wanted to abandon them. I said over and over again that we would regret it. What are they doing now in the forest? God in heaven, the wolves may already have eaten them! What a monster you are for having abandoned your children."

The woodcutter finally lost his patience, for she had repeated more than twenty times that he would regret it and that she had told him so. He threatened to beat her if she did not hold her tongue. It was not that the woodcutter was any less distressed than his wife, but she drove him crazy, and he was of the same opinion as many other people, who like women to say the right thing, but are troubled when they are always right. The woodcutter's

7. *The woodcutter sent his wife off to the butcher at once.* Peasants living in seventeenth-century France often subsisted on porridges, gruels, and stews, rarely having the opportunity to eat meat, which was considered a real luxury.

wife burst into tears: "Alas, where are my children now, my poor children?"

She said it so loudly that the children, who were at the door, heard it and began to cry out at once: "Here we are! Here we are!"

She rushed to open the door for them, and, as she kissed them, she said: "How happy I am to see you again, dear children! You must be very tired and very hungry. And you, little Pierrot, how muddy you are! Come and let me wash you!"

Pierrot was the oldest son, whom she loved more than

GUSTAVE DORÉ,
"Tom Thumb," 1861

Tom Thumb is the first to eat after the seven boys return home. The others strain to get some food in their bowls. Note how the six boys are now all the same size and that the mother's features have softened considerably from the first illustration in this series. The centrality of food in fairy tales is emphatically affirmed in this portrait of Tom Thumb's family.

all the others because he was something of a redhead, and she herself had reddish hair.

They sat down at the table and ate with an appetite that gave pleasure to their father and mother. They all talked at once as they told of how frightened they had been in the forest.

The good people were overjoyed to have their children back with them again, but the pleasure lasted only as long as the ten crowns. When the money was spent, they lapsed back into their earlier despair. Once again they decided to abandon the children, and to make sure they would not fail this time, they took them much farther away than the first time. But they were not able to talk about it quietly enough to escape being heard by Tom Thumb, who made up his mind to get out of this difficulty just as he had on the previous occasion. Although he was up early in the morning to go and collect his little stones, this time he could not carry out his plan because he found the door to the house had a double lock on it.

He could not think what to do until the woodcutter's wife gave them each a piece of bread for breakfast. Then it occurred to him to use the bread instead of the stones, by scattering crumbs along the path they were taking. He tucked his piece tightly into his pocket.

The father and mother took them into the deepest and darkest part of the forest, and as soon as they got there, they slipped off on a side path and abandoned them. This did not cause Tom Thumb much distress, for he was sure that he would be able to find the way back by following the bread crumbs he had scattered on the path. But to his dismay he could not find a single crumb. Birds had come along and eaten them all up.

They were in real trouble now, for with every step they went farther astray and plunged deeper and deeper into the forest. Night fell, and a strong wind arose, which made them feel anxious and scared. Everywhere they seemed to hear the howling of wolves that were coming toward them to eat them up. They hardly dared to talk with each other or even to turn their heads. Then it began raining so heavily that they were soaked to the bone. At every step they tripped and fell into the mud, getting up again all covered with mud and not knowing what to do with their hands.

Tom Thumb climbed to the top of a tree to take a look around. Surveying the area, he could see a little light that

GUSTAVE DORÉ,
"Tom Thumb," 1861

Tom Thumb may be diminutive, but he is both spirited and fearless. Climbing to the top of a tree, he catches sight of the ogre's abode, while his brothers await his descent.

GUSTAVE DORÉ,
"Tom Thumb," 1861

The ogre's wife puts the spotlight on the seven boys, six of whom huddle together in fear of the unknown. Tom doffs his cap and begs the ogre's wife for a night's lodging. The bat presiding over the entrance and the twin skulls on each side of the door do not bode well for the safety of the petitioners.

8. *a good woman opened the door.* The ogre's wife, as in "Jack and the Beanstalk," is a benevolent figure who takes pity on the children and offers them shelter.

looked like a candle far away on the other side of the forest. He climbed down the tree and was disappointed to find that, once back on the ground, he couldn't see the light any more. After walking some distance in the direction of the light, however, he caught a glimpse of it, as they were about to leave the forest. At last they reached the house where the light was burning, not without a good deal of anxiety, for they lost sight of it every time they had to go down into a hollow. They knocked at the door, and a good woman opened the door.**8** She asked them what they wanted.

Tom Thumb explained that they were poor children who had lost their way in the forest and who had come begging for a night's lodging. Noticing what lovely children they were, the woman began to weep: "Alas, my poor children! Don't you realize where you are? Haven't you ever heard that this house belongs to an ogre who eats little children?"

"Alas, Madam!" answered Tom Thumb, who was trembling as visibly as his brothers. "What shall we do? If you don't take us in, the wolves in the forest will surely devour us this very night. That being the case, we might as well be eaten by your husband. If you plead for us, maybe he will take pity on us."

The ogre's wife, who thought she might be able to hide them from her husband until the next morning, let them come in and warm themselves by a roaring fire, where a whole sheep was cooking on the spit for the ogre's supper. Just as the boys were beginning to get warm, they heard three or four loud bangs at the door. The ogre had returned. His wife hid the boys quickly under the bed and went to open the door.

The ogre had asked right away whether supper was ready and whether the wine had been drawn. Then he sat down to eat dinner. Blood was still dripping from the sheep, but it seemed all the better for that. He sniffed to the right, then to the left, insisting that he could smell fresh meat. His wife said: "You must be smelling the calf that I just dressed."

"I'll tell you again that I smell fresh meat," the ogre responded, looking at his wife suspiciously, "and there's something going on here that I don't get."

At that he got up from the table and went straight to the bed. "Aha!" he said. "So that's how you deceive me, you cursed woman! I don't know what's stopping me from eating you too! It's lucky for you that you're an old beast! I'm expecting three ogre friends for a visit in the next few days, and this excellent game will come in handy to entertain them!"

He pulled the children out from under the bed, one after another. The poor things fell to their knees, begging for mercy, but they were dealing with the most cruel of all ogres. Far from feeling pity for them, he was already devouring them with his eyes. He told his wife that if she

GUSTAVE DORÉ,
"Tom Thumb," 1861

A massive ogre seizes one of the boys, hoping to turn him into a tasty morsel for dinner. Thanks to the resourcefulness of the wife, the ogre decides to fatten them up before dining on them. Tom can no longer be distinguished from his other siblings.

cooked them with a tasty sauce, they would make dainty morsels. He went to get a big knife, which he sharpened on a long stone in his left hand as he walked toward the poor children. He had already grabbed one of them when his wife said to him: "Why are you doing this now? Can't it wait until tomorrow?"

"Hold your tongue," replied the ogre. "They will be all the more tender."

"But you already have plenty of meat on your plate," his wife countered. "There's a calf, two sheep, and half a pig."

"You're right," said the ogre. "Give them a good supper to eat so they won't lose any weight and put them to bed."

The good woman was overjoyed and brought them a tasty supper, but the boys were so overcome with fear that they couldn't eat a thing. As for the ogre, he went back to his drinking, thrilled at the prospect of having such a treat to regale his friends. He drank a dozen glasses more than usual, and had to go to bed early, for the wine had gone to his head.

Now, the ogre had seven daughters who were still just little children. These ogresses all had the most lovely complexions, because, like their father, they ate fresh meat. But they had little gray eyes that were completely round, crooked noses, and very large mouths, with long and dreadfully sharp teeth, set far apart. They were not yet terribly vicious, but they showed great promise, for already they were in the habit of killing little children to suck their blood.

They had gone to bed early, and all seven were in one large bed, each wearing a crown of gold upon her head. In that same room was another bed of the same size. The ogre's wife had put the seven boys into it. Then she lay down next to her husband and went to sleep.

Tom Thumb was afraid that the ogre might suddenly regret not having cut the throats of the boys that evening. Having noticed that the ogre's daughters all had golden crowns upon their heads, he got up in the middle of the night and gently put his own cap and those of his brothers on their heads, after having removed the crowns of gold and put them on his own and on his brothers' heads. In this way the ogre would take them for his daughters[9] and his daughters for the boys whom he wanted to eat.

Everything worked just as Tom Thumb had predicted. The ogre, waking up at midnight, regretted having postponed until tomorrow what he could have done that night. He leaped headlong out of bed and grabbed a knife, saying: "Now then, let's see how the little rascals are faring. I won't make the same mistake twice!"

He stole his way up to the room where his daughters were sleeping and walked over to the bed with the seven little boys, who were all asleep except for Tom Thumb. When the ogre's hand moved from the heads of each of his brothers to his own head, Tom Thumb was paralyzed with fear.

"Well, well," said the ogre, when he felt the golden

9. *In this way the ogre would take them for his daughters.* In a collection of second-century Latin myths, by Hyginus, an exchange of clothing leads to the murder of the wrong children.

GUSTAVE DORÉ,
"Tom Thumb," 1861

Eyes bulging, the ogre is about to slit the throats of his daughters, whom he believes to be Tom and his brothers. Note the remnants of the chicken dinner left on the coverlet.

GUSTAVE DORÉ,
"Tom Thumb," 1861

Not realizing that he has slain his daughters, the ogre decides to play a trick on his wife by telling her to go upstairs and "dress" the seven sleeping boys. Like his daughters, he manages to pick everything off the bones. More like a grand seigneur than a fairy-tale monster, this ogre always has a knife or fork at hand.

crowns. "I almost made a mess of this job! It's obvious that I had a little too much to drink last night!"

He went straight to the bed where his daughters were sleeping, and after feeling the boys' little caps, he cried: "Aha, here are the little rascals. Now let's get down to work!"

At that, without a moment's hesitation, he cut the throats of his seven daughters. Completely satisfied with his work, he got back into bed and lay down next to his wife.

As soon as Tom Thumb heard the ogre snoring, he woke his brothers up and told them to get dressed fast and to follow him. They crawled quietly down to the garden and jumped over the walls. They ran almost all night, trembling with fear and having no idea where they were going.

When the ogre woke up, he said to his wife: "Go upstairs and dress those little rascals who were here last night."

The wife was surprised by her husband's good will, never once suspecting the manner in which he was ordering her to have them dressed. She thought that he was telling her to go and put on their clothes. When she got upstairs, she was horrified to find her seven daughters with their throats cut, bathed in blood. She fainted instantly (the first response of almost all women in similar circumstances). The ogre, fearing that his wife was taking too long to carry out his orders, went upstairs to help her. He was no less horrified than his wife at the terrible spectacle that met his eyes.

"What have I done?" he shouted. "I will make those wretches pay, and it will be now."

He threw a jugful of water in his wife's face, and after reviving her, said: "Fetch me my seven-league boots[10] so that I can catch the children."

He got right down to it and, after having run far and wide in all directions, came to the road the poor children were traveling. They were not more than a hundred steps from their father's house when they saw the ogre striding from one mountain to the next, and stepping across rivers as though they were nothing but little brooks. Tom Thumb, who noticed a cave in some rocks close to where they were, hid his six brothers there and squeezed inside, always keeping an eye on the ogre's movements.

Now the ogre was feeling exhausted after having traveled so far in vain (for seven-league boots are very fatiguing to their owner), and he wanted to rest for a while. By chance, he happened to sit down on the very rock beneath which the boys were concealed. Since he could go no farther, he fell asleep after a while and began snoring so dreadfully that the poor children were no less frightened than when he had put his long knife to their

10. *seven-league boots.* In the Grimms' story "Sweetheart Roland," a witch mistakenly kills her own daughter and puts on similar boots. The seven-league boots are part of the standard paraphernalia of folklore.

GUSTAVE DORÉ,
"Tom Thumb," 1861

Worn out by his pursuit of the seven rascals who fled his house, the ogre takes a nap and loses his seven-league boots to Tom Thumb. Note the knife and fork tucked into his belt.

ARTHUR RACKHAM,
"Tom Thumb," 1933

An impish ogre dozes peacefully while Tom pulls off his second boot. The boys, wearing matching red caps, disperse out of fear that the cannibalistic fiend will awaken.

throats. Tom Thumb was not as alarmed, and he told his brothers to race at once to the house while the ogre was still sleeping so soundly. They were not to worry about him. The brothers took his advice and got home fast.

Tom Thumb went over to the ogre and gently pulled off his boots and put them on his own feet. The boots were very roomy and very long, but since they were enchanted, they had the power to become larger or smaller according to the feet wearing them. As a result they fit his feet and his ankles as if they had been made expressly for him. He went straight to the ogre's house, where he found the ogre's wife weeping over her murdered daughters.

"Your husband," said Tom Thumb, "is in great danger, for he has been captured by a band of thieves who have sworn to kill him if he does not hand over all his gold and silver. Just as they were putting a dagger to his throat, he caught sight of me and begged me to come to you and to alert you to the plight he is in. He said that you should give me everything he has of value, without holding back anything, otherwise he'll be slain without mercy. Since time is of the essence, he wanted me to take his seven-league boots, to make haste, and also to show you that I am no impostor."

The ogre's wife was terribly frightened and immediately gave Tom Thumb everything she had, for the ogre had always been a very good husband, even though he ate little children. Loaded down with the ogre's entire wealth, Tom Thumb returned to his father's house, where he was welcomed with open arms.

MANY PEOPLE DO not agree about this last adventure and claim that Tom Thumb never stole money from the ogre, just the seven-league boots, about which he had no qualms, since they had been used to chase little children. These people insist that they are in a position to know, having been wined and dined at the woodcutter's cottage. They claim that when Tom Thumb put on the ogre's boots, he went to the royal court, where he knew there was great anxiety about the army and about the outcome of a battle being fought two hundred leagues away. They say that Tom Thumb went to look for the king and told him that if he was interested he could get news of the army before the day was out. The king promised him a large sum of money if he were to succeed.

Tom Thumb brought news that very night, and this first errand having made his reputation, he could then earn as much as he wanted. The king paid him handsomely to carry orders to the army, but countless ladies gave him any price he named to get news of their lovers, and this became his best source of income. Some wives entrusted him with letters to their husbands, but they paid him so badly, and this activity brought him in so little, that he didn't even bother to keep track of what he made from it.

After working as courier for some time and amassing a small fortune, Tom Thumb returned to his father's house, where everyone was overjoyed to see him again. He saw to it that the entire family lived comfortably, buying newly created positions for his father and brothers. In this way he got them all established at the same time that he managed to do perfectly well for himself at the court.

MORAL

You never worry about having too many children
When they are handsome, well bred, strong,
And when they shine.
But if one is sickly or mute,
He is despised, scorned, ridiculed.
And sometimes it is the little runt
Who makes the family's happiness.

22

THE EMPEROR'S NEW CLOTHES

Hans Christian Andersen

Less fairy tale than fable about the consequences of collective hypocrisy, Andersen's story bears a message that has become a proverbial truth encapsulated in the saying "It's the emperor's new clothes." Choosing to ignore what is in plain sight and blindly acting as if there were nothing wrong are the targets of Andersen's satirical barbs. That it takes an "innocent" child to divine the truth that "His Majesty" is unable to discern is a reminder of the stultifying effects of social proprieties and the way in which culture and civilization produce duplicity and hypocrisy.

Although no one has identified oral sources for this particular story, Andersen is mining a rich, folkloric vein that shows rogues turning the tables on royalty and tricksters outwitting townspeople, clergymen, and innkeepers. The narrator adopts no clear point of view, neither endorsing the ingenuity of the swindlers nor defending the vanity of the emperor, though the tale is carefully constructed to convey a clear moral. Andersen,

From Hans Christian Andersen, "Keiserens nye Klæder," in *Eventyr, fort-alte for Børn* (Copenhagen: C. A. Reitzel, 1837).

a man of humble origins who despised the affectations of the aristocracy, would have aligned himself with the tale's innocent child, whose voice reveals the truth to the assembled crowd.

As the tale unfolds, it becomes clear that the fabrications of the swindlers, their acts of seduction and deception, are invested with a certain truth value, though one diametrically opposed to what is asserted by the thieves. Those who see the clothes are, in fact, either stupid or unfit for office, or both. Only the child of the pure, unclouded brow has the courage to assert that the emperor is wearing nothing at all. In its celebration of the child's wisdom and candor and its revelation of adult hypocrisies, this tale has a special appeal as bedtime reading.

1. *show off his new clothes.* For Andersen vanity was the cardinal sin of human nature. Excessive attachment to dress appears particularly absurd in a monarch who allows it to interfere with his royal duties. Tall and gawky, Andersen was always self-conscious about his own physical appearance and found the airs of the aristocracy particularly offensive.

2. *two swindlers arrived in the city.* The two charlatans belong to a rich folkloric tradition of tricksters who get the better of naïve villagers or townspeople. In this case the swindlers know exactly how to play on the insecurities and weaknesses of the upper crust.

MANY YEARS AGO there lived an emperor who was so devoted to fine new clothes that he spent all his money on elegant attire. He took no interest whatsoever in the army, nor did he care to attend the theater or take carriage rides through the country, unless of course it meant that he could show off his new clothes.[1] He had different garments for every hour of the day, and, just as you usually say of a king that he is sitting in council, so it was always said of this emperor: "He's in his dressing room right now."

There were plenty of diversions in the city where the emperor lived. Strangers were always coming and going, and one day two swindlers arrived in the city.[2] They claimed to be weavers and said that they knew how to weave the very finest fabrics imaginable. Not only were the colors and designs they created unusually attractive, but the clothes made from their fabrics also had the unique characteristic of turning invisible to anyone who was unfit for his job or hopelessly stupid.

RIE CRAMER,
"The Emperor's New Clothes," early 20th century

This Dutch version of Andersen's emperor emphasizes once again the protagonist's vanity. The emperor is engaged in his favorite activity, inspecting himself in the mirror and being attended by servants while trying on clothes.

"I say! Those must be wonderful clothes!" thought the emperor. "If I had some like that, I could tell which officials were unfit for their posts, and I would also be able to distinguish the wise ones from the foolish ones. Yes, I must have some of that fabric woven for me at once." And he paid the swindlers a large sum of money so that they could get to work right away.

The swindlers assembled a couple of looms and pretended to be working, though there was absolutely nothing on their looms. They shrewdly demanded the most delicate silk and the finest gold thread, which they promptly stowed away in their own bags. Then they worked far into the night on their empty looms.

"Well, now, I wonder how the weavers are getting on with their work," the emperor asked himself. But on one point he began to feel some anxiety, namely, that someone who is stupid or unfit for his post would never be able to see what was being woven. Not that he had any fears about himself—he felt quite confident on that score—but all the same it might be better to send someone else out first, to see how things were progressing. Everyone in the city had heard about the fabric's mysterious power, and they were all eager to determine the incompetence or stupidity of their neighbors.

"I will send my able prime minister to the weavers," the emperor thought. "He's the obvious choice to inspect the cloth, for he has plenty of good sense, and no one is better qualified for his post than he."

EDMUND DULAC,
"The Emperor's New Clothes," 1911

"They pointed at the empty frames, but although the poor minister opened his eyes wider and wider, he couldn't see a thing, for there was nothing there." For all his good will and his ocular efforts, the minister is unable to find any evidence of the work performed by the two weavers.

So off went the able minister to the workshop where the two swindlers were working with all their might at the empty looms. "Lord bless my soul," thought the minister, with eyes starting out from his head. "Why, I can't see a thing!" But he was careful not to let on.

The two swindlers begged him to take a closer look— didn't he find the colors and designs attractive? They pointed at the empty frames, but although the poor minister opened his eyes wider and wider, he couldn't see a thing, for there was nothing there. "Good Lord!" he thought. "Is it possible that I'm an idiot? I never once suspected it, and I mustn't let on that it is a possibility. Can it be that I'm unfit for my office? No, it will never do for me to confess that I can't see the fabric."

"Well, what do you think of it?" asked the chap who was pretending to be weaving.

"Oh, it's enchanting! Quite exquisite!" said the old minister, peering over his spectacles. "What a pattern and what coloring! I shall report to the emperor without delay how pleased I am with it."

"Ah, we shall be much obliged to you," said the impostors, and they described the colors and extraordinary design in detail. The old minister listened attentively so that he would be able to repeat their account when he returned to the emperor—which he duly did.

The swindlers demanded more money, more silk, and more gold thread, which they needed to continue weaving. They put it all in their pockets—not a thread was put on the loom—while they went on working the empty frames as before.

After a while the emperor sent a second official to see how the weaving was getting on and whether the cloth would soon be ready. What had happened to the minister also happened to him. He looked as hard as he could, but since there was nothing there but an empty loom, he couldn't see a thing.

"There, isn't this first-rate work!" said the swindlers, as they pointed out the beauty of the design, which didn't even exist.

"I know I'm not stupid," thought the man. "That can mean only that I'm not fit for my position. Some people will find that funny, so I'd better make sure it doesn't get out." And so he praised the cloth he could not see and declared that he was delighted with its enchanting hues and beautiful design. "Yes, it's quite exquisite," he said to the emperor, when he returned.

The splendid fabric became the talk of the town. And now the emperor himself wanted to see it while it was still on the loom. Accompanied by a select group of people, including the two old officials who had already been there, he went to see the loom. The two crafty swindlers were weaving for all they were worth without using a bit of thread.

"Look, isn't it magnificent?" said the two trustworthy officials. "If Your Majesty will but take a look. What a splendid design! What glorious colors!" And they pointed at the empty loom, feeling certain that all the others could see the cloth.

"What's this?" thought the emperor. "I can't see a thing! This is appalling! Am I stupid? Am I unfit to be emperor? This is the worst thing that could happen to me. . . ."

"Oh, it's quite enchanting!" he said to them. "It has our most gracious approval." And he gave a satisfied nod, as he inspected the empty loom. He wasn't about to say that he couldn't see anything. The courtiers who had come with him looked as hard as they could, but they could not see any better than the others. Still, they all said exactly what the emperor had said: "Oh, it's quite enchanting!" They advised him to have some clothes made from this splendid new fabric and to wear them for the first time in the grand parade that was about to take place. "Magnificent!" "Delightful!" "Superb!" were the words bandied about. Everyone was highly pleased with the weaving. The emperor knighted each of the two swindlers and gave them badges to wear in their buttonholes, along with the title "Imperial Weaver."

On the eve of the parade, the rogues sat up all night with something like sixteen lighted candles. People could see how busy they were finishing the emperor's new clothes. They pretended to remove the cloth from the loom, snipped away at the air with huge scissors, and stitched with needles that had no thread. Then at last they announced: "There! The emperor's clothes are ready at last!"

The emperor, with his most distinguished courtiers, went in person to the weavers, who each stretched out an arm as if holding something and said: "Just look at these trousers! Here is the jacket! This is the cloak." And so on. "They are all as light as spider webs. You can hardly tell you are wearing anything—that's the virtue of this delicate cloth."

"Yes, indeed," the courtiers declared. But they were unable to see a thing, for there was absolutely nothing there.

"Now, will Your Imperial Majesty kindly remove your clothes?" said the swindlers. "Then we can fit you with the new ones, over there in front of the tall mirror."

And so the emperor took off the clothes he was wearing, and the swindlers pretended to hand him each of the new garments they claimed to have made, and they held him at the waist as if they were fastening something on . . . it was his train. And the emperor twisted and turned in front of the mirror.

"Goodness! How splendid His Majesty looks in the new clothes. What a perfect fit!" they all exclaimed. "What a cut! What colors! What sumptuous robes!"

The master of ceremonies came in with an announcement. "The canopy for the parade is ready and waiting for Your Majesty."

"I am quite ready," said the emperor. "Don't these clothes fit well!" And he turned around one last time in front of the mirror, for he really had to make them all believe that he was gazing at his fine clothes.

The chamberlains who were supposed to carry the train groped around on the floor as if they were picking it up. As they walked, they held out their hands, not daring to let on that they couldn't see anything.

The emperor marched in the parade under the beautiful canopy, and everyone in the streets and at the win-

EDMUND DULAC,
"The Emperor's New Clothes," 1911

"The emperor marched in the parade under the beautiful canopy, and everyone in the streets and at the windows said: 'Goodness! The emperor's new clothes are the finest he has ever worn. What a wonderful train! What a perfect fit!'" The proud emperor struts through the streets in his underwear, putting himself on display to enact the role of vain fool.

ARTHUR RACKHAM,
"The Emperor's New Clothes," 1911

The artist neatly avoids the problem of how to represent a naked emperor by giving us the entourage in silhouette, while a child points at the monarch, revealing the true state of affairs. Others quickly join in, once the girl makes evident what is in plain sight.

ARTHUR RACKHAM,
"The Emperor's New Clothes," 1932

The artist's second effort to represent the parade scene in Andersen's story led to a silhouette of the naked emperor and two servants, strutting through the streets with aristocratic pride.

3. *"But the emperor has nothing at all on!" a little child declared.* That it takes a child to cut through the hypocrisy of the adult world is a powerful insight that will be particularly appealing to child readers, many of whom will identify with the heroic child.

dows said: "Goodness! The emperor's new clothes are the finest he has ever worn. What a wonderful train! What a perfect fit!" They would not let on that there was nothing at all to see, because that would have meant they were either unfit for their jobs or very stupid. Never had the emperor's clothes made such a great impression.

"But the emperor has nothing at all on!" a little child declared.**3**

"Goodness gracious! Did you hear the voice of that innocent child!" cried the father. And the child's remark was whispered from one person to the next.

"He really isn't wearing anything at all! There's a child here who says that he hasn't got anything on."

WILLIAM HEATH ROBINSON,
"The Emperor's New Clothes"

Bearing the caption "The Rogues Flee," this illustration reveals that the loot is substantial.

ARTHUR RACKHAM,
"The Emperor's New Clothes," 1925

"'But the emperor has nothing at all on!' a little child declared." The faces of observers register the shock of "discovering" that the emperor is wearing no clothes. Jaws drop and fingers point as the monarch passes by.

"Yes, he isn't wearing anything at all!" the people shouted at last. And the emperor felt very uncomfortable, for it seemed to him that everyone was right. But somehow he thought to himself: "I must go through with it now, parade and all."**4** And he drew himself up all the more proudly, while his chamberlains walked after him carrying a train that wasn't there.

4. *"I must go through with it now, parade and all."* The emperor's tenacity and his unwillingness to concede an error, along with the chamberlains' insistence on carrying a train that does not exist, reveal the degree to which Andersen faulted the aristocracy for its resistance to embrace the truth or to change in any way at all.

23

THE LITTLE MATCH GIRL[1]

Hans Christian Anderson

1. *the little match girl.* The attribute "little" before the name of a girl in a story for children often spells the character's doom. The little match girl, like Harriet Beecher Stowe's Little Eva, Charles Dickens's Little Nell, and Andersen's little mermaid, is destined never to become big.

Few children's stories celebrate suffering with the kind of passion brought to Hans Christian Andersen's tale of a match seller. The frail waif who freezes to death on New Year's Eve has become something of a cultural icon, the victim of a brutal father (far more cruel than the ogres of fairy tales) and of a heartless social world. Even nature turns its back on her, offering neither shelter nor sustenance. The fairy-tale magic is gone, and rescue comes only in the form of divine intervention.

The narrator of the match girl's story takes us into the heroine's mental world, allowing us to feel her pain as the temperature drops and the wind howls. We also share her visions, first of warmth, then of nourishment, then of beauty, and finally of human affection and compassion. If the final image of the story gives us a frozen corpse, the little match girl's death is still a "beautiful death," the site of radiant spirituality and transcendent meaning. Whether we read her sufferings as "tortures, disguised as pieties" (as did P. L. Travers, the author of Mary

Hans Christian Andersen, "Den lille Pige med Svovlstikkerne," in *Nye Eventyr* (Copenhagen: C. A. Reitzel, 1845).

Poppins) *or consider her wretchedness as the precondition for translation into a higher sphere, the story haunts our cultural imagination and remains one of the most memorable stories of childhood.*

Many will agree that the one requirement for a good children's book is the triumph of the protagonist. "The Little Match Girl," with its death scene, has been adapted and rewritten many times over the last century, most notably in an edition of 1944, which proclaimed on the dust jacket: "Children will read with delight this new version of the famous Hans Christian Andersen tale. For in it the little match girl on that long ago Christmas Eve does not perish from the bitter cold, but finds warmth and cheer and a lovely home where she lives happily ever after." Andersen, who wrote this story during a decade of social unrest and political upheaval, would no doubt have been distressed by the positive turn to a story that can be read as a powerful critique of social inequities.

I T WAS DREADFULLY cold. Snow was falling, and before long it would be dark. It was the last day of the year: New Year's Eve. In the cold, dark streets you could see a poor little girl wearing nothing on her head and walking in bare feet.[2] Yes, it's true, she was wearing slippers when she'd left home. But what good were they? They were great big slippers that had belonged to her mother, so you can imagine the size of them. The little girl had lost them while scurrying across the road to avoid two carriages hurtling by at a terrifying pace. One slipper was nowhere to be found, and a boy ran off with the other, saying that he could use it as a cradle when he had children of his own someday.

The little girl walked on in her tiny, bare feet, which were raw and turning blue with cold. She had a bundle of matches in her hand and some more in her apron. She

2. *bare feet.* As the son of a shoemaker, Andersen made a special point of focusing on his characters' footware. The bare feet of the little match girl make her a particularly abject figure, though girls who place a premium on their shoes also run into trouble (see Andersen's "Girl Who Trod on the Loaf," whose protagonist refuses to dirty her shoes, and "The Red Shoes," whose protagonist takes pride in wearing ostentatious footwear).

3. *the picture of misery.* Andersen often gives us tableaux of suffering. The loving elaboration of the girl's wretched condition suggests a tendency to aestheticize pain, to create beauty through elaborate descriptions of misery and distress.

4. *She didn't dare go home.* Andersen reported that the story was inspired in part by his own mother's experience of being sent out to beg and told not to return until she had received some money. Andersen's sympathies were always with the downtrodden, and the little match girl gives us a figure who is pure victim.

had not sold a thing all day long, and no one had given her even a copper. Poor mite, she looked like the picture of misery[3] as she trudged along, hungry and shivering with cold. Snowflakes settled on her long, fair hair, which curled itself sweetly around her neck. But you can be sure that she wasn't thinking about her looks. Lights were shining in every window, and the lovely smell of roast goose drifted out into the streets. You see, it was New Year's Eve. That's what she was thinking about.

In a corner between two houses, one of which jutted out into the street, she crouched down and huddled in the cold, with her legs tucked under her. But she just got colder and colder. She didn't dare go home,[4] for she hadn't sold any matches and didn't have one penny to take back home. Her father was certainly going to beat her, and besides, it was almost as cold at home as it was here. They had only the roof to protect them, and the wind howled right through it, although the worst cracks had been stopped up with straw and rags. The girl's little hands were almost numb from the cold. Ah! Maybe a burning match would do some good. If only she dared pull one from the bunch and strike it on the wall, just to warm her fingers. She pulled one out—scratch!—how it sputtered as it burned! Such a bright warm light, just like a little candle, as she held her hand over it. Yes, what a strange light it was! The little girl imagined that she was sitting in front of a big iron stove, with shiny brass knobs and brass feet. How warmly the fire was burning! She was just stretching out her toes to warm them up, too, when—out went the flame, and the stove vanished. There she sat with the stub of a burned-out match in her hand.

She struck another match against the wall. It burst into flames, and the wall that it lit up became as transparent as a veil. She could see right into the room, where a table was covered with a snowy white cloth that had delicate china on it. Right there, you could see a steaming roast goose, stuffed with apples and prunes. And what was even more amazing, the goose jumped right off the dish and waddled across the floor, with a carving knife and a fork still in its back. It marched right up to the poor little girl. But then the match went out, and nothing was left but the cold, damp wall in front of her.

She lit another match. Now she was sitting beneath a beautiful Christmas tree. It was even bigger and more beautiful than the one she had seen last Christmas through the glass door of a rich merchant's house. Thou-

ARTHUR RACKHAM,
"The Little Match Girl," 1932

"She lit another match. Now she was sitting beneath a beautiful Christmas tree." The second match brings the vision of a grand tree, lit up with candles, providing the pleasures of a feast that the little match girl could enjoy only as distant witness.

sands of candles were burning on the green branches, and colored pictures, just like the ones she'd seen in shop windows, looked down upon it all. The little girl stretched both hands up in the air . . . and the match went out. The Christmas candles rose higher and higher until she saw that they were bright stars. One of them turned into a shooting star, leaving behind it a sparkling streak of fire.

"Someone is dying," the little girl thought, for her grandmother, the only person who had been kind to her and who was now dead, had told her that when you see a shooting star, it is a sign that a soul is going up to God.

She struck another match against the wall. The light shone all around her, and right there in the midst of it stood her old grandmother, looking so bright and gentle and loving. "Oh, Grandma," the little girl cried out. "Do take me with you! I know you will vanish when the match burns out—just as the warm oven did, and the lovely roast goose, and the tall, glorious Christmas tree." And she quickly lit the whole bundle of matches, for she so wished to keep her Grandma right there where she was.

HONOR C. APPLETON,
"The Little Match Girl," 1920

"The light shone all around her, and right there in the midst of it stood her old grandmother, looking so bright and gentle and loving." Barefoot, the little match girl sits on a snow-covered step, welcomed into the arms of her loving grandmother after lighting a match for warmth.

And the matches flared up so powerfully that it was suddenly brighter than broad daylight. Never had Grandma looked so tall and beautiful. She took the little girl into her arms and together they flew in brightness and joy up, up, above the earth to where there is no cold, no hunger, no pain. They were with God.

At dawn the next morning, the little girl lay huddled between the two houses,[5] with rosy cheeks and a smile on her lips. She had frozen to death on the last night of the old year. The New Year dawned on the frozen body of the little girl, who was still holding matches in her hand, one bundle used up. "She was trying to get warm," people said. No one could imagine what beautiful things she had seen and in what glory she had gone with her old Grandma to the happiness of the New Year.

5. *the little girl lay huddled between the two houses.* Although the frozen body of the girl presents a grotesque warning to passersby, her "rosy cheeks" and "smile" suggest that her death is a beautiful one and that she has transcended worldly things.

24

THE PRINCESS AND THE PEA

Hans Christian Andersen

The casual, conversational tone and humorous touches in this story about a pathologically sensitive princess redeem many features that might offend modern sensibilities. The prince's insistence on finding a "real" princess and the equation of nobility with sensitivity challenge our own cultural values about character and social worth. And yet the sensitivity of the princess can also be read on a metaphorical level as a measure of the depth of her feeling and compassion. And Andersen also gives us a feisty heroine, who defies the elements and shows up on the doorstep of a prince, whom she has succeeded in tracking down.

Andersen claimed to have heard this story as a child, although there are no recorded Danish versions of the tale. A Swedish analogue ("The Princess Who Lay on Seven Peas") presents a similar scenario, though in it, an orphan girl passes herself off as a princess by claiming to have slept poorly. While

From Hans Christian Andersen, "Prindsessen paa Ærten," in *Eventyr, fortalte for Børn* (Copenhagen: C. A. Reitzel, 1835).

the folktale heroine uses deceit to raise her social rank, Andersen's princess is the "real" thing and does not have to misrepresent her physical state.

A 1960 musical, Once upon a Mattress, starring Carol Burnett as the irrepressible princess Winnifred, enjoyed popular success on Broadway for many years. The story remains among the favorite Andersen tales, and the princess has become an emblem of supremely delicate sensibilities.

ONCE UPON A TIME there was a prince. He went in search of a princess of his own, but he wanted her to be a true princess. And so he traveled all over the world in order to find one, but something was always wrong. There were plenty of princesses around, but he could never quite figure out whether they were real princesses. Each time something wasn't quite right. He returned home, feeling sad and weary, for his heart had been set on marrying a real princess.

One evening a terrible storm settled over the land.[1] Lightning flashed, thunder roared, and rain came down in buckets—it was really dreadful! Out of the blue there was a knock at the city gate, and the king himself went to open it. There was a princess standing outside.[2] But goodness gracious! What a sight she was out in the rain in this kind of weather! Water was running down her hair and her clothes. It flowed in through the tips of her shoes and back out again through the heels. And still, she insisted that she was a real princess.

"Well, we shall see about that soon enough!" thought the queen. She did not utter a word, but went straight to the bedroom, removed all the bedclothes, and put a pea on the bare bedstead. On top of the pea she piled twenty

1. *One evening a terrible storm settled over the land.* As in "The Little Mermaid," a storm signals a life-threatening situation, but it typically produces an opportunity for a fortunate romantic alliance.

2. *There was a princess standing outside.* Like Donkeyskin and Cinderella, this princess conceals her nobility until it is put to a test. Rather than matching a foot to a shoe or a finger to a ring, this princess must reveal her sensitivity.

KAY NIELSEN,
"The Princess and the Pea," 1924

A windswept princess seeks shelter in the castle and is welcomed by the king, who has the foresight to bring an umbrella when he lets in this "real" princess.

3. *she had felt the pea.* The feminist writer and essayist Vivian Gornick has read the princess's sensitivity as a form of dissatisfaction that will define her life and goad her into action: "She's not after the prince, she's after the pea. That moment when she feels the pea beneath the twenty mattresses, that is *her* moment of definition. It is the very meaning of her journey, why she has traveled so far, what she has come to declare: the dissatisfaction that will keep her life at bay."

mattresses and then put another twenty of the softest featherbeds on top of the mattresses. That's where the princess slept for the night.

In the morning, everyone asked how she had slept. "Oh, just wretchedly!" said the princess. "I hardly got a wink of sleep all night long! Goodness knows what was in that bed! I was lying on something so hard that I'm just black and blue all over. It's really awful!"

Then of course everyone could see that she really was a princess, because she had felt the pea[3] right through the twenty mattresses and twenty featherbeds. Nobody but a real princess has skin as tender as that.

KAY NIELSEN,
"The Princess and the Pea," 1924

The princess kneels atop the many mattresses in a room governed by extraordinary compositional symmetry. The single light in the chandelier, the mirror over one chair, and the design on the bedstead, along with the princess herself, disrupt the symmetries.

EDMUND DULAC,
"The Princess and the Pea," 1911

The massive timbers of the ceiling and the posters of the bed contain the tiny figure of the princess. The many mattresses beneath the princess provided the artist with an opportunity to create layer upon layer of decorative touches.

And so the prince married her, because now he knew that he had a true princess. And the pea was sent to a museum, where it is still on display,[4] unless someone has stolen it.

There. That's something of a story, isn't it?

4. *the pea was sent to a museum, where it is still on display.* For Andersen the material objects of everyday life—needles, pincushions, or whistles—are endowed with special whimsical human qualities. Here the pea is never endowed with human feelings, but it becomes an icon signaling the princess's special sensitivity, presumably not only to a pea under the mattress but also to the wishes of her human subjects.

25

THE UGLY DUCKLING[1]

Hans Christian Andersen

1. *ugly duckling.* The phrase has become a catchword for the unpromising figure who ends up surpassing everyone else. In fairy tales the despised prove their worth; the slow triumph over the swift; the stupid win over the clever.

This classic story of a duckling's metamorphosis into a beautiful swan has been evoked for generations as a source of comfort to those suffering from a sense of inadequacy and isolation. It has attained a kind of moral authority that merits close attention, for the story sends a very clear message about self-worth, social status, and the promise of transformation. The ugly duckling transcends his lowly condition through no real effort on his part. He simply endures humiliations, privation, and perils until his time comes. Then he spreads his wings and joins the majestic kin who float along the waters, serving as a source of visual delight to the children in the park.

Small, powerless, and often treated dismissively, children are likely to identify with Andersen's unsightly creature, who, like many a fairy-tale hero, is the youngest in the brood, in this case the last to hatch from the egg. The ugly duckling, like the proverbial tortoise or the tiny Tom Thumb, may be unpromising, but with time he surpasses the promising. As Bruno Bet-

From Hans Christian Andersen, "Den grimme Ælling," *Nye Eventyr* (Copenhagen: C. A. Reitzel, 1844).

telheim points out in The Uses of Enchantment, Andersen's protagonist does not have to submit to the tests, tasks, and trials usually imposed on the heroes of fairy tales. "No need to accomplish anything is expressed in 'The Ugly Duckling.' Things are simply fated and unfold accordingly, whether or not the hero takes some action." Andersen suggests that the ugly duckling's innate superiority stems from his being of a different breed. Unlike the other ducks, he has been hatched from a swan's egg. This implied hierarchy in nature—majestic swans versus the barnyard rabble—suggests that dignity and worth, along with aesthetic and moral superiority are determined by nature rather than by accomplishment.

Whatever the pleasures of a story that celebrates the triumph of the underdog, it is worth thinking about the ethical and aesthetic issues raised by that victory. Andersen's story not only perpetuates cultural stereotypes linking royalty and aristocracy with beauty; it also promotes a cult of suffering, one that sees virtue in physical distress and spiritual anguish. It could be argued that the ugly duckling undergoes a test of his character and fortitude. Staunchly enduring taunts from others and defying the physical challenges of nature, he survives, victorious, yet neither proud nor vain in his glory. In the pond the ugly duckling suffers glacial incarceration: he becomes a frozen ornament, dead to the world. For Andersen a turn away from carnality (sometimes taking the extreme form of mortification of the flesh and physical paralysis) becomes the prerequisite for spiritual plenitude and salvation.

Yet if the ugly duckling triumphs in the end and reigns supreme as the "most beautiful of all," as well as the fairest (for he does not have a proud heart), he is once again reduced to the rank of an ornament, skimming on the surface of the pond as he is admired by children who reward his preening with bits of bread. Many scholars have argued that "The Ugly Duckling" is the most deeply personal of Andersen's stories, a narrative that traces the trajectory of Andersen's own painful rise from humble origins to literary aristocracy. A target of derision even as an author (reviewers often disparaged his writings), Andersen acquired fame and admiration in his last years.

2. *chattering away in Egyptian.* Legend has it that storks were once men and that they returned to their human state in Egypt during the winter. That storks bring babies is a familiar superstition. It was believed that they picked up infants from marshes, ponds, and springs, where the souls of unborn children dwelled. Storks and birds appear frequently in Andersen's stories, and he wrote one tale entitled "The Storks."

3. *huge burdock leaves.* The burdock plant is a coarse, broad-leaved weed bearing prickly heads of burr. Its unattractiveness contrasts with the beauty of nature and introduces the theme of unsightliness.

IT WAS A LOVELY summer day in the country, and the golden corn, the green oats, and the haystacks piled up in the grassy meadows looked beautiful! There was a stork on long red legs, chattering away in Egyptian,[2] a language he had learned from his mother. The fields and meadows were surrounded by vast woods, dotted with deep lakes.

Yes, it certainly was lovely to walk about in the country. An old farmhouse close to a deep river was bathed in sunshine, and huge burdock leaves[3] covered the stretch from the house down to the water. The largest were so high up that little children could stand upright beneath them. The place was as tangled and twisted as a dense forest. It was here that a duck was sitting on her nest. The time had come for her to hatch her little ducklings, but it was such a slow job that she was nearing exhaustion. She hardly ever had any visitors. The other ducks preferred swimming about on the river to climbing the slippery slope to come over and sit under a burdock leaf just for the sake of a quack with her.

Finally the eggs cracked open, one by one: "Cheep, cheep." From each egg emerged a living creature that lifted its head up and cried out: "Peep, peep."

"Quack, quack!" said the mother duck, and the little ones scurried out as quickly as they could, poking around under the green leaves. The mother let them look around as much as they liked, for green is always good for the eyes.

"Oh, how large the world is!" said the ducklings, for they realized that they now had much more room than when they were curled up in an egg.

"Do you think that this spot is the whole world!" said their mother. "Why it reaches way past the other side of the garden, right into the parson's field. But I've never ventured that far. Well, you're all hatched now. I hope . . ."—

and she got up from her nest—"no, not all. The largest egg is still here. I wonder how long it is going to take. I can't be bothered with this much longer." And she went back to sit down in the nest.

"Well, how are you getting on?" asked an old duck who had come to pay a visit.

"One egg is still not hatched,"**4** said the duck. "It simply won't open. But take a look at the others—the loveliest ducklings I've ever seen. They all take after their father—the scoundrel! He never even comes to pay a visit."

"Let's have a look at that egg that won't crack," said the old duck. "I'll wager it's a turkey's egg. That's how I was once bamboozled. The little ones gave me no end of trouble, for they were afraid of the water—imagine that! I just couldn't get them to go in. I quacked and clacked, but it didn't do any good. Let's have a look at that egg. Oh, yes, that's a turkey's egg for sure, you can bet on it. Leave it alone and start teaching the others to swim."

"I think I'll sit on it just a little longer," said the duck. "I've been sitting so long that it can't hurt to sit a little longer."

"Please yourself!" said the old duck, and away she waddled.

Finally the big egg began to crack. There was a "cheep, cheep!" sound coming from the young one as he tumbled out, looking ever so large and ugly. The duck took a look and said: "My, what a great big duckling that is! None of the others looks at all like that. Still, it's not a turkey chick, I'm sure of that. . . . Well, we shall soon see. He will go into the water, even if I have to push him in myself!"

The following day, the weather was glorious, and the sun shone brightly on all the green burdock leaves. The mother duck came down to the water with her entire family and jumped in with a splash. "Quack, quack," she said, and one after another the ducklings leaped in after her. The water closed over their heads, but in an instant they were back up again, floating along beautifully. Their legs paddled along on their own, and now the whole group was

4. *"One egg is still not hatched."* The duckling is not only singular in his looks; he is also the youngest in the brood. His ugliness contrasts with the "loveliness" of the other ducklings.

5. *She's the most genteel of anyone here.* Note that Andersen's farmyard has its hierarchies and social rankings. Andersen himself suffered perpetually under the burden of his low social origins. Some critics see in the farmyard a symbolic representation of the stultifying atmosphere of Odense, Copenhagen, Slagelse, and Elsinore, places where Andersen endured countless humiliations.

in the water—even the ugly gray duckling joined in on the swimming.

"He's not a turkey, that's for sure," said the duck. "Look how beautifully he uses his legs and how straight he holds himself. He's my own little one all right, and he's quite handsome, when you take a good look at him. Quack, quack! Now come along with me and let me show you the world and introduce you to everyone in the barnyard. But pay attention and stay close to me so that nobody steps on you. And keep a good lookout for the cat."

They all made their way into the barnyard. There was a frightful din over there, for two families were fighting over an eel's head. In the end it was the cat that got it. "You see, that's the way of the world," said the mother duck, and she whetted her bill, because she too had been hoping to get the eel's head. "Come now, use your legs and look sharp," she said. "Make a nice bow to the old duck over there. She's the most genteel of anyone here.**5** She has Spanish blood; that's why she is so plump. And can you see that crimson flag she's wearing on one leg? It's extremely fine. It's the highest distinction any duck can earn. It's as good as saying that no one is thinking of getting rid of her. Man and beast are to take notice! Look alive, and don't turn your toes in! A well-bred duckling turns its toes out, like its father and mother . . . . That's it. Now bend your neck and say 'quack!' "

They all obeyed. But the other ducks there looked at them and said out loud: "There! Now we've got to have that rabble as well—as if there weren't enough of us already! Ugh! What a sight that duckling is! We can't possibly put up with him." And one of the ducks immediately flew at him and bit him in the neck.

"Leave him alone," said the mother. "He's not doing any harm."

"Yes, but he's so gawky and odd," said the one who had pecked him. "He will just have to be turned out."

"What pretty children you have, my dear!" said the old duck with the flag on her leg. "All but that one, who doesn't seem quite right. I just wish you could do something to improve him."

"That's impossible, my lady," said the ducklings' mother. "He's not attractive, but he's so good-tempered and he can swim just as well as the others—I daresay even a bit better. I think his looks will improve when he grows up, or maybe in time he'll shrink a little. He was in the egg for too long—that's why he isn't quite the right shape." And then she stroked his neck and smoothed out his feathers. "Anyway, he's a drake, and so it doesn't matter as much," **6** she added. "I feel sure he'll turn out pretty strong and be able to take care of himself."

"The other ducklings are charming," said the old duck. "Make yourselves at home, my dears, and if you should find anything that looks like an eel's head, you can bring it to me." And so they made themselves comfortable, but the poor duckling, who had been the last to creep out of his shell and who looked so ugly, got pecked and jostled and was teased by ducks and hens alike. "The great gawker!" they all clucked. And the turkey, who had been born with spurs and who fancied himself an emperor, puffed himself up like a ship in full rigging and went straight at him. Then he gobble gobbled until he was quite red in the face. The poor duckling didn't know where to turn. He was quite upset at being so ugly and at becoming the laughingstock of the barnyard.

That's how it was the first day, and things only got worse from there. Everyone started pushing the poor duckling around. Even his own brothers and sisters treated him badly and would say: "Oh, you ugly creature, if only the cat would get you." His mother said she wished he were not around. The ducks nipped at him, the chickens pecked him, and the maid who had to feed the poultry let fly at him with her foot.

Finally he ran away, frightening the little birds in the hedge as he flew off. "They are afraid of me because I am ugly," he said. And he closed his eyes and flew farther on until he reached some broad marshes inhabited by wild

6. *he's a drake, and so it doesn't matter as much.* In fairy tales, looks count less for the heroes than for the heroines, who usually live happily ever after because of their perfect beauty. By contrast, even a beast can win a fair princess.

7. *He wasn't dreaming about marriage.* While many fairy-tale heroes rise in social station through marriage, the duckling aspires to social acceptance rather than to social elevation through marriage. For those who read the story in biographical terms, it is worth noting that Andersen remained a bachelor all his life.

8. *wild geese.* One critic has identified the wild geese as the young bohemian poets with whom Andersen associated during his schooldays at Slagelse. In this reading the swans that appear at the end of the story would be the great writers of Europe.

ducks. He stayed there all night, feeling utterly tired and dispirited.

In the morning, when the wild ducks flew up into the air, they stared at their new companion. "What kind of duck could you possibly be?" they all asked, looking him up and down. He bowed to them and was as polite as he could be, but he did not reply to their question.

"You are exceedingly ugly," said the wild ducks, "but that doesn't matter, as long as you don't try to marry into our family." Poor thing! He wasn't dreaming about marriage.[7] All he wanted was a chance to lie quietly among the rushes and to drink some water on the marshes.

After he had been there for two whole days, a couple of wild geese,[8] or rather two wild ganders, came along. They had not been out of the egg for long and were very frisky. "Look here, old pal," one of them said to the duckling. "You are so ugly that we rather like you. Will you go with us and become a bird of passage? Not far off in another marsh there are some very nice wild geese, none of them married, and they all quack beautifully. Here's a chance for you to make a hit, ugly as you are."

"Bang! Bang!" shots suddenly rang out above them, and the two wild geese fell dead into the rushes. The water turned red with their blood. "Bang! Bang!" Shots sounded once more, and flocks of wild geese rose up from the rushes. The sounds came from all directions, for a big shoot was on. The hunting party had surrounded the marshlands. Some of the men were even seated on branches of trees, overlooking the marshes. Blue smoke from the guns rose like clouds over the dark trees and floated down over the water. Hounds came splashing through the mud, bending back reeds and rushes as they leapt. How they terrified the poor duckling! He turned away his head and was about to hide it under his wing when he suddenly became aware of a fearsomely large dog with lolling tongue and grim, glaring eyes. It lowered its muzzle right down to the duckling, bared its sharp teeth and—splash—went off again without touching him.

"Thank goodness," the duckling sighed with relief. "I'm

so ugly that even the dog is not interested in biting me." And he lay there quite still, while bullets rattled through the reeds and rushes, and shot after shot was heard.

By the time the noises had died down, it was late in the day. But the poor young duckling didn't dare get up yet. He waited quietly for several hours and then, after taking a careful look around him, took off from the marsh as fast as he could. He scrambled over meadows and fields, but the wind was so strong that he had a hard time making any progress.

Toward evening he reached a poor little cottage that was in a state of such disrepair that it remained standing only because it could not figure which way to collapse first. The wind blew so powerfully around the duckling that he had to sit on his tail so as not to be blown over. Soon the wind grew even fiercer. The duckling noticed that the door had come off one of its hinges and was hanging at an angle that allowed him to make his way into the house through a crack. He slipped in quietly and found shelter for the night.

There was an old woman living in the cottage with her tomcat and hen. The tomcat, whom she called Sonny, could arch his back and purr. He could even give off sparks, if you stroked his fur the wrong way. The hen had such short legs that she was called Chickabiddy Shortlegs. She was a good layer of eggs, and the old woman loved her like a child.

First thing in the morning the tomcat and hen noticed the strange duckling, and the cat began to purr and the hen began to cluck. "What's all this noise about?" asked the old woman, looking around the room. But her eyes weren't very good, and she took the ugly duckling for a plump duck that had strayed from home. "My, what a find!" she exclaimed. "I shall be able to have some duck eggs, as long as it's not a drake! We'll just have to wait and see."

And so the duckling was taken on trial for three weeks, but there was no sign of an egg. Now, the tomcat was master of the house, and the hen was mistress, and they

9. *But it's such a delight to swim about on the water.* The duckling, unlike the hen, has absolutely no use value. Even as a swan, he will produce nothing but pleasure, for himself and for his admirers.

always used to say: "We and the world," for they fancied that they made up half the world, and, what's more, the better half too. The duckling thought that there might be two opinions about that, but the hen wouldn't hear of it.

"Can you lay eggs?" she asked.

"No."

"Well, then, hold your tongue, will you!"

The tomcat asked: "Can you arch your back or purr or give off sparks?"

"No."

"Well, then, your opinion is not wanted when sensible people are speaking."

The duckling sat in a corner, feeling quite dejected. Then suddenly, he remembered the fresh air and the sunshine, and he began to feel such a deep longing for a swim on the water that he could not help telling the hen about it.

"What an absurd idea," said the hen. "You have too much time on your hands. That's why you get such foolish ideas in your head. They would vanish if you were able to lay eggs or purr."

"But it's such a delight to swim about on the water,"**9** said the duckling, "and so refreshing to duck your head in and dive down to the bottom."

"Delightful, I'm sure!" said the hen. "Why, you must be crazy! Ask the cat; he is the cleverest animal I know. Ask him how he feels about swimming or diving. I won't even give my views. Ask our mistress, the old woman—there's no one in the world wiser than she is. Do you think she likes to swim or to dive down into the water?"

"You don't understand me," said the duckling.

"Well, if we don't understand you, I should like to know who does. Surely you'll never try to say that you are wiser than the cat and the mistress, not to mention me. Don't be silly, child! Be happy for the good fortune that brought you here. Haven't you found a nice, warm room, along with a group of friends from whom you can learn something? But you're just stupid, and there's no fun in having you here. Believe me, if I say unpleasant things, it's only for your own good and a proof of real friendship. But take my advice. See to it that you lay eggs and learn how to purr or throw off sparks."

"I think I'll go back out into the wide world," said the duckling.

"Yes, do," said the hen.

And so the duckling departed. He dove down into the water and swam about, but no one else would have anything to do with him, because he was so ugly. Autumn arrived, and the leaves in the forest turned yellow and brown. As they fell to the ground, the wind caught them and whirled them around. The sky above had a frosty look. The clouds hung heavy with hail and snow, and a raven was perched on a fence, crying "Caw! Caw!" It gave you the shivers. Yes, the poor duckling was certainly having a hard time.

One evening there was a lovely sunset, and a large flock of majestic birds suddenly emerged from the bushes. The duckling had never seen such beautiful birds, dazzlingly white with long, graceful necks. They were swans. They uttered extraordinary cries, spread out their magnificent wings, and flew away from these cold regions to warmer countries across the sea.

As the ugly little duckling watched them mount higher and higher up in the air, he felt a strange sensation. He whirled round and round in the water and craned his neck in their direction, letting out a cry that was so shrill and strange that it frightened him when he heard it. How could he ever forget those beautiful birds who were so fortunate! When they were out of sight, he dived down to the bottom of the waters, and when he surfaced, he was almost beside himself with excitement. He had no idea who these birds were, nor did he know anything about their destination. Yet they were more precious to him than any birds he had ever known. He was not at all envious of them. After all, how could he ever aspire to their beauty? He would be quite satisfied if the ducks would just tolerate him—poor, gawky creature that he was.

What a cold winter it was! The duckling had to keep

10. *the duckling was afraid they would harm him.* Andersen's dislike of small children is well documented. In the plan for a commemorative statue in Copenhagen, he asked that the children looking over his shoulder be removed from the design. As a child he was an avid reader, who stayed away from other children. "I never played with the other boys," he reported in a letter to his benefactor Jonas Collin. "I was always alone."

swimming about in the water to keep it from freezing around him. Every night the area in which he swam grew smaller and smaller. At length the water froze so solidly that the ice creaked as he moved, and the duckling had to keep his feet moving all the time to prevent the space from closing up completely. At last he grew faint with exhaustion and lay quite still and helpless, frozen fast in the ice.

Early the next morning, a peasant who was passing by observed what had happened. He broke the ice with his

MABEL LUCIE ATTWELL,
"The Ugly Duckling"

"The woman screamed at him and struck him with the tongs, and the children tumbled all over each other trying to catch him. How they laughed and shouted! It was lucky that the door was open. The duckling darted out into the bushes and sank down, dazed, in the newly fallen snow." The ugly duckling's gawkiness gets him into trouble and leaves him without food or shelter for the winter.

wooden clog and carried the duckling home to his wife. There they revived him. The children wanted to play with him, but the duckling was afraid they would harm him.**10**

He started up in a panic, fluttering right into the milk bowl so that the milk splashed all over the room. When the woman screamed at him and clapped her hands, he flew into the butter tub, and from there into the flour bin and out again. Dear, dear, what a state he was in! The woman screamed at him and struck him with the tongs, and the children tumbled all over each other trying to catch him. How they laughed and shouted! It was lucky that the door was open. The duckling darted out into the bushes and sank down, dazed, in the newly fallen snow.

It would be dreary if I were to describe all the misery and hardship endured by the duckling in the course of that hard winter. . . . He remained sheltered among the reeds on the marshes. One day, the sun began to shine again, and the larks began to sing. Spring had arrived in all its beauty.

Then all at once he decided to try his wings. They whirred much louder then before, and they carried him away swiftly. Almost before he knew it, he found himself in a large garden. The apple trees were in full blossom, and the fragrant lilacs bent their long green branches down on a stream that wound its way across a smooth lawn. It was so lovely here in all the freshness of early spring! From a nearby thicket, three beautiful white swans emerged, ruffling their feathers and floating lightly over the still waters. The duckling recognized the splendid creatures and was overcome by a strange feeling of melancholy.

"I will fly over to those royal birds. Maybe they will peck me to death for daring to approach them, ugly as I am. But it doesn't matter. Better to be killed by them than to be nipped by the ducks, pecked by the hens, kicked by the maid who feeds the poultry, or to suffer hardship in the winter."

And he flew out on the water, swimming toward the beautiful swans. When they caught sight of him, they rushed to meet him with outstretched wings. "Yes, kill me, kill me," cried the poor bird,[11] and he bowed his head down to the water, awaiting death. But what did he dis-

11. *"Yes, kill me, kill me," cried the poor bird.* The duckling's suffering is so intense that it moves him toward self-immolation. It is telling that he looks on death as salvation, so long as the beautiful swans are the executioners.

cover in the clear surface beneath him? He saw his own image, and he was no longer a clumsy, gray bird, ugly and unpleasant to look at—no, he was himself a swan!

There's nothing wrong with being born in a duck yard, as long as you are hatched from a swan's egg. He now felt positively glad to have endured so much hardship and adversity. It helped him appreciate all the happiness and beauty surrounding him. . . . The three great swans swam around the newcomer and stroked his neck with their beaks.

Some little children came into the garden and threw bread and grain onto the water. The youngest cried out: "There's a new swan!" The other children were delighted and shouted: "Yes, there's a new swan!" And they clapped

JOHN HASSALL,
"The Ugly Duckling," 1932

"Some little children came into the garden and threw bread and grain onto the water. The youngest cried out: 'There's a new swan!' The other children were delighted and shouted: 'Yes, there's a new swan!'" The ugly duckling savors his new identity.

their hands and danced about and ran to fetch their fathers and mothers. Bits of bread and cake were thrown on the water, and everyone said: "The new one is the most beautiful of all. He is so young and handsome." And the old swans bowed their heads before him.

He felt quite humbled, and he tucked his head under his wing—he himself hardly knew why. He was so very happy, but not a bit proud, for a good heart is never proud.[12] He thought about how he had been despised and persecuted, and now everybody was saying that he was the most beautiful of all the birds. And the lilacs bowed their branches toward him, right down to the water. The sun shone warm and bright. Then he ruffled his feathers, raised his slender neck, and rejoiced from the depths of his heart. "I never dreamed of such happiness when I was an ugly duckling."

12. *a good heart is never proud.* For Andersen pride and vanity are the cardinal sins of humanity. Those with a humble heart are the true heroes of mankind, and they are often oppressed by the haughty, arrogant, and proud. Children from prosperous families scorned the young Andersen and mocked him with the cry "Look, there's the playwright!" In his memoirs Andersen recalls that he went home, hid in a corner, and "cried and prayed to God." Later in life he suffered countless insults from his patron Jonas Collin and his children, who always made him aware that he was their social inferior. Danish reviewers of Andersen's work tended to be critical and condescending.

26

THE LITTLE MERMAID

Hans Christian Andersen

Cruelty and violence have often been seen as the trademark of German fairy tales, but P. L. Travers, the author of the Mary Poppins books, found Hans Christian Andersen to be a master in the art of torture. "How much rather would I see wicked stepmothers boiled in oil . . . ," she declared, "than bear the protracted agony of the Little Mermaid or the girl who wore the Red Shoes." For Andersen suffering is the badge of spiritual superiority, and his downtrodden protagonists emerge triumphant by enduring seemingly endless humiliations. And yet the little mermaid has worldly ambitions that suggest more than silent suffering. Drawn to the upper world, she is eager to sail the seas, climb mountains, and explore forbidden territory. Donning boy's clothing, she goes horseback riding with the prince, transgressing gender boundaries in unprecedented ways. And for all her passion for adventure and life, she is, despite her pagan nature, a creature of compassion, unwilling to sacrifice the prince's life for her own.

From Hans Christian Andersen, "Den lille Havfrue," in *Eventyr, fortalte for Børn* (Copenhagen: C. A. Reitzel, 1837).

To gain full mobility in the human world, Andersen's mermaid must sacrifice her voice to the sea witch, a figure who, in her linkage with biological corruption and grotesque sensuality, is diametrically opposed to the promise of eternal salvation. The marsh in which she resides and the bones of the human folk supporting her house all point to a regime that emphatically displays human mortality and bodily decay. Initially attracted to what the sea witch can provide and willing to brave the dangers of a visit to her abode, the little mermaid ultimately renounces her black arts when she flings the knife meant for the prince into the sea and is rewarded with the possibility of earning immortality.

F AR OUT AT SEA the water's as blue as the petals of the prettiest cornflower and as clear as the purest glass. But it's very deep, deeper than any anchor can reach. Many church steeples would have to be piled up, one on top of the other, to reach from the bottom of the sea up to the surface. Down there live the sea people.[1]

Now, you mustn't for a moment imagine that there's nothing but bare, white sand down there. Oh, no! The most wonderful trees and plants grow at the bottom of the sea. Their stalks and leaves bend so easily that they stir with the slightest movement of the water, as if they were alive. All the fish, large and small, glide between the branches, just as birds fly through the trees up here. Down in the deepest spot of all is the castle of the sea king.[2] Its walls are built of coral, and the long, pointed windows are made of the clearest amber. The roof is formed of shells that open and close with the current. It's a pretty sight, for each shell has a dazzling pearl, any one of which would be a splendid ornament for a queen's crown.

The sea king had been a widower for some years, and

1. *Down there live the sea people.* The underwater realm of the sea people is described as a benign paradise, something of a parallel universe, but with more leisure and natural beauty. Disney's little mermaid, known by the name Ariel, lives in a realm in which the undersea people seem to do little more than sing and dance.

2. *the castle of the sea king.* The underwater monarchy may be a utopia in which art (song, dance, and spectacle) meets natural beauty, but it also has strict hierarchical distinctions, as becomes clear from the number of oysters worn on the tail of the sea king's mother.

ARTHUR RACKHAM,
"The Little Mermaid," 1932

The pleasures of the aquatic world become evident in this jump-roping scene, in which three of the sisters are playing games in their oceanic paradise.

EDMUND DULAC,
"The Little Mermaid," 1911

"The sea king had been a widower for some years, and his aged mother kept house for him. She was an intelligent woman, but proud when it came to her noble birth. That's why she wore twelve oysters on her tail, while everyone else of high rank had to settle for six." The king feeds his subjects in his undersea realm.

JEANNIE HARBOUR,
"The Little Mermaid," 1932

As unhappy fish swim beneath her, the little mermaid contemplates the bubbles rising to the surface of the ocean. Hair streaming through the waters and tail decorated with flowers, she dreams of another life.

his aged mother kept house for him. She was an intelligent woman, but proud when it came to her noble birth. That's why she wore twelve oysters on her tail, while everyone else of high rank had to settle for six. Otherwise she deserved great praise, for she was very devoted to her granddaughters, the little sea princesses. They were six pretty children, but the youngest was the loveliest of them all. Her skin was clear and delicate as a rose leaf. Her eyes were as blue as the deepest sea. But, like all the others, she had no feet and her body ended in a fish tail.

All day long the sea princesses played in the great halls of the castle, where flowers grew right out of the walls. The large amber windows were open, and the fish swam in, just as swallows fly into our homes when we open the windows. The fish glided right up to the princesses, fed from their hands, and waited to be patted.

Outside the castle there was a beautiful garden with trees of deep blue and fiery red. Their fruit glittered like gold, and their blossoms were like flames of fire, with leaves and stalks that never stayed still. The soil itself was the finest sand, but blue like a sulfur flame. A strange blue glow permeated everything in sight.[3] Standing down there, you really wouldn't know that you were at the bottom of the sea, but might imagine that you were high up in the air with nothing but sky above you and below you. When there was a dead calm, you could catch a glimpse of the sun, which looked like a purple flower with light streaming from its calyx.

Each of the little princesses had her own plot in the garden, where she could dig and plant as she pleased. One arranged her flower bed in the shape of a whale; another thought it nicer to make hers look like the figure of a little mermaid; but the youngest made hers quite round like the sun,[4] and she wanted nothing but flowers that shone red like it. She was a curious child, quiet and thoughtful. While her sisters decorated their gardens with the wonderful things they obtained from sunken ships, she would have nothing but rose-red flowers that were like the sun high above, and a beautiful marble statue. The statue was of a handsome boy, chiseled from pure white stone, and it had come down to the bottom of the sea after a shipwreck. Next to it the little princess had planted a rose-colored weeping willow, which grew splendidly and draped its fresh foliage over the statue down to the blue, sandy ocean bottom. Its shadow took on a violet tinge and, like the branches, was never still. The roots and crown of the tree seemed always at play, trying to kiss each other.

Nothing pleased the princess more than to hear about the world of humans above the sea. Her old grandmother had to tell her all she knew of the ships and towns, the people and the animals. One thing especially amazed her with its beauty, and this was that the flowers had a fra-

3. *A strange blue glow permeated everything in sight.* Blue and red are the dominant colors in the narrative, the one associated with the depths of the sea and the heights of the heavens, the other linked with sunlight, passion, suffering, and blood.

4. *The youngest made hers quite round like the sun.* The little mermaid's aspirations are clear early on. She is upwardly mobile, reaching for the sun and striving to transcend her nature.

ARTHUR RACKHAM,
"The Little Mermaid," 1932

Embracing the statue, the little mermaid blends into the marble forms
of the human world even as her hair
becomes one with the elements in
the undersea world.

WILLIAM HEATH ROBINSON,
"The Little Mermaid," 1913

The little mermaid's longing for the
world of humans is expressed in her
devotion to the statue kept underwater. The statuesque prince has
the look of a classical god who
delights in children sporting about
him.

grance—at the bottom of the sea they had none—and
also that the trees in the forest were green and that the
fish flying in the trees could sing so sweetly that it was a
pleasure to hear them. Her grandmother called the little
birds fishes. Otherwise the small sea princesses, never
having seen a bird, would not have understood her.

"When you are fifteen," the grandmother told them,
"we will let you rise to the surface and sit on the rocks in
the moonlight while the great ships sail past. You will see
both forests and towns." The following year one of the sisters was to have her fifteenth birthday, but the rest of
them—well, they were each a year younger than the
other, so the youngest of them had a whole five years to
wait before she could rise to the surface from the depths
and see how things are with us. But each promised to tell
the others what she had seen and what she had found the

most interesting on that first visit. Their grandmother never really told them enough. There were so many things they were longing to hear about.

None of the mermaids was more curious than the youngest, and she, who was so silent and thoughtful, also had the longest wait. Many a night she stood at the open window and gazed up through the dark blue waters, where the fish splash with their fins and tails. She could see the moon and the stars, even though their light was rather pale. Through the water they looked much larger than they do to us. If a black cloud passed above her, she knew that it was either a whale swimming over her head or a vessel filled with passengers. These people never imagined that a pretty little mermaid was standing beneath them, stretching up her white arms toward the keel of the ship.

As soon as the eldest princess was fifteen years old, she was allowed to rise to the surface of the ocean. When she returned, she had dozens of things to talk about. The loveliest moment, she said, was lying on a sandbank close to the shore in the moonlight while the sea was calm. Then you could look at the big town where the lights were twinkling like a hundred stars. You could hear the sounds of music and the noise and clatter of carts and people. You could see all the towers and spires of the churches and hear the bells ringing. And just because she could not get close to all those wonderful things, she longed for them all the more. Oh, how the youngest sister drank it all in! And later in the evening, when she stood at the open window gazing up through the dark blue waters, she thought of the big town with all its noise and clatter, and she even fancied that she could hear the sound of the church bells ringing down to her.

A year later, the second sister was allowed to go up through the water and swim wherever she liked. She arrived at the surface just as the sun was setting, and that, she said, was the most beautiful sight of all. The whole sky looked like gold, she said, and the clouds—well, she just couldn't describe how beautiful they were as they sailed, in crimson and violet hues, over her head. Even more rap-

5. *a flock of wild swans flew like a long white veil across the water.* For Andersen swans are creatures that move from a state of gawky awkwardness to one of majestic splendor, as in his story "The Ugly Duckling." Like butterflies, the romantic symbol par excellence for transcendence and transformation, they are able to metamorphose into a higher state. The transformation of the little mermaid from sea creature to mermaid in human form to a creature of the air reflects Andersen's constant engagement with mutability and changes in identity.

idly than the clouds, a flock of wild swans flew like a long white veil across the water[5] toward the setting sun. She swam off in that direction, but the sun sank, and its rosy light was swallowed up by sea and cloud.

Another year passed, and the third sister went up. She was the boldest of them all, and she swam up a wide river that emptied into the sea. She saw beautiful green hills covered with grape vines; manors and farms peeked out from magnificent woods; she heard the birds singing; and the sun was so hot that she often had to dive under the water to cool her burning face. In a small cove she came upon a whole troop of little human children, sporting about, quite naked, in the water. She wanted to play with them, but they were terrified and fled. Then a little black animal came to the water. It was a dog, but she had never seen one before. The animal barked at her so dreadfully that she became frightened and made for the open sea. But she said that she would never forget the magnificent forest, the green hills, and the pretty little children, who could swim in the water, even though they had no tails.

The fourth sister was not as bold. She stayed far out in the wild waste of ocean, but it was just that, she told them, that made her visit so wonderful. You could see for miles and miles around you, and the sky hung over you like a big glass bell. She had seen ships, but at a distance so great that they looked like seagulls. The dolphins were sporting in the waves, and enormous whales spouted water so powerfully from their nostrils that they seemed to be surrounded by a hundred fountains.

And now it was the turn of the fifth sister. Since her birthday fell in winter, she saw things the others had not seen the first time they went up. The sea looked quite green, and large icebergs were floating in it. Each looked like a pearl, she said, but they were larger than the church towers built by human beings. They appeared in the most fantastic shapes, and they glittered like diamonds. She had sat down on one of the largest, and all the ships seemed to be afraid of it, for they gave it a wide berth and sailed rapidly past where she was sitting, with the wind playing in her long hair.

Later that evening the sky became overcast. Thunder rolled and lightning flashed, and the dark waves lifted the great blocks of ice right up out of the water, so that they flashed in the fierce red lightning. All the ships took in sail, and amid the general horror and alarm, the mermaid sat calmly on the floating iceberg, watching the blue lightning zigzag into the glittering sea.

The first time any one of the sisters went up to the surface, she would always be delighted to see so many new and beautiful things. But later, when the princesses grew older and could go up as often as they liked, they became less enthusiastic. They longed to go back down again. And after a month had passed, they said that, after all, it was much nicer down below—it was such a comfort to be home. Yet often, in the evening hours, the five sisters would link arms and float up together out of the water. They had lovely voices,[6] more beautiful than any human being's.

Before the approach of a storm, when they expected a shipwreck, the sisters would swim in front of the vessel and sing sweetly of the delights to be found in the depths of the sea. They told the sailors not to be afraid of sinking down to the bottom, but the sailors never understood their songs. They thought they were hearing the howling of the storm. Nor did they ever see any of the delights the mermaids promised, because if the ship sank, the men were drowned, and only as dead men did they reach the palace of the sea king.

When the sisters floated up, arm in arm, through the water in this way, their youngest sister would always stay back all alone, gazing after them. She would have cried, but mermaids have no tears and suffer even more than we do. "Oh, if only I were fifteen years old," she would say. "I know that I will love the world up there and all the people who live in it."

Then at last she turned fifteen. "Well, now you'll soon

6. *They had lovely voices.* Having a voice and the ability to display its art figure importantly in this tale. That the little mermaid later loses her voice, the power to express herself, reveals the drawbacks of the exchange made with the sea witch. The mermaid's voice, even though it has emotive strength, is linked above all with artistic expression. It is what makes her appealing to both merfolk and humans.

be off our hands," said the old dowager queen, her grand-mother. "Come, let me dress you up like your other sisters," and she put a wreath of white lilies in her hair, and each flower petal was half a pearl. And the old woman ordered eight big oysters to nip tight onto the princess's tail to show her high rank.

"Ow! That hurts," said the little mermaid.

"Yes, beauty has its price," the grandmother replied. How she would have liked to shake off all this finery and put away the heavy wreath! The red flowers in her garden suited her much better, but she didn't dare make any changes. "Farewell," she said as she rose through the water as lightly and clearly as a bubble moves to the surface of the water.

The sun had just set as she lifted her head above the waves, but the clouds were still tinted with crimson and gold. Up in the pale, pink sky the evening star shone clear and bright. The air was mild and fresh, and the sea dead calm. A large three-masted ship was drifting in the water, with only one sail hoisted because not a breath of wind was stirring. The sailors were lolling about in the rigging and on the yards. There was music and singing on board, and when it grew dark, a hundred lanterns were lit. With their many colors, it looked as if the flags of all nations were fluttering in the air.

The little mermaid swam right up to the porthole of the cabin, and, every time a wave lifted her up, she could see a crowd of well-dressed people through the clear glass. Among them was a young prince, the handsomest person there, with large dark eyes. He could not have been more than sixteen. It was his birthday, and that's why there was so much of a stir. When the young prince came out on the deck, where the sailors were dancing, more than a hundred rockets swished up into the sky and broke into a glitter, making the sky as bright as day. The little mermaid was so startled that she dove down under the water. But she quickly popped her head out again. And look! It was just as if all the stars up in heaven were falling down on her. Never had she seen such fireworks. Great suns went spinning around; gorgeous fiery fishes swooped into the blue air, and all this glitter was reflected in the clear, calm waters below. The ship itself was so brightly illuminated that you could see not only everyone there but even the smallest piece of rope. How handsome the young prince looked as he shook hands with the sailors! He laughed and smiled as the music sounded through the lovely night air.

It grew late, but the little mermaid could not take her eyes off the ship or the handsome prince. The colored lanterns had been extinguished; the rockets no longer rose in the air; and the cannon had ceased firing. But the sea had become restless, and you could hear a moaning, grumbling sound beneath the waves. Still, the mermaid stayed on the water, rocking up and down so that she could look into the cabin.[7] The ship gathered speed; one after another of its sails was unfurled. The waves rose higher, heavy clouds darkened the sky, and lightning flashed in the distance. A dreadful storm was brewing. So the sailors took in the sails, while the great ship rocked and scudded through the raging sea. The waves rose higher and higher until they were like huge black mountains, threatening to bring down the mast. But the ship dove like a swan between them and then rose again on their lofty, foaming crests. The little mermaid thought it must be fun for a ship to sail like that, but the crew didn't think so. The vessel groaned and creaked; the stout planks burst under the heavy pounding of the sea against the ship; and the mast snapped in two like a reed. The ship lurched to one side as the water came rushing into the hold.

The little mermaid suddenly realized that the ship was in danger. She herself had to be careful of the beams and bits of wreckage drifting in the water. One moment it was so dark that she couldn't see a thing, but then a flash of lightning lit up everyone on board. Now it was every man for himself. She was looking for the young prince, and, just as the ship was being torn apart, she saw him disappear into the depths of the sea. For just a moment she was

7. *rocking up and down so that she could look in the cabin.* The little mermaid's curiosity about human beings draws her to the world of the prince. Fascinated by what is above the surface, by the unknown, and by the forbidden, she shows an investigative curiosity lacking in many fairy-tale heroines.

EDMUND DULAC,
"The Little Mermaid," 1911

"His limbs were failing him, his beautiful eyes were closed; and he would certainly have drowned if the little mermaid had not come to his rescue." With his head only slightly above water, the prince is rescued by the mermaid in a spectacular ocean of blues and foam.

quite pleased, for she thought he would now live in her part of the world. But then she remembered that human beings could not live underwater and that only as a dead man could he come down to her father's palace. No, no, he mustn't die. So she swam in among the drifting beams and planks, oblivious to the danger of being crushed. She dove deep down and came right back up again among the waves, and at last she found the young prince. He could hardly swim any longer in the stormy sea. His limbs were failing him; his beautiful eyes were closed; and he would certainly have drowned if the little mermaid had not come to his rescue. She held his head above water and then let the waves carry her along with him.

By morning the storm had died down, and there was not a trace of the ship. The sun rose red and glowing up out of the water and seemed to bring color back into the prince's cheeks; but his eyes remained closed. The mermaid kissed his fine, high forehead and smoothed back his wet hair. He seemed to her like the marble statue in her little garden. She kissed him again and made a wish that he might live.

Soon the mermaid saw the mainland before her, with its lofty blue mountains covered with glittering white snow that looked like nestling swans. Near the coast were lovely green forests, and close by was a large building, whether it was a church or a convent she could not say. Lemon and orange trees were growing in the garden, and at the door there were tall palm trees. The sea formed a small bay at this point, and the water in it was quite still, though very deep. The mermaid swam with the handsome prince to the beach, which was covered with fine, white sand. There she placed him in the warm sunshine, making a pillow for his head with the sand.

Bells sounded in the large white building, and a number of young girls came through the garden. The little mermaid swam farther out from the shore, hiding behind some large boulders that rose out of the water. She covered her hair and chest with sea foam so that no one could see her. Then she watched to see who would come to help the poor prince.

Not much later a young girl came along. She seemed quite frightened, but only for a moment, and ran to get help from others. The mermaid saw the prince come back to life, and he smiled at everyone around him. But there was no smile for her, because he had no idea that she had rescued him. After he was taken away to the large building, she felt so miserable that she dove into the water and returned to her father's palace.

She had always been silent and thoughtful, but now more so than ever. Her sisters asked her what she had seen during her first visit to the surface, but she told them nothing. Many a morning and many an evening she rose up to the spot where she had left the prince. She saw the fruits in the garden ripen and watched as they were harvested. She saw the snow melt on the peaks. But she never saw the prince, and so she always returned home, filled with even greater sorrow than before. Her one comfort was sitting in her little garden, with her arms around the beautiful marble statue, which was so like the prince. She gave up tending her flowers, and they grew into a kind of wilderness out over the paths, twining their long stalks and leaves around the branches of the trees until the light was quite shut out.

At length she could keep it to herself no longer and told one of her sisters everything. The others learned about it soon afterward, but no one else, except a few other mermaids who didn't breathe a word to anyone but their best friends. One of them was able to give her news about the prince. She, too, had seen the festival held on board and told more about the prince and the location of his kingdom.

"Come, little sister," said the other princesses. And with their arms on each other's shoulders, they rose in one long row to the surface, just in front of where the prince's castle stood. The castle was built of a pale yellow shining stone, and it had long flights of marble steps, one of which led straight down to the sea. Splendid gilded domes rose above the roof, and between the pillars that surrounded the entire building were lifelike sculptures in marble. Through the clear glass of the tall windows you could see magnificent rooms hung with sumptuous silk curtains and tapestries. The walls were covered with large paintings that were a pleasure to contemplate. In the center of the largest room was a fountain that threw its sparkling jets high up to the glass dome of the ceiling, through which the sun shone down on the water and on the beautiful plants growing in the large pool.

Now that the little mermaid knew where the prince lived, she spent many an evening and many a night at that spot. She swam much closer to the shore than any of the others dared. She even went up the narrow channel to reach the fine marble balcony that threw its long shadow across the water. Here she would sit and gaze at the young prince, who thought that he was completely alone in the bright moonlight.

Often in the evening the little mermaid saw him go out to sea in his splendid vessel, with flags hoisted, to the strains of music. She peeked out from among the green rushes, and, when the wind caught her long silvery white veil and people saw it, they just fancied it was a swan, spreading its wings.

On many nights, when the fishermen were out at sea with their torches, she heard them praising the young prince, and their words made her even happier that she had saved his life the day he was drifting about half dead on the waves. And she remembered how she had cradled his head on her chest and how lovingly she had kissed him. But he knew nothing about any of this and never even dreamed she existed.

The little mermaid grew more and more fond of human beings and longed deeply for their company. Their world seemed so much larger than her own. You see, they could fly across the ocean in ships and climb the steep mountains high above the clouds. And the lands they possessed, their woods and their fields, stretched far beyond where she could see. There was so much that she would have liked to know,[8] and her sisters weren't able to answer all her questions. And so she went to visit her old grandmother, who knew all about the upper world, as she so aptly called the countries above the sea.

"If human beings don't drown," asked the little mermaid, "can they go on living forever? Don't they die, as we do down here in the sea?"

"Yes, yes," replied the old woman. "They too must die, and their lifetime is even shorter than ours. We sometimes live to the age of three hundred, but when our life here comes to an end, we merely turn into foam on the water. We don't even have a grave down here among those we love. We lack an immortal soul, and we shall never have another life.[9] We're like the green rush. Once it's been cut, it stops growing. But human beings have souls that live forever, even after their bodies have turned to dust.

8. *There was so much that she would have liked to know.* The little mermaid is a creature intent on broadening her horizons. What she sees on earth stimulates her desire for challenges. She wants, above all, to explore the world and to discover what is beyond the realm of "home."

9. *We lack an immortal soul, and we shall never have another life.* Andersen was deeply invested in conveying Christian messages about immortal souls and eternal life even as he and his characters clearly delighted in worldly pleasures.

They rise up through the pure air until they reach the shining stars. Just as we come up out of the water and survey the lands of human beings, so they rise up to beautiful, unknown realms—regions we shall never see."

"Why can't we have an immortal soul?" the little mermaid asked mournfully. "I would gladly give all three hundred years I have to live to become a human being for just one day and to share in that heavenly world."

"You mustn't go worrying about that," said the grandmother. "We're much happier and better off than the human beings who live up there."

"So then I'm doomed to die and float like foam on the sea, never to hear the music of the waves or see the lovely flowers and the red sun. Isn't there anything at all I can do to win an immortal soul?"

"No," said the old woman. "Only if a human loved you so much that you meant more to him than father and mother. If he were to love you with all his heart and soul and let the priest place his right hand in yours as a promise to be faithful and true here and in all eternity—then his soul would glide into your body and you, too, would obtain a share of human happiness. He would give you a soul and yet keep his own. But that can never happen. Your fish tail, which we find so beautiful, looks repulsive to people on earth. They know so little about it that they really believe the two clumsy supports they call legs look nice."

The little mermaid sighed and looked mournfully at her fish tail.

"We must be satisfied with what we have," said the old woman. "Let's dance and be joyful for the three hundred years we have to live—that's really quite time enough. After that we'll rest all the better and get our fill of sleep after we die. Tonight we are going to have a court ball."

That was something more splendid than anything we ever see on earth. The walls and ceiling of the great ballroom were made of thick, but transparent, crystal. Several hundred enormous shells, rose red and grass green, were ranged on either side, each with a blue flame that lit up the entire room and, by shining through the walls, also lit up the sea. Countless fish, large and small, could be seen swimming toward the crystal walls. The scales on some of them glowed with a purple-red brilliance, and on others like silver and gold. Through the middle of the ballroom flowed a broad stream, and in it mermen and mermaids were dancing to their own sweet song. No human beings have voices so lovely. The little mermaid sang more sweetly than anyone else, and everyone applauded her. For a moment there was joy in her heart, for she knew that she had the most beautiful voice of anyone on land or in the sea. But then her thoughts turned to the world above her. She was unable to forget the handsome prince and her great sorrow that she lacked the immortal soul he had. So she crept out of her father's palace, and while everyone inside was singing and making merry, she sat grieving in her own little garden.

Suddenly she caught the sound of a horn echoing through the water, and she thought: "Ah, there he is, sailing up above—he whom I love more than my father or my mother, he who is always in my thoughts and in whose hands I would gladly place my happiness. I would venture anything to win him and an immortal soul. While my sisters are dancing away in Father's castle, I will go to the sea witch. I've always been dreadfully afraid of her, but perhaps she can help me and tell me what to do."

And so the little mermaid left her garden and set off for the place where the witch lived, on the far side of the foaming whirlpools. She had never been over there before. There were no flowers growing there and no sea grass. There was nothing but the bare, gray, sandy bottom stretching right up to the whirlpools, where the water went swirling around like roaring mill wheels and pulled everything that it could get down with it to the depths. She had to pass through the middle of those churning eddies in order to get to the domain of the sea witch. For a long stretch there was no other way than over hot, bubbling mud—the witch called it her swamp.

The witch's house lay behind the swamp in the middle

10. *a house, built with the bones of shipwrecked human folk.* Like the Russian Baba Yaga and the witches of other folkloric regimes, the sea witch has a house constructed of human bones. Affiliated with the grotesque and the monstrous, her realm is one of decay, death, and destruction.

of a fantastic forest. All the trees and bushes were polyps, half animal and half plant. They looked like hundred-headed serpents growing out of the ground. They had branches that looked like long slimy arms, with supple wormlike fingers. Joint by joint from the root up to the very tip, they were constantly on the move, and they wound themselves tightly around anything they could seize from the sea, never letting go. The little mermaid was terrified and paused at the edge of the wood. Her heart was throbbing with fear, and she was close to turning back. But then she remembered the prince and the human soul, and her courage returned. She fastened her long flowing hair tightly around her head so that the polyps couldn't grab it. Then she folded her arms across her chest and darted forward like a fish shooting through the water, in among the hideous polyps, which reached out for her with their agile arms and fingers. She noticed how each of them had caught something and held it fast with a hundred little arms that were like hoops of iron. The white skeletons of humans who had perished at sea and sunk down into the deep waters looked out from the arms of the polyps. Ship rudders and chests were gripped tight in their arms, along with the skeletons of land animals and—most horrifying of all—a small mermaid, whom they had caught and strangled.

Now she came to a large slimy marsh in the wood, where big, fat water snakes were rolling in the mire, showing their hideous, whitish-yellow bellies. In the middle of the marsh stood a house, built with the bones of shipwrecked human folk.**10** There sat the sea witch, letting a toad feed from her mouth, just the way people sometimes feed a canary with a piece of sugar. She called the hideous water snakes her little chicks and let them crawl all over her chest.

"I know exactly what you're after," said the sea witch. "How stupid of you! But you shall have your way, and it will bring you misfortune, my pretty princess. You want to get rid of your fish tail and in its place have a couple of stumps to walk on like a human being so that the young prince will fall in love with you and you can win an immortal soul." And with that the witch let out such a loud, repulsive laugh that the toad and the snakes fell and went sprawling on the ground. "You've come at just the right time," said the witch. "Tomorrow, once the sun is up, I wouldn't be able to help you for another year. I shall prepare a drink for you. You will have to swim to land with it before sunrise, sit down on the shore, and swallow it. Your tail will then divide in two and shrink into what human beings call 'pretty legs.' But it will hurt. It will feel like a sharp sword passing through you. All who see you will say that you are the loveliest little human being they have ever seen. You will keep your graceful movements—no dancer will ever glide so lightly—but every step taken will make you feel as if you were treading on a sharp knife, enough to make your feet bleed.[11] If you are prepared to endure all that, I can help you."

"Yes," said the little mermaid, and her voice trembled. But she turned her thoughts to the prince and the prize of an immortal soul.

"Think about it carefully," said the witch. "Once you take on the form of a human, you can never again be a mermaid. You won't be able to swim down through the water to your sisters and to your father's palace. The only way you can get an immortal soul is to win the prince's love and make him willing to forget his father and mother for your sake. He must have you always in his thoughts and allow the priest to join your hands to become man and wife. If the prince marries someone else, the morning thereafter your heart will break, and you will become foam on the crest of the waves."

"I'm ready," said the little mermaid, and she turned pale as death.

"But you will have to pay me," said the witch. "And you're not getting my help for nothing. You have the loveliest voice of anyone who dwells down here at the bottom of the sea. You probably think that you can charm the prince with that voice, but you will have to give it to me. I am going to demand the best thing you possess as

11. *enough to make your feet bleed.* Feet and footware figure prominently in fairy tales, but are especially central to Andersen's stories. Perhaps inspired by the example of Snow White's stepmother, who dances to death in red-hot iron shoes, Andersen, the son of a shoemaker, often located suffering in the feet of his protagonists. Like Karen in "The Red Shoes," the little mermaid must endure agonizing pain while dancing.

12. *Put out your little tongue and let me cut it off as my payment.* That the little mermaid loses the ability to speak and sacrifices her voice for the promise of love has been read as the fatal bargain women make in Andersen's culture and in our own. But the mermaid's willingness to give up her voice is driven not only by her love for the prince but also by her desire to enter a richer and more enriching domain, one that will allow a greater range and play for her adventurous spirit.

13. *she cut off the little mermaid's tongue.* Like Philomela in Ovid's *Metamorphoses*, the little mermaid loses the power to speak and sing.

14. *"just throw a single drop of this potion on them, and their arms and fingers will be torn into a thousand pieces."* The instructions of the sea witch foreshadow the brutal act later proposed by the little mermaid's sisters. In both cases the little mermaid abstains from violence, the first time because it is not necessary, the second time because she makes a deliberate decision to do no harm.

the price for my potion. You see, I have to mix in some of my own blood so that the drink will be as sharp as a double-edged sword."

"But if you take away my voice," said the little mermaid, "what will I have left?"

"Your lovely figure," said the witch, "your graceful movements, and your expressive eyes. With those you can easily enchant a human heart. . . . Well, where's your courage? Put out your little tongue and let me cut it off as my payment.[12] Then you shall have your powerful potion."

"So be it," said the little mermaid, and the witch placed her cauldron on the fire to brew the magic potion.

"Cleanliness before everything," she said, as she scoured the vessel with a bundle of snakes she had tied together in a large knot. Then she pricked herself in the breast and let the black blood drop into the cauldron. The steam that rose created strange shapes, terrifying to behold. The witch kept tossing fresh things into the cauldron, and when the brew began to boil, it sounded like a crocodile weeping. At last the magic potion was ready, and it looked just like clear water.

"There you go," said the witch, as she cut off the little mermaid's tongue.[13] She was now dumb and could neither speak nor sing.

"If the polyps should seize you as you return through the wood," said the witch, "just throw a single drop of this potion on them, and their arms and fingers will be torn into a thousand pieces."[14] But the little mermaid had no need for that. The polyps shrank back in terror when they caught sight of the glittering potion that shone in her hand like a twinkling star. And so she passed quickly through the wood, the marsh, and the roaring whirlpools.

The little mermaid could see her father's palace. The lights in the ballroom were out. Everyone there was sure to be asleep by this time. But she did not dare to go in to see them, for now she was dumb and about to leave them forever. She felt as if her heart was going to break from grief. She stole into the garden, took one flower from the

EDMUND DULAC,
"The Little Mermaid," 1911

"But the little mermaid had no need for that. The polyps shrank back in terror when they caught sight of the glittering potion that shone in her hand like a twinkling star." The little mermaid, eager to win the love of the prince, makes her way through the aquatic wasteland that is the domain of the sea witch.

15. *rose up through the dark blue waters.* A motherless child, the little mermaid rises up to join the world of humans and to find her bridegroom. Unlike Persephone, who is carried off by a bridegroom into nether regions and rescued by her mother, she is on her own.

16. *her fish tail was gone.* The metamorphosis of the little mermaid moves her from the realm of sea creatures to that of humans. Unlike most fairy-tale heroes and heroines, who undergo transformations from the human to the bestial, the little mermaid is a hybrid figure, half animal and half beast. Her transformation, like that of the seal maidens and swan maidens of Scandinavian folklore, is reversible, but at some cost, as the ending to the story reveals.

beds of each of her sisters, blew a thousand kisses toward the palace, and then rose up through the dark blue waters.**15**

The sun had not yet risen when she caught sight of the prince's palace and climbed the beautiful marble steps. The moon was shining clear and bright. The little mermaid drank the sharp, burning potion, and it seemed as if a double-edged sword was passing through her delicate body. She fainted and fell down as if dead.

The sun rose and, shining across the sea, woke her up. She felt a sharp pain. But there in front of her stood the handsome young prince. He fixed his coal-black eyes on her so earnestly that she cast down her own and realized that her fish tail was gone**16** and that she had as pretty a pair of white legs as any young girl could wish for. But she was quite naked and so she wrapped herself in her long, flowing hair. The prince asked who she was and how she had come there, and she could only gaze back at him sweetly and sadly with her deep blue eyes, for of course she could not speak. Then he took her by the hand and led her to the palace. Every step she took, as the witch had predicted, made her feel as if she were treading on sharp knives and needles, but she willingly endured it. She walked as lightly as a bubble by the prince's side. The prince and all who saw her marveled at the beauty of her graceful movements.

She was given costly dresses of silk and muslin after she arrived. She was the most beautiful creature in the palace, but she was dumb and could neither speak nor sing. Beau-

EDMUND DULAC,
"The Little Mermaid," 1911

"The prince asked who she was and how she had come there, and she could only gaze back at him sweetly and sadly with her deep blue eyes, for of course she could not speak." The prince, wearing oriental garb and leaning against a pillar, gazes down at the girl who has been washed up on the steps.

tiful slave girls dressed in silk and gold came out and danced before the prince and his royal parents. One sang more beautifully than all the others, and the prince clapped his hands and smiled at her. This saddened the little mermaid, for she knew that she herself could sing far more beautifully. And she thought, "Oh, if only he knew that I gave my voice away forever in order to be with him."

The slave girls then danced a graceful, gliding dance to the most enchanting music. And the little mermaid raised her lovely white arms, stood on the tips of her toes, and glided across the floor, dancing as no one had danced before. She looked more and more lovely with every step, and her eyes appealed more deeply to the heart than did the singing of the slave girls.

Everyone was enchanted, especially the prince, who called her his little foundling. She kept on dancing, even though it felt as if she were treading on sharp knives every time her foot touched the ground. The prince said that she must never leave him, and she was given permission to sleep outside his door, on a velvet cushion.[17]

The prince had a page's costume made for her[18] so that she could go riding with him on horseback. They rode together through the sweet-scented woods, where the green boughs grazed her shoulders, and the little birds sang among the cool leaves. She climbed with the prince to the tops of high mountains, and, although her tender feet bled and everyone could see the blood, she only laughed and followed the prince until they could see the clouds beneath them that looked like a flock of birds traveling to distant lands.

Back at the prince's palace, when everyone in the household was asleep, she would go out on the broad marble steps and cool her burning feet in the cold seawater. And then she would think of those down there in the depths of the sea. One night her sisters rose up arm in arm singing mournfully as they floated on the water. She beckoned to them, and they recognized her and told her how unhappy she had made them all. After that they used to

17. *on a velvet cushion.* Sleeping outside the prince's door on a cushion implies that the little mermaid is something of a waif, an exotic pet for the prince.

18. *The prince had a page's costume made for her.* The critics who bemoan the self-effacing nature of the little mermaid often neglect to note that she is also more adventurous, spirited, and curious than most fairy-tale heroines. Cross-dressing is a sign of her willingness to transgress gender boundaries and to take risks in order to see the world.

visit her every night, and once she saw in the distance her old grandmother, who had not been to the surface of the sea for many years, and also the old sea king with his crown on his head. They both stretched out their hands toward her, but they did not venture so near to the shore as her sisters.

With time, she became more precious to the prince. He loved her as one loves a little child, but it never occurred to him to make her his queen. And yet she had to become his wife or else she would never receive an immortal soul, and on his wedding morning, she would dissolve into foam on the sea.

"Do you like me best of all?" the little mermaid's eyes seemed to say when he took her in his arms and kissed her lovely brow.

"Yes, you are very precious to me," said the prince, "for you have the kindest heart of anyone. And you are more devoted to me than anyone else. You remind me of a young girl I once met, but shall probably never see again. I was in a shipwreck, and the waves cast me ashore near a holy temple, where several young girls were performing their duties. The youngest of them found me on the beach and saved my life. I saw her just twice. She is the only one in the world whom I could ever love. But you are so like her that you have almost driven her image out of my mind. She belongs to the holy temple, and my good fortune has sent you to me. We will never part."

"Ah, little does he know that it was I who saved his life," thought the little mermaid. "I carried him across the sea to the temple in the woods, and I waited in the foam for someone to come and help. I saw the pretty girl that he loves better than he loves me"—and the mermaid sighed deeply, for she did not know how to shed tears. "He says the girl belongs to the holy temple and that she will therefore never return to the world. They will never again meet. I am by his side, and I see him every day. I will take care of him and love him and give up my life for him."

Not long after that, there was talk that the prince would marry and that the beautiful daughter of a neighboring king would be his wife, and that was why he was rigging out such a splendid ship. The prince was going to pay a visit at a neighboring kingdom—that was how they put it, meaning that he was going to look at his neighbor's daughter. He had a large entourage, but the little mermaid shook her head and laughed. She knew the prince's thoughts far better than anyone else.

"I shall have to go," he told her. "I have to visit this beautiful princess, because my parents insist upon it. But they cannot force me to bring her back here as my wife. I could never love her. She is not at all like the beautiful girl in the temple, whom you resemble. If I were forced to choose a bride, I would rather choose you, my dear mute foundling, with the expressive eyes." And he kissed her rosy mouth, played with her long hair, and laid his head against her heart so that it dreamed of human happiness and an immortal soul.

"You are not afraid of the sea, are you, my dear mute girl?" he asked as they stood on the deck of the splendid ship that was carrying them to the neighboring kingdom. And he told her of powerful storms and dead calms, of the strange fishes in the deep, and what divers had seen down there. She smiled at his tales, for she knew better than any one else about the wonders at the bottom of the sea.

At night, when there was an unclouded moon and everyone was asleep but the helmsman at his wheel, the little mermaid sat by the ship's rail, gazing down through the clear water. She thought she could see her father's palace, with her old grandmother standing on top of it with the silver crown on her head, gazing through the swift current at the keel of the vessel. Then her sisters came up on the waves and looked at her with eyes full of sorrow, wringing their white hands. She beckoned to them and smiled and would have liked to tell them that she was happy and that all was going well for her. But the cabin boy came up just then, and the sisters dove down, so that the boy was sure that the white something he had seen was only foam on the water.

The next morning the ship sailed into the harbor of the

neighboring king's magnificent capital. The church bells were ringing, and from the towers you could hear a flourish of trumpets. Soldiers saluted with gleaming bayonets and flying colors. Every day there was a festival. Balls and entertainments followed one another, but the princess had not yet appeared. People said that she was being brought up and educated in a holy temple, where she was learning all the royal virtues. At last she arrived.

The little mermaid was eager for a glimpse of her beauty, and she had to admit that she had never seen a more charming person. Her skin was clear and delicate, and behind long, dark eyelashes her laughing blue eyes shone with deep sincerity.

"It's you," said the prince. "You're the one who rescued me when I was lying half dead on the beach." And he clasped his blushing bride in his arms. "Oh, I am so very happy," he said to the little mermaid. "My dearest wish—more than I ever dared hope for—has been granted. My happiness will give you pleasure, because you're more devoted to me than anyone else." The little mermaid kissed his hand, and she felt as if her heart were already broken. The day of his wedding would mean her death, and she would turn into foam on the ocean waves.

All the church bells were ringing as the heralds rode through the streets to proclaim the betrothal. Perfumed oil was burning in precious silver lamps on every altar. The priest swung the censers, while the bride and bridegroom joined hands and received the blessing of the bishop. Dressed in silk and gold, the little mermaid stood holding the bride's train, but her ears never heard the festive music, and her eyes never saw the holy rites. She was thinking about her last night on earth and about everything that she had lost in this world.

That same evening bride and bridegroom went on board ship. The cannon roared, the flags were waving, and in the center of the ship a sumptuous tent of purple and gold had been raised. It was strewn with luxurious cushions, for the wedded couple was to sleep there on that calm, cool night. The sails filled with the breeze, and the ship glided lightly and smoothly over the clear seas.

When it grew dark, colored lanterns were lit, and the sailors danced merrily on deck. The little mermaid could not help thinking of that first time she had come up from the sea and gazed on just such a scene of joyous festivities. And now she joined in the dance, swerving and swooping as lightly as a swallow that avoids pursuit. Cries of admiration greeted her from all sides. Never before had she danced so elegantly. It was as if sharp knives were cutting into her delicate feet, but she felt nothing, for the wound in her heart was far more painful. She knew that this was the last night she would ever see the prince for whom she had forsaken her family and her home, given up her lovely voice, and suffered hours of agony without his suspecting a thing. This was the last evening that she would breathe the air with him or gaze on the deep sea and starry sky. An eternal night, without thoughts or dreams, awaited her who had no soul and would never win one. All was joy and merriment on board until long past midnight. She laughed and danced with the others while the thought of death was in her heart. The prince kissed his lovely bride, while she played with his dark hair, and arm in arm they retired to the magnificent tent.

The ship was now hushed and quiet. Only the helmsman was there at his wheel. And the little mermaid leaned with her white arms on the rail and looked to the east for a sign of the rosy dawn. The first ray of the sun, she knew, would bring her death. Suddenly she saw her sisters rising out of the sea. They were as pale as she, but their long beautiful hair was no longer waving in the wind—it had been cut off.

"We have given our hair to the witch," they said, "to help us save you from the death that awaits you tonight. She has given us a knife—look, here it is. See how sharp it is? Before sunrise you must plunge it into the prince's heart. Then, when his warm blood splashes on your feet, they will grow back together and form a fish tail, and you will be a mermaid once more. You will be able to come back down to us in the water and to live out your three hundred years before being changed into the foam of the salty sea. Make haste! Either he or you will die before sunrise. Our old grandmother has been feeling such sorrow that her white hair has been falling out, as ours fell under the witch's scissors. Kill the prince and come back to us! But make haste—look at the red streaks in the sky. In a few minutes the sun will rise, and then you will die." And with a strange deep sigh, they sank down beneath the waves.

The little mermaid drew back the purple curtain of the tent, and she saw the lovely bride sleeping with her head on the prince's breast. She bent down and kissed his handsome brow, then looked at the sky where the rosy

EDMUND DULAC,
"The Little Mermaid," 1911

"With a last glance at the prince from eyes half dimmed in death, she threw herself from the ship into the sea and felt her body dissolve into foam." Bearing a distinct resemblance to Ophelia, the little mermaid perishes in the element that was once her home.

dawn was growing brighter and brighter. She gazed at the sharp knife in her hand and again fixed her eyes on the prince, who whispered the name of his bride in his dreams—she alone was in his thoughts. The little mermaid's hand trembled as she held the knife—then she flung it far out over the waves. The water turned red where it fell, something that looked like drops of blood came oozing out of the water. With a last glance at the prince from eyes half dimmed in death, she threw herself from the ship into the sea and felt her body dissolve into foam.

And now the sun came rising up from the sea. Its warm and gentle rays fell on the death-chilled foam, but the little mermaid did not feel as if she were dying. She saw the

HONOR C. APPLETON,
"The Little Mermaid," 1922

"The little mermaid saw that she had a body like theirs and that she was rising higher and higher out of the foam." The rising sun heralds the rebirth of the little mermaid, who, as a daughter of the air, can earn an immortal soul by performing good deeds for three hundred years.

19. *you too can earn for yourself an immortal soul.* The three hundred years of good deeds mark the life span of merfolk. The little mermaid herself has achieved immortality in the real world, not only through her story but also through the bronze statue of her that has become Copenhagen's most popular tourist attraction.

bright sun and, hovering around her, hundreds of lovely creatures—she could see right through them, see the white sails of the ship and the rosy clouds in the sky. And their voice was the voice of song, yet too ethereal to be heard by mortal ears, just as no mortal eye could behold them. They had no wings, but their lightness bore them up as they floated through the air. The little mermaid saw that she had a body like theirs and that she was rising higher and higher out of the foam.

"Where am I?" she asked, and her voice sounded like that of the other beings, more ethereal than any earthly music could sound.

"Among the daughters of the air," answered the others. "A mermaid does not have an immortal soul, and she can never have one unless she wins the love of a human being. Eternity, for her, depends on a power outside her. Nor do the daughters of the air have an everlasting soul, but through good deeds they can earn one for themselves. We shall fly to the hot countries, where the stifling air of pestilence means death for humans. We shall bring cool breezes. We shall carry the fragrance of flowers through the air and send comfort and healing. When we have tried to do all the good we can in three hundred years, we shall win an immortal soul and have a share in mankind's eternal happiness. You, poor little mermaid, have tried with your whole heart to do as we are doing. You have suffered and endured and have raised yourself into the world of the spirits of the air. Now, with three hundred years of good deeds, you too can earn for yourself an immortal soul."[19]

The little mermaid raised her crystal arms toward God's sun, and for the first time she knew what tears felt like.

On the ship there was much bustling about and sounds of life. The little mermaid saw the prince and his beautiful bride searching for her. With great sadness, they gazed at the pearly foam, as if they knew that she had thrown herself onto the waves. Unseen, she kissed the forehead of the bride, smiled at the prince, and then mounted onto a rose-red cloud that was sailing to the sky with the other children of the air.

"So we shall float for three hundred years, until at last we arrive at the heavenly kingdom."

"And we may reach it even sooner," whispered one of her companions. "Unseen, we float into human homes where there are children, and for every day we find a good child who makes mother and father happy and earns their love, God shortens our time of trial. The child never knows about that when we fly through the room and smile with joy, and then a year is taken away from the three hundred. But when we see a child who is naughty or spiteful, then we shed tears of sorrow, and every tear adds one more day to our time of trial."[20]

20. *every tear adds one more day to our time of trial.* The conclusion adds a disciplinary twist to the tale, suggesting to the children outside the book that an invisible presence monitors their behavior. This lesson can be far more frightening than the descriptions of the tortures to which the little mermaid is subjected.

BIOGRAPHIES OF AUTHORS

AND COLLECTORS

ALEXANDER AFANASEV (1826–1871)
"Vasilisa the Fair"

BORN IN A small town in Russia, Alexander Afanasev studied law at Moscow University and worked in the state archives from 1849 to 1856. In the 1850s he began studying Slavic folklore and, inspired by the example of the Brothers Grimm, collected and published Russian folktales. He initially planned to issue single editions of the tales, with extensive commentary, but ended up producing a comprehensive anthology. *Russian Fairy Tales*, which was issued in eight installments between 1855 and 1863, became the authoritative volume of Russian folklore. The work included over six hundred stories, along with variant forms, and made an effort to capture the "poetic voice" of the Russian people.

While Afanasev himself recorded about a dozen tales from storytellers, he relied mainly on stories passed on to him in written form. Many of the folktales had been gathered by the Russian Geographical Society; others were sent to him by teachers, army officers, and provincial governors. Over two hundred of the stories in *Russian Fairy Tales* came from the pen of Vladimir Dahl, a scholar who had spent years collecting folklore. Afanasev insisted on the scholarly integrity of his collection and resisted the notion of rewriting and embellishing the tales in order to make them more appealing to a popular audience. His was a scholarly venture, and he sought to rescue storytelling traditions by developing systematic methods for collecting, transcribing, and editing Russian folktales.

Afanasev's endorsement of folkloric authenticity brought him into repeated conflict with censors, who took issue with the earthy humor and ribald content of many tales. The Moscow metropolitan Filaret decreed the Russian stories to be "thoroughly blasphemous and immoral." The tales offended "pious sentiment and propriety" with their "profanity." Afanasev courageously responded by declaring: "There is a million times more morality, truth, and human love in my folk legends than in the sanctimonious sermons delivered by Your Holiness."

Afanasev embraced not only the peasant culture that produced the stories but also the language in which the tales were clothed. Like Pushkin, who believed that "our language is inherently beautiful" and that it finds its "breadth of expression" in folktales, Afanasev hoped that the revival of fairy tales would promote the triumph of the Russian language over the French language, which had been adopted by the aristocracy. The playwright Maxim Gorky also remarked, some decades later, on the powerful poetic language of the fairy tales in Afanasev's collection: "In the tales, people fly through the air on a magic carpet, walk in seven-league boots, build castles overnight. The tales opened up for me a new world where some free and fearless power reigned and inspired in me the dream of a better life. The immortal oral poetry of the common people . . . has greatly helped me understand the fascinating beauty and wealth of our language."

For all his enthusiasm for the robust imaginative world of the fairy tale, Afanasev took a strangely reductive interpretive approach to Russian folklore. For him the tales enacted meteorological dramas, with characters symbolizing the sun, the wind, the rain, the ocean, or the stars. In "Vasilisa the Fair" he perceived a battle between sunlight (Vasilisa) and storm (the stepmother) and other dark clouds (the stepsisters). Folktales, he reasoned, were primitive man's way of understanding nature, with the sun in the role of hero and darkness in any form as its adversary.

Like the Grimms, who hoped to reach a broad audience by publishing an abbreviated version of the *Nursery and Household Tales*, Afanasev published a compact edition entitled *Russian Fairy Tales for Children*. He eliminated bawdy tales and everything unsuitable for children and substituted standard Russian for dialecticisms. In 1872 stories that had been deemed "unprintable" by censors were published anonymously in Switzerland under the title

Russian Forbidden Tales. Afanasev's collection was used as the basis for Vladimir Propp's *Morphology of the Folktale,* a pioneering study of the structure of fairy tales.

In 1860 police raided the publishing house responsible for printing *Russian Fairy Tales* and arrested its owner. The second edition of the tales was confiscated and burned. Accused of illegally appropriating work from the public archives, Afanasev lost his government post and lived in poverty for the rest of his life. He was forced to sell his private library and lamented that "books once nourished me with ideas, now—with bread." Afanasev died of consumption at the age of forty-five in 1871.

HANS CHRISTIAN ANDERSEN (1805–1875)
"The Emperor's New Clothes"
"The Little Match Girl"
"The Princess and the Pea"
"The Ugly Duckling"
"The Little Mermaid"

COPENHAGEN'S MOST RENOWNED national monument is a bronze statue of a mermaid, a tribute to Hans Christian Andersen's celebrated story about a creature from the sea who transcends her origins through silence, suffering, and self-sacrifice. Despite a powerful rise to fame and international celebrity in his own lifetime, Andersen identified, up to the end of his life, with his characters, smarting at the wounds inflicted on them and commiserating with their humiliations. "I suffer with my characters," Andersen wrote to a friend. "I share their moods, whether good or bad." While some readers fault Andersen for indulging in self-pity by producing stories in which bad things happen to good people (think of the little match girl) or bad people happen to good things (think of the steadfast tin soldier), many others have found a powerful redemptive force in his depictions of tragic destinies. Writing over one hundred and fifty tales, Andersen was single-handedly responsible for reinvigorating the fairy tale and stretching its limits to accommodate new desires and fantasies.

Andersen's own account of his life exists in several versions. There is the youthful autobiography written in 1832, just before he embarked on a grand tour. Some years later he published *The Fairy Tale of My Life* in German and had it translated into English. And finally the Danish version of his life was published with his collected works, a full eight years after Andersen's oeuvre

HANS CHRISTIAN ANDERSEN
1860

had been translated into German. From these writings Andersen's powerful social anxieties and personal insecurities emerge.

An upwardly mobile child born to a shoemaker and a washerwoman, Andersen both romanticized his youth and elaborated endlessly on its indignities. At age fourteen Andersen left Odense, the town of his birth, for Copenhagen, determined to become a success on the national stage. Without an education, with a voice that was changing, and with no real means of subsistence, Andersen was taking an enormous risk by making this move to the city. In a stroke of good fortune, influential friends obtained funds for him to remedy his lack of education. At age seventeen Andersen attended school with twelve-year-olds. He hated his teacher, who constantly berated him, as well as the students, who mocked his gawky gait and strange mannerisms. When Jonas Collin, his guardian in Copenhagen, arranged for him to return to the capital and to complete his studies at the university, the quality of his life improved dramatically, although Andersen was never short of complaints about the miseries of his personal life.

Andersen's first encounter with Danish folktales had been in the spinning room of the asylum in which his grandmother worked. The young boy entertained the women there with chalk drawings, and they rewarded him, he recalled, "by telling [him] tales in return." What Andersen discovered in the folklore of his native land was a world "as rich as that of the Thousand and One Nights," but a world that also gave rise to dread: "When it grew dark I scarcely dared to go out of the house." As early as 1830, in the preface to a story called "The Ghost," Andersen recalled what a "pleasure" it had been to listen to fairy tales and declared his intention to publish a cycle of Danish folktales. After publishing a travelogue and a fictional autobiography that enjoyed a modest success, he turned his attention to the tales, bringing out a thin pamphlet entitled *Tales, Told for Children* in 1835. In it are to be found "The Tinderbox," "Little Claus and Big Claus," "The Princess and the Pea," and "Little Ida's Flowers." While the subtitle declared the implied audience to be children, Andersen himself commented: "I seize an idea for the grown-ups, and then tell the story to the little ones while always remembering that Father and Mother often listen, and you must also give them something for their minds."

Andersen, like the Grimms before him, had to endure stern criticism of the fairy tales he had published. *The Danish Literary Times* reprimanded the author for adopting a colloquial style: "It is not meaningless convention that one does not put words together in print in the same disordered manner as one may do quite acceptably in oral speech." And the reviewer further groused about the condescending tone of the volume. Another reviewer objected to "The Tinderbox," complaining that its lack of moral fiber made it inappropriate for children. But children evidently believed otherwise, and Andersen was delighted to find that wherever he went he found children who had read his fairy tales.

By 1837 Andersen had three fairy-tale pamphlets in print, and it began to dawn on him that the stories he was writing—more than the poems, novels, plays, and travelogues with which he hoped to secure literary eminence—might pave the way to fame. In Weimar and in London he received the kind of acclaim he had never received in his native land. From London he wrote: "I cannot achieve more here in this metropolis than I already have. . . . It is a fact: I am 'a famous man.' The aristocracy here, so discouraging to its own poets, has welcomed me as one of its own circle." Dickens presented him with twelve volumes of his collected works, inscribed with the words "Hans Christian Andersen, from his friend and admirer Charles Dickens." Unlike Perrault and Grimm, Andersen staked a claim to authorship of the stories he told. Conceding that some were inspired by the tales he had heard as a child, he also asserted the power of his own genius and imagination to craft literary fairy tales. If the folkloric imagination is oriented toward romance, marriage, power, wealth, and finding a way back home, the literary fairy tales of Andersen are more up close and personal, focusing on human behavior, on virtues and vices, and on compassion and repentance. Fairy tales give us archetypal figures: everyman, everywoman, and everychild. But in Andersen's work we often find characters who are alter egos of the author, figures who reflect the personal anxieties, fantasies, and struggles of the proletariat youth who worked his way up to Denmark's literary aristocracy.

Andersen is stingy with the use of "happily ever after." Many of his tales, charged with tragic power, contain elaborate descriptions of bodily mortification and conclude in the graveyard. If fairy tales allow us to witness the conquest of ogres, stepmothers, and witches, Andersen's stories, by contrast, put the suffering of orphans and children on display. The *little* mermaid, the *little* match girl, and young Karen of "The Red Shoes" all perish in the name of Christian piety. Maurice Sendak's indictment of Andersen is harsh: "*The Red Shoes* is the worst of the lot. The arbitrary torments Andersen inflicts on Karen are sadistic and distasteful in the extreme and the tale's Christian sentiment rings false."

The celebrated author Ursula Le Guin also "hated all the Andersen stories with unhappy endings," but still she found them fascinating: "That didn't stop me from reading them, and rereading them. Or from remembering them." And there are many who find in Andersen's stories, beyond fascination, the promise of redemption through compassion and genuine repentance. For Andersen the fairy tale had a powerful ethical element, providing a kind of "court of justice over shadow and substance." In every fairy tale, he insisted, there is a kind of "double current": "an ironic top current that plays and sports with great and small things, that plays shuttlecock with what is high and low; and then the deep undercurrent, that honestly and truly brings all to its right place." For him the tales had a compensatory force, enabling him to right the wrongs of real life and to even out the scales of justice. And it was in the immortality the fairy tales bestowed on him that he found real poetic justice.

PETER CHRISTEN ASBJØRNSEN (1812–1885) AND JØRGEN MOE (1813–1882)
"East of the Sun and West of the Moon"

ASBJØRNSEN AND MOE developed a friendship while still attending school, and together they determined to do for Norwegian folklore what the Brothers Grimm had accomplished for German folklore. "No cultivated person now doubts the scientific importance of the folktales," Moe asserted. "They help to determine a people's unique character and outlook." Like the Grimms, Asbjørnsen and Moe sought to preserve a national treasure, one that both reflected and shaped national identity. By collecting "nature poems," Asbjørnsen believed, he and Moe were preserving the most profound expressions of the Norwegian soul.

The two collaborators pursued very different careers: Moe became an ordained clergyman, then a bishop, while Asbjørnsen earned his living as a zoologist. But both had grown up listening to stories: Asbjørnsen in his father's workshop, and Moe on a farm. They both strove to capture more than the spirit of the oral storytelling tradition. Initially they planned to write the stories down verbatim, but they soon understood the way in which the spoken word tended to fall flat on the printed page. Engaging in intensive fieldwork, they sought to identify variant forms and to construct composite tales that captured the essence of a story. Asbjørnsen and Moe preserved a robust folkloric tradition and did for Norway what the sagas did for Iceland and the *Kalevala* for Finland. Together they roamed the countryside, collecting the stories that were included in their *Norwegian Folktales*, published in 1841. Three additional installments followed.

While many of the stories in the *Norwegian Folktales* have European analogues, others show a distinctive character that aligns them with the prose and poetic *Eddas*. In addition, these stories reveal the degree to which every culture constructs its own heroes, heroines, helpers, and villains. If the French cower before ogres, the British fear giants, and the Germans dread wicked witches, the Norwegians are terrorized by trolls. "East of the Sun and West of the Moon," for all its reliance on the story of "Cupid and Psyche," is also given a Nordic flavor with its four winds and mountainous retreat.

Asbjørnsen and Moe's collection was translated into English by Sir George Dasent in 1859, and many of the tales in it found their way into Andrew Lang's *Fairy Books*. Still, the stories, with the exception of "East of the Sun and West of the Moon," never enjoyed the popularity of the collections published by the Brothers Grimm and by Charles Perrault.

JEANNE-MARIE LEPRINCE DE BEAUMONT (1711–1780)
"Beauty and the Beast"

JEANNE-MARIE LEPRINCE DE BEAUMONT was born in Rouen. Her marriage in 1741 to a notorious libertine was annulled after two years, and she left for England in 1745 to take a post as governess. There she married M. Pichon and raised several children. Between 1750 and 1775 she published a series of anthologies of stories, fairy tales, essays, and anecdotes: *Le Magasin des enfants* (1757), *Le Magasin des adolescents* (1760), *Le Magasin des pauvres* (1768), and *Le Mentor moderne* (1770). Each of these collections was designed to instill social virtues in children and young adults. In 1762 Madame de Beaumont returned to France, where she continued to publish widely until her death at her country estate in Haute-Savoie.

Le Magasin des enfants (translated into English as *The Young Misses' Magazine* in 1759) was a frame narrative with a storytelling governess surrounded by young girls. Madame de Beaumont's best-known tales appeared in it: "Beauty and the Beast," "Prince Charming," "and "Prince Desire." She based her version of "Beauty and the Beast" on a far longer version published by Madame de Villeneuve in 1740. Her abbreviated version, which has become part of the Western fairy-tale canon, enshrines diligence, self-effacement, kindness, modesty, and compassion as the cardinal virtues for girls.

JEANNE-MARIE LEPRINCE DE BEAUMONT
Anonymous

JACOB GRIMM (1785–1863) AND
WILHELM GRIMM (1786–1859)

"Little Red Riding Hood"
"Hansel and Gretel"
"Snow White"
"Sleeping Beauty"
"Rapunzel"
"The Frog King, or Iron Heinrich"
"Rumpelstiltskin"

IN 1944, WHEN the Allies were locked in combat with German troops, W. H. Auden decreed the Grimms' *Fairy Tales* to be "among the few indispensable, common-property books upon which Western culture can be founded." In collecting folktales from German-speaking regions, Jacob and Wilhelm Grimm had produced a work that ranks "next to the Bible in importance." Published in two volumes in 1812 and 1815, the Grimms' collection—along with Charles Perrault's *Tales of Mother Goose* (1697)—quickly established itself as the authoritative source of tales now disseminated across many Anglo-American and European cultures.

When Jacob and Wilhelm Grimm first developed the plan to compile German folktales, they had in mind a scholarly project. They wanted to capture the "pure" voice of the German people and to preserve in print the oracular poetry of the common people. Priceless folkloric treasures could still be found circulating in towns and villages, but the twin threats of industrialization and urbanization imperiled their survival and demanded immediate action.

Weighed down by a ponderous introduction and by extensive annotations, the first edition of the *Nursery and Household Tales* had the look of a scholarly tome rather than of a book for a broad audience. It contained not only the classic fairy tales that we associate with the name Grimm but also jokes, legends, fables, anecdotes, and all manner of other traditional tales.

The tales in the Grimms' collection have come to constitute a cultural archive of Germanic folklore, a repository of stories thought to mirror and model national identity. Many folklorists and literary historians remain heavily invested in perpetuating the notion that the Grimms' tales were rooted in a peasant culture and that they were spontaneously produced by folk raconteurs who were able to tap into the creative unconscious of the German people. In recent decades, however, scholars have begun to inter-

JACOB AND WILHELM GRIMM
Elisabeth Jerichau-Baumann, 1855

rogate the genesis of the collection, challenging the notion that the Grimms' folktales are examples of unmediated storytelling.

The Grimms relied on numerous sources, both oral and literary, to compile their collection. Their annotations to the tales reveal the degree to which they raided various national collections, drawing on literary sources and European analogues to construct the "definitive" folkloric version of a tale. While they may not have cast a wide net in their efforts to identify oral tales ("We were not able to make broad inquiries," they conceded in their introductory essay), they spent many years listening, taking notes, and drafting different versions of each tale. The vast majority of their informants were literate women from their own social class, but they also collected tales told by "untutored" folk raconteurs (Dorothea Viehmann, the daughter of an innkeeper of French Huguenot descent and widow of a tailor, was, ironically, the star witness for the folkloric authenticity of the collection). Although the Grimms were at pains to emphasize the "purity" of the language in their collection, they failed to acknowledge that the versions to which they were treated must have deviated sharply from what was told at harvesting time or in the spinning room. The "stable core" to which they refer in their introduction may have been intact, but the manner in which the tales were told must have been considerably altered, moving in a register vastly different from the crude language, ribald humor, and earthy strokes of folk versions. Who would be surprised to learn that informants of any social class might want to impress the dignified brothers with their good breeding and polite diction?

To a great extent the Grimms' scholarly ambitions and patriotic zeal guided the production of the first edition of the *Nursery and Household Tales*. But once the collection was in print, reviewers weighed in with critiques that took the brothers (Wilhelm in particular) back to the drawing board to revise, rescript, and redact. One critic denounced the collection as tainted by French and Italian influences. Another lamented the vast amounts of "pathetic" and "tasteless" material and urged parents to keep the volume out of the hands of children. The philosopher August Wilhelm Schlegel and the poet Clemens Brentano were disheartened by the raw tone of the folktales and recommended a bit of artifice to make the folktales more appealing.

In successive editions of the *Nursery and Household Tales*, Wilhelm Grimm fleshed out the texts to the point where they were often double their original lengths. He polished the prose so carefully that no one could complain of its rough-hewn qualities. More important, the Grimms suddenly changed their view about the implied audience for the tales. What had originally been designed as documents for scholars gradually turned into bedtime reading for children. As early as 1815 Jacob wrote to his brother that the two of them would have to "confer extensively about the new edition of the first part of the children's tales," and he expressed high hopes for strong sales of the second, revised edition.

While Wilhelm Grimm's son claimed that children had taken possession of a book that was not theirs to begin with, Wilhelm clearly helped the process along by deleting "every phrase unsuitable for children." In practice this meant removing virtually every reference to premarital pregnancy. In the first edition of the *Nursery and Household Tales*, Rapunzel's daily romps up in the tower with the prince have weighty consequences: "Tell me, God-mother, why my clothes are so tight and why they don't fit me any longer," a mystified maiden asks the enchantress. For the second edition of the *Nursery and Household Tales*, Rapunzel simply asks the enchantress why she is so much harder to pull up to the window than is the prince. "Hans Dumm," the story of a young man who has the power (and uses it) to impregnate women simply by wishing them to be with child, was eliminated from the first edition of the tales. "The Frog King, or Iron Heinrich," the first tale in the collection, no longer ends with the overjoyed couple retiring for the night on the princess's bed but with a prenuptial visit to the father-king.

The Grimms were intent on eliminating all residues of risqué humor in the tales they recorded, yet they had no reservations about preserving, and in some cases intensifying, the violence. Cinderella's stepsisters are spared their vision in the first recorded version of the story, but in the second edition of the *Nursery and Household Tales*, doves peck out their eyes and a moral gloss is added to the story: "So both sisters were punished with blindness to the end of their days for being so wicked and false." Rumpelstiltskin beats a hasty retreat on a flying spoon at the end of some versions of his story, but the Grimms chose to show how he is so beside himself with rage that he tears himself in two. In successive editions of the *Nursery and Household Tales*, the grisly particulars about the fate of Briar Rose's unsuccessful suitors become clearer. When they failed to scale the hedge surrounding the castle, "the briars clasped each other as if they were holding hands, and the young men who tried got caught in them and . . . died an agonizing death."

In 1823 Edgar Taylor published a translation of selected tales from the Grimms' collection under the title *German Popular Stories*. It was this edition, illustrated by George Cruikshank, that inspired the Grimms to prepare a so-called *Kleine Ausgabe*, or compact edition, of the *Nursery and Household Tales*. This collection of fifty tales, which appeared in time for Christmas in 1825, revealed that the new implied audience for the Grimms' collecting efforts was children. The original goal of producing a cultural archive of folklore gradually gave way to the desire to create an educational manual (*Erziehungsbuch*) for children.

Today adults and children read Grimms' *Nursery and Household Tales* in nearly every shape and form: illustrated or annotated, bowdlerized or embellished, faithful to the original German or fractured, parodied or treated with reverence. Even more impressively, the Grimms' stories have come to be disseminated across a wide variety of media. Little Red Riding Hood is mobilized to sell rental cars and Johnnie Walker Red Label; Disney's Snow White has sung on-screen about the prince who will rescue her to several generations of children; "Fitcher's Bird" has been reprinted with photographs by Cindy Sherman; selected tales have been illustrated by Maurice Sendak; and Humperdinck's *Hansel and Gretel* is performed in opera houses. The Grimms' stories have been recycled in countless literary works, ranging from Charlotte Brontë's *Jane Eyre* through Vladimir Nabokov's *Lolita* to Anne Sexton's *Transformations*.

JOSEPH JACOBS (1854–1916)
"Jack and the Beanstalk"
"Molly Whuppie"
"The Story of the Three Little Pigs"
"Kate Crackernuts"

BORN IN SYDNEY, Australia, and educated at Sydney University, at Cambridge University, and at the University of Berlin, Joseph Jacobs was both folklorist and historian. He first earned renown for a series of articles on the persecution of Jews in Russia and published many volumes in the field of Jewish history. In 1900 he became editor of the *Jewish Encyclopedia* and moved to New York City to carry out that work. At the Jewish Theological Seminary he served as professor of English.

Jacobs was prolific as a folklorist. He edited the prominent journal *Folk-Lore* from 1899 to 1900 and issued collections of fables and fairy tales from around the world. After turning his energy to Indian and Near Eastern folklore, Jacobs launched a series of fairy-tale collections designed to reclaim Britain's rich folkloric legacy. These collections were the British answer to Perrault in France and to the Brothers Grimm in Germany, aiming to capture an oral tradition before it died out and to reveal that the British could pride themselves on a powerful, imaginative native lore. "Who says that English folk have no fairy tales of their own?" Jacobs asked with a rhetorical flourish in the preface to *English Fairy Tales*. Like the Grimms, Jacobs saw his project as a patriotic venture, but in his case it was also an effort to bridge class differences, to close "the lamentable gap between the governing and recording classes and the dumb working classes of this country—dumb to others but eloquent among themselves." He appealed to readers to send him tales like those in the Grimms' collection so that England might take the lead in folklore research.

Disturbed by the fact that Charles Perrault had "captivated" English and

Scottish children with as much force as or, probably, with even more force than he had entranced French ones, Jacobs sought to restore British stories to the national consciousness. "What Perrault began," he lamented, "the Grimms completed. Tom Tit Tot gave way to Rumpelstiltskin, the Three Sillies to Hansel and Gretel, and the English Fairy Tale became a *mélange confus* of Perrault and the Grimms." What Jacobs accomplished with great flair was the establishment of a British canon, a written script that preserved the stories and promoted their use as bedtime reading. Not only did he preserve the cultural memory of fairy tales; he also prided himself on a volume with powerful entertainment value.

Jacobs tried to retell the stories "as a good nurse will speak when she tells Fairy Tales," but he also added notes and commentary for those interested in his sources. A warning page preceded the notes: "Oyez, oyez, oyez: the English fairy tales are now closed. Little boys and girls must not read any further." In a matter of a few years, Jacobs had issued four volumes in all: *English Fairy Tales* (1890), *Celtic Fairy Tales* (1892), *More English Fairy Tales* (1894), and *More Celtic Fairy Tales* (1894). All four volumes were illustrated by John D. Batten.

Jacobs's contributions to the promotion of British folklore rivaled those of his contemporary Andrew Lang, whose series of fairy books are still in print today. Jacobs, unlike Lang, tried to capture the "colloquial-romantic tone" of British storytelling. "This book," he wrote of *English Fairy Tales*, "is meant to be read aloud, and not merely taken in by the eye."

CHARLES PERRAULT (1628–1703)

"Cinderella"
"Bluebeard"
"Donkeyskin"
"Master Cat, or Puss in Boots"
"Tom Thumb"
"Little Red Riding Hood"

CHARLES PERRAULT WAS BORN into a prominent family, one that made a lasting mark in the French civil service. As sons of a member of the Paris parliament, Perrault and his four brothers distinguished themselves in fields ranging from architecture and theology to literature and law. Charles enrolled in the Collège de Beauvais, but stopped attending classes at age fifteen and prepared himself for his law examinations. After taking a

CHARLES PERRAULT
Anonymous, 1670

degree in law, he began work in the office of his brother, then tax receiver in Paris. The demands of his post were light, and Perrault amused himself by writing verse and designing buildings. In 1663 he went to work for Jean-Baptiste Colbert, France's most influential minister, and was assigned to the Department of Buildings, where he was responsible for selecting the architects who designed Versailles and the Louvre.

Perrault married late, in 1672, and his wife, Marie Guichon, died in child-birth after bearing three sons. The youngest son, Pierre, has been credited as being author of the first edition of Perrault's collected fairy tales (his name appeared on the title page), but most scholars now take the position that Pierre Perrault Darmancour, then eighteen, was unlikely to have written the stories. Perrault retired from civil service in 1683 and devoted himself to the education of his sons and to literary efforts.

Perrault's *Stories, or Tales from Past Times, with Morals* (*Histoires ou contes du temps passé, avec des moralités*) appeared in 1697. It was a book that emphatically aligned Perrault with the "moderns," that faction in French literary circles that embraced the robust energy of folklore and paganism in order to renew French cultural production. Unlike the "ancients," Perrault and his followers disavowed classical models and denounced the oppressive influence of classical authors. In his *Quarrel between the Ancients and the Moderns* (*Querelle des anciens et des modernes*), Perrault elaborated on his then radical position, which pitted him against such luminaries as Boileau and Racine, and ultimately against Louis XIV, who favored turning to classical antiquity to inspire contemporary writers.

Perrault's collection of fairy tales includes stories that have come to constitute the classical canon: "Sleeping Beauty," "Little Red Riding Hood," "Bluebeard," "Cinderella," "Tom Thumb," "The Fairies," "Ricky with the Tuft," and "Master Cat, or Puss in Boots." Uprooting folktales from their peasant origins and transplanting them into a courtly culture that valued a stylized literary form and whimsical touches, Perrault produced a volume with an unprecedented popular appeal. Stories that had once been vulgar and ribald, with grotesque twists and burlesque turns, were established at the center of a new literary culture, one that trained its sights on socializing, civilizing, and educating children. In the high jinks, escapades, adventures, and romances of fairy-tale characters, Perrault found a way to communicate what matters and how to secure it. His Bluebeard's wife not only inherits Bluebeard's estate; she also buys commissions for her brothers and uses her wealth to remarry. Tom Thumb takes care of his entire family, buying peerages for his father and all his brothers.

Perrault's *Tales of Mother Goose* is unique in inflecting the stories in it for both children and adults. On the one hand, the plots offer family conflict and whimsical melodrama that appeal powerfully to the imagination of the child. On the other, they offer sly asides and sophisticated commentary that are directed to adult readers. Perrault was an inspired broker between the adult storytelling culture of peasants and the nursery stories for children of sophisticated aristocrats. He encoded his tales with messages about behavior, values, attitudes, and ways of reading the world, but sweetened those messages with fanciful plots and affecting prose. His rendition of "Cinderella" so perfectly captured the imagination of children and adults alike that it has remained the master narrative to which all variants are endlessly compared. Disney turned to Perrault when he planned a feature-length animated film on the persecuted heroine who dresses and dances her way to riches.

In the preface to *Tales of Mother Goose*, Perrault emphatically repeated what he had stated in an earlier collection of tales. His fairy tales, like those written by his literary antecedents, contain "a praiseworthy and instructive moral" and show how "virtue is rewarded" and "vice is always punished." For Perrault it was important to show the advantages of being "honest, patient, prudent, industrious, obedient" and to reveal a direct correlation between obedience and good fortune. "Sometimes there are children who become great lords for having obeyed their father or mother, or others who experience terrible misfortune for having been vicious and disobedient."

Yet a close look at some of the tales themselves reveals competing behavioral and ethical discourses. For every Little Red Riding Hood who is punished for dawdling in the woods, gathering nuts, chasing butterflies, and picking flowers, there is a miller's son who is rewarded with a kingdom and a princess for lying, cheating, and stealing. Or a Tom Thumb who finds wealth by loading himself down with the treasure of an ogre and then amasses a second fortune by serving as a courier to ladies desiring news from their lovers. If Perrault never explicitly acknowledged the flawed morality of his fairy tales, he made it clear in the morals to the tales that he sometimes had trouble finding a message that squared with the philosophy of virtue rewarded and vice punished. "Sometimes it is the little runt who makes the family's happiness," he declared at the end of "Tom Thumb." "Pure water and brown bread are enough nourishment for young women, so long as they have beautiful clothes," he observed at the end of "Donkeyskin."

What Perrault's tales may transmit more powerfully than a naïve morality that rewards good behavior is a plot that is, in Robert Darnton's phrase, "good to think with." In Perrault's "Puss in Boots," Darnton sees "the embodiment of 'Cartesian' cunning," which continues to be celebrated today in the attributes *méchant* and *malin* (both "wicked" and "shrewd"). "France," Darnton concludes, "is a country where it is good to be bad," and it is at an early age, through their folklore, that the French learn that lesson.

Unlike the Grimms, Perrault never sought to emphasize the particular French flavor of the stories in *Tales of Mother Goose*. He was satisfied simply to retell the old wives' tales that had circulated in his own nursery and that continued to offer entertainment for his own children. Unaware of the degree to which he was mediating between popular and elite culture, yet fully aware that a sophisticated courtier could not attach his name to fairy tales, Perrault doubly disavowed his authorship by attributing the tales first to his son and ultimately to Mother Goose. Unintentionally perhaps, he honored both the old wives who gave birth to many of the tales and the children whose desire for stories has nurtured the tales since their publication in 1697.

FURTHER READING ON AUTHORS AND COLLECTORS OF FAIRY TALES

Alexander Afanasev

Nikolajeva, Maria. "Aleksandr Afanasyev." In *The Oxford Companion to Fairy Tales*. Edited by Jack Zipes. Oxford: Oxford Univ. Press, 2000.

Riordan, James. "Commentary on Russian Folktales." In *Tales from Central Russia*. Retold by James Riordan. Harmondsworth: Penguin, 1976.

Hans Christian Andersen

Bredsdorff, Elias. *Hans Christian Andersen: An Introduction to His Life and Works*. Copenhagen: Reitzel, 1987.

Godden, Rumer. *Hans Christian Andersen: A Great Life in Brief*. New York: Knopf, 1955.

Rossel, Sven Hakon, ed. *Hans Christian Andersen: Danish Writer and Citizen of the World*. Amsterdam: Rodopi, 1996.

Spink, Reginald. *Hans Christian Andersen and His World*. London: Thames & Hudson, 1972.

Wullschlager, Jackie. *Hans Christian Andersen: The Life of a Storyteller*. New York: Knopf, 2001.

Peter Christen Asbjørnsen and Jørgen Moe

Christiansen, Reidar, ed. *Folktales of Norway*. Translated by Pat Shaw Iversen. Chicago: Univ. of Chicago Press, 1964.

DesRoches, Kay Unruh. "Asbjørnsen and Moe's Norwegian Folktales: Voice and Vision." In *Touchstones: Reflections on the Best in Children's Literature: Fairy Tales, Fables, Myths, Legends, and Poetry*, ed. Perry Nodelman. West Lafayette, Ind.: Children's Literature Association, 1985.

Jeanne-Marie Leprince de Beaumont

Clancy, Patricia. "A French Writer and Educator in England: Mme Le Prince de Beaumont." *Studies on Voltaire and the Eighteenth Century*, 201 (1982): 195–208.

Hearne, Betsy. *Beauty and the Beast: Visions and Revisions of an Old Tale.* Chicago: Univ. of Chicago Press, 1989.

Zipes, Jack. "The Origins of the Fairy Tale." In *Fairy Tale as Myth/Myth as Fairy Tale.* Lexington: Univ. of Kentucky Press, 1994.

Jacob and Wilhelm Grimm

Bottigheimer, Ruth. *Grimms' Bad Girls and Bold Boys: The Moral and Social Vision of the Tales.* New Haven: Yale Univ. Press, 1987.

Tatar, Maria. *The Hard Facts of the Grimms' Fairy Tales.* Princeton: Princeton Univ. Press, 1987.

Zipes, Jack. *The Brothers Grimm: From Enchanted Forests to the Modern World.* New York: Routledge, 1988.

Joseph Jacobs

Dorson, Richard M. *The British Folklorists.* Chicago: Univ. of Chicago Press, 1968.

Fine, Gary Alan. "Joseph Jacobs: A Sociological Folklorist." *Folklore* 98 (1987): 183–93.

Charles Perrault

Barchilon, Jacques, and Peter Flinders. *Charles Perrault.* Boston: Twayne, 1981.

Darnton, Robert. "Peasants Tell Tales: The Meaning of Mother Goose." In *The Great Cat Massacre and Other Episodes in French Cultural History.* New York: Random House, Vintage Books, 1985.

Philip Lewis, *Seeing through the Mother Goose Tales: Visual Turns in the Writings of Charles Perrault.* Stanford: Stanford Univ. Press, 1996.

Biographies of

Illustrators

Ivan Bilibin (1876–1942)

BORN IN ST. PETERSBURG to a physician and his wife, Bilibin earned a law degree, but also entered art school in 1895, then studied and traveled in Germany, Switzerland, and Italy. In 1899 he received an order for vignettes for an art journal and produced his first illustrations for Russian fairy tales. A commission from the Department for the Production of State Documents provided Bilibin with the opportunity to illustrate a group of Russian stories, including "Vasilisa the Fair." Abandoning the law career that his father had planned for him, Bilibin devoted himself almost exclusively to illustrating books (both fairy tales and *bylina*, or traditional folk epics) and designing theater sets and costumes. He collaborated on productions of *Boris Godunov, The Golden Cockerel*, and *Ruslan and Ludmila*. Bilibin left Russia to live abroad, but returned in 1936. He died during the siege of Leningrad, in the winter of 1942.

Bilibin considered himself not only an artist but also "a philologist, so to speak, or student of folklore." He saw fairy tales, along with *bylinas*, as part of a seamless folkloric whole, consisting of "embroidery, printed patterns on cloths, wood carvings, folk architecture, folk pictures, and so forth." In his illustrated work he made an effort to produce images that would form a cohesive whole, taking readers more deeply into the narrative rather than distracting them from it. His commission from the government department resulted in six slender, large-format paperbacks of classic Russian fairy tales. With intricate frames that are miniature works of art in their own right, the illustrations appear self-contained even as they figure as part of a larger storytelling sequence. Bilibin outlined figures, objects, and landscape details in India ink, then filled in the forms with monochromatic watercolors that produced the vibrant effects of folk art.

From his study of early Russian art, Japanese art, and woodcuts, Bilibin developed a style that mimicked primitive art, with its bright colors, small-scale patterns, and attention to detail. He saw his work as a craft, requiring the focused energy of the skilled draftsman and artisan. "To us," Bilibin wrote, "drawing at the beginning of the twentieth century was inconceivable without a great sense of discipline and a firm belief in the supremacy of the line." In some ways book illustration straddled the line between easel painting and applied art, for it required imagination and creativity even as it demanded close attention to the printing craft. Bilibin saw his drawings as a throwback to folk traditions: "The style is old Russian—derived from traditional art and the old popular print, but ennobled."

Bilibin's watercolors for "Vasilisa the Fair" are among the most powerful illustrative interpretations of a fairy tale. Each composition is dominated by single figures that arrest our attention with their searching gazes and haunted faces. Wedded to the landscape through the designs on their clothing, the wooden instruments they carry, or their bodily shapes and colors, they nonetheless arrest our attention through their determination. These are characters with a mission, and we wander with them through the Russian woods, contemplating its dark, intricate beauty.

EDWARD BURNE-JONES (1833–1898)

EDWARD BURNE-JONES became the quintessential Victorian artist, serious and high-minded with a powerfully romantic, ethereal bent. In 1853 the young Burne-Jones went to Oxford, with the plan to take holy orders. But by 1855 those plans had changed, and, after a visit to Paris with William Morris, he resolved to become a painter. "That was the most memorable night of my life," he later reported. Burne-Jones and Morris joined the Pre-Raphaelite community of artists in London, where Burne-Jones painted furniture, designed stained-glass windows, and participated in the collective

Pre-Raphaelite enterprise known as the Oxford murals. "I have my heart set on our founding a brotherhood," Burne-Jones wrote to a friend. "Learn Sir Galahad by heart. He is to be the patron of our Order."

Burne-Jones came to be known as much for his applied art as for his paintings. Many of the paintings had their origins in designs for other media, ranging from stained glass and embroidery to mosaics and tapestries. His most famous pronouncement about painting captures exactly what made fairy tales an ideal vehicle for his artistic talents: "I mean by a picture a beautiful romantic dream of something that never was, never will be—in light better than any light that ever shone—in a land no one can define, or remember, only desire."

In the 1860s Burne-Jones worked with Rossetti, Ford Madox Brown, and others for "The Firm," an artist's collective established by Morris. Members of the group contributed designs for individual projects, which were then farmed out to local craftsmen. Burne-Jones, with his instinct for decorative design, flourished in this regime. He produced stained-glass panels illustrating the tragic romance of Tristram and Isoude (sic). He studied furniture designs and painted tiles—one set illustrated "Sleeping Beauty," a tale to which he returned repeatedly in his painting. His public debut at the Old Watercolour Society in 1864 was less successful, meeting with a hostile critical reception that made the artist unwilling, for over a decade, to participate in any official exhibits or organizations of artists.

In the 1870s Burne-Jones took on mythical, religious, and folkloric projects on a grand scale, often producing a series of linked paintings. "I want big things to do and vast spaces," he told his wife. Illustrations for Arthurian romances, Greek myths, fairy tales, and Chaucer's tales preoccupied him even as he developed designs for needlework and tapestries for Morris and Company. With some trepidation, Burne-Jones agreed to exhibit his work at the first annual exhibit of the Grosvenor Gallery in 1877. It was received enthusiastically, turning him into an overnight celebrity. Henry James set the tone in his review of the exhibition: "In the palace of art there are many chambers, and that of which Mr. Burne-Jones holds the key is a wondrous museum. His imagination, his fertility of invention, his exquisiteness of work, his remarkable gifts as a colourist . . . all these things constitute a brilliant distinction."

In 1890 Burne-Jones completed a series of pictures that he had started in 1870 and that formed the capstone of his career. *Briar Rose* consisted of four paintings: *The Briar Wood, The Council Chamber, The Garden Court,* and *The Rose Bower*. Fascinated by the notion of aesthetic stasis, of sleeping forms forever preserved in their earthly perfection, Burne-Jones ended the cycle with the slumbering princess. "I want it to stop with the Princess asleep, and to tell no more, to leave all the afterwards to the invention and imagination of people, and to tell them no more." The model for the sleeping princess was his daughter Margaret.

The day before his death, Burne-Jones remarked that he should like to "paint and paint for seventeen thousand years. . . . Why seventeen? Why not seventy thousand years?" He died in London in 1898, shortly after completing *The Last Sleep of Arthur in Avalon*.

WALTER CRANE (1845–1915)

KNOWN AS "the father of the illustrated children's book," Walter Crane brought brightly colored, imaginatively designed, and inexpensively priced books into the nursery. The illustrator for nearly fifty children's books, Crane tried his hand at primers, alphabet books, and fairy tales that included "Cinderella," "Little Red Riding Hood," "Bluebeard," "Puss in Boots," and "Sleeping Beauty." His characteristic strong black lines, bright colors, flat decorative surfaces, and figures inspired by Greek vase painting resulted in designs that raised standards significantly for children's books. His work, which legitimized a turn to children's fare for serious artists, marked a real milestone in the aesthetic quality of children's books.

Crane's father recognized his son's artistic abilities early on and encouraged his efforts by introducing him to William James Linton, who owned the printing and engraving company for which John Tenniel had worked. A three-year apprenticeship with a wood engraver strengthened Crane's understanding of the craft and was followed by art classes at Heatherley's Art School. Edmund Evans, owner of the finest printing firm in England, worked with Crane on a series of picture books that came to be known as "toy books." These slim, large-format books consisted of eight pages, printed in color throughout and designed to use every bit of space from the pictorial front cover to the advertisements on the back cover. Crane's illustrations themselves had a strong architectural quality, filled to the edge with floor tiling, patterned carpets, lavish costumes, decorative vases, and tapestried walls. "I feel convinced that in all designs of a decorative character," he declared, "an artist works most freely and best without any direct reference to nature."

Crane's fully designed settings with their black contours and unified composition seem formal and stilted by comparison with what appears in contemporary book illustration for children. If the drawings are somewhat severe by today's standards, they also have a special appeal in the clarity of their lines and colors. As Crane himself put it, "Children, like the ancient Egyptians, appear to see most things in profile, and like definite statements in design. They prefer well-defined forms and bright, frank color. They don't want to bother about three dimensions. They can accept symbolic representations. They themselves employ drawing . . . as a kind of picture-writing, and eagerly follow a pictured story."

With Crane's toy books, which had to be produced in editions of 10,000 in order to make a profit at sixpence each, children's books began to take on the character of an industry. There is a touch of irony in this, for Crane himself had joined with William Morris and John Ruskin to take a leadership role in the Arts and Crafts movement. In 1884 he was elected president of the Art Workers' Guild, and he directed much of his energy toward breaking down the barriers between artists and craftsmen. Crane worked in a variety of media, ranging from oils and woodcuts to ceramics, textiles, tapestry, and wallpaper. A man who felt he carried socialism in his genes, he campaigned for socialist political causes and joined the Fabian Society in 1885.

While Crane's artwork may have a formal quality to it, the man himself had a quiet charm that won him many friends. At home, with his wife and children, he kept a menagerie that included, at various times, an owl, a mongoose, rabbits, and an alligator. For a while he worked with a squirrel perched on his shoulder. In his later years he called himself Commendatore Crane (the king of Italy had once given him that title) and playfully enjoyed the role of an "official." His signature, a crane encircled by his initials, adds a whimsical note to his many illustrations. In a statement about his love of the art of illustration, Crane revealed that he possessed the childlike heart of which he spoke so eloquently: "The best of designing for children is that the imagination and fancy may be let loose and roam freely, and there is always room for humor and even pathos, sure of being followed by that ever-living sense of wonder and romance in the child heart—a heart which in some cases, happily, never grows up or grows old."

GEORGE CRUIKSHANK (1792–1878)

IN HIS INTRODUCTION to *German Popular Stories* (1823), a translation by Edgar Taylor of selected fairy tales collected by the Brothers Grimm, John Ruskin observed that George Cruikshank, the volume's illustrator, had produced etchings that were "unrivalled in masterfulness of touch since Rembrandt." Cruikshank has since been recognized as one of the most important British graphic artists of the nineteenth century. Best known for illustrating Charles Dickens's *Sketches by Boz* and *Oliver Twist*, Cruikshank enjoyed great popularity for his ability to capture both the whimsy and the melodrama of literary scenes.

As the son of a political caricaturist, Cruikshank began his artistic training at an early age, following in his father's footsteps for a time, then branching out into book illustration. He produced the etchings for Adelbert von Chamisso's *Peter Schlemihl*, a story about a man who loses his shadow, around the time that he turned his attention to the fairy tales of the Brothers Grimm. In 1847 Cruikshank illustrated a story called "The Bottle," which charts the decline of a family through drink. This work inspired him to advocate abstinence and to infuse his artistic production with messages about the evils of alcohol.

Fairy tales may seem an unlikely venue for social propaganda, but Cruikshank wrote and illustrated four fairy tales in the years 1853–64 for *The Fairy Library*, a collection of tales designed to endorse the temperance movement. In "Hop o' My Thumb and the Seven League Boots," Hop's father loses his money to drink but reforms himself and introduces prohibition when he becomes prime minister. In "Cinderella," the father of the prince orders "fountains of wine" to be set up in the courtyards of the palace and in the streets. Cinderella's godmother, appalled by these plans, reminds the monarch that the wine will foment "quarrels, brutal fights, and violent death" and persuades the king to celebrate the wedding without alcohol.

Cruikshank's talent for drawing fantastic figures, often in a state of mild agitation, and his whimsical grotesqueries won him many admirers. Although the zeal for social reform (he passionately denounced the evils of drink, slavery, and cruelty to animals) began to affect his success as an artist, he remained active in later life, illustrating an English edition of Harriet Beecher Stowe's *Uncle Tom's Cabin* (1852) and experimenting with oil painting. When he died, in 1878, he left behind more than twelve thousand printed images in books, magazines, and pamphlets.

GUSTAVE DORÉ (1832–1883)

GUSTAVE DORÉ is without doubt among the most prolific of all book illustrators. With over ten thousand engravings, one thousand lithographs, four hundred oil paintings, and thirty sculptures to his credit, his artistic productivity is nothing short of staggering. His work has also been widely disseminated: the 238 Bible engravings he produced, for example, have appeared in nearly one thousand different editions. Their fame spread the world over, as becomes evident from Mark Twain's reference to it in *Tom Sawyer.*

Doré was born in Strasbourg in 1832 and grew up in the shadow of the city's famous Gothic cathedral. From the age of four he was always seen with pencil in hand, often with both ends sharpened. By twelve he was carving his own lithographic stones and making sets of engravings for illustrated books. His first book, *The Labors of Hercules,* for which he created both text and illustrations, was published when he was just fifteen. The young Doré took a position at the publishing firm of Aubert and Philipon, where he produced a page of caricatures in the manner of Cruikshank and Honoré Daumier on a weekly basis for the *Journal pour rire.* After only three years with the journal, he had produced seven hundred drawings and five albums.

Doré claimed that he had never taken art lessons. What he lacked in formal training, he made up for in natural talent and imaginative exuberance. A contemporary, the French writer Théophile Gautier, is reported to have declared that if you presented Doré with a subject like the influence of the flea on female sentimentality, he could come up with five hundred illustrations for it. Doré immersed himself in the social and artistic culture of Paris, attending the opera and theater, playing the piano and the violin, singing, and staging festive dinners. He worked in the grand style, producing gigantic canvases dashed off in a frenzy, then abandoned and repainted. As an illustrator, he was nearly manic in his ambitions, planning "to produce in a uniform style an edition of all the masterpieces in literature." At one point he announced a plan to create one thousand drawings for a complete Shakespeare. Doré was never one to turn down a commission, and he illustrated potboilers along with the classics. Yet he occasionally rued his success in the area of book illustration. "I must kill the illustrator and be known only as a painter," he declared, hoping in vain to build a powerful reputation as an artist. In his last years he gave up illustration almost completely, turning to oil, watercolors, and clay as preferred media.

Doré took on projects that included works by Rabelais, Balzac, Milton,

Gustave Doré
Self-portrait, 1872

Chateaubriand, Byron, Hugo, Shakespeare, and Tennyson. Although he had been obliged to subsidize the publication of the literary folio for Dante's *Inferno*, his publisher Louis Hachette quickly realized that Doré was right about the work's commercial possibilities. "Success! Come quickly! I am an ass!" read the famous telegram sent by Hachette to Doré shortly after the publication of the *Inferno*. Yet Doré never achieved in France the fame for which he longed. It was in London, where a Doré Gallery opened during the artist's lifetime, that he won the recognition he so craved from his native land.

Never one to focus on domestic interiors, Doré creates a world of what one critic has called "wild glades, mountain chasms, vast draughty castles, cobwebby dens, picnics of simple peasants round a fire." His is the art not of the drawing room, with all its cozy details, but of Gothic turrets and romantic vistas. In his illustrations for Perrault's *Tales*, the characters are often dwarfed by the trees in the forest, disoriented in a landscape that threatens to engulf them with its immense expanses. Doré captures the full range and play of the terror evoked by the French tales, never once hesitating to represent what our imagination sometimes fails to acknowledge. No one who has seen his etching of the ogre in "Tom Thumb," as he is about to slice the throats of his daughters, will read the tale again in the same way.

Doré died in 1883, at the age of fifty-one, just as he was finishing the engravings for his first U.S. commission, an edition of Edgar Allan Poe's "The Raven."

EDMUND DULAC (1882–1953)

A PASSION FOR pattern, texture, and pigment marks the illustrations produced by Edmund Dulac. Although Dulac was remarkably versatile as an artist—designing everything from postage stamps and paper money to theater costumes and furniture—he is best known today as one of the eminent illustrators working during the "golden age" of children's book illustration. For the decade preceding World War I, Arthur Rackham, Kay Nielsen, Charles Robinson, and W. Heath Robinson adorned children's books with stunning, tipped-in color plates. If Rackham remained faithful to his British roots and turned to Nordic mythology for his inspiration, Dulac, born in France in 1882, became a passionate Anglophile who looked to the Orient to enrich both the manner and the matter of his art. Rackham, it has been said, painted with his pencil, while Dulac, master of sensuous designs and exotic settings, drew with his brush.

A native of Toulouse, Dulac studied art while attending law classes at the university. Awarded a prize for his painting, he abandoned the study of law to devote himself fully to art school. An ardent admirer of William Morris, Walter Crane, and Aubrey Beardsley, Dulac changed the spelling of his first name from "Edmond" to the more British "Edmund," whereupon his friends began referred to him as "l'Anglais."

It was in London that Dulac got his start in the art of book illustration. The publishing house of J. M. Dent commissioned sixty watercolors for a complete set of the novels of the Brontë sisters. Encouraged by the offer, Dulac decided to stay in London, working as a contributing illustrator to the

Pall Mall Gazette, a monthly magazine. Like Rackham, he exhibited his work at the Leicester Galleries. The publishing house of Hodder & Stoughton, competing against William Heinemann, who had just signed on Rackham, hired Dulac to illustrate *The Arabian Nights*, a perfect match for the artist. Using varied shades of blue—indigo, cobalt, cerulean, lilac, lavender, and mauve—Dulac produced starry backgrounds with a magical quality so powerful that they dominated the composition. Dulac effaced differences between background and foreground, producing a visual plane that required the viewer to scan the entire surface. Increasingly, he liberated his art from Western artistic conventions, eliminating the conventional use of perspective and investing his energy in decorative surfaces with powerful hues and designs. "The end result of objective imitative art," he wrote, "is nothing less than colored photography."

Dulac's illustrations for "Beauty and the Beast," "Cinderella," "Bluebeard," and "Sleeping Beauty" were produced to accompany Sir Arthur Quiller-Couch's *Sleeping Beauty and Other Tales from the Old French*. During World War I, when business was slack, Dulac was commissioned to prepare illustrations for a book of fairy tales that became known as *Edmund Dulac's Fairy Book—Fairy Tales of the Allied Nations*. The volume, published in 1916, revealed Dulac's adaptability, for he was able to produce illustrations that captured the artistic styles of the different nations represented in the volume. Even though his interest in fairy-tale illustration waned as the years passed, he remained artistically active until his death in 1953, composing music, designing banknotes, and developing an interest in spiritualism.

KAY NIELSEN (1886–1957)

THE ART HISTORIAN Sir Kenneth Clark once confessed that Arthur Rackham's fairy-tale illustrations had stamped "images of terror" on his imagination. How much more troubled might he have been by the illustrations of Kay Nielsen, the Danish Aubrey Beardsley, whose heroes and heroines, bent with sinuous determination, make their way through powerfully eerie landscapes. If Rackham startles with his vivid three-dimensionality, Nielsen arrests our attention with his flattened perspectives and graceful linework in what appear to be vast, arctic terrains.

"They brought me up in a tense atmosphere of art," the artist reported of his parents. Born in 1886 in Copenhagen, Nielsen was the son of parents who were part of a robust theatrical culture. His mother was a leading lady of the Danish Royal Theater, while his father worked as managing director of another theater. As a child, Nielsen was accustomed to meeting such notables as Henrik Ibsen and Edvard Grieg on a regular basis. The young Nielsen was determined to become a physician, but by age seventeen his plans had changed, and he moved to Paris, where he studied art for nearly a decade.

Nielsen was fascinated not only by the work of the British artist Aubrey Beardsley but also by the Art Nouveau style in general and by Japanese woodcuts. In Paris he was commissioned to illustrate volumes of poems by Heinrich Heine and Paul Verlaine. In 1913 Nielsen produced twenty-four watercolors for a book of fairy tales retold by Sir Arthur Quiller-Couch. *In Powder and Crinoline* was subsequently published in the United States under the title *Twelve Dancing Princesses*. The volume secured Nielsen's reputation as an illustrator and led to additional commissioned works, the most important of which was *East of the Sun and West of the Moon*, a collection of Norwegian fairy tales that proved a congenial match for the Danish artist.

Nielsen's career lost its momentum with the onset of the war years, and he returned to Copenhagen, where set designs occupied his attention. For the Royal Theater he produced both sets and designs for a theatrical version of *Aladdin*, and he worked on productions of Shakespeare's *The Tempest* and *A Midsummer Night's Dream* as well. During the interwar years Nielsen illustrated two additional volumes of fairy tales, the one a collection of Andersen's fairy tales, the other an anthology of tales by the Brothers Grimm.

Nielsen spent the last two decades of his life in the United States. In 1936 he collaborated with Max Reinhardt on a production of *Everyman*. Los Angeles, which had the advantage of seemingly perpetual sunshine, proved attractive to Nielsen and his wife, and, despite straitened economic circumstances, they settled in the United States, where Nielsen worked briefly for Disney, designing the "Bald Mountain" sequence for *Fantasia*. Unwilling to compromise his artistic standards for commercial success, Nielsen was reduced to raising chickens for a time and managed to earn a meager living by painting murals at local high schools. He died in 1957 and left to family friends seemingly worthless paintings illustrating *The Thousand and One Nights*. These are among the most stunning of Nielsen's works, though they have never been incorporated into an edition of the tales.

MAXFIELD PARRISH (1870–1966)

ONE OF THE most prominent painters during the "golden age" of American illustration, Maxfield Parrish was a prolific artist whose romantic landscapes, sensual figures, and charming vignettes captured the public imagination. In magazines, calendars, advertisements, and book illustrations, Parrish produced photorealistic images haunted by a touch of the uncanny. *Daybreak*, a painting created specifically for reproduction as an art print, became so successful as a cultural icon that, for a time, it was said to be on display in one out of every four households in the United States. Though commercial art absorbed his energies for many years, Parrish also

MAXFIELD PARRISH
Maxfield Parrish, *The Artist, Sex, Male*, 1909

illustrated a number of children's books, most notably *Mother Goose in Prose* and *The Arabian Nights*.

Born in Philadelphia, Parrish grew up in a Quaker household. His father, Stephen Parrish, was a well-known etcher and landscape painter, with keen powers of observation and a shrewd business sense. Parrish studied painting at the Pennsylvania Academy of the Fine Arts. A firm believer in the power of beauty to promote moral change, he made a commitment to the popularization and democratization of art. From 1894 to 1896 Parrish served as instructor in interior and mural decoration and also continued his illustrative work, producing magazine covers, playbills, posters, menu covers, and advertisements. He married Lydia Austin in 1895, and after a summer of travel in Europe, where he visited the Louvre and spent time with painters, he returned to the United States, where a steady flow of commissions came his way.

Parrish established himself as an artist after painting a mural entitled *Old King Cole* in 1895 for the Mask and Wig Club, a thespian society at the University of Pennsylvania. In 1898 he left Philadelphia, moving to Plainfield, New Hampshire, where he purchased a plot of land near his parents' home and worked, with a local carpenter, for over ten years on the house. "The Oaks" grew to twenty rooms and included a fifteen-room studio, along with landscaped gardens. As one contemporary noted, "His surroundings possess the charm of his work, with the same interesting detail and the same poetic width of landscape."

Parrish's illustrations for Kenneth Grahame's *The Golden Age* (1899) established him as an internationally known illustrator of books. A review described the illustrations as displaying "photographic vision with the Pre-Raphaelite feeling" and observed the brilliant mix of styles in the paintings. Simultaneously modern, medieval, and classical, Parrish's illustrations defied categorization and represented a powerful new tradition in which the painter was more, as the artist himself put it, "annotator than illustrator."

For several years Parrish worked for *Collier's*, a prominent popular magazine that included many color illustrations. It was while under contract with *Collier's* that he produced two important series: *The Arabian Nights* (1906–7) and *Greek Mythology* (1908–9). His success in the commercial realm reached its height in the 1920s, though the rage for Parrish calendars, posters, and greeting cards waned by the end of the decade. Parrish recognized that he was not necessarily selling a mere product. He shrewdly observed that "it's the unattainable that appeals."

Parrish stopped painting after Susan Lewin, his model for over fifty-five years, married at the age of seventy. He died at age ninety-six at "The Oaks," his fame secured not only by his paintings, illustrations, and magazine covers but also by the term "Parrish blue," the new artistic designation for cobalt.

ARTHUR RACKHAM (1867–1939)

THE FOURTH OF twelve children (five of whom died in infancy), Arthur Rackham, known for his "wide and elfish grin," was born in 1867 and grew up in a middle-class Victorian family. As a child, he showed a talent for drawing and would smuggle paper and pencil with him into bed. After being caught and monitored, he still managed to draw at night by sneaking a pencil into bed and using his pillowcase as a drawing surface.

On the recommendation of a physician, the sixteen-year-old Rackham took a long sea voyage, journeying to Australia in 1883 with family friends. On board ship and in Sydney, there were many opportunities for sketching, and Rackham returned to England with a stronger physical constitution and with watercolors of Vesuvius, Capri, the Suez Canal, and Sydney. Convinced that his real calling was at the easel, he entered the Lambeth School of Art, but was obliged to spend the years 1885–92 on a stool in an insurance office, where he kept meticulous accounts. By 1891 he was selling his drawings to illustrated papers in London. The following year he left the insurance office to become a full-time graphic journalist on a newly started London weekly, the *Westminster Budget*, where his *"Sketches from Life"* received critical and popular acclaim. In 1900 he met the portrait painter Edyth Starkie, whom he married three years later.

It was in 1900 that Rackham was invited to illustrate *The Fairy Tales of the Brothers Grimm*, a volume for which he felt "more affection" than for other works. By 1905, when he published an edition of *Rip Van Winkle*, his reputation as the Edwardian era's most prominent illustrator was firmly established. Rackham was in great demand and was invited to illustrate J. M. Barrie's *Peter Pan in Kensington Garden* and Lewis Carroll's *Alice in Wonderland*. He endorsed the importance of fantasy and whimsy in books for children and averred that he firmly believed in "the greatest stimulating and educative power of imaginative, fantastic, and playful pictures and writings for children in their most impressionable years." For Rackham, illustrations conveyed the pleasures of the text, communicating the "sense of delight or emotion aroused by the accompanying passage of literature."

ARTHUR RACKHAM
Self-portrait, *Transpontine Cockney*

Rackham's projects included illustrations for adult readers as well. Wagner's *Ring of the Nibelung* and Shakespeare's *Midsummer Night's Dream* ranked among his greatest critical and commercial successes. In the years following the First World War, the market for expensively produced books declined in England, and Rackham increasingly depended on gallery sales and occasional work for his income. In 1927 he sailed to New York, where his works were on exhibit and where he personally met with an enthusiastic reception. In his last years he completed the illustrations for Kenneth Grahame's *Wind in the Willows*, a work to which he had a powerful sentimental attachment.

Rackham illustrated nearly ninety volumes. Influenced by Albrecht

Dürer, George Cruikshank, John Tenniel, and Aubrey Beardsley, he is best known for his sure sense of line, his mastery of the three-color process with its muted hues, and the creation of a mysteriously whimsical world, filled with gnomes, nymphs, giants, elves, sea serpents, and fairies in intricate landscapes of gnarled branches, foaming waves, sinuous vines, and anthropomorphized trees. A firm believer in the partnership between author and illustrator, he endorsed the notion that illustrations "give the artist's view of the author's idea . . . or his independent view of the author's subject." Rackham exercised a strong influence on future generations of illustrators, most notably Disney Studios, whose feature film of *Snow White* contains scenes clearly inspired by Rackham's style. Rackham died of cancer in 1939, just a few weeks after he had put the final touches on *The Wind in the Willows*. His last drawing presents a scene in which Mole and Rat are loading the rowboat for a picnic.

FURTHER READING ON ILLUSTRATORS

Ivan Bilibin
Golynets, Sergei. *Ivan Bilibin*. Leningrad: Aurora Art Publishers, 1982.

Edward Burne-Jones
Ash, Russell. *Sir Edward Burne-Jones*. New York: Harry N. Abrams, 1993.

Fitzgerald, Penelope. *Edward Burne-Jones: A Biography*. London: Michael Joseph, 1975.

Mancoff, Debra N. *Burne-Jones*. San Francisco: Pomegranate, 1998.

Morgan, Hilary. *Burne-Jones: The Pre-Raphaelites and Their Century*. 2 vols. London: P. Nahum, 1989.

Wildman, Stephen, ed. *Edward Burne-Jones: Victorian Artist-Dreamer*. New York: Harry N. Abrams, 1998.

Walter Crane
Engen, Rodney K. *Walter Crane as Book Illustrator*. New York: St. Martin's Press, 1975.

Meyer, Susan E. "Walter Crane." In *A Treasury of the Great Children's Book Illustrators*. New York: Harry N. Abrams, 1983.

Smith, Greg, and Sarah Hyde. *Walter Crane, 1845–1915: Artist, Designer, and Socialist*. London: Univ. of Manchester, 1989.

Spencer, Isobel. *Walter Crane*. New York: Macmillan, 1975.

George Cruikshank

Patten, Robert L. *George Cruikshank's Life, Times, and Art.* 2 vols. New Brunswick, N.J.: Rutgers Univ. Press, 1992–96.

Gustave Doré

Gosling, Nigel. *Gustave Doré.* New York: Praeger, 1973.

Richardson, Joanna. *Gustave Doré: A Biography.* London: Cassell, 1980.

Rose, Millicent. *Gustave Doré.* London: Pleiades Books, 1956.

Edmund Dulac

Hughey, Ann Conolly. *Edmund Dulac: His Book Illustrations: A Bibliography.* Potomac, Md.: Buttonwood Press, 1995.

Larkin, David, ed. *Edmund Dulac.* New York: Peacock Press, 1975.

White, Colin. *Edmund Dulac.* New York: Scribner, 1976.

Kay Nielsen

Larkin, David, ed. *Kay Nielsen.* Toronto: Peacock Press, Bantam, 1975.

Meyer, Susan. "Kay Nielsen." In *A Treasury of the Great Children's Book Illustrators.* New York: Harry N. Abrams, 1983.

Poltarnees, Welleran. *Kay Nielsen: An Appreciation.* La Jolla, Calif.: Green Tiger Press, 1976.

Maxfield Parrish

Cutler, Laurence S., and Judy Goffman Cutler. *Maxfield Parrish: A Retrospective.* San Francisco: Pomegranate, 1995.

Gilbert, Alma. *Maxfield Parrish: The Masterworks.* Berkeley, Calif.: Ten Speed Press, 1992.

Yount, Sylvia. *Maxfield Parrish, 1870–1966.* New York: Harry N. Abrams in association with the Pennsylvania Academy of the Fine Arts, 1999.

Arthur Rackham

Gettings, Fred. *Arthur Rackham.* London: Studio Vista, 1975.

Hamilton, James. *Arthur Rackham: A Life with Illustration.* London: Pavilion, 1990.

Hudson, Derek. *Arthur Rackham: His Life and Work.* London: William Heinemann, 1960.

Meyer, Susan E. "Arthur Rackham." In *A Treasury of the Great Children's Book Illustrators.* New York: Harry N. Abrams, 1983.

APPENDIX 1

THE STORY OF GRANDMOTHER

Told by Louis and François Briffault

in Nièvre, 1885

THERE WAS ONCE a woman who had made some bread. She said to her daughter: "Take this loaf of hot bread and this bottle of milk over to Granny's."

The little girl left. At the crossroads she met a wolf, who asked: "Where are you going?"

"I'm taking a loaf of hot bread and a bottle of milk to Granny's."

"Which path are you going to take," asked the wolf, "the path of needles or the path of pins?"

The little girl had fun picking up needles. Meanwhile, the wolf arrived at Granny's, killed her, put some of her flesh in the pantry and a bottle of her blood on the shelf. The little girl got there and knocked at the door.

"Push the door," said the wolf. "It's latched with a wet straw."

"Hello, Granny. I'm bringing you a loaf of hot bread and a bottle of milk."

"Put it in the pantry, my child. Take some of the meat in there along with the bottle of wine on the shelf."

There was a little cat in the room who watched her eat and said: "Phooey! You're a slut if you eat the flesh and drink the blood of Granny."

Originally published by Paul Delarue in "Les Contes merveilleux de Perrault et la tradition populaire," *Bulletin folklorique de l'Ile-de-France* (1951): 221–22.

"Take your clothes off, my child," said the wolf, "and come into bed with me."

"Where should I put my apron?"

"Throw it in the fire, my child. You won't be needing it any longer."

When she asked the wolf where to put all her other things, her bodice, her dress, her skirt, and her stockings, each time he said: "Throw them into the fire, my child. You won't be needing them any longer."

"Oh, Granny, how hairy you are!"

"The better to keep me warm, my child!"

"Oh, Granny, what long nails you have!"

"The better to scratch myself with, my child!"

"Oh, Granny, what big shoulders you have!"

"The better to carry firewood with, my child!"

"Oh, Granny, what big ears you have!"

"The better to hear you with, my child!"

"Oh, Granny, what big nostrils you have!"

"The better to sniff my tobacco with, my child!"

"Oh, Granny, what a big mouth you have!"

"The better to eat you with, my child!"

"Oh, Granny, I need to go badly. Let me go outside!"

"Do it in the bed, my child."

"No, Granny, I want to go outside."

"All right, but don't stay out long."

The wolf tied a rope made of wool to her leg and let her go outside.

When the little girl got outside, she attached the end of the rope to a plum tree in the yard. The wolf became impatient and said: "Are you making cables out there? Are you making cables?"

When he realized that there was no answer, he jumped out of bed and discovered that the little girl had escaped. He followed her, but he reached her house only after she was already inside.

LITTLE RED RIDING HOOD

Charles Perrault

ONCE UPON A TIME there was a village girl, the prettiest you can imagine. Her mother adored her. Her grandmother adored her even more and made a little red hood for her. The hood suited the child so well that everywhere she went she was known by the name Little Red Riding Hood.

One day her mother baked some cakes and said to her: "I want you to go and see how your grandmother is faring, for I've heard that she's ill. Take her some cakes and this little pot of butter."

Little Red Riding Hood left right away for her grandmother's house, which was in another village. As she was walking through the woods, she met old Neighbor Wolf, who wanted to eat her right there on the spot. But he didn't dare, because some woodcutters were in the forest. He asked where she was going. The poor child, who did not know that it was dangerous to stop and listen to wolves, said: "I'm going to go see my grandmother. And I'm taking her some cakes and a little pot of butter sent by my mother."

"Does she live very far away?" asked the wolf.

From Charles Perrault, "Le Petit Chaperon rouge," *Histoires ou contes du temps passé, avec des moralités* (Paris: Barbin, 1697).

"Oh, yes," said Little Red Riding Hood. "She lives beyond the mill that you can see over there. Hers is the first house you come to in the village."

"Well, well," said the wolf. "I think I shall go and see her too. I'll take the path over here, and you take the path over there, and we'll see who gets there first."

The wolf ran as fast as he could on the shorter path, and the little girl continued on her way along the longer path. She had a good time gathering nuts, chasing butterflies, and picking bunches of flowers that she found on the way.

The wolf did not take long to get to Grandmother's house. He knocked: Rat-a-tat-tat.

"Who's there?"

"It's your granddaughter, Little Red Riding Hood," said the wolf, disguising his voice. "And I'm bringing you some cake and a little pot of butter sent by my mother."

The dear grandmother, who was in bed because she was not feeling well, called out: "Pull the bolt, and the latch will open."

The wolf pulled the bolt, and the door opened wide. He threw himself on the good woman and devoured her in no time, for he had eaten nothing for the last three days. Then he closed the door and lay down on Grandmother's bed, waiting for Little Red Riding Hood, who, before long, came knocking at the door: Rat-a-tat-tat.

"Who's there?"

Little Red Riding Hood was afraid at first when she heard the gruff voice of the wolf, but thinking that her grandmother must have caught cold, she said: "It's your granddaughter, Little Red Riding Hood, and I'm bringing you some cake and a little pot of butter sent by my mother."

The wolf tried to soften his voice as he called out to her: "Pull the bolt, and the latch will open."

Little Red Riding Hood pulled the bolt, and the door opened wide. When the wolf saw her come in, he hid under the covers of the bed and said: "Put the cakes and the little pot of butter on the bin and climb into bed with me."

Little Red Riding Hood took off her clothes and climbed into the bed. She was astonished to see what her grandmother looked like in her nightgown.

"Grandmother," she said, "what big arms you have!"

"The better to hug you with, my child."

"Grandmother, what big legs you have!"

"The better to run with, my child."

"Grandmother, what big ears you have!"

"The better to hear with, my child."

"Grandmother, what big eyes you have!"

"The better to see with, my child."

"Grandmother, what big teeth you have!"

"The better to eat you with!"

Upon saying these words, the wicked wolf threw himself on Little Red Riding Hood and gobbled her up.

MORAL

From this story one learns that children,
Especially young girls,
Pretty, well bred, and genteel,
Are wrong to listen to just anyone,
And it's not at all strange,
If a wolf ends up eating them.
I say a wolf, but not all wolves
Are exactly the same.
Some are perfectly charming,
Not loud, brutal, or angry,
But tame, pleasant, and gentle,
Following young ladies
Right into their homes, into their chambers,
But watch out if you haven't learned that tame wolves
Are the most dangerous of all.

APPENDIX 2

THE STORY OF THE THREE BEARS

Robert Southey

"A tale which may content the minds of learned men
and grave philosophers."
—GASCOYNE

ONCE UPON A TIME there were Three Bears, who lived together in a house of their own, in a wood. One of them was a Little, Small, Wee Bear; and one was a Middle-sized Bear; and the other was a Great, Huge Bear. They had each a pot for their porridge, a little pot for the Little, Small, Wee Bear; and a middle-sized pot for the Middle Bear; and a great pot for the Great, Huge Bear. And they had each a chair to sit in; a little chair for the Little, Small, Wee Bear; and a middle-sized chair for the Middle Bear; and a great chair for the Great, Huge, Bear. And they had each a bed to sleep in; a little bed for the Little, Small, Wee Bear; and a middle-sized bed for the Middle Bear; and a great bed for the Great, Huge Bear.

One day, after they had made the porridge for their breakfast, and poured it into their porridge-pots, they walked out into the wood while the porridge was cooling that they might not burn their mouths by beginning too soon to eat it. And while they were walking, a little old Woman came to the house.

From Robert Southey's *The Doctor* (London: Longman, 1837).

She could not have been a good, honest old Woman; for first she looked in at the window, and then she peeped in at the keyhole; and seeing nobody in the house, she lifted the latch. The door was not fastened, because the Bears were good Bears, who did nobody any harm, and never suspected that anybody would harm them. So the little old Woman opened the door, and went in; and well pleased she was when she saw the porridge on the table. If she had been a good little old Woman, she would have waited till the Bears came home, and then, perhaps, they would have asked her to breakfast; for they were good Bears,—a little rough or so, as the manner of Bears is, but for all that very good-natured and hospitable. But she was an impudent, bad old Woman, and set about helping herself.

KAY NIELSEN,
"The Story of the Three Bears," 1930

The old lady in Robert Southey's version of the story of the three bears hightails it out the window after trying out the porridge and chairs of the three bears.

So first she tasted the porridge of the Great, Huge Bear, and that was too hot for her; and she said a bad word about that. And then she tasted the porridge of the Middle Bear, and that was too cold for her; and she said a bad word about that too. And then she went to the porridge of the Little, Small, Wee Bear, and tasted that; and that was neither too hot, nor too cold, but just right; and she liked it so well, that she ate it all up: but the naughty old Woman said a bad word about the little porridge-pot, because it did not hold enough for her.

Then the little old Woman sat down in the chair of the Great, Huge Bear, and that was too hard for her. And then she sat down in the chair of the Middle Bear, and that was too soft for her. And then she sat down in the chair of the Little, Small, Wee Bear, and that was neither too hard, nor too soft, but just right. So she seated herself in it, and there she sat till the bottom of the chair came out, and down came hers, plump upon the ground. And the naughty old Woman said a wicked word about that too.

Then the little old Woman went upstairs into the bed-chamber in which the Three Bears slept. And first she lay down upon the bed of the Great, Huge Bear; but that was too high at the head for her. And next she lay down upon the bed of the Middle Bear; and that was too high at the foot for her. And then she lay down upon the bed of the Little, Small, Wee Bear; and that was neither too high at the head, nor at the foot, but just right. So she covered herself up comfortably, and lay there till she fell fast asleep.

By this time the Three Bears thought their porridge would be cool enough; so they came home to breakfast. Now the little old Women had left the spoon of the Great Huge Bear, standing in his porridge.

"Somebody has been at my porridge!"

said the Great, Huge Bear, in his great, rough, gruff voice. And when the Middle Bear looked at his, he saw that the spoon was standing in it too. They were wooden spoons; if they had been silver ones, the naughty old Woman would have put them in her pocket.

"Somebody has been at my porridge!"

said the Middle Bear, in his middle voice.

Then the Little, Small, Wee Bear looked at his, and there was the spoon in the porridge-pot, but the porridge was all gone.

"Somebody has been at my porridge, and has eaten it all up!"

said the Little, Small, Wee Bear, in his little, small, wee voice.

Upon this the Three Bears, seeing that some one had entered their house, and eaten up the Little, Small, Wee Bear's breakfast, began to look about them. Now the little old Woman had not put the hard cushion straight when she rose from the chair of the Great, Huge Bear.

"Somebody has been sitting in my chair!"

said the Great, Huge Bear, in his great, rough, gruff voice.

And the little old Woman had squatted down the soft cushion of the Middle Bear.

"Somebody has been sitting in my chair!"

said the Middle Bear, in his middle voice.

And you know what the little old Woman had done to the third chair.

"Somebody has been sitting in my chair, and has sat the bottom of it out!"

said the Little, Small, Wee Bear, in his little, small, wee voice.

Then the Three Bears thought it necessary that they should make further search; so they went upstairs into their bed-chamber. Now the little old Woman had pulled the pillow of the Great, Huge Bear, out of its place.

"Somebody has been lying in my bed!"

said the Great, Huge Bear, in his great, rough, gruff voice

And the little old Woman had pulled the bolster of the Middle Bear out of its place.

"Somebody has been lying in my bed!"

said the Middle Bear, in his middle voice.

And when the Little, Small, Wee Bear came to look at his bed, there was the bolster in its place; and the pillow in its place upon the bolster; and upon the pillow was the little old Woman's ugly, dirty head,—which was not in its place, for she had no business there.

"Somebody has been lying in my bed and here she is!"

said the Little, Small, Wee Bear, in his little, small, wee voice.

The little old Woman had heard in her sleep the great, rough, gruff voice of the Great, Huge Bear; but she was so fast asleep that it was no more to her than the roaring of wind, or the rumbling of thunder. And she had heard the middle voice of the Middle Bear, but it was only as if she had heard some one speaking in a dream. But when she heard the little, small, wee voice of the Little, Small, Wee Bear, it was so sharp, and so shrill, that it awakened her at once. Up she started; and when she saw the Three Bears on one side of the bed, she tumbled herself out at the other, and ran to the window. Now the window was open, because the Bears, like good, tidy Bears, as they were, always opened their bed-chamber window when they got up in the morning. Out the little old Woman jumped; and whether she broke her neck in the fall; or ran into the wood and was lost there; or found her way out of the wood, and was taken up by the Constable and sent to the House of Correction for a vagrant as she was, I cannot tell. But the Three Bears never saw any thing more of her.

APPENDIX 3

WALTER CRANE'S ILLUSTRATIONS

"THE THREE BEARS,"
in *Walter Crane's Toy Books*
(London: Routledge, 1873)

Crane's popular version of "The Three Bears" presents the heroine Silverlocks as a girl in search of adventure, who manages to escape only because the youngest of the three bears protects her from the two ferocious parents.

And, as the door stood open, in walked boldly,
　This child, whose name was Silverlocks, I'm
There was nobody there to treat her coldly, [told;
　No friend to call her back, no nurse to scold.
She found herself within a parlour charming;
　And there upon the table there were placed
Three basins, sending up a smell so warming,
　That she at once felt hungry, and must taste.
The largest basin first, but hot and biting
　The soup was in it, and the second too;
The smallest basin tasted so inviting,
　That up she ate it all, with small ado.

And next she saw three chairs, and tried to sit in
　The biggest, but it was too hard and high;
The middle one she scarcely seemed to fit in,
　But in the smallest chair sat easily;
And rocked herself, her ease and comfort taking,
　Singing the pretty songs she knew so well;
When, oh! the little chair cracked loud, and,
　　breaking,
　Gave way all suddenly, and down she fell.

'Ah, well," she thought, "there may be beds to lie on
Upstairs; I think I'll go at once and see."
And so there were; she said aloud, "I'll try one,
For I am tired and sleepy as can be."
The biggest bed was not of feathers, surely,
It was so hard; and so she tried the next,
And found it little better; but securely
She slept upon the smallest one, unvext.
　The little house belonged to bears, not persons;
　　The Father Bear, so very rough and large;
　　　The Mother Bear (I have known
　　　　many worse ones);

And then the little Cub, their only charge.
They had gone for a walk before their dinner;
Returning, Father growled, "Who's touched my soup?'
"Who's touched my soup?" said Mother, with voice
"But mine," said little Cub, "is finished up!" [thinner;
They turned to draw their chairs a little nearer;
"Who's sat in my chair?" growled the Father Bear;
"Who's sat in my chair?" said
　　the Mother, clearer;
And squeaked the little
　Cub, "Who's broken
　my small chair?"

They rushed upstairs, and Father Bruin,
    growling,
Cried out, "Who's lain upon my bed?"
"Who's lain on mine?" cried Mother
    Bruin, howling;

"But some one *lies* on mine!" the small
    Bear said.
"We'll kill the child, and eat her for our
    dinner,"
The Father growled; but said the Mother,
    "No;
For supper she shall be, and I will skin
    her."
"No," said the little Cub, "we'll let her
    go."

So Silverlocks, in sudden terror flying,
Reached home; and when the Nurse the
    story hears,
She says, "You are in luck, there's no
    denying,
To get away in safety from

THREE BEARS."

"LITTLE RED RIDING HOOD,"
in *Walter Crane's Toy Books*
(London: Routledge, 1875)

The red cape of the heroine dominates Walter Crane's illustrations for the Grimms' version of the story. The formal elegance of the compositions stands in striking contrast to the disturbing violence of Little Red Riding Hood's adventure at Grandmother's house.

Out set Riding Hood, so obliging and
sweet,
And she met a great Wolf in the wood,
Who began most politely the maiden to
greet,
In as tender a voice as he could.

He asked to what house she was going,
and why;
Red Riding Hood answered him all:
He said, "Give my love to your Gran; I
will try
"At my earliest leisure to call."

Off he ran, and Red Riding Hood went on her way,
But often she lingered and played,
And made as she went quite a pretty nosegay
With the wild flowers that grew in the glade.

But in the meanwhile the Wolf went, with a grin,
At the Grandmother's cottage to call;
He knocked at the door, and was told to come in,
Then he eat her up—sad cannibal!
Then the Wolf shut the door, and got into bed,
And waited for Red Riding Hood;
When he heard her soft tap at the front door, he said,
Speaking softly as ever he could:

"CINDERELLA,"
in *Walter Crane's Toy Books*
(London: Routledge, 1873)

In Crane's version of Perrault's "Cinderella," the two stepsisters are reformed when they witness the heroine's triumph. Vowing to turn from idleness to industry, they have learned that hard work "really seems to pay."

THERE was an honest gentleman, who had a daughter dear;
His wife was dead, he took instead a new one in a year;
She had two daughters—Caroline and Bella were their names;
They called the other daughter Cinderella, to their shames,
Because she had to clean the hearths and black-lead all the grates;
She also had to scrub the floors, and wash the dinner plates.
But though the others went abroad, did nothing, smiled, and drest,
Yet Cinderella all the time was prettiest and best.
The King who ruled in that country, he had an only son,
Who gave a ball to all the town, when he was twenty-one;
And Caroline and Bella were invited, and they said,
"Cinderella shall leave scrubbing, and act as ladies' maid."

They dressed themselves so fine in silks, and pearls, and
    flowers, and lace,
Poor Cinderella hadn't time to wash her pretty face.
When they started for the ball, full of haughtiness and pride,
Poor Cinderella felt quite sad, and sat her down and cried.
She had not cried much longer than a quarter of an hour,
When a wonderful bright creature appeared upon the floor,
Looked compassionately on her, and said in accents mild,
"I am your Fairy Godmother, so cry no more, my child:
I know that you are sad, and that your sisters are unkind:
Now go and fetch for me the largest pumpkin you can find."
She went and fetched the pumpkin, and the Fairy shook her
    wand,
And changed it to a splendid coach, with cushions rich and
    grand.

Now fetch the mouse-trap from the shelf—there are six
    mice inside;"
She changed them to six prancing steeds, all harnessed side
    by side.
"Now fetch the rat-trap," and there was therein a large
    black rat,
So he was made the coachman, with silk stockings and
    cocked hat.
Six lizards happening to be there, all ready to the hand,
Were changed to powdered footmen, staff and bouquet all
    so grand.
"Now, Cinderella, here's your coach to take you to the
    ball."
"Not as I am," she cried; "like this I cannot go at
    all."

And then the Fairy raised her wand, and touched the shabby
    gown,
It turned to satin, trimmed with lace, and jewels, and swans-
    down.
Her face was clean, her gloves were new, her hair was nicely
    curled,
And on her feet were shoes of glass, the neatest in the world.
"Now, Cinderella, you may go; but take care to return
Before the clock strikes twelve, or else you'll see your carriage
    turn
Into a pumpkin once again, your horses into mice;
Your coachman, footmen, will become rat, lizards, in a trice,
And you yourself the cinder-girl will once again become;
So mind that when the clock strikes twelve you must be safe
    at home."

She promised, and with joyful heart she gained the palace
    hall,
And danced, and laughed, and looked indeed the fairest of
    them all.
The King's son danced with her, and praised her lovely shape
    and air;
All treated her as if she were the greatest lady there:
But in good time she slipped away, and waited safe at home,
In kitchen corner sitting till her sisters back should come;
And when they came they told her all about the stranger fair,
And what she wore, and how she looked, and how she did
    her hair.
Next night another ball was held—the sisters dressed, and
    went,
And pretty Cinderella, too, by Godmother was sent.

The Prince danced with her every dance, and praised her
    more and more,
And laughed and talked so much, that when the clock 'gan
    strike the hour—
The fatal hour of twelve—it took her greatly by surprise;
She turned and fled so quick before the Prince's wondering
    eyes,
That in her haste to reach her coach she dropped her crystal
    shoe;
She had no time to pick it up, as towards home she flew.
The sisters later home returned, and told her all they knew
About the lady and the Prince, and all of it was true.
As Cinderella heard them talk, she turned away her head,
Nor said a word that might not fit her place of kitchen-
    maid.

Next day was proclamation made: "Whereas, a crystal shoe
Has been discovered at the ball, who is the owner—who?
All ladies now must try it on; the Prince will marry her,
Whoe'er it be, who easily the crystal shoe can wear."
No foot was found to fit the shoe; they tried throughout the
    town;
At last they came unto this house, and called the ladies down.
The sisters try to get it on, and pull, and push, and squeeze,
When Cinderella calmly said, "Allow me, if you please."
The sisters scorned her for the thought, and much surprise
    they knew,
When Cinderella from her pocket pulled the fellow shoe.
She tried them on—they fit—and she, no longer kitchen-
    maid,
Stands up to meet the Prince in all her beauty fair arrayed.

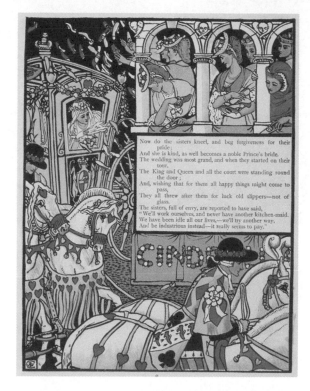

Now do the sisters kneel, and beg forgiveness for their
    pride;
And she is kind, as well becomes a noble Prince's bride.
The wedding was most grand, and when they started on their
    tour,
The King and Queen and all the court were standing round
    the door;
And, wishing that for them all happy things might come to
    pass,
They all threw after them for luck old slippers—not of
    glass.
The sisters, full of envy, are reported to have said,
"We'll work ourselves, and never have another kitchen-maid.
We have been idle all our lives,—we'll try another way,
And be industrious instead—it really seems to pay."

"THE FROG PRINCE,"
in *Walter Crane's Toy Books*
(London: Routledge, 1875)

The illustrations for the Grimms' tale captures the transformation scene in a whimsical manner. A dignified princess, caught between her father's orders and her own instincts, is faced with a problem that does not lend itself easily to resolution.

"BLUEBEARD,"
in *Walter Crane's Toy Books*
(London: Routledge, 1875)

Crane's version of Perrault's story presents Bluebeard's wife as a daughter of Eve, who cannot resist the temptation to disobey her husband's orders. Often presented as an oriental tyrant, with turban and scimitar, Crane's Bluebeard remains European in his appearance, but becomes increasingly diabolical with each new representation.

For a month after the wedding they
lived and had good cheer,
And then said Bluebeard to his wife,
"I'll say good-bye, my dear;
"Indeed, it is but for six weeks that I
shall be away,
"I beg that you'll invite your friends,
and feast and dance and play;
"And all my property I'll leave con-
fided to your care;
"Here are the keys of all my chests,
there's plenty and to spare,

"But this small key belongs to one small
room on the ground-floor,—
"And this you must not open, or you
will repent it sore.
And so he went; and all the friends
came there from far and wide.
And in her wealth the lady took much
happiness and pride;
But in a while this kind of joy grew
nearly satisfied,

And oft she saw the closet door, and longed
to look inside.
At last she could no more refrain and turned
the little key.
And looked within, and fainted straight the
horrid sight to see;
For there upon the floor was blood, and on
the walls were wives,
For Bluebeard first had married them, then
cut their throats with knives.

And this poor wife, distracted, picked the key
up from the floor,
All stained with blood; and with much fear
she shut and locked the door.
She tried in vain to clean the key and wash
the stain away
With sand and soap,—it was no use. Bluebeard came back that day;
At once he asked her for the key,—he saw
the bloody stain,—

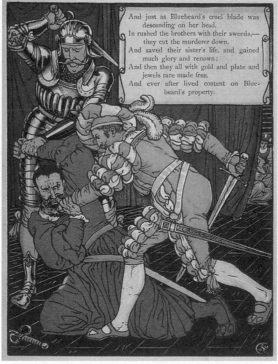

"BEAUTY AND THE BEAST,"
in *Walter Crane's Toy Books*
(London: Routledge, 1875)

Madame de Beaumont's story of Beauty and the Beast is treated with powerfully vivid illustrations in Crane's *Toy Book*. Beast, who walks upright although he appears as a four-footed boar, is first presented in a floral setting and nearly expires in the same kind of milieu. The monkey servants add a whimsical touch that serves as a counterpoint to the melodramatic events of the story.

"JACK AND THE BEANSTALK,"
in *Walter Crane's Toy Books*
(London: Routledge, 1875)

Crane's illustrations follow Jack from his "idle" days at home with his "kind" mother to his acquisition of riches and his decision to "settle down, stay at home, climb no more beanstalks."

Jack and the Bean-stalk.

IN the days of good King Alfred
lived a widow with her son;
She was kind, and he was idle, so
at last their wealth was done,
Nothing left remaining but a cow,
which must be sold for bread;
Jack, who was to sell, exchanged
her, and got only beans instead,—
Beans, which when his angry mother
saw, she flung away in scorn:
Think how great her Jack's surprise was, when, on getting up
next morn,

He perceived the beans had sprout-
    ed,—grown so very tall and high,
That the topmost of their branches
    seemed to lose itself in sky.
"I must climb," cried Jack, delighted,
    " it seems strong enough to bear;"
When his mother would prevent him,
    no remonstrance would he hear.
Up he goes among the branches,
    easy as a winding stair ;
Climbing on for hours, he reaches
    desert lands and bleaker air.
Was no sight or sound to cheer him,
    and he very hungry grew ;
As he wandered, sick and weary, an
    old woman came in view :
She was old, her garments tattered,
    and half blind she seemed, and
    lame,

But she asked of Jack his business,
    and how he in that land came.
Jack then told her all his hist'ry,
    though it presently appeared
She knew rather more than he did,
    and some mysteries she cleared,
As to who his father was, and how
    he lost his life and wealth.
Through the baseness of a giant,
    who disposed of him by stealth,
Making off with all his riches ; " In
    this very land," said she,
" Lives he,—all is yours, and you
    must claim your property.
I will help you,—I'm a Fairy ;
    turn directly to the right ;
If with speed you journey on,
    you'll reach his house before
    the night."

On he went, and reached the giant's house, and found him
    not at home ;
Wife permitted Jack to enter, as to call so far he'd come ;
Meat and drink she gave him also, showed him over all the
    house,
And at last she hid him, lest he'd tempt the hunger of her
    spouse.
Who, on entering, loudly stated that he plainly smelt fresh
    meat,
But was by his wife persuaded quietly his meal to eat,
(Grieved I am that it consisted solely of the flesh of men) ;
And when he his supper ended, in was brought a splendid
    hen,
Who a golden egg produced whene'er the giant shouted
    " Lay!"
When the giant fell asleep, Jack seized the hen and ran away.

Down the bean-stalk home he hastened, and
    upon the magic pelf
Long he lived, his mother also, till at last he
    found himself
Quite inclined for greater riches, as he knew
    an easy road ;
Up he climbed the bean-stalk ladder, and
    returned with *such* a load !
But the giant nearly wakened with the bark-
    ing of a dog,—
(Very lucky 'twas for Jack, that way of sleep-
    ing like a log).

Bags of gold and silver Jack took
    home, but still his mind did lean
Towards another prize, and journey
    up the lucky stalk of bean.
Hidden in his usual corner in the
    giant's house, he spied,
Bought for that great man's amuse-
    ment, playing sweetly by his side
While he slept, a golden harp, which
    Jack at once caught up, and ran,
But the harp with human voice cried,
    " Master, master, stop this man !"
But so tipsy was the giant, though
    he tried to run and bawl,
That, with all his pains, he could not
    stop the flight of Jack at all.

Down the road and down the bean-
    stalk swiftly ran and clambered
    Jack,
Joy was in his manly bosom, and
    the harp upon his back.
Down the giant scrambles after
    Jack, but little does *he* reck,—
With an axe he cuts the bean-
    stalk, and the giant breaks his
    neck.
After this, I need not tell you,
    Jack resolved to settle down,
Stay at home, climb no more bean-
    stalks, be respected in the town.

"SLEEPING BEAUTY,"
in *Walter Crane's Toy Books*
(London: Routledge, 1876)

Using what he referred to as his "classical style," Crane shows Sleeping Beauty as a young woman of Grecian beauty in a setting marked by static images. The self-contained scenes are often framed by pillars, giving them a portrait-like quality.

THE SLEEPING BEAUTY.

LONG, long ago, in ancient times, there lived a King and Queen,
  And for the blessing of a child their longing sore had been;
At last, a little daughter fair, to their great joy, was given,
And to the christening feast they made, they bade the Fairies seven—

The Fairies seven, who loved the land—that they the child might bless;
Yet one old Fairy they left out, in pure forgetfulness.
And at the feast, the dishes fair were of the reddest gold:
Aut when the Fairy came, not one for her, so bad and old.
Angry was she, because her place and dish had been forgot,
And angry things she muttered long, and kept her anger hot,

Until the Fairy godmothers their gifts and wishes gave:
She waited long to spoil the gifts, and her revenge to have.
One gave the Princess goodness, and one gave her beauty rare;
One gave her sweetest singing voice; one, gracious mien and air;
One, skill in dancing; one, all cleverness; and then the crone
Came forth, and muttered, angry still, and good gift gave she none;

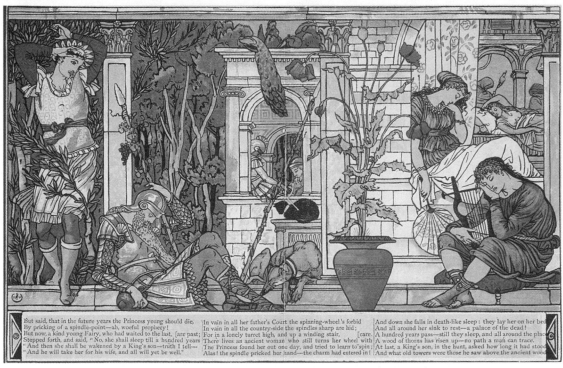

But said, that in the future years the Princess young should die,
By pricking of a spindle-point—ah, woeful prophecy!
But now, a kind young Fairy, who had waited to the last, [are past;
Stepped forth, and said, "No, she shall sleep till a hundred years
"And then she shall be wakened by a King's son—truth I tell—
"And he will take her for his wife, and all will yet be well."

In vain in all her father's Court the spinning-wheel's forbid
In vain in all the country-side the spindles sharp are hid;
For in a lonely turret high, and up a winding stair, [care.
There lives an ancient woman who still turns her wheel with
The Princess found her out one day, and tried to learn to spin
Alas! the spindle pricked her hand—the charm had entered in!

And down she falls in death-like sleep: they lay her on her bed
And all around her sink to rest—a palace of the dead!
A hundred years pass—still they sleep, and all around the place
A wood of thorns has risen up—so path a man can trace.
At last, a King's son, in the hunt, asked how long it had stood
And what old towers were those he saw above the ancient wood

An aged peasant told of an enchanted palace, where
A sleeping King and Court lay hid, and sleeping Princess fair,
Through the thick wood, that gave him way, and past the thorns that drew
Their sharpest points another way, the King's son presses through.
He reached the guard, the court, the hall,—and there, where'er he stept,
He saw the sentinels, and grooms, and courtiers as they slept.

Ladies in act to smile, and pages in attendance wait;
The horses slept within their stalls, the dogs about the gate.
The King's son presses on, into an inner chamber fair,
And sees, laid on a silken bed, a lovely lady there;
So sweet a face, so fair—was never beauty such as this;
He stands—he stoops to gaze—he kneels—he wakes her with a kiss.

He leads her forth; the magic sleep of all the Court is o'er,—
They wake, they move, they talk, they laugh, just as they did of yore,
A hundred years ago. The King and Queen awake, and tell
How all has happed, rejoicing much that all has ended well.
They hold the wedding that same day, with mirth and feasting good—
The wedding of the Prince and Sleeping Beauty in the Wood.

APPENDIX 4

GEORGE CRUIKSHANK'S ILLUSTRATIONS

"Puss in Boots,"
London: Routledge, Warne, and Routledge, 1864.

Tom Puss, consoling his Master, and asking for a Pair of Boots, & a suit of Clothes.

Tom Puss telling the King that his Master — the Marquess of Carabas, is in the River!

Tom Puss, after his master is dressed, introduces him to the King — as the Marquess of Carabas!

The Ogre turns himself into an Elephant! _____ Tom Puss pretends to be frightened _____

The Ogre turns himself into a Lion!. Tom Puss, is still more frightened & asks the Ogre to change into a Mouse!.

The Ogre turns himself into a Mouse _____ Tom Puss springs upon him & kills him!

Tom Puss receiving the King — the Princess & his Master at the Castle —

The Wedding Feast — and Tom Puss making a Speech! — Designed & Etched by George Cruikshank

"Cinderella and the Glass Slipper," London: Bogue 1854.

Cinderella scouring the Pots and Kettles

Cinderella helping her Sisters to Dress, for the Royal Ball

The Pumpkin, and the Rat, and the Mice, and the Lizards, being changed by the Fairy, into a Coach, Horses, and Servants, to take Cinderella to the Ball at the Royal Palace—

The Fairy changing Cinderella's Kitchen dress, into a beautiful Ball dress. &c.&c.

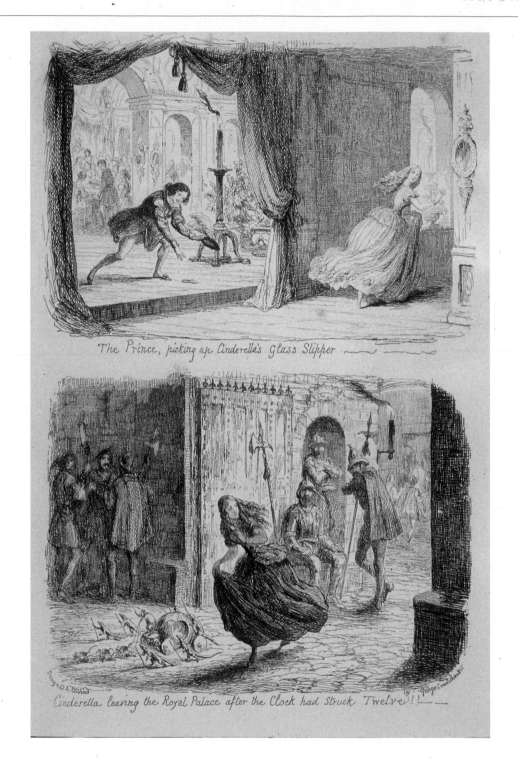

The Prince, picking up Cinderella's Glass Slipper

Cinderella leaving the Royal Palace after the Clock had Struck Twelve!!!

The Heralds proclaiming the Prince's wish, that all the Single Ladies, should try on the Glass Slipper!

Cinderella having fitted on the Glass Slipper produces it's fellow

The Marriage of Cinderella, to
The Prince___

"The History of Jack and the Bean Stalk," London: Bogue, 1854.

The Fairies tie the Giant up in the Bean Stalk.

Jack. climbing the Bean Stalk.

Jack gets the Golden Hen, away from the Giant

Jack and the Fairy Harp, escaping from the Giant.

Jack brings the Giant prisoner to King Alfred.

"Hop o' My Thumb and the Seven League Boots," London: Bogue, 1854.

The Giant Ogre, discovers Hop'o my Thumb & his Brothers whom his Wife had endeavoured to conceal from him

The Giant Ogre in his Seven League Boots,
pursuing Hop o' my Thumb & his Brothers, who hide in a Cave.

The Giant Ogre falls asleep, Hop o' my Thumb, pulls off
the Seven League Boots whilst his Brothers run away —

Hop'o my Thumb leads his Brothers out of the Wood

Hop'o my Thumb puts on the Seven League Boots — escapes from the Giant and goes home.

Hop'o my Thumb arrives at home before his Brothers, shows the Seven League Boots to his Father & tells him all about the Giant Ogre !.

George Cruikshank fecit

Hop'o my Thumb presenting the
Seven League Boots to the King

BIBLIOGRAPHY

FURTHER READING ON FAIRY TALES

Aarne, Antti, and Stith Thompson. *The Types of the Folktale: A Classification and Bibliography*. Helsinki: Academia Scientiarum Fennica, 1961.

Apo, Satu. *The Narrative World of Finnish Fairy Tales: Structure, Agency and Evaluation in Southwest Finnish Folktales*. Helsinki: Academia Scientiarum Fennica, 1995.

Ashliman, D. L. "Symbolic Sex-Role Reversals in the Grimms' Fairy Tales." In *Forms of the Fantastic: Selected Essays from the Third International Conference on the Fantastic in Literature and Film*, ed. Jan Hokenson and Howard Pearce. New York: Greenwood Press, 1986.

————. *A Guide to Folktales in the English Language: Based on the Aarne-Thompson Classification System*. New York: Greenwood Press, 1987.

Attebery, Brian. *The Fantasy Tradition in American Literature: From Irving to Le Guin*. Bloomington: Indiana University Press, 1980.

Avery, Gillian, and Angela Bull. *Children and Their Books: A Celebration of the Work of Iona and Peter Opie*. Oxford: Clarendon Press, 1989.

Bacchilega, Christina. "Introduction: The Innocent Persecuted Heroine Fairy Tale." *Western Folklore* 52 (1993): 1–12.

————. *Postmodern Fairy Tales: Gender and Narrative Strategies*. Philadelphia: University of Pennsylvania Press, 1997.

Barchilon, Jacques. "Beauty and the Beast: From Myth to Fairy Tale." *Psychoanalysis and the Psychoanalytic Review* 46 (1959): 19–29.

————. "Confessions of a Fairy-Tale Lover." *The Lion and the Unicorn* 12 (1988): 208–23.

Barchilon, Jacques, and Peter Flinders. *Charles Perrault*. Boston: Twayne, 1981.

Barzilai, Shuli. "Reading 'Snow White': The Mother's Story." *Signs: Journal of Women in Culture and Society* 15 (1990): 515–34.

———. "'Say That I had a Lovely Face': The Grimms' "Rapunzel," Tennyson's "Lady of Shalott," and Atwood's *Lady Oracle*. *Tulsa Studies in Women's Literature* 19 (2000): 231–54.

Baughman, Ernest W. *Type and Motif Index of the Folktales of England and North America*. The Hague: Mouton, 1966.

Bauman, Richard. "Conceptions of Folklore in the Development of Literary Semiotics." *Semiotica* 39 (1982): 1–20.

Behlmer, Rudy. "They Called It 'Disney's Folly': Snow White and the Seven Dwarfs (1937)." In *America's Favorite Movies: Behind the Scenes*. New York: Ungar, 1982.

Beitter, Ursula E. "Identity Crisis in Fairy-Tale Land: The Grimm Fairy Tales and Their Uses by Modern-Day Imitators." In *Imagination, Emblems and Expressions: Essays on Latin American, Carribean, and Continental Culture and Identity*, ed. Helen Ryan-Ransom. Bowling Green, Ohio: Bowling Green State University Popular Press, 1993.

Bell, Elizabeth, Lynda Haas, and Laura Sells, eds. *From Mouse to Mermaid: The Politics of Film, Gender, and Culture*. Bloomington: Indiana University Press, 1995.

Benjamin, Walter. "The Storyteller." In *Illuminations*, trans. Harry Zohn. New York: Harcourt, Brace and World, 1968.

Benson, Stephen. "Stories of Love and Death: Reading and Writing the Fairy Tale Romance." In *Image and Power: Women in Fiction in the Twentieth Century*, ed. Sarah Sceats and Gail Cunnigham. New York: Longman, 1996.

Bernheimer, Kate, ed. *Mirror, Mirror on the Wall: Women Writers Explore Their Favorite Fairy Tales*. New York: Anchor Press, 1998.

Bettelheim, Bruno. *The Uses of Enchantment: The Meaning and Importance of Fairy Tales*. New York: Vintage Books, 1976.

Bilmes, Jack. "The Joke's on You, Goldilocks: A Reinterpretation of 'The Three Bears.'" *Semiotica* 39 (1982): 269–83.

Birkhauser-Oeri, Sybille. *The Mother: Archetypal Image in Fairy Tales*. Toronto: Inner City Books, 1988.

Bluhm, Lothar. "A New Debate about 'Old Marie'? Critical Observations on the Attempt to Remythologize Grimms' Fairy Tales from a Sociohistorical Perspective." *Marvels and Tales* 14 (2000): 287–311.

Book, Fredrik. *Hans Christian Andersen: A Biography*. Trans. George C. Schoolfield. Norman: University of Oklahoma Press, 1962.

Bottigheimer, Ruth B. "Tale Spinners: Submerged Voices in Grimms' Fairy Tales." *New German Critique* 27 (1982): 141-50.

———. *Grimms' Bad Girls and Bold Boys: The Moral and Social Vision of the Tales*. New Haven, Conn.: Yale University Press, 1987.

———. "'Beauty and the Beast.'" *Midwestern Folklore* 15 (1989): 79–88.

———. "Cupid and Psyche vs. Beauty and the Beast: The Milesian and the Modern." *Merveilles et contes* 3 (1989): 4–14.

———. "Fairy Tales and Children's Literature: A Feminist Perspective." In *Teaching Children's Literature: Issues, Pedagogy, Resources*, ed. Glen Edward Sadler. New York: Modern Language Association of America, 1992.

———, ed. *Fairy Tales and Society: Illusion, Allusion, and Paradigm*. Philadelphia: University of Pennsylvania Press, 1986.

Bredsdorff, Elias. *Hans Christian Andersen: An Introduction to His Life and Works*. Copenhagen: H. Reitzel, 1987.

Brewer, Derek. *Symbolic Stories: Traditional Narratives of Family Drama in English Literature*. Cambridge, England: D. S. Brewer, 1980.

Briggs, Charles, and Amy Schuman, eds. "Theorizing Folklore: Toward New Perspectives on the Politics of Culture." *Western Folklore* 52 (1993).

Briggs, Katherine Mary. *The Fairies in English Tradition and Literature*. Chicago: University of Chicago Press, 1967.

———. *A Dictionary of British Folk-tales in the English Language*. 4 vols. London: Routledge & Kegan Paul, 1970–71.

Bronner, Simon, ed. *Creativity and Tradition in Folklore: New Directions*. Logan: Utah State University Press, 1992.

Bryant, Sylvia. "Re-Constructing Oedipus through 'Beauty and the Beast.' " *Criticism* 31 (1989): 439–53.

Campbell, Joseph. *The Hero with a Thousand Faces*. New York: Pantheon, 1949.

———. *The Flight of the Wild Gander: Explorations in the Mythological Dimension*. New York: Viking, 1969.

Canepa, Nancy, ed. *Out of the Woods: The Origins of the Literary Fairy Tale in Italy and France*. Detroit: Wayne State University Press, 1997.

———. *From Court to Forest: Giambattista Basile's 'Lo cunto de li cunti' and the Birth of the Literary Fairy Tale*. Detroit: Wayne State University Press, 1999.

Canham, Stephen. "What Manner of Beast? Illustrations of 'Beauty and the Beast.' " In *Image and Maker: An Annual Dedicated to the Consideration of Book Illustration*, ed. Harold Darling and Peter Neumeyer. La Jolla, Calif.: Green Tiger Press, 1984.

Canton, Katia. *The Fairy-Tale Revisited: A Survey of the Evolution of the Tales from Classical Literary Interpretations to Innovative Contemporary Dance-Theater Productions*. New York: Lang, 1994.

Caracciolo, Peter L., ed. *The Arabian Nights in English Literature: Studies in the Reception of "The Thousand and One Nights" into British Culture*. Houndmills, Basingstoke, Hampshire: Macmillan, 1988.

Cardigos, Isabel. *In and Out of Enchantment: Blood Symbolism and Gender in Portugese Fairytales*. Helsinki: Academia Scientiarum Fennica, 1996.

Carter, Angela, ed. "About the Stories." In *Sleeping Beauty and Other Favorite Fairy Tales*. Boston: Otter Books, 1991.

Cashdan, Sheldon. *The Witch Must Die: How Fairy Tales Shape Our Lives*. New York: Basic Books, 1999.

Cech, Jon. "Hans Christian Andersen's Fairy Tales and Stories: Secrets, Swans and Shadows." In *Touchstones: Reflections on the Best in Children's Literature*, ed. Perry Nodelman. Vol. 2. West Lafayette, Ind.: Children's Literature Association, 1987.

Chase, Richard. *The Jack Tales*. Cambridge, Mass.: Houghton, 1943.

Chinen, Allan B. *In the Ever After: Fairy Tales and the Second Half of Life*. Wilmette, Ill.: Chiron Publications, 1989.

Clarkson, Atelia, and Gilbert B. Cross. *World Folktales: A Scribner Resource Collection*. New York: Scribner's, 1980.

Clodd, Edward. *Tom Tit Tot: An Essay on Savage Philosophy in Folk-Tale*. London: Duckworth, 1898.

Cocchiara, Guiseppe. *The History of Folklore in Europe*. Trans. John N. McDaniel. Philadelphia: Institute for the Study of Human Issues, 1981.

Cohen, Betsy. *The Snow White Syndrome: All about Envy*. New York: Macmillan, 1986.

Cooks, Leda M., and Mark P. Orbe and Carol S. Bruess. "The Fairy Tale Theme in Popular Culture: A Semiotic Analysis of *Pretty Woman*." *Women's Studies in Communication* 16 (1993): 86–104.

Cox, Marian Roalfe. *Cinderella: Three Hundred and Forty-five Variants of Cinderella, Catskin, and Cap o'Rushes*. London: David Nutt, 1893.

Darnton, Robert. "Peasants Tell Tales: The Meaning of Mother Goose." In *The Great Cat Massacre and Other Episodes in French Cultural History*. New York: Basic Books, 1984.

De Graff, Amy Vanderlin. *The Tower and the Well: A Psychological Interpretation of the Fairy Tales of Madame d'Aulnoy*. Birmingham, Ala.: Summa, 1984.

Dégh, Linda. *Folktales and Society: Storytelling in a Hungarian Peasant Community*. Trans. Emily M. Schossberger. Bloomington: Indiana University Press, 1969.

———. "Beauty, Wealth and Power: Career Choices for Women in Folktales, Fairytales and Modern Media." *Fabula* 30 (1989): 43–62.

Dieckmann, Hans. *Twice-Told Tales: The Psychological Use of Fairy Tales*. Foreword by Bruno Bettelheim. Wilmette, Ill.: Chiron, 1986.

Dobay Rifelj, Carol de. "Cendrillon and the Ogre: Women in Fairy Tales and Sade." *Romantic Review* 81 (1990): 11–24.

Dorson, Richard M. *Folklore: Selected Essays*. Bloomington: Indiana University Press, 1972.

———. *Folklore and Fakelore: Essays toward a Discipline of Folk Studies*. Cambridge, Mass.: Harvard University Press, 1976.

Douglas, Mary. "Red Riding Hood: An Interpretation from Anthropology." *Folklore* 106 (1995): 1–7.

Duffy, Maureen. *The Erotic World of Faery*. London: Cardinal, 1989.

Dundes, Alan. *The Study of Folklore*. Englewood Cliffs, N.J.: Prentice-Hall, 1965.

———. *Cinderella: A Casebook*. Madison: University of Wisconsin Press, 1988.

———. *Folklore Matters*. Knoxville: University of Tennessee Press, 1989.

———. "Bruno Bettelheim's Uses of Enchantment and Abuses of Scholarship." *Journal of American Folklore* 104 (1991): 74–83.

———, ed. *Little Red Riding Hood: A Casebook*. Madison: University of Wisconsin Press, 1989.

Eastman, Mary H. *Index to Fairy Tales, Myths and Legends*. Boston: Faxon, 1926.

Edwards, Carol L. "The Fairy Tale 'Snow White.' " In *Making Connections across the Curriculum: Readings for Analysis*. New York: St. Martin's Press, 1986.

Edwards, Lee R. "The Labors of Psyche: Toward a Theory of Female Heroism." *Critical Inquiry* 6 (1979): 33–49.

Egoff, Sheila, ed. *Only Connect: Readings on Children's Literature*. 2nd ed. Oxford: Oxford University Press, 1965.

Ellis, John M. *One Fairy Story Too Many: The Brothers Grimm and Their Tales*. Chicago: University of Chicago Press, 1982.

Erb, Cynthia. "Another World or the World of an Other? The Space of Romance in Recent Versions of 'Beauty and the Beast.' " *Cinema Journal* 34 (1995): 50–70.

Estés, Clarissa Pinkola. *Women Who Run with the Wolves: Myths and Stories of the Wild Woman Archetype*. New York: Ballantine, 1992.

Farrer, Claire, ed. *Women and Folklore*. Austin: University of Texas Press, 1975.

Favat, F. Andre. *Child and Tale: The Origins of Interest*. Urbana, Ill.: National Council of Teachers of English, 1977.

Fine, Gary Alan, and Julie Ford. "Magic Settings: The Reflection of Middle-Class Life in 'Beauty and the Beast.' " *Midwestern Folklore* 15 (1989): 89–100.

Fohr, Samuel Denis. *Cinderella's Gold Slipper: Spiritual Symbolism in the Grimms' Tales*. Wheaton, Ill.: Quest Books, 1991.

Franz, Marie-Louise von. *Problems of the Feminine in Fairytales*. New York: Spring Publications, 1972.

———. *Shadow and Evil in Fairy Tales*. Rev. ed. Boston: Shambhala, 1990.

———. *The Interpretation of Fairy Tales*. Rev. ed. Boston: Shambhala, 1996.

———. *Archetypal Patterns in Fairy Tales*. Toronto: Inner City Books, 1997.

Gilbert, Sandra M., and Susan Gubar. *The Madwoman in the Attic: The Woman Writer and the Nineteenth-Century Literary Imagination*. New Haven, Conn.: Yale University Press, 1979.

Girardot, N. J. "Initiation and Meaning in the Tale of Snow White and the Seven Dwarfs." *Journal of American Folklore* 90 (1977): 274–300.

Goldberg, Christine. "The Composition of 'Jack and the Beanstalk.' " *Marvels & Tales* 15 (2001): 11–26.

Goldenstern, Joyce. "Connections That Open Up: Coordination and Causality in Folktales." *Marvels & Tales* 15 (2001): 27–41.

Goldthwaite, John. *The Natural History of Make-Believe: A Guide to the Principal Works of Britain, Europe, and America*. New York: Oxford University Press, 1996.

Grace, Sherrill. "Courting Bluebeard with Bartók, Atwood, and Fowles: Modern Treatments of the Bluebeard Theme." *Journal of Modern Literature* 11 (1984): 245–62.

Haase, Donald. "Gold into Straw: Fairy Tale Movies for Children and the Culture Industry." *The Lion and the Unicorn* 12 (1988): 193–207.

———. "Yours, Mine, or Ours? Perrault, the Brothers Grimm and the Ownership of Fairy Tales." In *Once Upon a Folktale: Capturing the Folklore Process with Children*, ed. Gloria T. Blatt. New York: Teachers College, Columbia University, 1993.

———, ed. *The Reception of Grimms' Fairy Tales: Responses, Reactions, Revisions*. Detroit: Wayne State University Press, 1993.

Hains, Maryellen. "Beauty and the Beast: 20th-Century Romance?" *Merveilles et contes* 3 (1989): 75–83.

Hallett, Martin, and Barbara Karasek. *Folk and Fairy Tales: Their Origins, Meaning, and Usefulness*. Peterborough, Ontario: Broadview Press, 1991.

Hanks, Carole, and D. T. Hanks Jr. "Perrault's 'Little Red Riding Hood': Victim of the Revisers." *Children's Literature* 7 (1978): 68–77.

Hannon, Patricia. *Fabulous Identities: Women's Fairy Tales in Seventeenth-Century France*. Amsterdam: Rodopi, 1998.

Hartland, E. Sidney. "The Forbidden Chamber." *Folk-Lore Journal* 3 (1885): 193–242.

Hearn, Michael Patrick, Trinkett Clark, and H. Nichols Clark. *Myth, Magic, and Mystery: One Hundred Years of American Children's Book Illustrations*. Boulder, Colo.: Roberts Rinehart, 1996.

Hearne, Betsy. *Beauty and the Beast: Visions and Revisions of an Old Tale*. Chicago: University of Chicago Press, 1989.

Henein, Eglal. "Male and Female Ugliness Through the Ages." *Merveilles et contes* 3 (1989): 45–56.

Henke, Jill Birnie, Diane Zimmerman Umble, and Nancy J. Smith. "Construction of the Female Self: Feminist Readings of the Disney Heroine." *Women's Studies in Communication* 19 (1996): 229–49.

Heuscher, Julius E. *A Psychiatric Study of Fairy Tales: Their Origin, Meaning, and Usefulness*. 2nd rev. ed. Springfield, Ill.: Charles C. Thomas, 1974.

Hoggard, Lynn. "Writing with the Ink of Light: Jean Cocteau's *Beauty and the Beast*." In *Film and Literature: A Comparative Approach to Adaptation*, ed. Wendell Aycock and Michael Schoenecke. Lubbock: Texas Tech University Press, 1988.

Holbek, Bengt. *The Interpretation of Fairy Tales: Danish Folklore in a European Perspective*. Helsinki: Academia Scientiarum Fennica, 1987.

Holliss, Richard, and Brian Sibley. *Walt Disney's Snow White and the Seven Dwarfs and the Making of the Classic Film*. New York: Simon and Schuster, 1987.

Hood, Gwyneth. "Husbands and Gods as Shadowbrutes: 'Beauty and the Beast' from Apuleius to C. S. Lewis." *Mythlore* 15 (1988):33–43.

Hoyme, James B. "The 'Abandoning Impuse' in Human Parents." *The Lion and the Unicorn* 12 (1988): 32–46.

Jacoby, Mario, Verena Kast, and Ingrid Reidel, eds. *Witches, Ogres and the Devil's Daughter: Encounters with Evil in Fairy Tales*. Boston: Shambhala, 1992.

Jenkins, Henry. " 'It's Not a Fairy Tale Anymore': Gender, Genre and *Beauty and the Beast*." *Journal of Film and Video* 43 (1991): 90–110.

Johnson, Faye R., and Carole M. Carroll. " 'Little Red Riding Hood': Then and Now." *Studies in Popular Culture* 14 (1992): 71–84.

Jones, Steven Swann. "On Analyzing Fairy Tales: 'Little Red Riding Hood' Revisited." *Western Folklore* 46 (1987): 97–106.

———. *The New Comparative Method: Structural and Symbolic Analysis of the Allomotifs of "Snow White."* Helsinki: Academia Scientiarum Fennica, 1990.

———. "The Innocent Persecuted Heroine Genre: An Analysis of Its Structures and Themes." *Western Folklore* 52 (1993): 13–41.

———. *The Fairy Tale: The Magic Mirror of the Imagination*. New York: Twayne, 1995.

Kamenetsky, Christa. *The Brothers Grimm and Their Critics: Folktales and the Quest for Meaning*. Athens: Ohio University Press, 1992.

Kast, Verena. *Fairy Tales for the Psyche: Ali Baba and the Forty Thieves and the Myth of Sisyphus*. Trans. Vanessa Agnew. New York: Continuum, 1996.

Kertzer, Adrienne. "Reclaiming Her Maternal Pre-Text: Little Red Riding Hood's Mother and Three Young Adult Novels." *Children's Literature Association Quarterly* 21 (1996): 20–27.

Knoepflmacher, U. C. *Ventures into Childland: Victorians, Fairy Tales, and Femininity*. Chicago: University of Chicago Press, 1998.

Kolbenschlag, Madonna. *Kiss Sleeping Beauty Good-Bye: Breaking the Spell of Feminine Myths and Models*. San Francisco: Harper & Row, 1988.

Kravchenko, Maria. *The World of the Russian Fairy Tale*. Bern: Lang, 1987.

Kready, Laura F. *A Study of Fairy Tales*. Boston: Houghton Mifflin, 1916.

Laruccia, Victor. "Little Red Riding Hood's Metacommentary: Paradoxical Injunction, Semiotics & Behavior." *Modern Language Notes* 90 (1975): 517–34.

Le Guin, Ursula. "The Child and the Shadow." In *The Open-Hearted Audience: Ten Writers Talk about Writing for Children*, ed. Virginia Haviland. Washington, D.C.: Library of Congress, 1980.

Leach, Maria, and Jerome Fried, eds. *Funk & Wagnalls Standard Dictionary of Folklore, Mythology, and Legend*. Rev. ed. New York: Harper & Row, 1972.

Lederer, Wolfgang. *The Kiss of the Snow Queen: Hans Christian Andersen and Man's Redemption by Woman*. Berkeley: University of California Press, 1986.

Lewis, Philip. *Seeing through the Mother Goose Tales: Visual Turns in the Writings of Charles Perrault*. Stanford, Calif.: Stanford University Press, 1996.

Lieberman, Marcia. "Some Day My Prince Will Come: Female Acculturation through the Fairy Tale." *College English* 34 (1972): 383–95.

Livo, Norma. *Who's Afraid . . . ? Facing Children's Fears with Folktales*. Englewood, Colo.: Teacher Ideas Press, 1994.

Lundell, Torborg. *Fairy Tale Mothers*. New York: Lang, 1990.

Lurie, Alison. *Don't Tell the Grown-Ups. Subversive Children's Literature*. Boston: Little, Brown, 1990.

Lüthi, Max. *The European Folktale: Form and Nature*. Trans. John D. Niles. Philadelphia: Institute for the Study of Human Issues, 1982.

———. *The Fairytale as Art Form and Portrait of Man*. Trans. Jon Erickson. Bloomington: Indiana University Press, 1984.

———. *Once Upon a Time: On the Nature of Fairy Tales*. Trans. John Erickson. Bloomington: Indiana University Press, 1984.

MacDonald, Margaret Read. *The Storyteller's Sourcebook: A Subject, Title, and Motif Index to Folklore Collections for Children*. Detroit: Gale, 1982.

Mallet, Carl-Heinz. *Fairy Tales and Children: The Psychology of Children Revealed through Four of Grimms' Fairy Tales*. Trans. Joachim Neugroschel. New York: Schocken Books, 1984.

Maranda, P. *Soviet Structural Folkloristics*. The Hague: Mouton, 1974.

Marin, Louis. *Food for Thought*. Trans. Mette Hjort. Baltimore: Johns Hopkins University Press, 1989.

Marshall, Howard Wight. "Tom Tit Tot: A Comparative Essay on Aarne-Thompson Type 500—The Name of the Helper." *Folklore* 84 (1973): 51–57.

Mavrogenes, Nancy A., and Joan S. Cummins. "What Ever Happened to Little Red Riding Hood? A Study of a Nursery Tale." *Horn Book* (1979): 344–49.

McCarthy, William. *Jack in Two Worlds*. Chapel Hill, N.C.: University of North Carolina Press, 1994.

McGlathery, James M. *The Brothers Grimm and Folktale*. Urbana: University of Illinois Press, 1988.

———. *Fairy Tale Romance: The Grimms, Basile, and Perrault*. Urbana: University of Illinois Press, 1991.

———. *Grimms' Fairy Tales: A History of Criticism on a Popular Classic*. Columbia, S.C.: Camden House, 1993.

McMaster, Juliet. "Bluebeard: A Tale of Matrimony." *A Room of One's Own* 2 (1976): 10–19.

Meinhardt, Lela, and Paul Meinhardt. *Cinderella's Housework Dialectics: Housework as the Root of Human Creation*. Nutley, N.J.: Incunabula Press, 1977.

Metzger, Michael M., and Katharina Mommsen, eds. *Fairy Tales as Ways of Knowing: Essays on Märchen in Psychology, Society, and Literature*. Bern: Lang, 1981.

Michaelis-Jena, Ruth. *The Brothers Grimm*. London: Routledge, 1970.

Mieder, Wolfgang. "Modern Anglo-American Variants of the Frog Prince (AT 440)." *New York Folklore* 6 (1980): 111–35.

———. "Survival Forms of 'Little Red Riding Hood' in Modern Society." *International Folklore Review* 2 (1982): 23–40.

———. *Disenchantments: An Anthology of Modern Fairy Tale Poetry*. Hanover, N.H.: University Press of New England, 1987.

———. *Tradition and Innovation in Folk Literature*. Hanover, N.H.: University Press of New England, 1987.

Miller, Martin. "Poor Rumpelstiltskin." *Psychoanalytic Quarterly* 54 (1985): 73–76.

Morgan, Jeanne. *Perrault's Morals for Moderns*. New York: Lang, 1985.

Moss, Anita. "Mothers, Monsters, and Morals in Victorian Fairy Tales." *The Lion and the Unicorn* 12 (1988): 47–60.

Murphy, G. Ronald. *The Owl, the Raven, and the Dove: The Religious Meaning of the Grimms' Magic Fairy Tales*. New York: Oxford University Press, 2000.

Natov, Roni. "The Dwarf Inside Us: A Reading of 'Rumpelstiltskin.' " *The Lion and the Unicorn* 1 (1977): 71–76.

Neemann, Harold. *Piercing the Magic Veil: Toward a Theory of the Conte*. Tübingen: Gunter Narr, 1999.

Nenola-Kallio, Aili. "Lucky Shoes or Weeping Shoes: Structural Analysis of Ingarian Shoeing Laments." *Finnish Folkloristics* 1 (1974): 62–91.

Nicolaisen, W. F. H. "Why Tell Stories about Innocent Persecuted Heroines?" *Western Folklore* 52 (1993): 61–71.

Olrik, Axel. *Principles for Oral Narrative Research*. Trans. Kirsten Wolf and Jody Jensen. Bloomington: Indiana University Press, 1992.

Ong, Walter J. *Orality and Literacy: The Technologizing of the World*. New York: Methuen, 1982.

Opie, Iona, and Peter Opie. *The Classic Fairy Tales*. New York: Oxford University Press, 1974.

Panttaja, Elisabeth. "Going up in the World: Class in 'Cinderella.' " *Western Folklore* 52 (1993): 85–104.

Peppard, Murray B. *Paths through the Forest: A Biography of the Brothers Grimm*. New York: Holt, Rinehart, and Winston, 1971.

Philip, Neil. *The Cinderella Story*. London: Penguin, 1989.

Preston, Cathy Lynn. " 'Cinderella' as a Dirty Joke: Gender, Multivocality, and the Polysemic Text." *Western Folklore* 53 (1994): 27–49.

———, ed. *Folklore, Literature, and Cultural Theory: Collected Essays*. New York, Garland, 1995.

Propp, Vladimir. *Morphology of the Folktale*. Trans. Laurence Scott. Austin: University of Texas Press, 1975.

———. *Theory and History of Folklore*. Trans. Ariadna Y. Martin and Richard P. Martin. Ed. Anatoly Liberman. University of Minnesota Press, 1984.

Purkiss, Diane. *The Witch in History: Early Modern and Twentieth-Century Representations*. London: Routledge, 1996.

Radner, Joan N., and Susan S. Lanser. *Feminist Messages: Coding in Women's Folk Culture*. Urbana: University of Illinois Press, 1993.

Roberts, Warren E. *The Tale of the Kind and the Unkind Girls: AA-TH 480 and Related Tales*. Berlin: de Gruyter, 1958.

Röhrich, Lutz. *Folktales and Reality*. Trans. Peter Tokofsky. Bloomington: Indiana University Press, 1991.

Rooth, Anna Birgitta. *The Cinderella Cycle*. Lund: C.W.K. Gleerup Press, 1951.

Rose, Ellen Cronan. "Through the Looking Glass: When Women Tell Fairy Tales." In *The Voyage In: Fictions of Female Development*, ed. Elizabeth Abel, Marianne Hirsch, and Elizabeth Langland. Hanover, N.H.: University Press of New England, 1983.

Rovenger, Judith. "The Better to Hear You With: Making Sense of Folktales." *School Library Journal* (1993): 134–35.

Rowe, Karen E. "Feminism and Fairy Tales." *Women's Studies: An Interdisciplinary Journal* 6 (1979): 237–57.

Rusch-Feja, Diann. *The Portrayal of the Maturation Process in Girl Figures in Selected Tales of the Brothers Grimm*. New York: Peter Lang, 1995.

Sale, Roger. *Fairy Tales and After: From Snow White to E. B. White*. Cambridge, Mass.: Harvard University Press, 1978.

Sax, Boria. *The Frog King: On Legends, Fables, Fairy Tales and Anecdotes of Animals*. New York: Pace University Press, 1990.

———. *The Serpent and the Swan: The Animal Bride in Folklore and Literature*. Blacksburg, Va.: McDonald and Woodward, 1998.

Schectman, Jacqueline. *The Stepmother in Fairy Tales: Bereavement and the Feminine Shadow*. Boston: Sigo, 1993.

Scherf, Walter. "Family Conflicts and Emancipation in Fairy Tales." *Children's Literature* 3 (1974): 77–93.

Schickel, Richard. *The Disney Version: The Life, Times, Art and Commerce of Walt Disney.* New York: Simon and Schuster, 1968.

Schneider, Jane. "Rumpelstiltskin's Bargain: Folklore and the Merchant Capitalist Intensification of Linen Manufacture in Early Modern Europe." In *Cloth and Human Experience,* ed. Annette B. Weiner and Jane Schneider. Washington, D.C.: Smithsonian Institution Press, 1989.

Schwartz, Emanuel K. "A Psychoanalytic Study of the Fairy Tale." *American Journal of Psychotherapy* 10 (1956): 740–62.

Seifert, Lewis Carl. *Fairy Tales, Sexuality, and Gender in France, 1690–1715: Nostalgic Utopias.* New York: Cambridge University Press, 1996.

Sendak, Maurice. "Hans Christian Andersen." In *Caldecott and Co.: Notes on Books and Pictures.* New York: Farrar, Straus and Giroux, Michael di Capua Books, 1988.

Shavit, Zohar. "The Concept of Childhood and Children's Folktales: Test Case—'Little Red Riding Hood.' " *Jerusalem Studies in Jewish Folklore* 4 (1983): 93–124.

Silver, Carole. " 'East of the Sun and West of the Moon': Victorians and Fairy Brides." *Tulsa Studies in Women's Literature* 6 (1987): 283–98.

Stone, Harry. *Dickens and the Invisible World: Fairy Tales, Fantasy, and Novel-Making.* Bloomington: Indiana University Press, 1979.

Stone, Kay F. "Things Walt Disney Never Told Us." *Journal of American Folklore* 88 (1975): 42–49.

———. "Fairy Tales for Adults: Walt Disney's Americanization of the Märchen." In *Folklore on Two Continents: Essays in Honor of Linda Dégh,* ed. Nikolai Burlakoff and Carl Lindahl. Bloomington, Ind.: Trickster, 1980.

——— "The Misuses of Enchantment: Controversies on the Significance of Fairy Tales." In *Women's Folklore, Women's Culture,* ed. Rosan A. Jordan and Susan J. Kalcik. Philadelphia: University of Pennsylvania Press, 1985.

———. "And She Lived Happily Ever After?" *Women and Language* 19 (1996): 14–18.

———. *Burning Bright: New Light on Old Tales Told Today.* Peterborough, Ontario: Broadview Press, 1998.

Sutton, Martin. *The Sin-Complex: A Critical Study of English Versions of the Grimms' Kinder- und Hausmärchen in the Nineteenth Century.* Kassel: Brüder-Grimm-Gesellschaft, 1996.

Taggart, James M. *Enchanted Maidens: Gender Relations in Spanish Folktales of Courtship and Marriage.* Princeton, N.J.: Princeton University Press, 1990.

Tatar, Maria. *The Hard Facts of the Grimms' Fairy Tales.* Princeton, N.J.: Princeton University Press, 1987.

———. *Off with Their Heads! Fairy Tales and the Culture of Childhood.* Princeton, N.J.: Princeton University Press, 1992.

———. *Classic Fairy Tales.* New York: W. W. Norton, 1999.

Taylor, Peter, and Hermann Rebel. "Hessian Peasant Women, Their Families and the Draft: A Social-Historical Interpretation of Four Tales from the Grimm Collection." *Journal of Family History* 6 (1981): 347–78.

Thomas, Joyce. *Inside the Wolf's Belly: Aspects of the Fairy Tale.* Sheffield, England: Sheffield Academic Press, 1989.

Thomson, David. *The People of the Sea: A Journey in Search of the Seal Legend.* Washington, D.C.: Counterpoint, 2000.

Thompson, Stith. *Motif Index of Folk-Literature.* Bloomington: Indiana University Press, 1955–58.

Tolkien, J. R. R. "On Fairy-Stories." In *The Tolkien Reader.* New York: Ballantine, 1966.

Tomkowiak, Ingrid, and Ulrich Marzolph. *Grimms Märchen International.* 2 vols. Paderborn: Ferdinand Schöningh, 1966.

Travers, P. L. *About the Sleeping Beauty*. New York: McGraw-Hill, 1975.

———. "The Black Sheep." In *What the Bee Knows: Reflections on Myth, Symbol, and Story*. Wellingborough, Northamptonshire: Aquarian, 1989.

Tucker, Nicholas. *The Child and the Book: A Psychological and Literary Exploration*. Cambridge, England: Cambridge University Press, 1982.

Ulanov, Ann, and Barry Ulanov. *Cinderella and Her Sisters: The Envied and the Envying*. Philadelphia: Westminster Press, 1983.

Verdier, Yvonne. "Little Red Riding Hood in Oral Tradition." *Marvels and Tales* 11 (1997): 101–23.

Vessely, Thomas R. "In Defense of Useless Enchantment: Bettelheim's Appraisal of the Fairy Tales of Perrault." In *The Scope of the Fantastic—Culture, Biography, Themes, Children's Literature: Selected Essays from the First International Conference on the Fantastic in Literature and Film*, ed. Robert A. Collins and Howard D. Pearce. Westport, Conn.: Greenwood Press, 1985.

Vos, Gail de, and Anna E. Altmann. *New Tales for Old: Folktales as Literary Fictions for Young Adults*. Englewood, Colo.: Libraries Unlimited, 1999.

Waelti-Walters, Jennifer. "On Princesses: Fairy Tales, Sex Roles and Loss of Self." *International Journal of Women's Studies* 2 (1981): 180–88.

———. *Fairy Tales and the Female Imagination*. Montreal: Eden Press, 1982.

Waley, Arthur. "The Chinese Cinderella Story." *Folk-Lore* 58 (1947): 226–38.

Walter, Virginia A. "Hansel and Gretel as Abandoned Children: Timeless Images for a Postmodern Age." *Children's Literature in Education* 23 (1992): 203–14.

Ward, Donald. " 'Beauty and the Beast': Fact and Fancy, Past and Present." *Midwestern Folklore* 15 (1989): 119–25.

Wardetzky, Kristin. "The Structure and Interpretation of Fairy Tales Composed by Children." Trans. Ruth B. Bottigheimer. *Journal of American Folklore* 103 (1990): 157–76.

Warner, Marina. *From the Beast to the Blonde: On Fairy Tales and Their Tellers*. London: Chatto & Windus, 1994.

———. *Six Myths of Our Time*. New York: Vintage, 1995.

Weber, Eugen. "Fairies and Hard Facts: The Reality of Folktales." *Journal of the History of Ideas* 63 (1981): 93–113.

Weigle, Marta. *Spiders and Spinsters*. Albuquerque: University of New Mexico Press, 1982.

Yolen, Jane. "America's Cinderella." *Children's Literature in Education* 8 (1977): 21–29.

———. *Touch Magic: Fantasy, Faerie and Folklore in the Literature of Childhood*. New York: Philomel, 1981.

Zago, Ester. "Some Medieval Versions of 'Sleeping Beauty.' " *Studi Francesci* 69 (1979): 417–31.

Zarucchi, Jeanne Morgan. *Perrault's Morals for Moderns*. New York: Lang, 1985.

Ziolkowski, Jan M. "A Fairy Tale from before Fairy Tales: Egbert of Liège's 'De puella a lupellis seruata' and the Medieval Background of 'Little Red Riding Hood.' " *Speculum* 67 (1992): 549–75.

Zipes, Jack. *Breaking the Magic Spell: Radical Theories of Folk and Fairy Tales*. Austin: University of Texas Press, 1979.

———. *Fairy Tales and the Art of Subversion: The Classical Genre for Children and the Process of Civilization*. New York: Methuen, 1983.

———. "A Second Gaze at Little Red Riding Hood's Trials and Tribulations." *The Lion and the Unicorn* 7/8 (1983/84): 78–109.

———. *The Brothers Grimm: From Enchanted Forests to the Modern World*. New York: Routledge, 1988.

———. "The Changing Function of the Fairy Tale." In *The Lion and the Unicorn* 12 (1988): 7–31.

———. "On the Use and Abuse of Folk and Fairy Tales with Children: Bruno Bettelheim's Moralistic Magic Wand." In *How Much Truth Do We Tell the Children: The Poetics of Children's Literature*, ed. Betty Bacon. Minneapolis, Minn.: Marxist Editions Press, 1988.

———. *The Trials and Tribulations of Little Red Riding Hood.* 2nd ed. New York: Routledge, 1993.

———. *Fairy Tales as Myth, Myth as Fairy Tales.* Lexington: University of Kentucky Press, 1994.

———. *Creative Storytelling: Building Community, Changing Lives.* New York: Routledge, 1995.

———. *Happily Ever After: Fairy Tales, Children, and the Culture Industry.* New York: Routledge, 1997.

———. ed. *The Oxford Companion to Fairy Tales. The Western Fairy Tale Tradition from Medieval to Modern.* Oxford: Oxford University Press, 2000.

ANTHOLOGIES OF FAIRY TALES

Abrahams, Roger D. *African American Folktales: Stories from Black Traditions in the New World.* New York: Pantheon, 1999.

Afanasev, Alexander. *Russian Fairy Tales.* Trans. Norbert Guterman. New York: Pantheon, 1945.

Andersen, Hans Christian. *Eighty Fairy Tales.* Trans. R. P. Keigwin. New York: Pantheon, 1976.

Arabian Nights. Trans. Husain Haddawy. New York: W. W. Norton, 1990.

Asbjørnsen, Peter Christian, and Jörgen Møe. *Popular Tales from the Norse.* Trans. Sir George Webbe Dasent. New York: D. Appleton, 1859.

———. *Norwegian Folktales.* New York: Pantheon, 1960.

———. *East of the Sun and West of the Moon.* New York: Macmillan, 1963.

Baker, Augusta. *The Talking Tree: Fairy Tales from Fifteen Lands.* Philadelphia: Lippincott, 1955.

Barbeau, Marius. *The Golden Phoenix and Other French Canadian Fairy Tales.* New York: Walck, 1958.

Barchers, Suzanne I. *Wise Women: Folk and Fairy Tales from Around the World.* Englewood, Colo.: Libraries Unlimited, 1990.

Basile, Giambattista. *The Pentamerone of Giambattista Basile.* Trans. Benedetto Croce. Ed. N. M. Penzer. 2 vols. London: John Lane the Bodley Head, 1932.

Berry, Jack. *West African Folk Tales.* Evanston, Ill.: Northwestern University Press, 1991.

Bierhorst, John. *The Red Swan: Myths and Tales of the American Indians.* Albuquerque: University of New Mexico Press, 1992.

Blecher, Lone Thygensen, and George Blecher. *Swedish Tales and Legends.* New York: Pantheon, 1993.

Booss, Claire. *Scandinavian Folk and Fairy Tales: Tales from Norway, Sweden, Denmark, Finland, Iceland.* New York: Gramercy Books, 1984.

Briggs, Katharine M. A *Dictionary of British Folk-Tales in the English Language.* 4 vols. London: Routledge and Kegan Paul, 1970–71.

———, and Ruth L. Tongue. *Folktales of England.* Chicago: University of Chicago Press, 1965.

Bushnaq, Inea. *Arab Folktales.* New York: Pantheon, 1986.

Calvino, Italo. *Italian Folktales.* Trans. George Martin. New York: Pantheon, 1980.

Carlson, Ruth Kearney. *Folklore and Folktales Around the World.* Newark, Del.: The Association, 1972.

Carter, Angela. *The Virago Book of Fairy Tales.* London: Virago Press, 1990.

———. *The Second Virago Book of Fairy Tales.* London: Virago Press, 1992.

———. *Strange Things Sometimes Still Happen: Fairy Tales from Around the World.* Boston: Faber and Faber, 1993.

Chase, Richard. *American Folk Tales and Songs.* New York: Signet, 1956.

Christiansen, Reidar Thorwald. *Folktales of Norway*. Trans. Pat Shaw Iversen. London: Routledge & Kegan Paul, 1964.

Clarkson, Atelia, and Gilbert B. Cross. *World Folktales: A Scribner Resource Collection*. New York: Charles Scribner's Sons, 1980.

Coffin, Tristram Potter, and Hennig Cohen. *Folklore from the Working Folk of America*. Garden City, N.Y.: Anchor Press, 1973.

Cole, Joanna. *Best-Loved Folktales of the World*. New York: Anchor Press, 1983.

Cott, Jonathan. *Beyond the Looking Glass: Extraordinary Works of Fairy Tale and Fantasy*. New York: Stonehill, 1973.

Crossley-Holland, Kevin. *Folktales of the British Isles*. New York: Pantheon, 1988.

Curtin, Jeremiah. *Irish Folk-Tales*. Dublin: Talbot Press, 1964.

Dasent, George Webbe. *East o' the Sun and West o' the Moon*. New York: Dover, 1971.

Dawkins, R. M. *Modern Greek Folktales*. Oxford: Clarendon, 1953.

Dégh, Linda. *Folktales of Hungary*. Trans. Judit Halasz. Chicago: University of Chicago Press, 1965.

Delarue, Paul. *Borzoi Book of French Folk Tales*. New York: Knopf, 1956.

Dorson, Richard. *Buying the Wind: Regional Folklore of the United States*. Chicago: University of Chicago Press, 1964.

Douglas, Sir George Brisbane. *Scottish Fairy and Folk Tales*. London: Scott, 1893.

———. *American Negro Folktales*. New York: Fawcett Publications, 1968.

———. *Folktales Told Around the World*. Chicago: University of Chicago Press, 1975.

Eberhard, Wolfram. *Folktales of China*. Chicago: University of Chicago Press, 1965.

El-Shamy, Hasan M. *Folktales of Egypt*. Chicago: University of Chicago Press, 1980.

Feldmann, Susan. *The Storytelling Stone: Myths and Tales of the American Indians*. New York: Dell, 1965.

Friedlander, George. *Jewish Fairy Tales and Stories*. London: Routledge, 1918.

Glassie, Henry. *Irish Folk Tales*. New York: Pantheon, 1985.

Griffis, William Elliott. *Japanese Fairy Tales*. New York: T.Y. Crowell, 1923.

Grimm, Jacob, and Wilhelm Grimm. *The Complete Fairy Tales of the Brothers Grimm*. Trans. Jack Zipes. New York: Bantam, 1987.

Hallett, Martin, and Barbara Karasek. *Folk and Fairy Tales*. Peterborough, Ontario: Broadview Press, 1991.

Hearn, Michael Patrick. *Victorian Fairy Tale Book*. New York: Pantheon, 1988.

Haviland, Virginia. *Favorite Fairy Tales Told in England*. Boston: Little, Brown, 1959.

———. *Favorite Fairy Tales Told in Ireland*. Boston: Little, Brown, 1961.

———. *Favorite Fairy Tales Told in Norway*. Boston: Little, Brown, 1961.

———. *Favorite Fairy Tales Told in Russia*. Boston: Little, Brown, 1961.

———. *Favorite Fairy Tales Told in Poland*. Boston: Little, Brown, 1963.

———. *Favorite Fairy Tales Told in Scotland*. Boston: Little, Brown, 1963.

———. *Favorite Fairy Tales Told in Spain*. Boston: Little, Brown, 1963.

———. *Favorite Fairy Tales Told in Italy*. Boston: Little, Brown, 1965.

———. *Favorite Fairy Tales Told in Czechoslovakia*. Boston: Little, Brown, 1966.

———. *Favorite Fairy Tales Told in Sweden*. Boston: Little, Brown, 1966.

———. *Favorite Fairy Tales Told in Japan*. Boston: Little, Brown, 1967.

———. *Favorite Fairy Tales Told in Denmark*. Boston: Little, Brown, 1971.

———. *Favorite Fairy Tales Told in India*. Boston: Little, Brown, 1973.

Jacobs, Joseph. *English Fairy Tales*. London: David Nutt, 1890.

———. *Celtic Fairy Tales*. London: David Nutt, 1892.

———. *Indian Fairy Tales*. New York: Putnam's, 1892.

————. *More English Fairy Tales*. London: David Nutt, 1894.

Jones, Gwyn. *Scandinavian Legends and Folk-tales*. London: Oxford University Press, 1956.

Lang, Andrew. *The Blue Fairy Book*. London: Longmans, Green, 1889.

————. *The Red Fairy Book*. London: Longmans, Green, 1890.

————. *The Green Fairy Book*. London: Longmans, Green, 1892.

————. *The Yellow Fairy Book*. London: Longmans, Green, 1894.

————. *The Pink Fairy Book*. London: Longmans, Green, 1897.

————. *The Grey Fairy Book*. London: Longmans, Green, 1900.

————. *The Violet Fairy Book*. London: Longmans, Green, 1901.

————. *The Brown Fairy Book*. London: Longmans, Green, 1904.

————. *The Orange Fairy Book*. London: Longmans, Green, 1906.

————. *The Olive Fairy Book*. London: Longmans, Green, 1907.

Lurie, Alison. *Clever Gretchen and Other Forgotten Folktales*. New York: Crowell, 1980.

————. *The Oxford Book of Modern Fairy Tales*. Oxford: Oxford University Press, 1993.

MacMillan, Cyrus. *Canadian Fairy Tales*. London: John Lane The Bodley Head, 1928.

Manning-Sanders, Ruth. *The Glass Man and the Golden Bird: Hungarian Folk and Fairy Tales*. New York: Roy Publishers, 1968.

Massignon, Geneviève. *Folktales of France*. Trans. Jacqueline Hyland. Chicago: University of Chicago Press, 1968.

Megas, Georgios A. *Folktales of Greece*. Chicago: University of Chicago Press, 1970.

Mieder, Wolfgang. *Disenchantments. An Anthology of Modern Fairy Tale Poetry*. Hanover, N.H.: University Press of New England, 1985.

Minard, Rosemary. *Womenfolk and Fairy Tales*. Boston: Houghton Mifflin, 1975.

Montgomerie, Norah, and William Montgomerie. *The Well at the World's End: Folk Tales of Scotland*. Toronto: The Bodley Head, 1956.

Noy, Dov. *Folktales of Israel*. Trans. Gene Baharav. Chicago: University of Chicago Press, 1963.

O'Sullivan, Sean. *Folktales of Ireland*. London: Routledge & Paul, 1966.

Opie, Iona, and Peter Opie. *The Classic Fairy Tales*. New York: Oxford University Press, 1974.

Paredes, Americo. *Folktales of Mexico*. Chicago: University of Chicago Press, 1970.

Perrault, Charles. *Perrault's Complete Fairy Tales*. Trans. A. E. Johnson et al. New York: Dodd, Mead, 1961.

Phelps, Ethel Johnston. *The Maid of the North: Feminist Folk Tales from Around the World*. New York: Holt, Rinehart and Winston, 1981.

————. *Tatterhood and Other Tales*. Old Westbury, N.Y.: Feminist Press, 1978.

Philip, Neil. *The Cinderella Story: The Origins and Variations of the Story Known as "Cinderella."* London: Penguin, 1989.

Pino-Saavedra, Yolanda. *Folktales of Chile*. Chicago: University of Chicago Press, 1968.

Pourrat, Henri. *French Folktales*. Trans. Royall Tyler. New York: Pantheon, 1989.

Rackham, Arthur. *Arthur Rackham Fairy Book*. Philadelphia: J. B. Lippincott Co., 1933.

Ramanujan, A. K. *Folktales from India*. New York: Random House, 1991.

Randolph, Vance. *Sticks in the Knapsack and Other Ozark Folk Tales*. New York: Columbia University Press, 1958.

————. *Pissing in the Snow and Other Ozark Folktales*. Urbana: University of Illinois Press, 1976.

Ragan, Kathleen. *Fearless Girls, Wise Women, and Beloved Sisters: Heroines in Folktales from Around the World*. New York: Norton, 1998.

Ranke, Kurt. *Folktales of Germany*. Trans. Lotte Baumann. Chicago: University of Chicago Press, 1966.

Riordan, James. *The Sun Maiden and the Crescent Moon: Siberian Folk Tales*. New York: Interlink Books, 1991.

————. *Korean Folk-tales*. New York: Oxford University Press, 1994.

Roberts, Moss. *Chinese Fairy Tales and Fantasies*. New York: Pantheon Books, 1979.

Rugoff, Milton A. *A Harvest of World Folk Tales*. New York: Viking, 1949.

Seki, Keigo. *Folktales of Japan*. Chicago: University of Chicago Press, 1963.

Simpson, Jacqueline. *Icelandic Folktales and Legends*. Berkeley: University of California Press, 1972.

Straparola, Giovanni Francesco. *The Facetious Nights of Straparola*. Trans. W. G. Waters. 4 vols. London: Society of Bibliophiles, 1901.

Thompson, Stith. *Tales of the North American Indians*. Bloomington: Indiana University Press, 1929.

————. *One Hundred Favorite Folktales*. Bloomington: Indiana University Press, 1968.

Tong, Diane. *Gypsy Folktales*. San Diego: Harcourt Brace Jovanovich, 1989.

Travers, P. L. *About the Sleeping Beauty*. New York: McGraw-Hill, 1975.

Walker, Barbara G. *Feminist Fairy Tales*. New York: HarperCollins, 1996.

Weinrich, Beatrice Silverman. *Yiddish Folktales*. New York: Pantheon, 1988.

Yolen, Jane. *Favorite Folktales from Around the World*. New York: Pantheon, 1986.

Zipes, Jack. *Beauties, Beasts and Enchantment: Classic Fairy Tales*. New York: New American Library, 1989.

————. *Spells of Enchantment: The Wondrous Fairy Tales of Western Culture*. New York: Viking, 1991.

BIBLIOGRAPHY OF ILLUSTRATIONS

Arthur Rackham's Book of Pictures. London: Heinemann, 1913.

Charles Perrault's Classic Fairy Tales. Illus. Harry Clarke. London: George G. Harrap, 1922.

Cinderella and the Glass Slipper. Illus. George Cruikshank. London: David Bogue, 1854.

Les Contes de Perrault. Illus. Gustave Doré. Paris: J. Hetzel, 1862.

The Fairy Book: The Best Popular Fairy Stories Selected and Rendered Anew by the Author of "John Halifax, Gentleman." Illus. Warwick Goble. London: Macmillan and Co., 1923.

Fairy Tales by Hans Andersen. Illus. Arthur Rackham. London: George G. Harrap, 1932.

The Fairy Tales of the Brothers Grimm. Illus. Arthur Rackham. Trans. Mrs. Edgar Lucas. London: Constable & Company Ltd., 1909; New York: Doubleday, Page and Co., 1916.

Hansel and Gretel and Other Stories by the Brothers Grimm. Illus. Kay Nielsen. London: Hodder and Stoughton, 1925.

The History of Jack and the Bean Stalk. Illus. George Cruikshank. London: David Bogue, 1854.

Hop o' My Thumb and the Seven League Boots. Illus. George Cruikshank. London: David Bogue, 1853.

In Powder and Crinoline: Old Fairy Tales. Retold by Arthur Quiller-Couch. Illus. Kay Nielsen. London: Hodder and Stoughton, 1913.

Little Brother and Little Sister. Illus. Arthur Rackham. New York: Dodd, Mead & Co., 1917.

Puss in Boots. Illus. George Cruikshank. London: Routledge, Warne, and Routledge, 1864.

Red Magic: A Collection of the World's Best Fairy Tales from All Countries. Illus. Kay Nielsen. Ed. Romer Wilson. London: J. Cape, 1930

Sleeping Beauty and Other Fairy Tales from the Old French. Retold by A. T. Quiller-Couch. Illus. by Edmund Dulac. New York and London: Hodder and Stoughton, 1910.

The Snow Queen and Other Stories from Hans Andersen. Illus. Edmund Dulac. London: Hodder and Stoughton, 1911.

Walter Crane's Toy Books. *Beauty and the Beast*. London: Routledge, 1875.

———. *Bluebeard*. London: Routledge, 1875.

———. *Cinderella*. London: Routledge, 1873.

———. *The Frog Prince*. London: Routledge, 1875.

———. *Jack and the Beanstalk*. London: Routledge, 1875.

———. *Little Red Riding Hood*. London: Routledge, 1875.

———. *Sleeping Beauty*. London: Routledge, 1876.

———. *The Three Bears*. London: Routledge, 1873.

JOURNALS

Children's Literature: Annual of the Modern Language Association Division on Children's Literature

Children's Literature Association Quarterly

Fabula

Folklore and Mythology Studies

International Folklore Review

Journal of American Folklore

The Lion and the Unicorn

Marvels and Tales

Midwestern Folklore

Western Folklore

ABOUT THE AUTHOR

MARIA TATAR is the John L. Loeb Professor of Germanic Languages and Literatures at Harvard University, where she teaches courses in German studies, folklore, and children's literature. She is the author of *Classic Fairy Tales* (W. W. Norton), *The Hard Facts of the Grimms' Fairy Tales*, and *Off with Their Heads! Fairy Tales and the Culture of Childhood*. She is the recipient of fellowships from the National Endowment for the Humanities, the John Simon Guggenheim Foundation, and the Humboldt Foundation. She also received the German Studies Association book award in 1992.